PRAISE FOR BONE MOUNTAIN

"Quick-draw opening; never-quit antagonists; spilled blood: Greed meets buried bones in a thriller humming with Big Sky atmosphere, nonstop action, smart dialogue, and detection detail. Dig in!"

> —Arthur Plotnik, author of *Spunk & Bite: A Writer's Guide to Bold, Contemporary Style, The Elements of Expression,* and others

"Big sky, big bones, and big story—Robert D. Hughes' fast-paced debut mystery has it all."

> —Michael Bracken, author of *All White Girls*

"Bone Mountain is a hella fast-paced high plains thriller."

> —Elwood Reid, Executive Producer of the hit FX series, *The Bridge*

BONE MOUNTAIN

A NOVEL

ROBERT D. HUGHES

C J KEENAN Publishing

Publisher's Note

This book is a work of fiction. Names, characters, places and incidents are either products of the author's imagination or used fictitiously. Any resemblance to actual persons, living or dead, businesses, events or locales is purely coincidental.

The scanning, uploading, and distribution of this book via the Internet or via any other means without the permission of the publisher is illegal and punishable by law. Please purchase only authorized electronic editions, and do not participate in or encourage the electronic piracy of copyrighted materials.

Cover photographs: © Robert D. Hughes

Cover design: Mary Jane Corrigan

Author photograph (About the Author): Loneman Photography

ISBN: 978-0-9993392-2-0

C J KEENAN Publishing

For Sally, my constant inspiration

Three may keep a secret, if two of them are dead.

—Benjamin Franklin, *Poor Richard's Almanac*

1

Darcy McKay noticed the huge man with the rifle when she glanced up from the fossil bone she'd been unearthing with hand tools. She sat cross-legged near the hilltop, dizzy from the intense high-altitude sun. The bone looked intact. Maybe there'd be more of them nearby. How cool it would be to find an entire duckbill skeleton. She set down her digging implements, a small paintbrush for whisking away loose soil and an ice pick for dislodging rock. She extended a bronzed arm to the plastic water bottle next to her right knee. As she tipped her head back to drink, she studied the guy standing motionless at the bottom of the ridge, now staring up at her. A straw cowboy hat cast shadow over the top part of his face. He held a bolt-action rifle loosely in hands the size of catchers' mitts.

Could he be a hunter? Nah—even a city girl knew the deer and elk season didn't open until fall. Maybe he owned this side of the hill and she was trespassing. If it turned out to be something like that, she'd just apologize and return to the group working the *T. rex* bones. No harm, no foul. Darcy had learned the power of a smile. She grinned and waved as she got to her feet.

The man didn't return the greeting. He raised his rifle and pointed it in her direction. Sun glinted off the lens of the telescopic scope atop the weapon. Darcy imagined herself magnified in the crosshairs. Jesus! The guy might—she began to edge sideways toward a large boulder. The rifle barrel tracked her movement like a movie camera panning on an actor.

Before Darcy had gotten ten feet, something nipped at her left shoulder, the sensation like a bee sting. A split-second later, a sharp cracking noise came from the place where the man stood. She leapt sideways and sprawled facedown behind the refrigerator-sized boulder, shielded now from the threat below. She glanced at her throbbing left shoulder, stunned to see blood soaking through her tee shirt. Adrenaline began to fuel the primal fight-or-flight instinct. Her heart was pounding like a bass drum.

Darcy kept down and remained motionless despite the temptation to jump up and run like hell. Had the guy taken off? She wasn't about to stick her head out to check. She noticed her cap had come off when she left her feet. Mechanically, she retrieved it with her right hand and tugged it in place on her head, working her blonde ponytail through the hole above the adjusting strap in back. There had to be some mistake—why would anyone shoot her? She'd only been working a duckbill dinosaur bone she'd spotted during an exploratory hike on the first day onsite. She didn't even know anybody out here except the other crew members.

Blood from her shoulder formed a small crimson pool on the ground. She'd need help, and fast. They kept a first-aid kit in the headquarters tent on the other side of the hill, but she didn't dare leave the safety of the rocks. What if the shooter was still down there, waiting for her to make a move? Easy, she told herself. Keep it together.

Then she heard the sound of methodical footfalls coming up the hill, the man taking his time. She moved into shadow further behind the boulder. Maybe he'd think she'd run for it. But no, he'd have seen her if she had, and he'd know she was still there. She closed her eyes for a moment and tried to think of a way out, but nothing came.

During her entire lifetime in Chicago, Darcy had never heard a gun fired. This was ridiculous, out in Montana, working on a museum-sponsored dinosaur dig, to be shot by some nut on a bright summer day. This gun stuff was more her uncle's kind of thing—too bad he wasn't here now.

The footfalls became louder. The son of a bitch would be there any second; she had to do something. She fumbled in a pocket of her cargo shorts for the small notebook and pencil stub she carried on the dig, found them and began scribbling a note as fast as she could.

A gravelly voice came from just below her. "Come on out now. I ain't gonna hurt you."

Darcy ripped the page from the pad and palmed the note and pencil as the man came around the edge of the boulder. His high-heeled, pointy-toed boots caused him to step awkwardly among the shifting rocks. He stood hip-cocked above her, his bulk blocking out the light. In silhouette, his face was a dark blur. Darcy noticed three pearl snap buttons lining one of the man's shirt cuffs. For a crazy instant, an odd question occurred to her—why did they put those weird-looking buttons on western shirts?

"Didn't think you were hurt bad," The stranger said. "I was only trying to scare you, but you must've moved just as I fired." He shrugged.

3

Darcy struggled to a sitting position, wedging the small piece of paper under a rock behind her. She eased the pencil back into a pocket. She looked around in a short arc. Hemmed in by rocks, she could only get out by going through the shooter, who outweighed her by a hundred pounds, easy. In the distance, tumbleweed bounced by in front of reddish-brown rock and stunted sagebrush. She could hear the rasping clicks of grasshoppers.

As Darcy watched, the guy fingered the Winchester's polished wooden stock with idle familiarity, as if caressing a lover he'd known for years.

"Look, I don't know what this is about," Darcy said, rising to her feet. "Hey, if I'm trespassing, I'm sorry." Thinking, this guy's whacko—got to figure out how to play him.

The man stood mute, his silence more terrifying than words. What *was* it with this guy? He wasn't angry. He wasn't happy. He was just...there.

Darcy tried again. "If you're after money, you're out of luck. I don't—"

"Shhhhh." The man put a finger to his lips, as if hushing a child. He paused, apparently considering his options. Then, "Be a damn shame, kill a girl pretty as you." He was silent for a moment. "Well, looks like you're going with me."

"What? I'm not going anywhere." Darcy backed off a step. The wind whipped a free strand of hair in front of her face, partially obscuring the gunman.

Another pause, then, "I kinda hate to do this, but..." He shifted his grip on the Winchester and abruptly slapped the wooden butt at the side of Darcy's head. She saw the blow coming, but it caught her just behind the right ear as she turned away.

Her knees gave out and she sank to the ground. Still hanging onto a thread of consciousness, she felt rough hands grab her under her shoulders and legs, lift her up. She threw an elbow back into the ribs of her attacker, but it didn't seem to have any effect. Her shoulder throbbed. She felt stunned, as if she'd fallen from a height. Her head lolled against a hard chest, and she could feel the thumping beat of the man's heart against her ear as he labored down the hillside. For a moment, she rallied, twisting and thrashing like an animal caught in a trap. Then everything went black.

At the bottom of the other side of the ridge, a group of men and women ranging in age from late teens to forties strolled toward a cluster of vehicles in an impromptu parking lot. They were at the terminus of the narrow road leading to the main dig area, the place where the huge *T. rex* skeleton had come to rest in the Cretaceous highlands of south-central Montana 65 million years earlier. It was the end of another day's draining work in the July sun. Time to party, for those with the energy.

"It's beer-thirty," somebody yelled.

"Yowsah," someone else called out.

At the rear of the procession, Doctor Scott Noble Stevens, paleontologist in charge of the dig, stopped abruptly.

"Did you hear that noise, Bill? Sounded like an explosion or something." Stevens addressed a nearby young man wearing wire-rimmed glasses.

"Yeah, Doc. Sounded like it came from over the hill. Like a gunshot. Want me take a look?"

Stevens glanced at his watch and sighed. He was eager to get back to his tent and online so he could type in the latest installment of *From the Lair of T. rex*, which would appear on his popular blog. And the people from the Discovery Channel were supposed to show up the next day. But this could be something serious. He couldn't afford to take a chance. "Ah, hell. Why don't you come with me," he said. "We'll both check it out."

Stevens led the way along the winding trail to the vertex of the windswept ridge with Bill French at his heels. They might have been brothers, with their curved-billed ball caps, tee shirts, baggy shorts, scuffed work boots, lanky builds and tanned skin. When Stevens crested the ridge top, he peered down the talus slope on the other side. A late-model white pickup truck with a large cab caught his eye as it faded from sight over a rise on the gravel road barely visible in the distance. There was something ungainly about the pickup—did it have dual rear tires? Not being a truck guy, Stevens wasn't sure. He dismissed it and turned to French.

"Darcy McKay was working up here by herself," Stevens said. "But where the hell is she?"

French shrugged. "Beats me like a drum."

"Ah, shit. I knew it was dumb, letting her go off on her own." Stevens kicked at a stone like a sullen youth. "Well, let's fan out and look around."

They separated and began to search the area for a sign of the young crew member.

A few minutes later, French called, "Doc, over here!"

Stevens hurried to French, who held up a plastic-handled paintbrush and an ice pick. "Gotta be Darcy's stuff,"

French said. "And here's a bone, nice duckbill skull, looks like."

"Holy shit!" Stevens yelled. "Look at this." He squatted down and pointed to a small mass of red liquid on the ground nearby.

French scratched his chin. "I wonder if she's hurt. Maybe she went to the HQ tent for first aid."

The note Darcy had left lay in the shade of the large boulder she'd taken cover behind, held down by a rock. In the lengthening shadows of late afternoon, it escaped the notice of the two men.

They searched for a few more minutes, yelling Darcy's name as they worked lower on the loose rock and gravel of the steep slope. Finally, they converged and looked at each other helplessly.

Stevens frowned. "She wouldn't miss dinner—no one does. Let's check back at HQ. If she's not there, she's missing." He kicked at a stone. "And we've got a problem."

2

The squad room of the Federal Bureau of Investigation's White Collar Crime unit in the Chicago Field Office was divided into square cubicles twelve feet on a side with shoulder-height partitions. Each cube contained a work surface, personal computer, four-drawer metal file cabinet and, in a few cases, an agent. Some of the cubes were meticulously neat, others a rat's nest of loose paper, overflowing file folders, flash drives and electronic devices. The few office-bound agents were on the phone, online or working with documents. The outer walls of the large room were covered with wanted posters, maps with color-coded dots representing crime scenes and memos from the Special Agent in Charge. The air smelled of stale coffee.

Brian McKay swiveled his chair around to face the man who'd just appeared at his cubicle opening.

"Hey Mon, want to buy some ganja?" The speaker, a young black man, was stocky, impeccably dressed in a dark Italian suit and a pale gray shirt with matching silk tie. He grinned broadly.

"No thanks, James, I've already got a shitload of the stuff. Why do you think I've stayed in this job all these years? Sure as hell wasn't the pay."

The reference to marijuana was a running joke between the two agents. It had originated a year earlier when the pompous Special Agent In Charge of the Chicago Field Office, a man named John Elgar, and known to all the local agents as J. Edgar, had had dinner at a Jamaican restaurant in Brian's North Side neighborhood. The SAC and his wife were walking to their car when the waiter caught up with them and spoke to Elgar in a hushed voice, like a doctor consulting on a difficult case, "Hey Mon, want to buy some ganja?" Elgar had gone ballistic, lecturing the waiter and the restaurant manager on the evils of marijuana and other illegal drugs. The following day, agents swept into the restaurant with a search warrant, but any ganja that might have been around was long gone. A Chicago Tribune columnist had gotten wind of the episode and mocked Elgar viciously. The incident remained a sore spot with the SAC.

The men agreed to meet later for an after-work drink and James St. Claire left. Brian resumed packing his personal stuff into a cardboard box on his desk. There were a couple of framed snapshots—his parents and his niece, an iPod with ear-buds, computer manuals, a dictionary, a Lucite paperweight commemorating his first ten years of service.

He'd decided to leave the FBI after twelve years: four in Violent Crimes and Major Thefts, followed by eight with the White-Collar Crime unit. Gradually, boredom had set in—he'd had his fill of investment brokers' transactions listings, auditors' reports, bank statements and tax returns. And he didn't enjoy nor was he much good at office politics, which limited his suitability for the top echelons. As he'd explained to James when he broke the news, he was tired of eating, sleeping, dressing and shitting FBI gray. It was time to move on.

A single man living simply, he'd managed to tuck away a few thousand dollars. His only luxuries—if you could call them that—were a seldom-used vintage Porsche hidden away in a windowless garage off the alley near his apartment, a ton of books, mostly mystery novels, and an extensive collection of hundreds of CDs and vinyl, heavy on classic rock and blues. He'd assembled a huge collection of tunes on his iPod as well. Though he'd been born in the late-seventies, he'd always loved classic rock.

Brian had nearly finished packing his desk contents when the landline rang with an outside call. He reached a long arm over the box, grabbed the receiver and said, "Supervisory Special Agent McKay."

A mellifluous male voice came on the line. "Brian McKay? This is Doctor Scott Noble Stevens." A pause, then: "The paleontologist."

Brian had heard of Stevens, a hotshot professor at the University of Illinois. He frowned at the receiver. "Yeah?"

"Hey Brian, I have to give you some bad news. One of my...your niece, seems to have uh, disappeared. We checked the records, and she indicated your name as next of kin."

Brian had never liked the expression "next of kin." It reminded him of old black and white movies on late-night TV where a sad-faced man in uniform stands in the doorway of a neat frame house and tells a wholesome-looking woman her husband won't be coming home from the war.

"You're talking about Darcy?"

"Yeah, she's been working with us on the *T. rex* dig here in Montana."

"What's going on? What's this 'disappeared' stuff?"

10

"We don't know yet. I mean, she was working by herself and there was a noise and then she was gone. We don't—"

"What do you mean 'gone?'" Don't you keep track of your staff? What the hell happened?"

Brian pressed the phone hard against his ear and listened as Stevens rambled on about the "unfortunate incident," the fact that the stakes were sky-high on such an important dig, that there might be poachers trying to get the bones. The bottom line: Darcy had gone off to work by herself the previous afternoon and they'd heard a noise—possibly a gunshot. They'd tried to find her, but only located her digging tools and what appeared to be blood by the time it got dark. The county sheriff and deputies searched the area that morning and confirmed it was human blood near where Darcy's digging implements had been found. Search and rescue was on the scene now. The sheriff said it would be treated as a missing person case. But, Brian knew, since Darcy was a young adult, it would get less attention then if she were a juvenile. The nearest town was a place called Clarkville.

Brian asked Stevens a few more questions, and then replaced the handset softly. He felt as though his ribs and guts were being flattened together like pages in a book. He retrieved the framed photo of Darcy from the cardboard box, examined it for a moment. In the head-and-shoulders shot taken the summer before, Darcy smiled confidently at the camera, intelligence and mischief mirrored in her eyes. Blonde hair framed an oval face. In the protective glass over the photo, Brian caught his own reflection. Definitely a family resemblance. But the worry lines under his eyes seemed to have deepened since he'd shaved that morning. He carefully removed the color print from the frame and made a few color photocopies.

He could feel the blood rushing to his head. He banged his hand on the desktop. He wanted to slam a fist through the wallboard partition. Better to do something useful, though. He thought of the Chicago street maxim: Don't get mad, get even.

Brian went to James' cubicle in a daze. When the younger agent looked up and saw Brian's face, his expression clouded.

"Man, you don't look right. You sick?"

"Yeah. Just found out my niece has disappeared out in Montana."

"Ah, shit. What happened?"

Brian shook his head. "This guy called, her boss on the dinosaur dig, says they heard a noise—maybe a shot—and Darcy's gone. Said the local law's got nothing. I'm going out there."

"Sounds like a plan. When?"

"Next flight's at 4:50."

"Need a lift to O'Hare? Got my ride in the parking garage."

Brian had taken a cab to work. "Yeah, thanks." He glanced at his watch. "We better hit the road pretty soon."

He stood outside the main entrance to the FBI head-quarters building at 2111 West Roosevelt holding his box of personal items. James St. Claire wheeled his spotless jet-black Ford F-150 pickup into a no-parking zone at the curb and beeped his horn. Brian smiled. The truck was James's first love—substitute for a wife, the way Brian saw it. He placed his storage box from the office in the back seat and climbed aboard at shotgun.

They swung by Brian's Lakeview apartment first, so he could drop off the box and throw together a duffel bag of necessities for the trip. On the way, Brian called his girlfriend, Michelle Emerson, to let her know he'd be out of town for a few days. The secretary told him she was in a meeting with some other lawyers and couldn't be interrupted. No surprise there—the woman busted her butt trying to make partner. He left her a brief message, clicked off the phone and tucked it into his canvas brief case. A few minutes later, they entered the Kennedy expressway, where four lanes of traffic crawled toward O'Hare and the vast constellation of northwest suburbs.

"I've got another favor to ask," Brian said. "If the bureau gets involved, I'll have zero access. But I'd appreciate it if you'd keep track of who's doing what on this."

"You got it. Gonna call in?"

"Yeah." He was silent for a moment. "Something's bugging me. I remember a murder case out there, about a year ago. Unsolved."

"Yeah? I'll see what's in the system."

"Good. And Stevens makes a valid point when he says there's a lot at stake. If they pull this thing off, this new outfit could ace out the Field Museum."

"Dinosaurs ain't my thing, man. What's the big deal?"

"The Field shelled out eight million for Sue the *T. rex* back in '97. Since then, the bone market's gone through the roof. If Stevens can score a world-class *rex*, it'll put him on the map big-time."

"You serious? No way a pile of damned dinosaur bones is worth eight mil."

"I hear you. But, at the time, Sue was the biggest and baddest *T. rex* anybody'd dug up so far. There was a big mother of a battle over who got the bones, remember?"

"Oh yeah—the bureau grabbed the bones. Worst publicity since they found out Hoover wore dresses," James said.

"There you go. The bureau seized the bones and locked 'em up in a warehouse, which, of course, pissed off everybody involved. Years later, they got auctioned off. I've been following this stuff through Darcy, mainly."

"You two're still tight, then?"

Brian sighed. "Yeah. She's on her own, and I've been kinda keeping an eye on her. Sees me as a big brother, I guess."

A woman yakking on a cell phone cut them off. James nailed the brakes and gave a blast on the horn, prompting her to take her hand off the wheel to flip him the bird. As she did so, her Cadillac drifted into the lane to the right, nearly striking a semi, which emitted another ear-splitting horn blast.

"Fuckin' idiot," James said. "You guys don't have any other family, right?"

"Yep."

"She must be a good kid, making it through college by her own self."

"Damn right. She's got a full ride, you know."

"No shit?"

"Yep. Softball. Takes after her uncle."

James looked dubious. "Man, I know you played baseball in college, but that was what, a hundred years ago?"

"Well, it *was* in the last century."

"Doesn't Darcy have games in the summer?"

"Nah. They wrapped up the season in May. They start fall training in September, but that's a ways off." He shook his head. "She's smart, doesn't do drugs, not a big drinker, never been in much trouble. I hope to Christ she's okay."

James eased the truck in next to the Delta signs on the departures level at O'Hare International at 3:50 p.m. A pale-faced young steroid-abuser in Chicago Police uniform rapped on the half-open driver's window with his metal parking ticket book.

"Can't park it here, pal."

James badged him. "Official business, pal."

The cop shrugged and moved on to the next vehicle in line.

"Take care, big guy," James said.

"Okay, man. Look, I'll check in with you."

They got out and shook hands—a formal gesture, Brian thought, but it seemed appropriate, since he'd just ended his career, and they probably wouldn't see each other any time soon. Brian had been James's first and only boss with the bureau. As Brian cleared the revolving door into the terminal, he glanced over his shoulder. James stood next to his truck, watching and absentmindedly buffing a fender with a shirt cuff. Brian gave him a two-fingered salute, turned and plunged into the crowd.

He made his way to the check-in routine, always irritating. Resignedly, he stripped off his belt and shoes and got in the long line to the metal detectors.

Once he'd buckled into his seat, a wave of anxiety washed over him. Someone must've snatched Darcy from that dinosaur dig. But why? Could this be related to the dig? A random act of some crazy? He hated to think about the possi-

15

bility of an unknown predator, a rapist who'd use a woman and dispose of her like Kleenex. He'd have to work fast. From first-hand experience, he knew that, after 48 hours, the odds of finding a kidnap victim alive were negligible. Half that time had already elapsed.

As James had said, Brian and Darcy were each other's only living relatives. Both sets of their parents had died in a horrendous car accident while vacationing together in Florida a few years earlier. And they were both only children. Uncle and niece had grown closer ever since. They relied on each other as good friends. Darcy looked up to her uncle as a trusted advisor as well. Brian knew that he couldn't stop worrying about her. He just couldn't stop.

He settled in for the long flight to Minneapolis and then on to Bozeman, Montana. He inserted his earbuds, thumbed on his iPod and got as comfortable as he could in the leg-constricting coach seat. But even the music he loved couldn't blot out his fears about Darcy. More than six leg-cramping, back-pinching hours later, the plane descended over mountains just visible through the clouds in the moonlight, and arrowed down to Bozeman Yellowstone International Airport. On the tarmac, Brian set his watch back an hour to Mountain Daylight Time and waited as the front section of the plane emptied out. When the aisle ahead cleared, he retrieved his duffel from the overhead compartment and trudged off the plane.

The car rental counters were closed for the night, so Brian called the local cab company and headed outside to wait at the deserted cabstand. The cool night air smelled clean, with a hint of dry grass. There was no discernible pollution—quite a contrast with O'Hare. A few minutes later, a minivan with a TAXI sign on the roof pulled up. After a fifteen-minute drive to Bozeman, Brian followed the cabby's recommendation and checked into a small downtown motel with a Triple-A sign out front.

For a couple of hours, he tossed and wrestled with the blankets, trying to drop off. Thoughts of Darcy and fears of the worst outcome wouldn't allow him the solace of sleep. Finally, his consciousness switched over to fishing in a clear mountain stream on a summer's day, and he sank into a fitful sleep.

He awoke sweating during the short night. The fishing dream had gone bad—a monstrous grizzly bear had grabbed the trout on Brian's line and was reeling the freaked-out fisherman in toward a gaping maw of dagger-like teeth. Although he quickly realized it was just a dream, probably caused by indigestion from the taco he'd had in the Salt Lake City airport lying lump-like in his stomach, he felt as if someone had taken a paring knife to his nerves. He didn't get back to sleep until nearly dawn.

3

Darcy drifted slowly into consciousness. A shaft of sunlight sliced through the window to her left, casting parallel lines of shadow across her bare legs. She lay on her back on a sagging mattress. Her first thought: why was she in a bed and not in her sleeping bag at the dig? Disoriented, she looked around the unfamiliar space. Where was she? Her left shoulder hurt like hell. How had she injured it? This place looked like some kind of a log cabin. How had she gotten here? Had she been drugged?

She took a deep breath and concentrated. Okay, now she remembered finding a duckbill jawbone sticking out of the ground high on the far side of Bone Mountain. She'd been by herself, brushing loose soil from the bone with a small paintbrush, carefully, taking it slow, doing it the way they'd taught her in orientation. She'd stopped for a break and been surprised to see a man with a gun standing at the bottom of the hill looking up at her. Then, the incredible shock of being shot in the shoulder, the strange conversation with the creep who'd done it, the blow to her head, trying to fight the guy off, being carried down the hill, then...nothing.

The shoulder felt as if it contained a small fire, burning low and steady. She flexed her arms and legs one by one to see if they worked. The only problem was the shoulder, and at least she could move it. She turned her head to look at the wound, and saw that it had been sloppily wrapped in white gauze held fast by a tan elastic bandage with a Velcro fastener. Blood had leaked through to the outer layer and hardened into a dime-sized scab. Her cap lay beside her on the pillow. She felt like crying, but willed herself to keep calm. There'd be time to cry later—if she survived.

She attempted to sit up, nearly blacked out. *Let's try it again, Babe, slower this time. Yeah, that's it.* She managed to push back with her good arm until she was sitting upright with her back against the wooden headboard.

She inventoried the room. The walls were made of varnished logs, the floor and ceiling of pine boards. She had the impression, from the room's shape, that this was part of a log building of several rooms.

A canteen stood on the table next to the bed. Darcy picked it up, unscrewed the cap and sniffed the contents. She took a small sip of tepid water and waited. Seemed okay. She had a long swallow then, nearly draining the container. That helped.

She eyed the window. Half-inch-thick black metal bars spanned the outside of it, like the burglar bars now standard equipment on ground-floor apartments in her Chicago neighborhood. Had her captor planned this? Was there some sick reason for the bars? She shuddered.

Outside, it was light, but either very overcast or near one end of the day or the other. Tall, jagged lodgepole pines shivered in a light wind. Thick clouds clogged the sky. She struggled to her feet. She felt unsteady at first, but then, equilibrium returned. Her wounded shoulder began a metronomic throb.

Darcy walked to the door, dropped her hand to the knob and tried to turn it. Locked. She realized she was still wearing her watch. The digital face registered 7:17 a.m. She must have been taken here last night, then slept or been unconscious in this damned cabin for more hours than she normally slept in two nights. Yep, she must have been drugged. Thoughts of date rape came to mind. But she was sure she hadn't been assaulted. She felt all right, other than the shoulder and general sluggishness. Her shirt was smeared with dirt where she'd sprawled after being shot. A little blood had dripped onto her New Balance running shoes and dried on the laces.

Darcy had to go to the bathroom pretty badly. An antique chamber pot occupied a corner of the room. She went to it, lowered her shorts and panties and peed. She hurriedly reassembled her clothing. The last thing she wanted was to be caught naked by the shooter. She assumed he was the one who'd brought her here. He probably wasn't far away.

She suddenly became aware that she was starving. If the bastard left a canteen for her, maybe he left some food. There was nothing on the table or the shelf beneath. She stood and did a thorough search, intent on anything either edible or capable of serving as a weapon.

The only other objects were a small wooden chair and, in the corner opposite the chamber pot, a tall knotty pine closet with two narrow doors. She pulled the doors open. The closet yawned empty except for a few hangers on a metal clothes bar enclosed at each end by circular brackets attached to the side walls with slotted screws. The bar looked promising, but it would take some work to get it down. Darcy always carried a

20

Swiss Army knife in a pocket of her cargo shorts. She patted the pocket. The knife was gone. So was her phone.

She appraised her surroundings again. There were no light fixtures or electric outlets. Was this dude some kind of hermit, living without electricity? She positioned herself on the bed, the only place in the room where she could look straight ahead at the door and also see out the window to the left. Her stomach rumbled.

A few minutes later, Darcy heard a muffled noise outside the door, then the metallic rasp of a key being inserted in the lock. The door swung open into the room. Nobody there at first. Darcy sat bolt upright, jazzed, ready to move.

The man who'd beaten her unconscious the day before walked in, smiled and said, "Some goddamn people'd sleep all day, you let 'em."

Darcy scrabbled backward and pressed against the wall. She drew her feet up toward her butt, ready to lash out with her legs. The man stood at the foot of the bed, hands on hips, a nasty grin on his broad face. He went about six-four, heavyset, with pale unblinking eyes under bushy eyebrows. There was something wrong with the eyes. They seemed...vacant, devoid of feeling. Darcy was reminded of a boy in her high-school class that nobody liked. He'd been called "The Perv" by the girls in the class, a real loser.

The man's mustache was ragged and he needed a shave. He wore a green tee shirt with the caption, "Beer: It's Not Just for Breakfast Anymore." A hard-looking basketball-sized potbelly pushed out the shirtfront. He propped a boot on the footboard and crossed his arms over the raised thigh. Darcy cringed.

"Aw, I ain't gonna hurt ya. I'da killed ya already, I'd

21

wanted to."

He stepped around to the bedside, sat on the edge near the foot. The mattress sank down several inches, the springs groaning under his weight. He raised a hand and scratched the top of his head. At the motion, Darcy held up her hands as if to ward off a blow.

The man smirked. "Hey, you're pretty jumpy."

When he spoke, Darcy thought of a professional wrestler she'd seen recently while channel surfing, an overbearing skinhead doing his damndest to project a menacing image.

"What do you want? I told you I don't have any money."

"They said I was to keep an eye out for anybody messin' around over there, and that's what I did." He looked proud of himself. "I had second thoughts, though." He raked his mustache with the tips of sausage-like fingers. "You should be happy I didn't kill ya. How about showing a little gratitude?" His voice had become husky, agitated.

"Gratitude? For shooting me and taking me hostage? Gratitude? What the hell is your problem?"

The big man suddenly leaned forward and grabbed Darcy's upper arms, pinning them to her sides. He ground his mouth against hers in a sloppy pantomime of a kiss. She twisted in his grasp, trying to break the grip of hard fingers pinching off the flow of blood to her hands. Her wounded shoulder blazed. The man released a hand from one of her arms and began to tug the hem of her tee shirt up. In desperation, Darcy cuffed him on an ear, connecting solidly. It didn't seem to have any effect. She lifted her right foot, tensed her leg muscles and kicked at the man's crotch as though booting a soccer ball from midfield toward an open goal. She could feel spongy flesh give way beneath the toe of her shoe. The man gasped and released his grip on her arms. He struggled to his feet, took a step away from the bed and bent forward holding both hands over his groin and moaning softly.

"Holy shit," he said. "Why'd ya have to do that?"

Darcy got to her feet on the bed. She backed against the wall, half-sitting on the headboard. "Try that again and you'll be a soprano."

He straightened slowly. "You got attitude, girl, I'll give you that. But I ain't done with you. Be back later. That's a promise." He staggered out of the room.

Darcy heard the door being locked again from outside, then receding footfalls. She slumped on the bed, trying to conserve energy. No way would she allow this barfbag to control her. If she could get out of the room, she'd have a chance. Otherwise...

She looked around with a renewed sense of urgency. She had to have a weapon, anything—couldn't be fussy. And she'd need the element of surprise. She got off the bed, went to hands and knees and peered underneath. Nothing. Then, out of the corner of an eye, she saw a small red object between a leg of the bed and the wall. She squirmed under the bed frame, stretched her fingers and touched the edge of the object. She managed to grasp it in her fingertips and pull it out into the light. Her Swiss Army knife—must have fallen from her shorts pocket.

She stood with the knife in her right hand. The two-inch blade wouldn't do much good, even if she slashed or stabbed with it. She'd probably just piss the guy off, cause him to hurt her even more. She walked to the closet, removed the hangers from the metal clothes rod and placed them on the floor. There were three sturdy screws anchoring the brackets at each end of the steel rod to the pine wall. The whole thing looked really old, way heavier than the wooden clothes rods common in modern bedrooms. She opened the stubby bottle-opener/screwdriver attachment on the knife, and began unscrewing one of the brackets.

The screws were balky and it took her quite a while to loosen them. Finally, she got all three out. She grabbed the metal rod and shook. The bracket came away from the wall and the heavy rod clattered to the floor, where it reverberated like a gong. Darcy listened intently to see if there'd be a reaction to the noise, but heard nothing.

She scrambled back from the closet, leaving the doors open. She now held a four-foot-long, inch-and-a-half-thick solid metal weapon. She returned to the bed and sat, staring at the door, listening, waiting. She wondered whether the people at the dig site were looking for her, whether they'd called the cops to report her missing. Maybe they'd think she'd just taken off. They didn't know her that well.

Around noon, the door opened a crack and a can of baked beans with a spoon sticking out of the top was shoved into the room along with a mason jar filled with water. Darcy clutched the metal bar, ready to strike. The door was slammed and locked. Darcy waited a few minutes, then wolfed down the beans and water.

She explored the room again, opened the window and tested the iron bars, which held despite her attempts to pry them loose with the closet rod and screwdriver. She checked the soundness of the door hinges, the walls, the floor—nothing offered hope of escape.

4

Tom Norton, security manager of the Sands Ranch, snatched the phone on his desk and quickly punched in the number for the Gruel brothers' cabin. After six rings, a man answered, "Hey."

"Hey, my ass," Norton shouted. "I've been trying to reach you guys for the last hour. Where the fuck you been?"

"Sorry 'bout that. We just went out to get some, uh, supplies."

"Well set down your beers and get your asses over to my office right now—the both of you."

Norton slammed the phone down and drummed thick fingers on the desktop. Those guys were about as useful as toxic waste. Hell of a lot harder finding experienced security men out here than it would be in Chicago, where there were armies of ex-cops and moonlighting cops—experienced, no-nonsense men with a work ethic. Harrison had recommended the Gruels—was that the best he could come up with? These guys would rather drink or hunt than work. Shane and Donny were supervised mostly by Ray Chafee, doing ranch chores, things like fence repairs and unclogging irrigation ditches. From what Norton had seen, they didn't screw up that stuff, but every time he'd given them a security-related assignment, he'd been as confident of them doing it right as he'd be of them taking the trophy on Dancing With The Stars.

Norton's gold cocker spaniel bumped him gently in the shin. When he looked down at her, she gazed into his face expectantly and wagged her tail. Norton's expression softened. "Least I can count on you, Annie," he said. He reached down and scratched the top of the dog's furry head. She dropped to the floor next to his feet and arranged herself with her tail over his shoe tops. While Norton studied an invoice for electronic hardware, he scratched the dog's head absentmindedly. Suddenly, she stiffened and got to her feet, alert to something outside.

A loud BANG came from nearby. Norton looked out the window in time to see a battered old Chevy pickup splotched with red primer paint over faded blue, and jacked up above oversized tires, lurch into the parking area near the door. As the driver cut the engine, it backfired again, dieseled for a moment, then gasped into silence. An overweight black Labrador retriever stood in the truck bed, barking. Then it circled, passed gas loudly and lay down.

Annie began a high-pitched yelping.

"Cool it, girl. You go sit in the corner now," Norton murmured. He guided the dog away from his desk.

Two wiry men wearing sweat-stained rodeo-style straw hats, white tee shirts and faded Wranglers sauntered into the office. They could have passed for twins, though Shane Gruel was three years older than his brother, Donny. Annie growled briefly at their entrance, then retreated to the corner and sat on her haunches, keeping a wary eye on the intruders.

Shane thumbed his hat back from dishwater blonde locks, squinted, shifted his toothpick to a corner of his mouth with his tongue. "Uh, what can we do ya for, Tom?"

Norton looked up, paused for a beat, held his seething temper in check. "Sit the fuck down and listen. I'm only gonna explain this once. Cody's been gone since yesterday afternoon. I sent him over to check on TBT, and haven't heard from him since. Also, some girl working on the dinosaur dig disappeared last night. Cody hasn't got a phone in that godforsaken place of his. I want you to go over there, get him and all three of you get back here on the double. If he's not home, look for him in town, but don't waste any time hanging around. Understand?"

"You bet," Shane said. "But ya can't drive all the way to his cabin. Last eight miles is just a trail, really. We could get up there with ATVs, though, we had 'em." The toothpick waggled as he spoke.

Donny cleared his throat. His prominent Adams apple bobbed in his thin neck. "Could we maybe use a couple a four-wheelers and a trailer to haul 'em?"

Norton considered. The Sands fleet of all-terrain vehicles was to be used strictly for ranch work, but this was an emergency. "Yeah, go get 'em from Chafee. I'll call and let him know it's okay."

"One other question. What does TBT mean, again?" Donny asked.

"Ticket to the big time. Now get going."

Norton stared out the window as the brothers strolled slowly to their truck, bantering. Donny punched Shane on the shoulder and ducked as Shane flicked a lazy backhand at his face. As the truck jerked away in a cloud of smoke, Norton noticed a bumper sticker on the tailgate: HORN BROKEN. WATCH FOR FINGER. He shook his head, sat down and reached for the phone.

5

Darcy rubbed her eyes. Bored and drowsy, she felt like sleeping, but forced herself to stay awake. Her clothes were wrinkled and dank. Her left shoulder still burned with pain. She sniffed an armpit. Yuck. She could use a shower. She heard a noise somewhere in the building. Getting closer. She raced to the door and stood next to it. When it opened, she'd be shielded behind it. As she got into position, she could hear faint footfalls approaching.

Darcy heard a key in the lock. She held the metal closet rod in front of her, chest-high. The door opened slowly and stopped an inch from her hands.

He stepped into the room, didn't see Darcy and passed his eyes over the interior until his gaze settled on the open closet door. "You ain't fooling me none," he said. He stepped toward the closet.

Darcy followed silently, on the balls of her feet. She wanted room to take a good cut. She recalled her UIC softball coach's advice: when you swing, plant your feet, keep your shoulders square and swing easy. Make contact with the ball. Let the bat and your body strength do the rest. Don't try to kill the ball. As she swung the heavy bar at the back of the man's head, she remembered all this advice except the last. In an adrenaline rush, she swung with all her might, a bit off-balance. The end of the stout shaft connected solidly with his skull, emitting a sound like a melon dropped from a counter-top.

He pitched forward onto his face, twitching spasmodi-cally. Although conscious, he was obviously hurt. He began to move an arm forward, as if trying to brace himself to get up. Darcy rushed the second swing, more of a downward hack, actually. It connected less solidly than the first, but the man jerked once, then went limp, his breath rasping like a second-hand bicycle pump. Blood seeped from the crown of his head. Darcy noticed a length of nylon rope and a bandana in his right hand. A roll of silver duct tape had fallen from his other hand and rolled across the room, coming to rest against a wall. The sick bastard had planned on tying her up and gagging her. Then what?

"You asshole!" she yelled. She dropped the closet rod to the floor, took the rope, gathered the man's hands at the small of his back and tied the thick wrists together securely. With her jackknife, she cut the tag end off the rope and tied it around the man's ankles. For good measure, she wound duct tape around both sets of tied limbs, and wrapped a few loops around his head so they covered his mouth. She regarded the prone figure for a moment. Her injured shoulder was throbbing with pain, worse than before. There was no time to worry about it now. She had to get moving. She left the room.

Darcy emerged into a short hallway, took it to the end and turned right into a small, messy kitchen. An opened bag of sour cream and onion potato chips sat on the counter. She snatched the bag, ate a handful, which stimulated her appetite. Ravenous, she ripped open the door of the propane refrigerator. There were a few candy bars on the middle shelf. She tore off the wrapper on one and ate it, then scooped up the rest and stuffed them into her cargo shorts pockets. She grabbed a can of Coke from another shelf and the bag of chips.

She hurried into the next room, which contained a few chairs and a crude table covered with a litter of pizza boxes, beer cans and magazines. A real boar's den. No TV or radio. A camp lantern hung from a chain attached to the ceiling. The one window was open. She looked in vain for a phone. A scuffed leather wallet, a ring of keys and a few coins were heaped on a table near the heavy entry door at the front of the building.

Darcy picked up the wallet, flipped it open. There were six twenties and some singles. In a laminated plastic sleeve, she found a Montana driver's license with a mug shot of the man she'd just brained. The name on the license was Cody Gilstrap. No address—just a post office box in town. She pocketed the license and bills and grabbed the keys.

She rushed to the door, pulled it open and went outside carrying the Coke and chips in one hand, the keys in the other. Three steps led to a rock-strewn yard. Sharp-edged mountains rimmed the horizon beyond a dense wall of pines and spruce. A red-winged blackbird lit on a branch and trilled raucously. Otherwise, it was dead quiet. Darcy took in the cabin's log walls, stone chimney and a barred window on the right side of the building, marking the room she'd escaped from.

A green all-terrain vehicle with a miniature pickup bed behind its yellow seat was parked out front, looking like a toy truck. A decal on the side caught her eye—a yellow alligator and the word GATOR.

She walked to the vehicle, got behind the wheel and

tried keys from the ring until she found one that fit the ignition. She noticed a Dodge truck key, but there was no vehicle in sight. She twisted the GATOR key to the right. A clicking noise came from under the hood. She tried again. More clicks. Dead battery. Christ, couldn't she catch a break? Disgusted, she threw the keys as far as she could into a clump of trees, turned and walked down the gravel drive, which devolved into a narrow rutted track dropping steeply below the cabin and disappearing into a thickness of trees and brush.

Darcy began to jog down the track, keeping to the left. She was in shady coniferous forest now. After a few minutes, she stopped to catch her breath, leaning against the scaly orange-brown trunk of a huge ponderosa at the side of the track. She guessed she'd put about a half-mile between herself and the cabin. It would take Gilstrap a while to recover from the blows she'd landed on his head—if he recovered at all. Maybe he'd die. But, then, he deserved it, the things he'd done and meant to do. Even if he was not seriously injured, it would take him hours to get loose from the ropes and duct tape, she thought with grim satisfaction. In any case, if he *did* get loose, he could only chase her on foot. Even if he had a spare key to the GATOR thing, it wasn't likely he'd have a way to charge the battery. With any luck, she'd be far away by then, maybe back at the dig site. It occurred to her she must have been brought to that cabin in the bed of the little vehicle she'd tried starting.

Suddenly, she heard the sound of high-pitched revving motors below. It reminded her of the four-wheeled all-terrain vehicle Doctor Stevens sometimes used at the dig site, only more than one. The high-pitched racket seemed to be ascending, getting closer. If she stayed there, the vehicles would overtake her in no time. Could they be friends of Gilstrap's? Darcy veered off the track, squatted down behind some bushes and waited, peering through a small gap in the branches.

A moment later, someone yelled, "Outa my way, ya dumb fuck!"

A pair of ATVs lurched into view around a bend below, perhaps two hundred feet away. It looked like they were racing each other, jockeying for position, but there wasn't room for them to ride two abreast. The riders gunned their engines and shot up the track, spewing gravel. Darcy ducked lower as the machines screamed by. All she could see of the drivers was straw cowboy hats bobbing up and down and back and forth like feathers in the wind as the noisy two-stroke vehicles bore upward. A cloud of smelly blue smoke drifted down the mountain in their wake.

6

The two Polaris Rangers careened up the gravel drive to Cody Gilstrap's rustic cabin and nearly collided as they slid to a stop a few feet shy of the front door. Shane and Donny Gruel dismounted.

"Think the dude's here?" Donny said in a whiny voice.

"Well, shit-for-brains, his truck's down below and his four-wheeler's setting right there yonder. That sorta indicates he might be here. C'mon."

Shane led the way to the cabin door, opened it without knocking and shouldered his way in. Donny kept on his heels, anxious to not miss anything. The brothers looked around the messy front room, then poked their heads into the slovenly kitchen.

"The man's a fucking pig, and that's a fact," Donny declared.

"Like you're not? Get real." Shane retorted, his toothpick waggling vigorously. He went into the hallway leading to the two bedrooms in back.

"Holy shit! The dude's in a world of hurt," Shane said, as he spotted Gilstrap lying facedown on the bedroom floor. There was a glazed smear of blood near the man's head, and his hat lay upside down a few feet away. He appeared to be alive, though. Breath labored in and out of his nose—his mouth was duct-taped. It looked like someone had beaten him with a club.

"Get some cold water to revive the son of a bitch," Shane ordered his younger brother.

"Who was your goddamn slave last year?" Donny rejoined.

Shane balled a fist and feinted at Donny's face. Donny laughed and backed toward the door. "Okay, okay, I'm getting it. Pretty goddamn sad, man can't take a fuckin' joke."

Shane worried about his younger brother sometimes. Donny acted dumber than he actually was. Why would a guy act stupid all the time? Because of it, everybody dumped on him, and it set Shane up as a kind of goddamned bodyguard, watching over the jagoff.

But there'd been times Donny'd surprised him, like when the two of them were kids at the Methodist church camp that summer, musta been damn-near twenty years ago. The preacher'd been keeping an eye on the brothers during his talks on living a Christian life, kind of like he knew their rep as troublemakers. Part of the deal was you were supposed to be "saved" during the weeklong retreat. Supposedly, you'd feel God's presence and know you could make it with His help. The preacher would sling a load of religious crap at the group, and then, random-like, he'd shout out a kid's name and ask him, "Have you been saved?"

Just about everybody came back with, "Yes, sir." Not Donny. The first two times, he'd told the preacher, "Nah, I don't think so." The third time, he'd said, "Well, maybe, a little." Short on either patience or interest, the preacher jumped all over Donny's half-assed answer like it was exactly the right one. "This young man's been saved!" he'd bawled, while

Donny stood there with a fuck-you smirk on his mug. Donny was one of those guys who never quite got with the program, and you had to like that, no matter how much the fucker screwed up.

Shane rolled Gilstrap over onto his back, then drew a razor-sharp hunting knife from the leather sheath on his belt. He squatted down and cut through the duct tape around Gilstrap's head, down near the floor. He took an edge of the tape between thumb and index finger and ripped it upward, yanking it off the big man's mouth along with a strip of skin and whiskers.

Blood spurted from Gilstrap's lower lip, and he muttered dazedly, "What the hell?" His eyes remained closed.

Shane grabbed the glass of water from Donny's hand and poured it on Gilstrap's broad face. He sputtered and licked the moisture off his lips. In a moment, his eyes flickered open. He quickly closed them again, and spoke through clenched teeth. "I must be having the worst damned nightmare on the planet."

"Man, who scrambled your eggs?" Shane asked.

"Yeah, who dropkicked your dipstick, cowboy?" Donny put in.

Gilstrap groaned. "Just what I need, a couple of rodeo clown rejects. How about stifling the wise-ass remarks and cutting me loose."

Shane set to work sawing through the bonds around Gilstrap's wrists and ankles. Donny kept his distance, as if afraid one of the others might hit him on general principles. Finally, Gilstrap was free. He massaged his wrists in an attempt to restore circulation. Then he sat up on the floor with his hands behind him for support, wiggling his toes for a moment.

With Shane's help, Gilstrap made it to his feet, staggered to the bed and sank down like a weighted diver entering the water backwards. The bedsprings protested with a shriek. He arranged his back against the rough wall, sighed deeply and said, "Look, I had a, uh misunderstanding with a girl, that's all. No big deal."

"No big deal? Man, you're in deep doodoo. Norton's been looking all over for ya. Said to bring your ass back to the ranch like pronto, Tonto," Donny said.

"Man, if brains was gunpowder, you couldn't blow your nose," Shane said to his brother.

Donny began to sing like a country artist, "If mah nose was runnin' money, Honey, Ah'd blow it all on yew. If mah nose—"

"Are you fucking done?" Gilstrap demanded.

There was silence for a moment, then Shane addressed Gilstrap. "You want to maybe work up a story for Norton? He seemed to think you were like, scoping out TBT."

Gilstrap gingerly fingered the knot on his head. He drew the fingers before his eyes and frowned when he saw blood on them. "Look, the guy told us to watch for people messin' around on the hill—right? This broad was digging around up in the rocks right near TBT. I fired my weapon to scare her, but winged her, didn't hardly hurt her at all. So, I bring her here to find out what the hell she's doing up there, see if she's seen anything she shouldn't have."

"You were supposed to 'observe and report' any trespassers to Norton, not fucking kidnap them," Shane said. "Man, you really stirred up a shit storm."

"Can't help that now. I grabbed the girl. It's done."

"Well, where's she at—under the bed?" Donny raised hands next to his shoulders and gave an exaggerated bug-eyed look.

"She belted me with that metal bar there," Gilstrap said. He nodded at the closet rod on the floor. "I musta been out for a while. Then you guys showed up. The girl musta took off. That's all she wrote."

"Is that your final answer?" Donny bellowed.

The other two men ignored him. Shane scratched his chin, as if deep in thought. Finally, he said, "We gotta find the bitch."

"Fuckin' A," Donny agreed.

"But we better check in with Norton," Shane said. He seemed to relish the idea of being in charge. "Let's boogie," he said, turning toward the door.

Gilstrap managed to hoist his bulk from the bed, scooped up his hat and followed the brothers to the front door. He paused at the table near the entryway. "She took my god-damned keys," he yelled. "I gotta find 'em."

After a few minutes' search, Gilstrap remembered the spare keys to the ATV and his truck squirreled away in a box of stuff in the kitchen. He retrieved the keys and said, "Okay, let's get the fuck out of here." They went outside and boarded their vehicles.

Gilstrap tried to start the GATOR but, when he turned the key in the ignition, a sick-sounding clicking noise came from under the hood.

"Ah, blow me," he said.

"Problem there, Chief?" Donny asked.

"Get your goddamned machine over here. I need a jump."

"Man, your problem is, you already done jumped the wrong damn gal," Donny drawled.

It took another twenty minutes to locate jumper cables, argue about what stupid thing Gilstrap might have done to cause the battery to die, argue further about the proper method of attaching the cables and finally, to get Gilstrap's machine started. When all three vehicles were running, the trio descended the trail, peering back and forth for a sign of Darcy. The Gruel brothers continued bantering while Cody Gilstrap simmered in silence, concentrating on keeping his machine on the rocky track. His head throbbed with a low-level pain that just wouldn't quit.

"Ya know, I could get into this detective shit," Donny yelled over the racket. "Maybe I'll apply for one of them deputy jobs they got."

Shane's laugh was nasty. "They'd never hire the likes of you, fuckwad. Besides, they're so goddamned picky in that town, Jesus Christ couldn't get a job as preacher."

After a ride of several miles, they reached the small gravel parking area at the bottom of the road without seeing the girl. The Gruels backed their four-wheelers onto the flatbed trailer they'd borrowed at the ranch, while Gilstrap stowed his in a small metal shed and padlocked the door. Shane and Donny piled into their old truck. Gilstrap boarded his big white one-ton crew cab and followed the brothers on the short drive to the Sands compound.

7

Brian stepped out into to a bright, crisp morning. It was only forty-six degrees according to the sign on the bank across the street when he picked up his four-wheel drive Jeep Grand Cherokee from Hertz. Bozeman, Montana sits at an elevation of 4,750 feet in the Gallatin River valley, surrounded by mountain ranges of the northern Rockies. Home to Montana State University, it's a Mecca for people who play in the mountains—hikers, fishermen, hunters, climbers, horseback riders, skiers—and the guides, retailers, restaurateurs and motel operators who make a living off them.

Brian's gray tee shirt, faded jeans and scuffed boots allowed him to blend in on the college town's streets. Logy from lack of sleep and tight-nerved with worry about Darcy, he forced himself to get the required errands done before going out to search for her.

He went to a tourist information center, where he got directions to the dinosaur dig site and a Montana highway map. Next, it was off to a supermarket for sliced turkey, rolls, cheese, crackers, apples, potato chips, pretzels, candy bars and bottled water, all of which he stowed in the rental. Michelle was always after him to eat healthy but, unlike her, he couldn't summon the willpower to pass up nutritiously bankrupt snack foods, especially on the road. A natural inclination toward leanness helped—he weighed the same 175 he had in his days as an outfielder at Michigan. He followed Main Street out to the Interstate and headed east just before ten A.M.

An hour later, Brian arrived in the small town of Clarkville on the Yellowstone River. According to a brochure he'd picked up at the information place, the town's leading industries were agriculture and tourism, catering especially to fly-fishermen. Brian tooled along the main drag, making a mental note of a funky-looking old hotel with a huge neon sign advertising both the hotel itself and the house bar, Murray's Hideout.

The dinosaur dig site, labeled on the map as Park Butte, but known to locals as Bone Mountain, lay in a mountain valley fifteen miles north, in the "checkerboard." Brian had learned from the woman at the tourist center that checkerboard meant alternating one-mile squares, or sections, of public and private land, a legacy of the government's setting aside a patchwork of land for the Northern Pacific Railroad. Recognizing there was no significant timber value, the railroad sold off its sections early in the twentieth century. Most of the private sections were vacant, but a few had cabins on them.

He'd also learned that Bone Mountain itself lay on National Forest land, covered several sections, was bordered on two sides by mixed checkerboard, with National Forest on the third side and a large private holding of thousands of acres on the fourth. The Crazy Mountains jutted upward to elevations of more than 11,000 feet just east of the dig site. This island mountain range had once been home to the Crow Indians, who called the Crazies the Bird Home Mountains, site of many vision quests. The Crows now mostly lived on a large reservation about a hundred miles east near Billings, Montana's largest city.

Brian drove north on two-lane blacktop for ten miles along the Shields River as it tumbled over rocks and wound through ranchland west of the Crazies. He turned right onto a poorly maintained gravel road. The Grand Cherokee juddered and squeaked as he climbed higher on the washboard surface. Clumps of Russian olives, cottonwoods and junipers appeared wherever there was water. Otherwise, the landscape was all grass, rocks and low sagebrush. Shortly, signs began to appear along the roadside: KEEP ON THE TRAVELED WAY, PRIVATE LAND NEXT 1.5 MILES and BONE MOUNTAIN SITE 1.0. Finally, after a seemingly endless spine-jarring ride, the way was barred by a gate constructed of treated pine posts and barbed wire and flanked by a brown metal sign with white lettering, BONE MOUNTAIN PALEONTOLOGICAL SITE. NO ADMITTANCE WITHOUT PERMIT.

Brian got out, worked the gate open, pulled it to one side and drove through. Then he saw the next sign: DON'T EVEN THINK OF LEAVING THE GATE OPEN! He secured the gate the way he'd found it, got back into the Grand Cherokee and drove on.

In another mile or so, he arrived at a grouping of three large canvas teepees. A recently used fire pit containing half-burnt logs was positioned in front of the central tent. Nearby were a bunch of smaller nylon tents, a scattering of picnic tables and a camp kitchen set up under a tarpaulin: gas refrigerator, Coleman stoves, coolers, utensils and metal plates. Several vehicles, mostly Subaru wagons and domestic SUVs, were parked haphazardly. Odd bits of paraphernalia were scattered about—rock hammers, clipboards, whiskbrooms, bags of plaster of Paris, plastic buckets, shovels. It looked like a group of rockhound gypsies had found a place to hide until the police came to roust them out.

The base camp was set in a shallow basin dotted with sagebrush and other dryland plants. The ground was parched and dusty, with rocks of all sizes strewn about like a child's playthings. A ground squirrel darted by, a few feet from Brian's boots. A pair of gray-blue pinyon jays flew close, perched on a stunted juniper and eyed him hopefully.

He walked to the teepee with the fire ring and called out, "Yo. Anybody home?"

In a moment, he heard rustling noises within the conical tent. A bare-chested man of about thirty emerged through the door flap. He was about Brian's height, stocky, with a shaved head, wispy mustache/goatee combination and blinking eyes set a bit too close together. An incongruous tattoo of a seahorse covered his meaty right biceps. He rubbed his eyes and blinked as if he'd just awakened. He scowled at Brian. "Help you?"

To Brian, he looked like a guy not naturally predisposed to helping strangers. "I'm Brian McKay, here to see Doctor Stevens."

The man from the tent considered that for a moment, then brightened. "Oh yeah? He said you'd probably be by? Uh, they won't be back down here for a while?" Statements generally came out as questions; he ended each sentence with rising inflection.

"How long is a while?"

"They like, stay up at the dig 'til maybe seven? You could like, just go up there, you want?"

"Okay, I'll do that," Brian said. "Which way?"

"You take that jeep trail there for maybe a mile? It climbs up and dead-ends near the dig? You'll see some vee-hicles, and you can drop yours there, too? You should run into somebody pretty quick."

Brian thanked him and followed the directions. The road above the tents was barely passable; it looked like it had been jury-rigged as a way to cut the commuting time for the dinosaur workers. Brian horsed the Grand Cherokee slowly around and over granite boulders. Even with the vehicle's high ground clearance, the bottom occasionally scraped stone. He was relieved to spot a few vehicles ahead in a flat area at the base of a layered hill that looked like a sienna and gray wedding cake made of rock.

The temperature had risen into the eighties. The dry heat felt good to Brian after the sweltering humidity of Chicago. He abandoned the Jeep and hiked up a narrow trail for about five minutes until, rounding a bend, he saw a young woman in tan shirt and shorts walking the same direction about twenty-five yards ahead. Brian sped up to overtake her. As he approached, she turned and regarded him with undisguised curiosity. She held a water bottle in one hand. A green nylon rucksack hung from her shoulders.

Mopping sweat from her brow with a forearm, she smiled and said, "Hey, did ya miss a turn somewhere?"

"Could be. I'm looking for Doctor Stevens."

"Follow me. I'll show ya where he is."

"Thanks."

As they rounded the next curve, a group of men and women working under the intense sun came into view to the left.

"That's our fearless leader," she said. "The guy in the yellow cap, bossing everyone else around. Good luck," she said, as she walked off.

The young woman's description was accurate. Stevens stood, hands on hips, watching the others work on various objects in the ground with small hand tools. Brian approached and offered a hand. "Brian McKay." He noticed that Stevens wore a chunky gold Rolex on his left wrist.

Stevens hesitated for a split-second, then extended a hand. "Oh yes, of course. Scott Stevens. Welcome to our dig, Brian. As you'll see, this is one of the most impressive paleontological sites in North America. We've got the most bad-ass *T. rex* known to man." Then, as if remembering the reason for Brian's presence, "Sorry it has to be under such shitty circumstances for you. Really a bummer. We'll uh, do everything we can to help. You know, you look less like a fed than the dudes who came out here last year." His speech was like a stream running swiftly over stones.

Brian wondered whether Stevens knew he'd left the FBI. He wasn't about to volunteer that information. A crew of a half dozen tanned workers crouched, sat or stood in a nearby roped-off area about sixty feet long and twenty-five feet wide. The crew members were mainly attired in tee shirts and cargo shorts or grimy jeans. Headgear ranged from ball caps to bandanas to floppy straws. They wielded brushes, ice picks, dental probes, rock hammers and chisels, painstakingly removing bits of dirt and rock from partially uncovered dark objects that Brian presumed, were dinosaur bones. One neckless young man who looked like a Big Ten lineman jabbed at the ground with an army surplus bayonet. The dig area was bracketed by a pair of three-foot-tall concrete pillars painted bright blue. Even to

Brian's untrained eyes, the long, knobby ridge they'd exposed looked like a gigantic curving spine. Stevens gestured at the ridge like the proud father of a newborn.

"They're working on the vertebrae there."

"What are the blue things?"

"We call them datum stakes. They're the reference points for everything we find. At the beginning of the process, we situated them using a very accurate GPS. As we uncover bones, we use a technique called radial mapping, recording the distance in meters and centimeters and the angle in degrees and minutes between the ends of each bone and the two stakes. Plus, we take still photos throughout. Documentation is key, just like provenance is for an old painting, say. It's slower than whale shit, but hey, you've gotta do it.

Brian broke in, "Fascinating. But where was Darcy working?"

Stevens looked a little miffed, but quickly recovered with an ingratiating smile. "Hey, I'm lecturing. You didn't come here for that. C'mon, let's head up."

As they walked a dusty path, Brian asked, "How much longer will this thing take?"

"Two to three weeks. We're in the home stretch."

"Can't just blast away with jackhammers, eh?"

"Believe it or not, we remove a lot of the overburden with paintbrushes. Points and hammers are only for the harder rock, and even then, away from the bone. Anyway, we barely got started last September, when the snows came early. We splash-casted the exposed bones and reburied them until a few weeks ago. We've got to get this baby done before we get forced out by the weather again."

"So what's at stake here, bottom line?"

"Let me put it this way: there are about 300 bones in a *T. rex*, and we think they're all here. No one's ever found more than ninety percent before. Man, this is a coup."

"You guys do all the bone-cleaning here, too?"

"Nah. We encase bone groupings in plaster. We'll chopper 'em down to a semi and truck 'em to Chicago. That's where our lab-bound buddies, the preparators, come in. They remove the rest of the material from the bone, make repairs, put it all together. For every day we spend in the field, it takes the prep guys twenty days of work." He made a wry face. "I can tell you, that's not my cup of cappuccino."

Brian was eager to get down to business. "Are we almost to the spot where Darcy disappeared?"

"Quite so," Stevens said. The guy's accent seemed to vary between American and English.

As they continued on, Stevens kept up a running commentary. "This part of Montana used to be hardwood forest and swamps. There were cypresses, sequoias, China firs. We know that from the material accompanying the fossils."

As they crested the hilltop, they stopped to catch their breath for a moment. Brian's interest was captured by the stunning vistas unfolding in all directions. To the east, there were miles of brown and red rock cliffs above the banks of a dry creek. Spread out below were incredibly rough striped and folded hillsides, cliffs and canyons of fast-eroding badlands. The rocky terrain was punctuated by stunted junipers, sagebrush, prickly pear cactus, grasses, thistles, wildflowers and an occasional gnarled cottonwood or fir. Grasshoppers were so plentiful, Brian felt compelled to keep his mouth closed to avoid sucking one in. A dirt road crossed a narrow thread of flat ground running in a line perhaps a mile-and-a-half from the base of the hill and separated from it by twisted ditches and deep rock-choked gorges. Past the road was a stark contrast: miles of verdant irrigated fields. He noticed pivot lines spraying water onto the land in circular patterns. He knew that center-pivot irrigation made growing of crops in dry country like this economically feasible. Each pivot had a center hub and an attached quarter-mile-long wheeled pipeline. An electric motor rotated the line in an arc around the hub, with line-mounted spray nozzles watering the ground. When viewed from an airplane, the circular irrigation pattern looked like green circles, sometimes called "crop circles."

"What's that place across the road?" Brian asked.

"A ranch. Private property."

"They grow crops?"

"Mostly, they grow bison. Those irrigated fields are alfalfa. The bison graze in the natural grasslands, and the ranch sells the alfalfa hay to other ranchers who raise cattle."

In the distance, the Crazy Mountains seemed to kiss the sky. Timber climbed the mountain flanks, much higher than the hilltop they stood on. Brian knew that with elevation came clouds and rain and snow. Still, the ability to view such diverse microclimates from a single point was amazing to his Midwestern-trained eyes.

Like a natural lecturer, Stevens commented, "The last ice age, about forty thousand years ago, scoured this land and exposed much of what you see below us. The glaciers were the bulldozers of the Pleistocene. That's pretty recent. On the other hand, the sedimentary rock in this area is part of the Livingston Group, about sixty-seven million years old. We're talking the last part of the Cretaceous. That's when *T. rex* ruled. The really cool thing is, nobody's ever found one in the Shields River valley before. But I realized this place had the two things you want—deposition and erosion. Deposition preserves the bones and erosion exposes them. My colleagues insisted this is too far west for any large theropods, let alone tyrannosaurids. They concentrate on the Hell Creek formation east of here. But they tend to follow the pack. I don't."

"So this is the place?" Brian asked.

"Almost there."

There was no trail on the other side, and they had to scramble, picking footholds carefully in the sliding scree. A little further on, Stevens moved off to the left and stopped near a head-high boulder. A shallow circular hole had recently been hollowed out in the ground around a dark stone object about the size of a coffee cup. A four-inch wide yellow tape bearing the legend GEYSER COUNTY SHERIFF DO NOT REMOVE had been placed on the ground around the boulder and the dark object, marking off a rough circle perhaps fifteen feet in diameter. Rocks anchored the tape to the ground.

Stevens stepped into the taped area. "That's part of a duckbill jaw down there." He toed the dark object. "She hadn't gotten that much of it exposed," he mused.

"And those spots are blood," Brian said.

"According to the sheriff. He had one of his people take a sample. Anyway, this is where she was."

"What was she doing over here by herself?"

For the first time since Brian had met the man, Stevens looked unsure of himself. "She talked me into letting her come over here, said she'd seen some bones and wanted to identify them." He shrugged. "I figured, what the hell, we could spare her for a couple hours. Of course, who'd've thought there was any danger? I mean, nothing like this has ever happened on a Stevens dig."

"What's the sheriff doing? Is there a search party looking for Darcy?"

"The sheriff and some of his people were here last night till dark, and the female deputy came back by herself this morning. And then a couple of guys from a search and rescue team stopped by and interviewed me: what was she wearing, what did she look like, did she have camping equipment with her, stuff like that. They went off to do some tracking or something, last I saw of them."

Brian pulled the Nikon from his daypack and took several overlapping photos of the bloody rocks, the immediately surrounding area. Once back on top of the divide, he took some shots of the panorama below, including just past the dirt road. He made mental notes of rough distances between features of the terrain he'd just photographed. He got out his binoculars and studied the area ranging down to the bottom of the hill. The proximity of the dirt road below bothered him.

"Is there any way to drive from that road there over to this hill? I mean, get over here without coming in through the gate on the other side?"

"I've never tried," Stevens said. "You can see it's pretty much impassable down there, with all those crevices and rocks, but I've heard that locals get through in the fall to hunt. It's not that far, so I guess you could walk in from the road, or maybe use an ATV. I just hope they don't start hunting dinosaur bones."

"I saw something recently about a professor from

some Midwestern university," Brian said. "The guy said ever since Sue sold for millions, fossil pirates have been coming out of the woodwork, following you dinosaur guys to see where you dig. Then they come in with everything from backhoes to shovels and steal."

Stevens frowned. "Yeah, that's right. Some places, but not here so far, knock on wood. And we actually have a security man with us."

"The bald guy in the tent?" Brian raised an eyebrow.

"He may not be a brain surgeon, but he's experienced, strong as an ox and he's armed."

"How's he do any good staying in the tent?"

"Colten sleeps during the day, goes on duty when we stop each evening. I mean, with the crew and me around, there's not much chance somebody would mess with our stuff. At any rate, he makes sure no unauthorized people come on-site after hours." Stevens shot a look at his watch. "Anything else?"

"Not now, but I might need to come back."

As they turned to leave, Brian noticed a rusted pile of old metal machine parts about sixty feet away and slightly above them on a steeper part of the hillside.

"What's that?" Brian gestured with a thumb.

"I understand it's old scrap metal, some kind of gold mining equipment left over from a century or so ago." He dismissed the subject with a shoofly wave.

"Do you know who Darcy was close to in your crew?"

"Let's see. Her tent-mate's a girl named Becky something from MSU. Want to meet her?"

"Yes, I would. MSU's Montana State—right?"

"Yup. Local college."

They retraced their steps down the other side.

When they reached the main dig area again, Stevens introduced Brian to Becky, whose last name turned out to be Stanton—an attractive brown-haired twenty-year-old in a red halter and faded cutoff jeans.

"How was Darcy doing last time you talked with her?" Brian asked.

"Darcy was okay in the morning when we started working," Becky said. "I mean, she didn't seem to have any problems. Everything was cool. Then she went over the hill. Last I saw her."

"Did she have any hassles with anyone, say, before yesterday?"

"Oh, no. Darcy gets along with everybody okay. Like, we're here working and stuff all the time. We don't really have the chance to meet anyone else around here."

"Any boyfriends you know of?"

"Not here. She said she was dating a guy at home once in a while, but she didn't really say that much about him." She shrugged. "I just can't see her taking off without saying anything. I'm like, super worried. Anything I can do to help, let me know."

"Thanks. You've helped already."

Brian asked Stevens if they had cell coverage onsite, and learned they had it plus there were solar panels for charging electronic devices. He asked the paleontologist to call him if anything came up. He returned to his truck and drove back to town, deep in thought and munching on crackers.

On the way, he replayed the morning's events. Something was bothering him...he'd seen something on the hillside where Darcy'd been, but now he couldn't remember. Something near the big boulder? The pile of scrap metal? It wouldn't come to him.

8

Darcy roused from sleep suddenly. Night surrounded her like a black shroud. She couldn't remember ever being in such impenetrable darkness. The stars and the crescent moon, veiled behind thick clouds, provided the only illumination. She was lying on the ground under a huge evergreen tree. And she was shivering in the cold high-altitude air.

The reality of the situation flooded in. She'd run from the big jerk in the cabin and raced away into the woods. As the two ATVs screamed toward her, she'd moved off the track and then continued downhill. Somehow, she'd gotten mixed up and lost her way. She'd dodged around wildly for quite some time, trying to find the track again, without success. Exhausted, dazed, her shoulder throbbing, scratched, covered with insect bites, she'd curled up under the thick branches of a sheltering fir and fallen asleep. Awake and starving, she sat erect and snarfed down the remaining candy bars she'd taken from the cabin.

Around 6:20 a.m., faint pastel orange stripes banded the eastern sky as night dissolved gradually into dawn. Darcy allowed herself a short respite to admire the beauty of the subtle play of light behind the craggy mountains. The far off peaks looked simultaneously weighty and like feathery islands floating near the sky. All around, ridges leapt upward, peaking, arching and diving from view like the backs of a school of fish frolicking in shallow water. The irregular rock formations looked like the streets of a town laid out by a lunatic. Maybe that's where the name Crazy Mountains came from. A meadow lay in front of her, brilliantly purpled with lupines. The gentle air enveloped her in softness and sweet fragrance. Sunlight washed over her, warm and healing. Darcy imagined for a moment that she was on vacation, untroubled and free. But soon she was on the move again, bearing downward, away from the rising sun. She guessed that there might be a road at the bottom of the mountain.

Mid-morning, she came to a large clearing in the woods. She guessed it was an old logging site, perhaps fifty acres in size. But there was no road. Had they used helicopters? Stumps of large firs and spruce rotted in the sunlight. Young trees in bright hues of green poked through the earth and attained heights of four to ten feet. Another range of snow-crested mountains was visible in the west, many miles distant. The intense sun provided welcome warmth. Puffy cirrus clouds scudded across an impossibly blue sky. A small creek meandered through the open space, gurgling and hissing as it wended its way down the mountain.

Darcy picked a few huckleberries from a low bush and sat on spongy ground next to the creek to rest for a few minutes. This would make an excellent lunch spot, if only she had a lunch. Her shoulder hurt; it might be infected, but she didn't want to pull off her shirt to look at it. She ate the berries and then reclined against a stump. In a few minutes, she was asleep.

A snorting sound awoke Darcy. Actually, it was more like a series of burps in quick succession. Someone was wandering around nearby. Someone very heavy. An alarm went off in her head. At some basic visceral level, she sensed danger. Fully awake now, adrenaline pumping, she sat motionless and listened. She spotted movement in a thicket of brush about thirty yards in front of her. Something the color and texture of a golden retriever moved between trees. The snorting/burping noise amplified, then a low woof came that made the hair on the back of her neck and arms stand up.

A huge hump-shouldered bear wandered into the far edge of the clearing on all fours, his golden fur aglow in the sunlight. The massive animal didn't seem to see her. About twenty yards distant, the bruin stood on its hind legs, reaching a height of well over seven feet. The bear tipped its head back and sniffed in all directions, testing the air. Darcy sat statue-like and waited, trembling, praying the bear's feeble eyesight would not allow it to see her, hoping it would give up and just go away.

The bear seemed to lose interest. Calmly and deliberately, it squatted its bulk down on massive haunches, facing slightly to Darcy's right.

She recognized the animal as a grizzly. Its dished face and the large hump of muscle between its shoulder blades were clear identifying characteristics. She'd seen grizzlies only in photographs and movies, but their reputation for awesome strength, occasional bloodlust toward humans and general unpredictability had been drummed into her during the orientation course the dig workers had attended on their first day in Montana. Darcy knew the drill: if a bear charges you, lie facedown with your hands locked behind your neck. If the animal bites or swats you, don't react. If it rolls you over, keep rolling until you're facing the ground again. Chances are, the bear will soon lose interest and go on its way. Of course, if it begins to devour you alive, fight your way free, if you can, and try to find a tree to climb. Adult grizzlies can't climb trees, but they can run faster than a horse for short bursts. Unless you're real close to a climbable tree, don't try to run for it, except as a last resort, because then, you'll look more like prey, and the bear can easily run you down.

The bear remained still, breathing deeply and looking into the far distance, as if meditating. Darcy could see flecks of bark and grass on its head. Six hundred pounds, she thought. Its claws extended at least two inches beyond the edges of its huge padded feet. The beast looked relaxed, almost contemplative. After a few minutes, it got onto all four feet and ambled slowly toward the motionless young woman.

Darcy held her breath. Drops of perspiration trickled down her neck and into the collar of her tee shirt. The bear's small eyes seemed to gain focus as it got closer. The animal stood squarely planted, and regarded Darcy impassively. Suddenly its short ears flattened back on its head. It opened its mouth, baring huge yellow canines with points like steak knives. Drool dripped from the corners of its mouth. Putrid breath fouled the air. The animal emitted a deep-throated roar that reverberated thunder-like through the clearing, then snapped its jaws shut with a decisive CLICK. It looked right at Darcy silently for a moment. Then it charged head-on.

Darcy ducked and rolled as the bear stormed by like a steamroller from hell. It swatted at her with a front paw as it swept past, knocking her onto her back. Darcy rolled onto her stomach and interlaced her fingers across the back of her neck. She lay still, afraid to even breathe. A few seconds elapsed before the grizzly returned. It slowly extended a paw and, almost gently, poked at her side a few times. Darcy smelled the sickeningly putrid breath, a cross between rotting flesh and the world's dankest locker room. She steeled herself to remain inert. Abruptly, the bear turned, disappeared from her peripheral vision and retreated. Darcy could hear steady breathing, in and out, like a fireplace bellows worked by a muscleman.

Minutes passed. Finally, she heard the sound of heavy feet moving into the woods. Darcy risked a quick turn of her head. She caught a glimpse of golden fur receding. The bear melted into the trees and was gone. For several minutes, Darcy heard branches snapping as the animal continued through the forest. Then it was quiet, save for the gurgling water in the creek, the gentle rustling of leaves and distant creaking from the swaying trunks of the towering firs surrounding the clearing. Darcy stood on rubbery legs and hurried away opposite the direction the bear had gone. She covered perhaps a quarter mile before stopping to get her bearings. Judging from the sun's position, she'd gone north. She corrected course and continued westward on her trek downhill. At orientation, they'd told her only black bears inhabited the Crazy Mountains, not grizzlies. So much for that theory.

In late afternoon, Darcy came across a trail cutting diagonally through her line of travel, a rocky pathway about a foot wide slashing through the woods along a gentle slope, obviously a designated trail for hikers. She stepped onto the trail and headed to the left and down. She'd walked for about ten minutes when she encountered another clearing. A large light-colored object appeared below the trail and off to the right perhaps fifty yards away. Darcy headed directly toward it. Soon, she could make out a rectangular canvas tent covering a space about twenty by fifteen feet. A galvanized smokestack jutted through the roof. Sturdy ropes stretched the walls out toward thick wooden stakes in the ground.

Nearly fresh horse manure lay in piles all around the clearing. A heap of firewood flanked the tent. Darcy hurried to the doorway flap, pushed it aside and stumbled into an interior dimly illuminated by sunlight through small plastic windows on two sides.

It took a moment for her eyes to adjust to the dull light. Four cots were arranged along the walls. Sleeping bags in nylon sacks sat on two of the cots. A black iron cook stove stood on curved legs in the center of the tent. Frying pans, saucepans, plastic dishes, cooking implements and a canvas drawstring sack covered a rough wooden table. Another such table was surrounded by six homemade wooden chairs, a couple of which had folded brightly striped Hudson's Bay blankets draped over the backs. Large green plastic drums lined a wall. Several pairs of old-fashioned wooden snowshoes hung on hooks suspended from a horizontal guy line near the entrance.

Darcy had never been hungrier in her life. She wrenched the lid off the nearest drum and peered inside. There were cans of soup, beans and potatoes, as well as a large tub of supermarket chocolate chip cookies. She grabbed several of the cans and deposited them on the table. She jerked open the drawstring sack to find mismatched silverware, a bottle opener and a gloriously welcome can opener. She opened a can of three-bean salad and devoured the contents with a tablespoon. Wiping her mouth with the back of a hand, she selected the next course, fruit cocktail in syrup. Moments later, the fruit was a pleasant memory.

She found an axe on a large flat rock in a corner of the tent, next to a few stubby pine logs. She chopped off some kindling strips, tossed them in the stove and got a little flame going with a strike-anywhere match from a box she'd found on the floor. The next order of business was to build the fire up and heat a pan of chicken noodle soup, which she gulped down, burning the roof of her mouth. A half dozen stale cookies completed the repast.

Darcy pulled the tops off each of the remaining drums, and found blankets, towels, tools, ropes, several cans of inexpensive pop and beer, along with a few articles of clothing—old but clean. She rummaged through the clothes and selected a long-sleeved cotton shirt and worn Levi's. She shucked off her shorts and donned the jeans—baggy in the waist, snug in the rear, but about right in length. She found a knife and chopped off a length of rope, which she threaded through the belt loops to form a makeshift cincture. She put on the shirt, folded back the cuffs once and tucked in the long tails.

She noticed a small galvanized washbasin on legs next to the hanging snowshoes. A mirror about the size of a sheet of letter paper hung on the wall above the sink. Darcy pulled the rubber band off her ponytail and faced the mirror with trepidation. A tangled mass of blonde hair framed a face deep red with sunburn. Her blue eyes were veined with red. There were lack-of-sleep pouches beneath each eye. Vivid scratches marred her forehead and both cheeks. She grimaced—she looked, as her Dad sometimes used to say about himself, like the wrath of God on a windy day.

Among the paraphernalia in the tent, Darcy discovered

a topographical map entitled Bear Basin, Montana. She unfolded it and spread it out on the floor near the stove. Sitting cross-legged, she studied it carefully. Someone had inscribed a penciled star at a point near the center of the map, with an accompanying caption: "Your ass is here." The star was situated on a point along a dashed line bearing the cartographer's label, "Hamilton Ridge Pack Trail." East of the star lay a circular clearing marked "Salvage Harvest." The dashed line led north into a series of jagged peaks of 10,000 feet and higher elevation. Toward the bottom of the map, the trail meandered in a southerly course, paralleling a thin blue line labeled "Specimen Creek." The trail intersected some sort of road at the very bottom of the document. Based on the mileage scale, the road was about eight miles away. The contour lines indicated the road's elevation as 3,000 feet lower than her current location.

Darcy checked her watch: 7:44 p.m. It would be dark soon, when the sun sank behind the nearby rock walls. Too late to head out. She decided to hang at the tent, get some sleep and take off in the morning.

9

Brian reached Clarkville just before dusk. It was now well into the second day since Darcy'd gone missing, the time limit for realistic hope of getting the victim back in one piece. Focus, he told himself. Worrying's not going to help one damn bit. Still, his subconscious wouldn't allow him a moment of ease.

He quickly located the county courthouse on Geyser Street, left the Grand Cherokee out front and entered the modern red brick structure. A directory just inside the entrance indicated the "Law Enforcement Offices" were downstairs. There was no one else in sight as Brian made his way to the basement and down a long silent corridor. Everything seemed to be closed up for the day until he came nearly to the end of the hall, where light leaked from under a door labeled "Law Enforcement." He entered and found himself in a Spartan waiting room with a few chairs and a low table. Across the room was a thick bulletproof glass panel with a pattern of pencil-sized circular holes in the center and a shallow metal tray at the bottom. A steel door flanked the panel.

A plump young woman with sandy hair and freckles sat behind the glass reading a paperback. Her tanned legs were crossed, and her skirt had hiked up to expose a generous expanse of thigh. Brian cleared his throat. The woman looked up, stuck a finger in her book to mark her place, and said, "Can I help you?"

"Yeah, I'm Brian McKay. Sheriff in?"

She blinked. "What's this regarding?"

"My niece was kidnapped from the dinosaur dig."

"Oh. Let me see if the sheriff is available." She picked up a handset and keyed in two digits. Brian turned away but listened to her side of the conversation.

"Sam, there's a Brian McKay here to see you." Pause. "I know, but he's standing right here. His niece is the one was kidnapped at the dinosaur dig. Okay. I'll do that. 'Bye." The last syllable dripped with honey.

"I'll buzz you in."

The receptionist pointed Brian toward a private office in the corner of the suite. On the way back, he passed six cubicles, all containing cheap desks, computer terminals, stacks of forms, and in one case, a deputy talking quietly on the phone. The room smelled of old coffee. He noticed the source, an overheated glass coffeepot with a brown crust caked in the bottom. Some things were the same everywhere.

As he approached the sheriff's office, he heard a deep male voice, apparently one side of a conversation. Affixed to the outside wall was a plaque reading: "Sheriff Sam Harrison." Brian rapped knuckles on the open walnut-veneer door. An overweight red-haired man in his mid-forties sat behind a battered metal desk, cradling a phone receiver between jaw and shoulder and listening. He held up a wait-a-minute finger and spoke into the phone. The sheriff had blunt features, a salt-and-pepper mustache and a baggy gray uniform with a silver badge pinned to the right pocket flap. A gray felt western hat hung from a rack in a corner.

"Yeah, uh huh, Okay, I hear ya," Harrison murmured into the mouthpiece. "Well, circumstances sometimes get the best of us. Like you say, things can get out of hand at times." A pause, then, "Sure. I understand. When can you come in? Tuesday? Okay. Make it morning. Say ten? All right. See you then." Pause. "I'll see what we can work out. No, you don't have to do that. Okay. See you Tuesday."

The sheriff hung up the phone as he looked at Brian, grinned broadly and said, "One of my criminals just confessed."

"Congratulations," Brian said.

"Thanks. That made my day. They're not all so easy. You're Mr. McKay, I take it." It wasn't a question. Harrison tilted back in his chair, crossed his feet on the desktop and waited as if he had all the time in the world.

Brian knew this was the tricky part. He was invading a local lawman's turf with a bunch of questions and nothing much to offer in return. Worst of all, he wasn't even with the FBI any more.

"Look, I'm Darcy's only relative. I'm worried as hell about her."

"That's understandable," Harrison said neutrally.

"I'd appreciate it if you'd answer a few questions. The main thing is, I'm wondering if there's anything concrete so far."

Harrison frowned. "I may just have a question or two for *you*."

"Sure. Maybe we can help each other out. What can you tell me?"

"Well, this is a strange one, them hearing a shot and

64

all. But it's not the first time a college girl's disappeared around here during the summer. Lotta times, the kid turns up unharmed, maybe just needed to get away, maybe took off with a boyfriend, that sorta thing."

Brian felt the color rising in his face. He hated to be patronized. "Aw, come on. If everything's kosher, they don't leave bloodstains behind."

Harrison held up a hand. "Look, I understand your concern, really I do. You're probably thinkin' the worst, that somebody took your niece off to hurt her. But in my experience, that's not necessarily the case. Besides, the amount of blood at the scene was pretty small. Probably something minor. Hell, it might not even be her blood."

"Has the sample been tested yet?"

"Gave it to the ET to check it out. You know your niece's blood type?"

"It's A."

Harrison scrawled a note on a pad on his desk.

"Did your niece use drugs, to your knowledge?"

"No."

"Any enemies, threats, feuds, relationships gone bad? Any reason you can think of someone would want to harm her?"

"None at all."

"She got a boyfriend?"

"I don't know. I'm looking into that."

Harrison made another notation. "Could you give me a detailed description?"

"Better yet." Brian took one of the copies of the picture of Darcy from his shirt pocket and placed it on the desk in front of the sheriff.

Harrison regarded the color print for a moment. "Can I keep this?"

"Sure."

"I suppose the FBI'll be coming in," Harrison said.

"If she was abducted, which it sure as hell looks like, then it'll be an FBI case. They use blunt instruments to kill flies, if you catch my drift."

Harrison looked at Brian blankly. "I catch it. Clarkville's a tourist town, and this kinda thing's not good for business. For what it's worth, I think you're right. I mean, it *does* look like an abduction." He glanced down at the picture of Darcy on the desk.

"Tell me, was a slug recovered from the scene? Any shell casings left behind?" Brian asked.

"We found a slug all right, but too banged up to match to a weapon."

"That's too bad. Would've been nice to have a slug in good shape."

"Yeah, but then, if a frog had side pockets, he could carry a jackknife. Anyway, we'll try to get her tested, but I wouldn't count on much. No shells."

"What's the deal with this dinosaur digging business, anyway? Isn't this the second shooting up there?"

"No indication the first one had anything to do with this."

"Wasn't the body found about where my niece disappeared?"

"Well, not exactly, but pretty close."

"I don't know about you, but I don't believe in coincidences when it comes to shootings. I mean, what's the common element, other than the dinosaur operation?"

"Beats me like a drum. Ya know, this dinosaur business is good for us here, pumps money into the economy. Lord knows it needs it. Last thing we'd want to do is scare people away. They've got a crew of ten or so, and they're here for a good chunk of the summer."

"Any incidents involving other people on the dig?"

"Nah."

"They get along with the locals?"

"They don't cause us any problems to speak of." He scratched his chin thoughtfully. "This Stevens guy is kind of obnoxious, but it seems we get more than our share of them around here, lately."

Brian wondered if the last remark was intended to reflect on him.

Harrison continued, "Those folks are pretty tame. We only get 'em in town here on Saturday nights. They send in a young bald-head guy picks up food and stuff every few days, but mainly, they stay up there at their dig."

"What exactly happened with that shooting at Bone Mountain last year?" Brian asked.

Harrison took his feet off his desk, sat up straight. "May before last, an old Indian was found up there, Crow fella by the name of William Old Horn. He'd been shot in the head and left in the brush. A couple schoolboys, out plinkin' gophers found him. The coyotes and magpies'd worked him over pretty good. Something those kids won't forget in a hurry."

"Is the case still open?"

Harrison gave him an admonishing look. "Hell yeah, till it gets solved."

"Any suspects?"

"Nope. Never came up with a motive either."

"Any of the old guy's relatives around?"

"Mr. Old Horn was not survived by any family, except a nephew over in Bozeman. Student at the university, I believe."

"What's his name?"

"Feather something. Eagle Feather, that's it."

"You talked to him, right?"

"Yup. Didn't help any."

"Did he inherit Old Horn's property?"

"Well, I guess he did. But it didn't amount to much—a broken-down shack on a few dried-up acres."

"At least it's a motive."

"Not much a one. But hey, you never know."

"Would you happen to have Eagle Feather's address?"

"Not off hand. He's prob'ly in the phone book."

"Where's Old Horn's shack?"

"On a piece of ground up near the dinosaur outfit."

"What's the land ownership like?" Brian asked. "Are we talking checkerboard?"

"Yeah, like that," Harrison replied. He glanced at the large clock on the wall to his left.

Brian knew the sheriff was antsy. He decided to take a chance. "Don't know about you, but I'm hungry. And thirsty. Care to be my guest for a bite to eat?"

Harrison shrugged, then reached for his Stetson and put it on. "Why not? I know a place up the street's got okay food at a good price."

BONE MOUNTAIN

The front room of the Cattleman Restaurant was a large and noisy bar full of men and a few women drinking beer and whiskey, and conversing loudly. Happy shouts and whoops punctuated the talk. Many of the customers sported well-worn western or farm clothes. A few obvious tourists were in evidence. Ranch hands fed coins into keno machines along one wall. Dwight Yoakam's "Guitars, Cadillacs" blared from the jukebox. Brian felt as if he'd stumbled onto a movie set. The noise level was like that of a Chicago Bulls playoff crowd. A white cardboard sign taped to the mirror behind the bar advised, LIQUOR IN THE FRONT, POKER IN THE BACK. Down-home humor.

Sheriff Harrison exchanged good-natured jibes with several men as he worked his way to the dining room in back with Brian in tow. A spindly man wearing walking shorts straddled a stool midway along the bar and smiled up at Harrison as he passed. Harrison eyed him with mock confusion and boomed, "Are those your legs, or are you ridin' a chicken?" This brought appreciative guffaws from the man and those on either side of him.

They entered a dining room paneled in knotty pine and took a booth in the corner. A waitress appeared wearing a uniform the color of leftover tuna salad. Harrison ordered bourbon on the rocks and Brian asked for a pint of a strong dark beer called Moose Drool.

The sheriff filled Brian in on the fruitless search for Darcy the previous evening and the follow-up work they'd done that morning. A "Hasty Team," made up of volunteer search and rescue people with specially trained dogs had come up empty so far. The sheriff asked routine questions regarding Darcy's height, weight, background, credit rating, life insurance, etc. Brian made a few inquiries of his own. Finally, he shut up and let the sheriff tell the story his own way.

Harrison removed his Stetson, set it upside down on the table at his elbow. "I grew up on a ranch in the Crazies, not far from that dinosaur place. To answer your question from before, land ownership up there's a mixed bag of private and National Forest. The dinosaur folks got a permit to dig up their bones from the feds—they're working on a Forest parcel."

"What about the gold mining stuff on the east slope? That on private property?"

Harrison hesitated. "It's Forest. Not much of a gold mine, though. Somebody sunk a shaft into the mountainside a ways and cleaned out a little vein. Before my time."

"What's on the surrounding land?"

"The feds got some hiking trails that go through public and private land on the way up into the high country. They don't maintain the trails too good or put up signs, so it's mostly locals use 'em for hunting in the fall. A couple outfitters've got tents in the woods. Then you've got your struggling cattle ranchers, mostly third or fourth-generation. A good year for them's to break even. There're your hobby ranches owned by millionaires from California and such, your Hollywood types, and there's a few weirdoes—hermits, survivalists, God knows what all." He grimaced.

Harrison paused to shake a filtered cigarette out of a pack and stuck it between his lips. He shook his head and frowned. "Can't light up in here. Whole state's smoke-free indoors." The cigarette waggled up and down in his mouth as he spoke.

Brian thought of the term oral gratification from a college psychology course. "What happened with the old Indian?"

"The Indian used to drop hints he'd found something. Folks'd see him poking around on the east side of Bone Mountain, but if he'd struck gold, you'd sure as hell never know it by the way he lived. Anyway, he never filed a claim. I checked."

"So he was looking around over the hill from where the dinosaur dig's going on?"

"That's where he was found, at the foot of the hill."

"Any forensic evidence at the scene?"

"A shell casing, .30-06. But hell, it coulda come from a lotta guys around here—hunters, I mean. Probably nothing to do with the old man."

"What about slugs?"

Harrison shook his head.

"And no idea about motive?"

"Nah. The old guy was a little strange, but basically harmless. He'd do handyman work on some of the ranches, and he'd come into town in his old rig every now and then, have a meal, buy some food, drink and swap lies till his money ran out and then go back home. I never heard of anyone having anything serious against him, but hey, shit happens. Anyway, we don't have the time to go back and rework old cases. We're understaffed as hell. Can't hardly keep up with the current stuff."

"What did the FBI come up with?"

Harrison snorted. "Pissants. Brought in a guy from Washington, some kinda bug expert. Studied the maggots on the body and somehow calculated the victim'd been lying there three weeks." His expression said he thought this was nonsense.

"Oh yeah, I've heard of him. A forensic entomologist name of Hayes, pretty sharp guy."

"If you say so. Not much call for 'em here."

Brian suppressed a smile. "Who's the private land-owner up there, I mean that big chunk of property across the road from the east slope?"

"That's a ranch owned by this rich dude from Chicago, name a Art Sands."

"Big place?"

"Depends on what the meaning of 'big' is." Harrison extracted the unlit cigarette from his mouth and picked a shred of tobacco from his lower lip. "Runs about eighty thousand deeded acres, and every damned perimeter foot's fenced in by the stoutest electric fence you'll ever see. This guy Sands, he's not there that much. He raises buffalo, smack dab in the middle of some of the best cattle country in the state. Kind of goes over with folks around here like a cement cloud. But then again, I'd rather see buffalo on that land than condos. A lot of cow outfits are folding up and getting subdivided into little bitty pieces."

"Can't make it ranching?"

"Nah. They're land-rich and cash-poor. I don't blame 'em for selling out. Ya can't eat the scenery."

"So, Sands isn't all bad then, preserving a big piece of land."

"Right. But people get jealous. The guy's got a jet air-plane, a landing strip on the place, businesses all over the country, more money than Midas is what I hear. Kinda like Ted Turner, I guess, but how would I really know?" He looked at the cigarette, put it into a shirt pocket and lifted his glass to drain the rest of the bourbon.

Brian recognized the name Arthur Sands. A wealthy Chicago businessman with alleged mob links, Sands headed a large politically connected construction company based in the Windy City, with offices in London, Munich, Cairo and Singapore. The company and its many subsidiaries built things worldwide—office towers, nuclear power plants, pipelines, docks, schools, roads, you name it. Sands had grown up in a working class New Town third-floor walkup shadowed by the elevated train tracks. His drive and street smarts had carried him far, but he was reputed to have stepped on more than a few toes on the way up. He was now on the board of the fledgling Chicago Museum of Natural History, the outfit sponsoring the *T. rex* dig. He gave freely and conspicuously to charities but, despite his prominence, he'd been hard-pressed to gain acceptance in Chicago society. He was of the wrong background, wrong religion and wrong temperament to comfortably rub elbows with the old-money movers and shakers of the North Shore. And some of his business associates were tied to organized crime in a very public manner. Brian remembered a file on him in the FBI Chicago Field office, something about alleged corruption of public officials in connection with keeping a union out of a speedboat manufacturing plant in Tennessee. He suspected there was more on Sands in the bureau's files, and he thought about James.

The waitress returned to their booth. "What are you havin', Sheriff?"

"We'll each have another drink and I'd like to get the prime rib medium and home fries."

"Same for me," Brian said.

The men continued to discuss Sands, his ranch, his

reputation and his women, of whom there'd been many. Harrison confessed he'd never actually met the man, though he'd seen him around. Brian requested and received directions to the Sands ranch.

The waitress brought fresh beverages. A few minutes later, the meals were served. Brian was astounded by the quantity: platters holding twenty-ounce slabs of fat-marbled red meat accompanied by mountains of greasy fried potatoes and huge salads containing exactly two ingredients—iceberg lettuce and grated carrots.

The waitress deposited this bounty on the table, and then scanned her work for possible omissions. "Oh my God. I forgot the condiment tray. Just a sec, I'll be right back."

A moment later she returned with a tray of bottles—steak sauce, various hot sauces, smoke-flavored sauce, barbecue sauce and a huge ketchup. "Prime ribs just ain't right without your condiments," she said.

"You're right, they ain't," the sheriff replied.

Brian made quick work of the food; he'd had little to eat since breakfast.

After apple pie a la mode and coffee, Brian took care of the bill. They left the Cattleman and paused briefly on the sidewalk out front, where Harrison set fire to a cigarette. "Wife's after me all the time to quit the cancer sticks," he said. "I'd rather keep the smokes than the wife, tell you the truth. Oh well. Brian, you might check in with me once in a while. Let me know what you find out, and I'll do the same for you. Deal?"

"Deal."

Brian drove to the Masters Hotel on Main Street, strode through a lobby where The Man With No Name would have felt at home and dinged the bubble-shaped chrome service bell at the unmanned registration counter. A few seconds later, a woman with weathered skin and a good-natured grin rushed into the small space behind the counter, wiping her hands on her apron.

"Howdy," she said. "Help you?"

"Yes, I'd like a single room for at least tonight, possibly longer."

"You bet. We can put you in a room with phone and TV for a hundred dollars. For an extra ten, you get breakfast and a sack lunch from our restaurant, the Rifleman."

"I'll take the room, no food, thanks."

Brian toted his duffel to the second floor, found 207 at the end of a narrow hall, and entered a small, high-ceilinged room that appeared to have been decorated in 1890 and maintained sporadically since. A few modern upgrades had been added—a small flat-screen TV shared a wall with a telephone on a black iron stand and a dented brass cuspidor. Plastic longhorns surmounted the high brass bed. Cowboy and Indian prints in plastic frames were screwed to the other two walls.

Brian turned on the TV. On the screen, a snowy-haired man in a white suit with a powder blue shirt and American flag-pattern tie grasped a microphone with both hands and gazed doe-eyed into the camera. In a quavering tenor he said, "Praise be to <u>Gawd</u>!"

Brian grimaced, turned off the set, stripped, had a hot shower and sank to the bed naked. As he pulled up the bedcovers, he noticed movement on the floor in a corner of the room. A tiny gray mouse darted behind the wastebasket. Brian swore softly, got out of bed and tried to find the intruder, not sure what he'd do if he succeeded. No sign of the little bugger. Then he saw a half-full box of d-Con on the floor behind the wastebasket. Too tired to worry about his non-paying room-mate, he dropped into bed and was asleep in minutes.

10

Michelle Emerson walked through the doorway of her town home in Chicago's tony Lincoln Park neighborhood, sighed, shouldered her heavy briefcase to the floor and kicked off dressy black leather pumps. She'd turned her cell phone off while on the el train coming home. Now, she checked for messages. There was one: Brian McKay's recorded voice, sounding metallic and distant: "Hey, not looking good. Nothing from Darcy yet. I'll be out here a while. Talk to you later." Pretty terse, but then, Brian had always disliked talking to machines.

Michelle went into the master bedroom and removed her pale yellow silk blouse and navy wool skirt. Wearing only a black bra and panties, she paused, turned sideways and assessed her trim figure in the full-length mirror next to the dresser. The three-times-a-week workouts at the health club seemed to be doing some good. Her weight never varied more than a pound week after week, though her work tied her to a desk. Was there the hint of crow's feet at the corners of her mouth? Practicing law as a member of the litigation department of a big firm meant endless hours of reading through page after page of tedious legal documents and sitting through seemingly interminable meetings. She disliked the meetings the most. Actual courtroom time was minimal—the exciting trial stuff didn't come up that often, even for the top litigation partners. But the pay was almost obscene and the work intellectually stimulating. She slid her long legs into a pair of faded jeans and donned a Tom Petty and the Heartbreakers concert tee shirt and Teva sandals. She walked to the built-in bar in the dining room and fixed herself a generous shot of The Macallan single malt Scotch, neat. She swirled the amber liquid around in the glass, took a sip, and went over to the large living room window overlooking Fullerton Parkway.

The grass in the tiny lawn below needed cutting—she'd have to call the kid who took care of it. A black wrought-iron fence edged the yard. Luxury sedans and sport-utility/crossover vehicles—Beamers, Mercedes and Lexuses—lined the busy street, some parked at the curb, some oozing by in traffic. Michelle's face would have been considered magazine-model-perfect, except that her large brown eyes were just a bit too far apart and her lips might have been considered a trifle too full. Straight brown hair brushed her collar. Her makeup was minimal—just a touch of neutral base and lipgloss. Tiny gold hoop earrings graced her ears. She abandoned the window and paced the living room.

Michelle frowned. Brian had been gone two days, and she hadn't heard from him until now. They'd both been so busy the last few weeks. It seemed they'd gradually been losing touch. She and Brian had been together for almost a year now. They'd met during a white collar fraud trial—he'd been a witness for the prosecuting Cook County State's Attorney, and she one of the lawyers representing the defendant, the chief executive of a discount electronics chain. The guy called himself, "Crazy Freddy" and appeared as a goggle-eyed huckster in TV ads. He hadn't been crazy—just crooked, orchestrating fictitious revenues, overstated inventories, off-balance sheet liabilities—anything to keep the creditors off his back. Brian's side had won. Crazy Freddy had been sentenced to seven years. Brian and Michelle had developed a friendship, which quickly turned to lust, then a relationship.

Lately, though, he'd seemed preoccupied. Probably related to leaving his job. He'd told her he needed to get out of the pit of government bureaucracy embodied by the FBI. He described the bureau as a machine that tends to run itself, an organization where the process is more important than the result, where loyalty and political skills are more valued than competence. He'd finally quit. Maybe he'd start his own business.

Michelle wondered if he'd thought of her at all that day. But then, he'd called. He'd have to be worried sick about Darcy. Not a man to wear his emotions on his sleeve, though. Always trying to be the cool professional, never showing fear, hiding uncertainty. But tenacious as a pit bull with a bone. He'd have to find Darcy. She just hoped the girl would be okay when he did.

Michelle sat on a large maroon couch, drink in hand, and scanned the Chicago Tribune. On page four of the first section there was a brief story, "Chicago Teen Missing in Montana." She read the piece quickly:

CLARKVILLE, MONTANA - Darcy McKay, 19, of Chicago, a paleontological assistant on the Chicago Museum of Natural History's *Tyrannosaurus rex* dig north of Clarkville, disappeared about 6:30 p.m. local time, Tuesday.

ROBERT D. HUGHES

Geyser County Sheriff Sam Harrison indicated McKay was last seen at Bone Mountain, site of the current Chicago Museum of Natural History-sponsored dinosaur-bones expedition led by noted University of Illinois at Chicago paleontologist Dr. Scott Noble Stevens. Stevens said, "As we were getting ready to knock off for the day, I heard what sounded like a gunshot from the other side of the hill where Darcy'd gone. We couldn't find her, but we're hoping for her speedy return."

Ms. McKay was believed to have been digging fossil bones by herself over the hilltop and out of sight of the group. Sheriff Harrison revealed that bloodstains were found where Ms. McKay had been working. "We suspect foul play," he said. "An investigation has been launched and we're working on leads." Becky Stanton, a co-worker and friend of the missing woman, said, "I'm like worried to death about Darcy. She's so together and so smart. No way did she just take off."

Ms. McKay is described as five feet, six inches tall, slender build, with blonde shoulder-length hair, usually worn in a ponytail, and blue eyes. She was last seen wearing tan shorts, a white tee shirt and white-and-red New Balance running shoes.

A search by sheriff's deputies and a local volunteer search and rescue team had turned up nothing by noon on Wednesday. The search was still in process at that time.

Ms. McKay's uncle, Brian McKay of Chicago, was at the

scene Wednesday evening. He declined comment.

Michelle set the newspaper down. Gunshot? Blood-stains? Foul play? Her hand shook as she built another drink.

11

James St. Claire's cell phone rang as he sat at his desk in the Chicago FBI office.

"It's Brian. Can you talk?"

"Yeah, sorta. What's shakin'?"

"I visited the dinosaur place. Learned a little bit. Local sheriff's a piece of work. Gave me some background on the dig site, land ownership in the neighborhood, info about the Indian got killed last year. A couple of threads to pull on. I'm sticking around. What's the buzz there?

"Nothing so far."

"Okay. Let me know when you find out what the bureau's doing. Also, how about checking the file on an Arthur Sands, residence Chicago—charges, convictions, recent activity. And one more thing, the killing of that Indian, William Old Horn, happened here in Geyser County last May. I know the bureau worked it—Salt Lake. See who the field agents were, what's in the file. You might run into access problems, but I'd appreciate anything you can get."

"No problem, big guy. Hey, keep the faith."

"Kind of hard to, considering."

"Yeah, I know, you're thinkin' about elapsed time. But hey, remember the Talman kid? Gone six days and we still got her back okay."

"Yeah, thanks." Brian appreciated James's attempt to

buck him up, but he could immediately think of three other kidnappings that hadn't ended well.

After they'd ended the call, James's desk phone rang, an inside call. He scooped up the receiver and said, "Hello."

"Special Agent St. Claire, is that the proper way to answer the telephone in this office?"

Christ, not that idiot. The Special Agent in Charge, John Elgar himself, was on the line.

"Yes, sir. I mean, no, not really. Uh, can I help you?"

"Would you like to come to my office, please?

I'd like to boot your sorry ass into Lake Michigan, he thought. "Right away, sir," he said.

James went to Elgar's outer office and smiled at Ginny Clements, the SAC's long-suffering secretary.

"Good luck," she said, rolling her eyes.

James waggled his eyebrows and gave her a thumbs-up. He knocked on the half-closed door of Elgar's spacious corner office.

Elgar glanced up at James and said, "Have a seat, Special Agent St. Claire. I'll be with you in just a moment."

James took a visitor's chair and looked around. Elgar's mammoth rosewood desktop was empty except for a telephone with more buttons than the cockpit of a 747, some pipe-smoking materials, and pieces of a fancy fountain pen, a Mont Blanc shaped like an elongated Goodyear blimp. A sleek Bang and Olufsen stereo system sat atop the credenza. Elevator music tinkled from the speakers. A portrait of the current Director gazed down solemnly from the wall behind the SAC. Good landscapes in oils and watercolors graced the other walls. James glanced out the window. Elgar's domain afforded a spectacular view of the cityscape, looking north to the Loop.

The SAC continued to fiddle with an ink refill cartridge, attempting to fit it into the barrel of the faux marble-finish pen. The refill wouldn't screw in properly. He held the cartridge up to the window light, peered at it accusingly and squeezed it. A stream of blue ink squirted from the tip of the refill, onto Elgar's beautiful red Hermes necktie and the breast of his white shirt. He sat motionless for a beat, holding the dripping object between index finger and thumb as if he had a dead rat by the tail. "Doggone," he said softly. James stifled a laugh, looked out the window and thought of a recent visit to the dentist—anything to avoid laughing out loud.

Elgar ignored the spreading blue stain on his tie and shirtfront. He looked up, focusing, it seemed, on a point just past the agent's left shoulder. James couldn't remember the SAC ever actually looking him in the eye. Elgar had been truly mediocre as a field agent, everybody said. But he was reputed to be the preeminent expert on bureau politics. He was said to know every nuance of FBI organization, from the Washington headquarters bureaucracy to the 56 field offices in major U. S. cities and the 380 smaller resident agency offices. Such details were the essence of his professional life. He excelled at office administration and intra-bureau intrigue. He prided himself on moving the endless stream of paperwork efficiently. Elgar displayed his capped white teeth and said, "St. Claire, I'm interested in speaking with former Supervisory Special Agent McKay." He raised an eyebrow and sat silently, apparently waiting for a response.

"Uh, sir, he's out of town. Took a trip."

"Where?"

"Out west, sir."

"Could you be more specific?"

"Uh, he said he was going to Montana."

"Is he investigating the disappearance of his niece?"

James was surprised by the question. How had the SAC glommed onto the Darcy situation so quickly? Why would he care? "Yes, sir. I believe he's looking into it. It's a personal matter for him."

"Has he communicated his findings to you?"

"Well, he said he's talked to the county sheriff, hasn't found out much. Sir, is the bureau involved?"

"Frankly, I'm not able to divulge that at this time." Like answering a TV reporter, James thought. "If this thing turns out to be a kidnapping, I'd like to volunteer to be Chicago office liaison with local field offices. I mean, with the apparent victim's Chicago connections, and my knowing her legal guardian, and—"

Elgar interrupted, "Special Agent St. Claire, I'll be frank with you." Like many politicians, he was fond of the words "frank" and "frankly," especially when he was being anything but. He pushed the fountain pen parts aside, picked up his pipe and inserted it into his mouth. A stickler for rules, he did not violate the no-smoking edict, but seemed to calm himself by sucking and chewing on his pipe stem. Finally he cleared his throat and said, "Quite frankly, the Salt Lake City divisional office has begun preliminary assessment. The Chicago field office's role, if any, is not knowable, at this time."

James chose his words carefully. "Whatever the Chicago office role ends up being, I'd be interested in working on it, whether it's here or in the field. You know, I worked closely with Brian McKay on the Talman kidnapping case last year. I'm qualified."

"I'm afraid your, ah, ethnicity would be conspicuous in a place such as rural Montana. I've actually been out there, you know, fly-fishing."

James pictured the man wearing one each of everything from the Orvis catalog, a fishing line hopelessly tangled around his hands.

"In any case, demographics, as well as your relative inexperience, deem you not the best fit for field agent activities related to this matter," Elgar continued. "Nonetheless, should circumstances permit, it is possible that you might carry out such Chicago office administrative or computer data-related duties as might arise."

"Okay."

"Meanwhile, should you receive any communication from Mr. McKay, please advise me ASAP. I'd like to speak with him. Are we squared away?"

"Yessir."

"Good. That will be all."

Elgar turned his attention to foraging about in a desk drawer. He found what he was looking for, another fountain pen refill, and reached for the barrel of the pen. James winced, stood quickly and got out of the SAC's office.

James stopped to chat with Ginny for a few minutes. The secretaries' network in the office knew everything. If you were plugged into it, you could find out anything. He asked her to let him know whatever she heard about the Darcy McKay kidnapping case. She didn't say no, and James was pretty sure he could count on her. A few minutes later, he took an elevator to the ground floor, stepped outside the building and pulled out his phone. He punched in Brian's number and got him in a moment.

"Our buddy J. Edgar called me in a few minutes ago, right after we spoke. Said he wants to talk to you if you call in."

"What else did he want?"

"Asked where you were and whether you're investigating the Darcy situation. Way he talked, I figured he might have listened in on our last conversation. It was like he knew what you were into. The man's gettin' jiggy."

"Maybe I was mentioned in the paper. I no-commented some reporter who tracked me down in Clarkville. Anyway, what did you tell him?"

"Just that you were in Montana looking for your niece. I couldn't lie since he might have already known. You know the name of that tune—never ask a question you don't already know the answer to. Anyway, next I volunteered to be assigned to the case at this end. He played down the Chicago office, said Salt Lake was running the show."

"Okay. The sheriff said two agents were there after the old Indian was shot last year. The lead guy was from Salt Lake. The sheriff didn't seem impressed. Implied they were seagulls—flew in, dropped shit all over the locals and flew away. Couldn't remember their names, which seems strange. I'd like to know who those two guys were."

"No problem, big guy."

"You got any contacts in Salt Lake?"

"Is the Pope a geriatric Catholic? My girl's cousin happens to be a secretary there. She married this white dude, insurance salesman, discovered he was a cowboy at the age of forty. So they up and moved out to the frontier. I haven't seen her in like, forever, but Linelle keeps in touch. Want me call

87

her?"

"Yeah. Ask her to keep you posted. I'll check in with you in a day or two."

"Look, man, you better call my cell from now on. Somebody might tap my bureau phone. Or monitor my e-mail. Or videotape me in the goddamned men's room." James chuckled. "That reminds me. Remember the 'Restroom Use Policy' someone posted on the bulletin board last year?"

"Yeah. And I figure you're the someone who wrote it and tacked J. Edgar's signature on the bottom."

James reminisced about the hoax memo that had the Chicago office agents in stitches for most of a Monday until the SAC had discovered it, blown a gasket, ripped it down and tried unsuccessfully to identify the culprit. The memo had specified no more than two daily trips to the office restroom, to be documented in a log. If an agent or other employee were to visit a restroom stall more than twice in a day, a digital "butt recognition monitor" would identify the transgressor, where-upon the stall door would automatically lock, a siren would sound and the agent's restroom privileges would be suspended for a week. The memo concluded: "This is serious business. Believe me, I know. Why do you think my eyes are brown? I'm still full of shit from the last time it happened to me."

"Man, J. Edgar was so fuckin' pissed off when he read that thing, he 'bout fell through his butt-hole and hanged himself," James said. "Jesus, the man was smokin'."

"James, it was funny at the time, but you've got to move on."

"Sad but true. I've got a question. How do fuckups like J. Edgar end up running the show, while the good guys get all frosted over and bail?"

"The bureau got too big. Too many agents, *way* too many administrative staff. The result's bureaucracy. Who eats that shit up? The politicians. The mucky-mucks are politicians. But hey, keep on pluggin', kid. Don't let the bastards get you down."

"Never happen. Well, I better get back to my desk. J. Edgar's been acting even weirder than usual, and I don't want to get him all jazzed to gig me. But I'll call the gal in SLC from here first."

"One other thing: how's the truck?"

"Doin' good. Leave her at home most times, though. Some dumb fuck in the parking structure put the wham-bam-thank you-ma'am on the rear bumper yesterday, left a smear of appliance-white paint, took me damn near an hour to get it off."

"Tough world, dude. Maybe a vehicular bodyguard'd be worthwhile, so you could rest easy."

"You think? Anyway, I gotta go. Keep it up there, big guy."

James then called Betty Payton in the Salt Lake City office, which covered Utah, Idaho and Montana. After minimal chitchat, James got to the point. "Betty, wonder if you could do me a favor."

"For you, anything. As long as it's borderline legal."

"I'm needing some info on a case you guys're supposedly just getting into. Don't even know what agents are assigned, but it's about a missing person, young lady name of Darcy McKay, from Chicago."

"She went missing here?"

"Actually, near some town in Montana name of

Clarkville."

"Haven't heard anything on that one yet."

"When you find out who the assigned agents are, how 'bout giving me a ring?"

"Sure."

"And one other thing. Who were the agents worked the murder of a William Old Horn, same location, little over a year ago? And what did they get? This is off the record, know what I'm saying? But whatever you find out about that field work, I'd sure appreciate it."

"Uh, you got a special interest here?"

"This girl, Darcy, she's the niece of my mentor, guy just left the Chicago office."

"Cool. I'll see what I can do. Gotta run now. Give my love to Linelle."

"Oh, you can bet I'll do that. Bye."

James returned to his office, refilled his oversized Chicago Blues Festival coffee mug, set it on his desk and switched on his computer. In a few moments, the database log-in screen appeared. Just as he was about to begin work at the keyboard, a voice boomed behind him. "James, how are you, sir?"

James turned to see Del Blevins, the Office Services Manager, standing just outside his cube. Blevins was an Assistant Special Agent in Charge, or ASAC (pronounced ay-sack), one of four reporting to Elgar. His main function seemed to be personnel, or what was called "Human Resources"—for James, the term called to mind a warehouse full of people stacked on shelves with little name tags tied to their toes. Since Blevins was one of the few who had extensive contact with

Elgar, the street agents considered him a snake and treated him accordingly.

Blevins grinned like a vinyl siding salesman, stepped in and sat in the lone visitor's chair. "Mind if I sit down for a minute?" he said.

"Guess not, especially since you already have." James was glad he hadn't logged on yet. Blevins was known for sneaking up and looking over people's shoulders, stealing peeks at what they were working on. James waited.

"Just thought I'd stop by and say hello," Blevins said.

Bullshit, James thought. "What you working on these days?" James replied.

"Well, you know, staff evaluations are due back in my office by Friday, and, with Brian McKay leaving, I was wondering whether he'd given you your evaluation."

"Nah, I'll just do it myself."

"Ha-ha. The problem is, without it, how can we get your raise processed?" He held his hands palms-up at shoulder level, his rubbery lips turned down.

"Del, my man, I'm sure a high-level executive such as yourself can figure out a way to deal with my raise without the form. I mean, people leave all the time, and forms still gotta get filled out. What do you normally do?"

"Well...there's a self-evaluation form we can give the agent to complete, but only if we can't contact the former supervisor."

"Have you tried to contact Brian?"

"Yes, but I couldn't get him. You wouldn't know where I could reach him, would you?"

"Nope. Understand the man's out of town. So you can just give me the form, and I'll complete it in spades." James winked.

Blevins hesitated, unsure if the last comment was meant to be funny. "I'll get back to you." He pasted a smile on his face, unfolded his lanky frame and headed in the direction of Elgar's office.

James sighed as he keyed in his ID and password, then clicked his mouse to enter the FBI automated database system. He decided to start with the Uniform Crime Reporting Program, better known as UCR. As the screens loaded and changed from one to the next, he thought about Brian. He'd never seen the guy so worried-looking as when he'd dropped him off at O'Hare, evening before last. Their phone conversation this morning hadn't been reassuring. Over two days had passed with nothing on his niece, a *very* bad sign in a kidnapping. And why would Elgar want to talk to an ex-agent? Not to get James's evaluation. He clicked a symbol on the screen and began to search for the information Brian had requested.

12

Brian got online and located the MSU student directory, where he found a phone number and email address for Russell Eagle Feather. Next, he went to a reverse lookup directory and found a physical address for the young man.

Brian pointed the Grand Cherokee to the Interstate en route to Bozeman and Russell Eagle Feather's apartment thirty miles to the west. He switched on the cruise control and cranked up the radio—he'd found an eclectic FM station based in Bozeman called KGLT. That day, they were featuring seminal folk-rock artists like the Byrds. He found himself tapping his left foot on the floorboard in time to the music. After stopping for directions at a gas station, he found the twelve-unit apartment building near the Montana State University campus. Dwarfing its neighbors, an old black Cadillac hearse with soaring tail fins occupied two spaces in the lot out front. The Montana license plate: "DROP DED." The apartment complex looked about ten years old, but already the wood siding had weathered and flecks of paint peeled from window trim. Bare patches spotted the grass. The sky-scraping mountains in the distance looked like a painted stage backdrop.

Brian rang the bell of unit two and waited. He could hear someone moving around inside. After a minute or so, a tall, broad-shouldered man in his mid-twenties, with medium brown skin, dark eyes and long raven-black hair rubber-banded into a ponytail opened the door. Movie star-handsome, he evoked pictures of the young Chief Joseph that Brian had seen recently in a magazine. The broad face featured high cheekbones and intense brown eyes. He wore a tight black tee shirt over beltless Levi's slung low on narrow hips.

He regarded Brian neutrally and said, "Help you?"

"I'm Brian McKay. You're Russell?"

"No, I'm Chief Thundercloud." Deadpan.

"Look, I don't mean to bother you, but I'm investigating the kidnapping of my niece from the same place where your uncle was found. Okay if I come in and talk for a few minutes?"

The young man reached to his side and brandished a wooden spear with a sharp steel tip affixed to the shaft by a rawhide strip. He moved the tip to within a couple of inches of Brain's face.

"This spear has poison in the tip. If I were to jab you with it, you would die. It would take a long time. What do you think of that?"

"Uh, I think you should move it away from me." Brian stepped back a pace. "Look. This is really important. Can I come in to talk with you for just a few minutes?"

A shrug. He set the spear to the side and gave a smile that didn't reach his eyes. "You don't scare easy, I'll say that for you. I guess we can talk, but only a little while. I've got some studying to do. And yes, my name is Russell Eagle Feather."

Brian followed the young Indian into a modest apartment decorated in early graduate student. The living room contained a threadbare brown couch facing the obligatory wide-screen TV, a pair of mismatched easy chairs perpendicular to the couch and a scarred walnut-veneer coffee table in the square formed by the furniture. A kitchen/dining area adjoined the living room. Homemade cinder block-and-board bookcases lined the walls. An old desk in a corner held an Apple laptop with a word processing document displayed on the screen. A nearby floor lamp shed scant illumination. Eagle Feather waved Brian to a seat in a chair where he couldn't see the screen and perched on a couch arm.

"I knew you'd be here soon," Eagle Feather said.

"Why's that?"

"That sheriff dude over in Geyser County called. Said you were trying to find your niece, said you might look me up." Eagle Feather hesitated. "He kind of like, coached me."

"Coached you?"

"Yeah. He said nothing ever came out of their investigation on my uncle. Said to tell you I didn't know anything that could help you find your niece."

"You think that's true?"

Eagle Feather smiled and shook his head as if appreciating some small private joke. A feather-shaped silver earring swayed from his left ear and flashed in the lamplight. "Who knows?" he said. "They told me before they never found diddly-squat about who killed my uncle. But did they try?"

"Any reason they wouldn't?" Brian asked.

"You might not understand this. There's two kinds of justice around here—one for whites, one for everyone else. That goes double for Indians."

"And, as a Native American, your uncle was treated accordingly?"

"Most of us don't like that term, 'Native American.' We prefer 'Indian.' Hell, we're just thankful Columbus was looking for India, and not Turkey."

Brian smiled. His impression of Russell Eagle Feather had just ratcheted up a notch. "Okay. What kind of man was your uncle?"

"A good guy. Never harmed a soul. Minded his own business. Used to say, 'You only live once, but, if you work it right, once is enough.' Look where it got him." Another head-shake. "You might have better luck with your niece. But I don't see how I can help. Maybe that sheriff's right, far as that goes."

"Tell me more about your uncle," Brian said. "What was he into that might make someone want to kill him?"

The young man shrugged. "Who knows?"

"What did he do to make ends meet?"

"Worked as a coal miner on the rez as a young guy, so he said. Far back as I can remember, he was a ranch hand off and on, did fencing, mechanical work, repairing tractors, stuff like that."

"What about his spare time?"

"He was what you'd call a historian of native peoples. Kept a history of the Crows and a journal, wrote in it every day. Kept a scrapbook, too. Collected pictures of Indians in traditional clothes, like at powwows and shit. I guess you could say he lived in the past."

"Was he an organizer?"

"You mean troublemaker? He believed in tribal soli-darity, economic self-determination, didn't want handouts from the Man. Uppity Indian. Organizer? He was no fucking

96

organizer. Might've been resented by some of his brothers, though—you'd be surprised, a lot of Indians don't want to stir things up."

"You think his attitude might have gotten him in trouble?"

"That's a stretch, but how the hell am I ever gonna know? Man, it's a done deal, far as I'm concerned. You get pissed off, cry a little, bury your feelings, move on."

"Did he collect Indian artifacts?"

"Well yeah, he was always looking for traces of ancient peoples. Found some pottery, tools, stuff like that."

"Any idea at all why somebody would want to hurt him?"

Eagle Feather looked at his feet. After a moment, he said, "Man, you don't give up easy." He fiddled with the silver earring. Brian wondered if he'd pushed too hard.

Finally, after several more seconds of silence, Eagle Feather said, "Well, I kinda think he *did* find something." He held his hands up, as if signaling for traffic to stop. "Now, don't go trying to pump me about what it was. I flat-out don't know, man. It's just that he was...in a better mood that last time I saw him. He said something like 'Never know what you'll find out there.' Meaning where he lived. Acted cagey, like he had a secret."

"When was this?" Brian asked.

"Couple days before they killed him, early part of May, last year."

"Why did you say 'they?'"

"No particular reason."

"Where are his journal and scrapbook?"

"I've got 'em."

"I'm thinking there's got to be a connection between your uncle's murder and my niece. If we can find a motive for your uncle, I might have something. Could I have a peek at his stuff?"

Eagle Feather looked uncertain. He shrugged. "Ah, hell, what's the difference now?"

The young man left the room and returned a few minutes later carrying a large pale-green cloth-covered scrapbook and a spiral-bound stenographer's notebook. Clippings and odd-sized scraps of paper peeped out from the edges of the scrapbook. He placed both volumes on the low coffee table in front of Brian.

"You can look through these, take notes if you like, knock yourself out. But I can't let them out of here. I've gotta do some reading for a class, man. Go to it." Eagle Feather walked to the desk, retrieved several books, a folder of notes and a yellow highlighter, and slumped onto the couch. He flipped open a large hardcover and began to read.

Brian started with the scrapbook. It was full of photos, mostly black-and-white, neatly affixed to heavy pages. There were pictures of Indians in costumes dancing, a picture of the tribal Chairwoman being sworn in. Every few pages, newspaper clippings had been tucked in the book—articles on Crow culture, the government-built dam on the Bighorn River, coal-mining on the reservation, leasing of Crow land to ranchers.

One article traced the sad history of the Crows. In 1825, the government agreed that 36 million acres of western land belonged to the Crows permanently. Treaties had been systematically broken by the government ever since, with Crow land reduced drastically each time. The current reservation in southeastern Montana contained about 2.5 million acres and 7,500 people. It encompassed the Little Big Horn Battlefield, where Custer got his. A handwritten copy of the words of a Crow war chief covered a separate page:

"The Crow Country is exactly in the right place. It has snowy mountains and sunny plains, all kinds of climates and good things for every season. When the summer heat scorches the prairies, you can draw up under the mountains, where the air is sweet and cool, the grass fresh and the bright streams come tumbling out of the snow banks. In the autumn, when your horses are fat and strong from the mountain pastures, you can go down into the plains and hunt the buffalo. When winter comes in, you can take shelter in the woody bottoms along the rivers. The Crow Country is exactly in the right place. Everything good is to be found there."

Eagle Feather looked up. "Anything?"

"I was just reading a piece about the Crow country being exactly in the right place."

"Huh. Used to be, until you whites stole most of it. We got the shitty end of the stick."

Brian flipped through the pages slowly. An article scissored from the Clarkville Times caught his eye: "Tribal Oral Historian Tells of Early Mining." Old Horn was quoted, "I worked in those mines from the age of fifteen, in the summer until I got out of school, and full-time for a few years after that. We used draglines and backhoes to dig out the coal. It was dirty and dusty work. At the end of the day, I'd gone from red to black. But it was worth it. I learned a trade. I learned how to get minerals from the earth." There was a picture of a youthful Old Horn in coveralls leaning on a shovel, standing next to a backhoe. It reminded Brian of the young man sitting nearby, engrossed in reading, but occasionally raising an eye to keep track of him.

Brian finished with the scrapbook, and picked up the steno notebook labeled "Journal." It began in January 1997 and ended in early May of the year Old Horn died. Most entries concerned Crow culture, politics and individuals. Toward the end, a series of references appeared regarding items "found." The entry for 4/16 of last year read: "Found pieces." A note headed 4/26 read: "Findings - 2 items, broke, same place as 4/16." The final entry, dated May 9th, read, "Found face pot."

Brian pulled a small notebook from a jeans pocket and jotted down the dates and text of the references. He pocketed his notebook and said, "The items found in there, towards the end—you think they were all pottery?"

"I wondered about that myself. Sounds like pottery."

"Do you have any of those items your uncle found?" Brian said.

Eagle Feather left the room again, for his sleeping quarters, Brian presumed, and returned with a plastic bag from a grocery store. He emptied the contents on the tabletop in front of his visitor without comment. Brian bent his head to examine them. There were shards of faded red clay pottery, along with arrowheads and crude stone tools. Then the young Indian placed a much larger object on the table, a dark rock about ten inches long with a large knob-like protrusion on one end.

Brian hefted the rock. It weighed several pounds and felt solid and dense." Any idea what this is?"

"Nah. Just a paperweight, far as I'm concerned.

"Could I borrow these things for a day or two?"

Eagle Feather frowned, and Brian quickly added, "I'd like to show them to an expert. I'm thinking this stuff could be interesting to a scientist. Maybe it'll help us figure out who killed your uncle."

Eagle Feather said, "All right, long as you let me know what you find out. And return that stuff."

"I will. By the way, what happened to your uncle's property?"

"I got his land and cabin. Besides that and his clothes and such, there wasn't much more than what you see here."

"Was there a will?"

"Nope."

"Property values rising up there?"

"I doubt it. Hey, I haven't been out to the cabin since I picked up that stuff. What? Am I a suspect?"

Brian shook his head. "Nah."

Eagle Feather glanced at the textbook on the couch. "Well, if there isn't anything else..."

"One more thing. You know anybody knowledgeable about Indian pottery around here?"

"Actually, yeah. I'm taking a course from a guy's written books on it. Name's Holt."

Eagle Feather gave Brian Holt's phone number. Brian quickly called Dr. Anton Holt, a professor in the Native American Studies program at MSU. They arranged to meet in Holt's office in a few minutes.

"What degree are you working on?" Brian asked.

"Master of Arts in Native American Studies." The young Indian's voice betrayed his pride.

"Sounds good. Well, thanks for your help," Brian said. "I'll be in touch, and I'll get these back to you as soon as I can. How about giving me a call if you think of anything else." He stood and, with a ballpoint from his shirt pocket, jotted his cell number on a piece of notepaper and handed it to Eagle Feather.

The enigmatic smile again. "Yeah, whatever."

13

D r. Anton Holt rotated the pottery shard in long, tapered fingers, examining the pale red fragment through a jeweler's loupe wedged into his right eye socket. He grunted a couple of times as he worked. After a few moments, he carefully set the piece on his desk blotter, removed his glasses and looked at Brian, his eyes bright.

"This is part of a pot made by Paleo-Indians of the northern Rockies, around two thousand years ago. These were folks with Asian blood who hunted for a living. Anyway, this looks like the stuff found over at Pictograph Cave back in the thirties."

"Where's that?"

"Not far from Billings. It's a state park, now.

"Are these valuable?" Brian asked.

"To an academic, maybe. To a collector, not particularly. You'd need a lot more of the pieces and you'd need to know exactly where they came from. If you had most of a pot like this, and you could document the provenance, you'd have something rather interesting, I'd suspect."

"Have any whole pots been found?"

"No, not that I'm aware of. We believe the Crows are descended from the prehistoric people who lived in the pictograph caves. Such a pot might exist on the reservation somewhere."

"How about these things?" Brian said. He eased the stone tools onto the desk, next to the pottery fragments.

"The points and scrapers are fairly common. They turn up around here now and then."

Brian removed the heavy black rock from the bag, and laid it on Holt's desk. "Here's the last item. Any ideas?"

Holt raised his eyebrows. "Well, now. It's not my field, but this does look interesting."

"What is it?"

"Unless I'm mistaken, you've got a dinosaur bone there. Looks like it came from a good-sized animal. That's about all I can tell you."

"Can you recommend someone here at the university that I could show it to?"

"Just a second." Holt picked up his desk phone and dialed a four-digit extension. After exchanging good-natured barbs with the person on the other end, he said, "I've got a fellow from Chicago in my office with some sort of dinosaur bone he wants an opinion on. No, he got it third-hand. Nope, doesn't have a clue. Yeah, I know, but would it be all right if he stopped by to show this thing to you? Uh huh. Thanks, Dave. I'll do that." He hung up.

"Dave Bakeno over in the paleontology department says he'll be happy to take a look at that."

"Appreciate it. By the way, did you know Mr. Old Horn personally?"

Holt smiled. "Indeed, I did. He was quite helpful in my work on Crow culture, pre-white settlement."

"Did Old Horn find any pottery pieces like these?"

"Well, now that you mention it, he did. Quite similar to what you have there. I told him the same thing I just told you. He was a little disappointed." Holt frowned. "Who'd want to kill a nice old guy like that?"

"I'd like to know the answer to that one, myself."

Following Doctor Holt's directions, Brian easily found Bakeno's office. A sign taped to the inside of the open door proclaimed: MORPHOLOGISTS HAVE HARDER BONES. A fortyish man wearing horn-rimmed glasses rose from a cluttered desk to greet Brian. After introductions, Bakeno waved Brian to a chair, sat and rubbed his hands together. "Where's this mysterious bone?" he said.

Brian placed it on the desktop.

"Where'd you get this?"

"It was found in the Crazies, I'm told."

"Looks to me like it's part of an upper arm, likely from a tyrannosaurid."

"Does that mean *T. rex*?"

"Could be, but a whole group of animals falls into the tyrannosaurid family. What you've got there is the upper end of a humerus, the bone between the shoulder and forearm." He beamed. "I happen to know that because I dug one up last summer over in the Hell Creek area. Mine came from a *T. rex*, but it was quite a bit smaller than this one. Could be this is a female. We think they were larger than the males, just as you find with predatory birds. But jeez, this thing is huge, about a quarter bigger than the largest such bones previously discovered. Maybe it's something else entirely. Now, who's the guy that found it?"

"His name was William Old Horn."

"Oh, yeah. An old Crow Indian."

105

"That's right. You knew him?"

"He stopped by here once."

"Did he bring any bones with him?"

"Nope, he just wanted some information about fossils, how we find them, how we dig them up, stuff like that. How'd you latch onto the bone, anyway?"

"I'm investigating Mr. Old Horn's murder. His nephew loaned me the bone to get an opinion on it."

"Huh. Where exactly in the Crazies did Old Horn find this?"

"I'm not sure, but I think it came from Bone Mountain."

"Hmmm. Then Stevens is probably going to come up short when he puts his *T. rex* skeleton together, I'd say. Does he know about this?"

"Not yet."

"Well, this is kind of up my alley. If you need more help, don't hesitate to call." Bakeno handed the bone back.

On the return trip to Clarkville, Brian reflected on the morning's events. The old Indian knew about mining, digging, and he'd sought out advice on fossils. Maybe the dinosaur bone or the pottery shards in the bag on the seat next to him were only the tip of the iceberg. Perhaps something else had been taken from the old man. Maybe Darcy had stumbled upon whatever the old guy'd been after.

An ancient pickup with squared-off fenders and random rust patches appeared ahead and loomed quickly as the Grand Cherokee closed on it. The driver's head was barely visible above the steering wheel. The truck couldn't be going more than forty miles an hour on a road with a speed limit of seventy. The man behind the wheel wore a high-crowned flat-brimmed black hat. Long gray braids protruded in back. A bumper sticker on the rear of the rickety vehicle read, CUSTER WORE AN ARROW SHIRT. As Brian overtook the truck, he glanced over at the occupant. The old walnut-hued driver looked at him, dipped his chin and smiled, revealing yellow teeth with a large gap in the middle. Brian smiled back and gave him a thumbs-up.

14

Darcy slept until the sun reached her eyes. She'd been so bone-deep tired, even the terrifying experience with the grizzly bear was blotted out by weariness. Fully awake now, she was reluctant to leave her cozy bed. The down-filled sleeping bag she'd zipped into felt good in the chill air. The fire in the wood stove had gone out during the night, but the remaining embers still infused the tent with warmth. The wind had picked up, and the canvas wall next to her head luffed in and out steadily. She heard birds singing outside. She studied the roof of the tent, noting the pattern of light filtered through the trees.

Her thoughts wandered to the real world and her life in Chicago a thousand years ago. She thought of her apartment, her classes at the University of Illinois at Chicago. Would she be back in time for the fall semester? The guy she'd been dating, Matt, would he be worried at the lack of communication from her? They'd texted back and forth a few times before her trip to Montana. But she knew the relationship was going nowhere in the long run. What about her tent-mate, Becky? Would she have sounded the alarm when Darcy didn't show up after the day's work? Doctor Stevens would have mounted a search, wouldn't he? She wasn't sure. What about Brian? Had they called him? God, she hoped so. Of all the people she knew, he was the most capable. Plus, his being an FBI agent couldn't hurt. If he'd gotten word, he'd be looking for her, no question. She wondered if she'd ever see him again.

Darcy rubbed her eyes, unzipped the sleeping bag, swung her legs over the side of the cot and dropped her feet to the plywood floor. Christ, it was cold. She grabbed her crew socks and running shoes and quickly put them on. The flannel shirt and jeans she'd slept in were rumpled and smelly. Her shoulder ached. She carefully stretched her left arm and rotated it. The ache intensified. She unbuttoned the outer shirt and took it off, then the grimy tee shirt. The cool air raised goose bumps on her bare skin.

She went to the makeshift sink in the corner and looked into the mirror above it. Her hair was a clumpy mess. There were bags under her eyes. Her face was tan but stressed-looking. She grasped the end of the elastic bandage and gently unwrapped it. The gauze Gilstrap had applied to her shoulder was stained through with blood and sweat. She peeled it off, exposing the wound to the air. The groove the bullet had carved in her flesh had sealed closed in a puckered crimp. There was a reddish puffiness and a wicked scab. She looked in the mirror again, over her shoulder and down to the small of her back, where a tattoo of a blue butterfly over red flowers and small green leaves contrasted with her pale skin. She'd gotten the tat at the same time as her friend Jan had the spring before. At first, she'd wondered if it had been a smart move, then, gradually, it felt like part of her identity, and she knew she'd have it for life.

Back to practical concerns. Darcy hunted around the tent for medical supplies, located a first-aid kit hanging by a strap next to the storage barrels. She found a packet of antiseptic cleansing wipes, ripped one open and swabbed the wound. She applied a three-by-four-inch trauma pad and secured it with first-aid tape. The shoulder seemed to feel a little better. She donned her tee shirt and flannel shirt and looked for something to eat.

After a can of fruit cocktail, Darcy put the remaining cookies in the small backpack she'd found in the tent. What else to take with her? A box of crackers, the map, of course, and some water. She picked up an empty plastic bottle, went outside and filled it with icy water from the little creek near the front of the tent.

Back inside, Darcy took a last look around. She'd been damned lucky to find this place. Whoever owned it would notice some things were missing. She felt bad about that. She fumbled out the bills she'd taken from Gilstrap's wallet and left a few of them on the table, weighted down with a rock. Outside, she turned and said, "Thanks for everything." Then she swung the pack onto her back, carefully arranging the straps to keep pressure off her injured shoulder as much as possible. She began to follow the steep trail down through a sea of evergreen trees and boulders.

She hiked for an hour, steadily descending through lodgepole forest, rocky slopes and grassy meadows. The only sounds were her footfalls, her breathing and the occasional calls of birds and squirrels. As she moved lower, the air warmed and sweat began to form on her forehead, chest and back. She removed the flannel shirt and stowed it in the pack. This seemed to be a good time to rest and peruse the map. After a moment of study, she was able to match the terrain with a place on the map where a cliff loomed above the pathway. She must have come about two miles, with about six more to go. After a couple of cookies and a swig of water, she struggled to her feet.

As Darcy walked on, she developed a steady rhythm, picked up the pace and began to feel confident she'd make the road she'd seen on the map that afternoon. But what then? Would it lead her to a town? Would it take her to the dig site? Maybe there'd be traffic, and she could flag down a ride. She kept slogging until the sun was directly overhead before she stopped for another break. It was a lot warmer now, probably near seventy. She stretched and took another reading from the map. Looked like she'd come about halfway to the road. After a lunch of a handful of crackers, the last of the stale cookies and some tepid water, she was underway again, determined to reach the road before dark.

Darcy's feet were killing her, especially her toes, which pressed against the front of her shoes with every downward step. No doubt, blisters had formed. She'd been at it for five hours. There'd been no visible wildlife other than the birds and squirrels. The water bottle was nearly empty. Her stomach growled. She'd picked and eaten wild berries from bushes along the trail, some she could identify, others—who knew? She shuffled along now, head bent, eyes on the ground. Suddenly, she heard a faint sound below. Could it be the crunch of tires on a gravel road? She quickened her pace.

She rounded a bend and slowed. The trail broke out of the woods into a grassy meadow. A thin brown line bisected the mid-distance, perhaps a mile away and quite a ways below. A small cloud of dust rose above the line and drifted toward the trees on the far side of the meadow. A vehicle on a dusty road? Darcy broke into a trot, stumbled and fell to her hands and knees. She stopped to appraise the damage—a skinned knee—and continued at a fast walk.

Darcy finally came to a potholed gravel road, empty to the horizon in both directions. No sign of the dust cloud she'd seen earlier. Could it have been the product of a gust of wind? A mirage? She examined the map—going north would take her back into the mountains, south to level ground. She adjusted the pack straps to put most of the load on her good shoulder and, verifying direction by the location of the late afternoon sun, headed south. In another mile she spotted a small green metal sign along the shoulder to the right of the road. A number was emblazoned in white: 8. It might mean eight miles, but from what? She resumed walking at a steady pace, despite her sore knee and aching legs and feet.

A six-foot-high fence with parallel strands of taut wire appeared on the left, forming the corner boundary of a property. A white sign with red letters was affixed to a fence post: DANGER! ELECTRIC FENCE. Darcy walked along the fence on prairie grass.

A little while later, a building came into view on the horizon. Darcy knew she shouldn't get her hopes up. She forced herself to remain calm, to keep going, but slowly. This was no time to panic, to stumble into another bad situation. As she got closer to the building, she could see that it was behind the electric fence. It was some sort of warehouse, with walls and roof of corrugated tan metal. Darcy detected movement at the far end of the building. A pair of all-terrain vehicles, piloted by men wearing broad-brimmed straw hats, disappeared through a garage door. She stood and watched. They looked like the men she'd seen blast by her near the cabin where she'd been held prisoner, but she couldn't be sure. She dropped to the ground, making it less likely they'd see her if they happened to look her way. A few minutes later, the duo exited the building on foot, sauntered to a pickup, closed a gate in the fence behind them and drove away.

Darcy approached the fence, debated whether to try to get in or to continue on the road. She was sore and starving, tired of walking. Maybe there was a phone inside. The guys who'd just left had been somehow connected with Gilstrap, but they were gone. What the hell, she'd take a chance.

She went to the wide metal gate. A chromed padlock and a chain covered in thick green vinyl hung from the gate, but the lock's shackle wasn't closed. She undid the chain and set it aside. Carefully gripping the insulating plastic handles on the gate that would protect her from the electric current surging through the fence, Darcy opened the barrier, stepped in, and closed it behind her. She reset the chain and lock as they'd been.

The place seemed to be part of a farm or ranch. An ocean of grass bent slightly in the breeze. The sun was now an orange ball, low in the sky and sinking as the air cooled perceptibly. She stopped to put on the heavy flannel shirt.

Darcy went over to the building. There was a silver Ford pickup truck parked outside. Nearby, a closed overhead garage door flanked a steel entry door. She twisted the doorknob, and it gave. A sudden gust of wind tore the cap from her head and sailed it away. She thought about chasing after it, decided to let it go. She entered and closed the door behind her. As her eyes grew accustomed to the dark interior, she could make out a row of farm equipment parked along the wall to her left—tractors, all-terrain vehicles, a bulldozer, a couple of flatbed trailers and a horse trailer, a service area containing a vehicle hoist and steel tables covered with mechanic's tools. Darcy went over to the nearest ATV and placed a hand on the hood. Still warm. She was pretty sure this machine and its neighbor were the ones she'd seen tearing up the trail beneath the cabin the night before last.

On the far side of the cavernous space, a floor-to-ceiling partition wall contained a closed door. Darcy walked over, found the door unlocked and went through. Now she was in a smaller space containing spools of smooth steel fencing wire and fence posts. A single light bulb illuminated the room. She'd yet to see a window in the structure. Along the opposite wall was a closed door to yet another room from which a high-pitched whine came. It reminded Darcy of a dentist's drill. Then came an intermittent percussive sound, like a sculptor chipping splinters from a rock. In the background, she heard recorded music, a country song with the refrain, "My wife thinks you're dead." A live male voice sang along.

Darcy moved closer to the room, keeping to the wall. Near the door, she inadvertently bumped into a metal table on casters with a toolbox on top. The table rolled a few feet and thudded into a support beam. The box moved slightly, the tools inside rattling around. The man stopped singing. Darcy crouched behind the fencing materials, just as the door to the room opened. Through a thin gap between fence post bundles, she saw a pudgy, unshaven man with a bald pate and gray ponytail gazing around. He wore a red vest over a white tee shirt and held a hammer in his right hand. He looked puzzled. He didn't seem to spot anything out of order, shrugged and returned to his room, leaving the door open. Another song came

114

on the radio, and the man resumed his inexpert caterwauling.

Darcy moved to a corner opposite the workroom doorway. There, she found a lumpy white plaster-coated package on a wooden pallet. It had the size and roughly the shape of a mummy. She shuddered—it looked like a body. Fossilized dinosaur bones were wrapped that way in preparation for transport. Had someone raided the dig site? The Stevens group had plaster-wrapped some of the *T. rex* bones and stored them in one of the teepees. Could Doctor Stevens have contracted with the owner of this building to store bones here? It would make sense to keep them in a safe place until the dig concluded—there were no secure indoor storage areas at the site. Maybe she'd somehow gotten back close to the dig, even though the surroundings didn't look familiar.

She was about to make a move toward the exit when suddenly the workroom door opened again. As Darcy sneaked a peek from behind the plaster cast, the man she'd seen with the hammer re-emerged, this time wearing a floppy-brimmed tan canvas hat like fishermen wore. A leather messenger bag hung from his shoulder. He turned, closed and locked the workroom door with a key on a chain attached to his belt. He passed through the door separating Darcy's room from the farm equipment room, shut the door and locked it. Darcy heard the sound of the third and final door closing, then footfalls outside. A vehicle started up and accelerated away. Finally, all was dark and quiet in the building.

Darcy moved to the dividing door, tried the knob. Locked. Same thing with the workroom door. There were no windows. Worst of all, she had no phone. She returned to the plaster package and sat down on it. She had a feeling she'd be spending another night in an unfamiliar place, hungry, scared, wondering when she'd get back to the dig site, wondering if she'd ever get home. Darcy sighed, let her head sag. She felt like screaming.

15

B rian got back to the Masters Hotel and checked for messages at the front desk. There were none. He bought a copy of the previous day's Clarkville Times, found a table in the nearly empty hotel restaurant and ordered a corned beef sandwich with chips.

As he waited for the food to arrive, he read the skimpy newspaper. The weekly "Constabulary Report" caught his eye. There was a series of sheriff's office-related vignettes with titles. Brian read, "CAR CHASER CATCHES QUARRY: A man reported that as he drove along the Frontage Road, a dog sprang out of the brush, attempting to bite the truck tires. The dog ran into the side of the truck, denting it. Since there was no ID on the dog, the man gently placed the unconscious canine into the ditch next to the road." Another story: "NO BULL: A woman, very upset, called the sheriff's office and reported there was a black bull standing on the railroad tracks and that a train was coming. The sheriff's office called the Burlington Northern dispatcher, who slowed the train to a crawl. Ranchers in the area were contacted to see if a bull was missing. The bull was not on the tracks when the train went by. The sheriff's office considers the matter closed."

Brian compared these stories to what he read in the Chicago newspapers every day—the knifings, shootings, decapitations, wife-beatings, child molestation, traffic altercation shootouts, liquor store robberies, indictments of politicians for extortion, unidentified corpses found in car trunks at O'Hare. He sighed and set the paper down as the waitress placed his food in front of him.

Two men in ball caps and Carhartts entered the restaurant and took seats at a nearby table. They ordered sandwiches and began talking about hunting.

"You ready for the season?" the bigger of the two men asked the other.

"Hell, yes."

"Where'd ya get yer elk last year? In the Crazies?"

"Nope, got her in the Belts."

"Man, I gotta get over there this year. Crazies are a tough place to get a clean shot."

Not tough enough, Brian thought.

Brian mulled over his meeting with Russell Eagle Feather. The young man had seemed sincere, if a little reluctant. He'd had a motive to kill his uncle—inheriting the land. But if he had, why would he volunteer the bone and other stuff the old man had found? And Brian's gut told him Eagle Feather was a solid citizen despite his attitude. He decided to relegate the young Indian to non-suspect status for now.

Darcy had been missing for three days. Brian considered the options. Continue plodding along in Montana? Return to Chicago? Push to find out what the bureau might be doing? Put out TV and print ads offering a reward for information? He decided to try to shake something loose locally.

He finished his meal and called the Geyser County sheriff's office. A woman answered, "Sheriff's. Kelly speaking."

"Sheriff Harrison, please," Brian said.

"He's out of the office today. Help you?"

"I'm the one that was there about my niece, the young woman who disappeared from the dinosaur dig. I wanted to speak with the sheriff about it."

"Afraid he's out 'til day after tomorrow. He's attending a law enforcement conference in Helena. I can leave a message if you'd like," she said.

"Is there someone in the office familiar with the case—a deputy, maybe?"

There was silence on the line for a couple of seconds. Then, "Just a moment."

"This is Laura Jensen. Can I help you?"

"Brian McKay here. Are you on the Darcy McKay case?"

"Well, yeah, I'm working on it."

"Could I stop by and talk?"

"You must be the uncle."

"That's right."

"I guess there's no harm to it. Come on by," she said.

The woman didn't sound jaded enough for a cop.

Laura Jensen greeted him as he cleared the door. "So you're the famous Mr. McKay from Chicago, eh?" She smiled. The deputy was about thirty, average height, slim figure. Curly blond hair, frank blue eyes, crisp, formfitting gray uniform. A nameplate pinned above her left breast read JENSEN in white block letters on a black background. She wore a wide black belt holding a brass badge, nightstick, holstered Smith & Wesson .38 service revolver, mace canister, Taser, cell phone, handcuffs, tactical radio and ammunition pouch.

"Good news travels fast." Brian noticed small laugh lines at the corners of the deputy's mouth. The nightstick stuck out from her body a little, supported by the graceful curve of her rump. She was the best-looking cop he'd seen in a long while.

He decided to try a bit of levity. "I was just reading the constabulary notes in the Times, and figured you folks might be too busy chasing wayward animals to even spare the time to talk," he said.

"We don't get the major-league criminals here like you guys do in Chicago, unless they're passing through on vacation," she replied.

"Ms. Jensen, I—"

"No one's called me Ms. Jensen since I quit substitute-teaching five years ago. It's Laura. You got anything on your niece?" Down to business. She took a seat behind a gray steel desk and Brian settled down in a chair across from her.

"I just met with William Old Horn's nephew in Bozeman this morning," Brian said. "He showed me the old guy's scrapbook and journal. Seems Old Horn was near the dinosaur dig, I mean on the same side of the hill where Darcy was digging, when he got shot. Assuming the body wasn't moved. According to the nephew, Old Horn might have found something interesting. It occurred to me there could be a connection with my niece."

"What do you suppose he found?"

Brian explained what Russell Eagle Feather had told him about his uncle, and mentioned the journal entries about "items" found and the "face pot." He didn't mention his sub-sequent visits with the two MSU professors.

"What's the sheriff's investigation turned up?" he asked.

"Didn't you meet with Sam already?"

"Yeah, but I'd value your take on this thing, too."

"You've no doubt already heard about the blood on the rocks and the boot tracks on the hillside. We've done some follow-up stuff here, contacted truck dealers state-wide, trying to put together a list of 2000 and later white extended and crew cab pickups registered in the state."

"So a witness saw a pickup at the scene?"

"The guy in charge of the dinosaur dig and a helper saw a big white late-model pickup going north when they went up to look for Darcy. Montana plates."

Brian wondered why Stevens hadn't mentioned this bit of information to him, then decided the paleontologist proba-bly didn't consider it important. "What else you got?" he said.

"We found a slug at the scene and are gonna get it tested by the crime lab in Missoula. The blood on the rocks was type A. Other than that, not much, so far. No fibers, hairs or anything, but it's windy up there and so that's not surpris-ing. We'll keep on it."

"Any idea when the ballistics results are due back?

"Nope. Just a second. I want to check something."

Laura walked to the sheriff's private office, opened a desk drawer and rummaged around. She picked up a plastic bag containing a small object and returned.

"You know, it's funny," she said. "He must have for-gotten to send this out. It's actually not in bad shape, consider-ing it was bouncing around in those rocks."

She shook a lump of gray metal the size of a fingertip from the small zip-closure bag. It looked like a rifle slug. Brian could make out lands and grooves on the surface. The tip was slightly deformed, but it was mostly intact. Why had the sheriff said it was flattened and smashed up? The fact that it was more or less intact gave Brian a scintilla of hope. If this were in fact the slug that had struck Darcy, it had probably either nicked her or passed through flesh, not hitting bone. With the small amount of blood at the abduction scene, he could hope it was the former.

"How did he find this up there among all those rocks? Seems like it'd be a needle in a haystack deal," Brian said.

"You mean how did *she* find it. I took a metal detector to the scene, buzzed it around, and bingo, there it was. Bagged it, gave it to the sheriff."

She carefully pushed the slug into the bag with the tip of a ballpoint and left it on her desk. "I'll send this out to Missoula ASAP," she said.

"What about shells?" Brian said.

She shook her head. "Didn't find anything."

"Oh, hell," Brian said. His cheeks reddened slightly.

"What?"

"The damned hole in the side of the hill, like a tunnel. I knew I saw something as I was leaving, but I couldn't remember what it was."

"I think what you saw is an abandoned mineshaft. It's nothing much."

"I'd like to go out and take another look on that hillside. Is there a way to get there other than through the dig and up and over?"

"The way I'd do it, I'd put my mountain bike in the bed of my truck, I'd drive over on the Castle Mountain road—that's the eastern access—and I'd ride my bike in there through the rocks," Laura said. "Or I'd walk in."

"Interested in joining me while I do that?" Brian asked.

Laura glanced at the large wall clock, hesitated a moment, then nodded as if she'd made a decision. "I can get out of here at five, assuming Jim makes it back when he's supposed to. We could stop by my house and pick up the bikes. My son's got a nicer bike than mine. Maybe we can talk him into lending it to you, seeing as how he's supposed to be doing his homework."

16

They reached Laura Jensen's modest 1950s bungalow on a quiet Clarkville street at five-thirty. An overgrown weeping willow took up a sizeable chunk of the small front yard. Brian parked at the curb as Laura eased her Tacoma pickup into the driveway outside a one-car garage. He noticed her license plate read "CRAZIES."

She opened the unlocked front door and invited Brian into the house. In the living room, a comfortable-looking couch and a couple of upholstered chairs surrounded a low coffee table littered with magazines and a copy of the latest Lee Child bestseller. A small river rock fireplace flanked by built-in bookcases dominated a wall. Paperback mysteries filled the shelves, entire series of detective novels, from Harry Bosch to Nero Wolfe.

"Ah, you read crime novels," Brian said.

"Yeah. I get teased about it at work."

"Don't you get enough of real crime in your job?"

"Well, novels are different. Everything's tied up in a neat bow at the end, the bad guy gets what he's got coming and the hero, often a highly-trained law-enforcement person such as myself, comes out looking golden."

"You know the four elements of a good novel?" Brian said.

"I have the feeling I'm about to find out."

"Yep. Religion, sex, royalty and mystery."

"So..."

"So, here's a good one-sentence novel: Oh my God, I'm pregnant, said the princess. I wonder who did it."

She laughed. "Not bad."

"Gotta admit, I stole that from W. Somerset Maugham."

They chatted about books for a few minutes. Brian gradually got the feeling he was being watched. He pivoted suddenly to see a stringbean boy of about thirteen standing in the arched opening between the living and dining rooms, keeping an eye on them.

"Hi there," Brian said.

The boy just stared.

"Brian, this is my son, Jerry. Jerry, can't you say hello to Mr. McKay?"

The boy tilted his chin up an inch, jammed his hands a little deeper into the back pockets of his voluminous cargo shorts.

"Hey, dude," he said. He turned and disappeared into the next room.

"Jerry's not much for meeting new people, especially adults." She raised her voice, "Jerry, we need to borrow your bike while you do your homework. Okay?" No response. She sighed, held up a wait-a-minute finger and went to the rear of the house.

She returned a few minutes later. "Jerry will be simply delighted to let you use his bike. He says he's, and here I quote him, 'like, bummed.' He reminds me it's a sweet bike and he doesn't want the rims taco'd. He requests that we wash it, lube the chain and air it out when we return. I told him he's lucky if we return. Have a seat while I change."

A few minutes later, Laura swept into the room wearing a blue short-sleeved tee shirt, snug cycling shorts and black Nikes with red laces. She wore a small fanny pack around her waist.

"I've got some water. Ready to rumble?" she said.

"I think so. Are these clothes okay? Anything I can carry?"

"You're fine. We'll clip your pants leg with rubber bands, so they won't get caught in the chain. Oh, and by the way, I've got my .38 in my pack, and some evidence bags, just in case."

They climbed into Laura's truck after lashing the mountain bikes down with shock cords in the bed. She headed north on the state highway for a few miles, then veered right on a narrow gravel road. A few minutes later, she made a left turn on another, bumpier dirt road and continued north. Brian feared the washboard surface might shake the gold fillings from his teeth, but Laura was a skillful driver—she had a knack for missing most of the larger potholes and rocks. Fifteen minutes later, she shunted the truck onto a narrow turnout on the left side.

A brush-choked creek meandered through dry, rocky terrain dotted with willows, alders and sage. Rocks, from pebble-size up to glacial boulders larger than vehicles, were scattered about like teeth from a hockey player's mouth. In the distance, Bone Mountain loomed over everything, steep-sided, crumbly, covered with multicolored rock top to bottom. Brian wondered how they'd manage to navigate the obstacle course to the base of the hill on bikes. The thick-framed cycles looked robust, with their rubber-coated reciprocating suspension forks and fat knobby tires.

"Okay, this should be a nice little ride, nothing too technical," Laura said. "I meant to ask, have you done much single-track riding?"

"I wouldn't know a single-track from a singles bar," Brian said.

"Just follow me. We'll take it slow, stay in the lower gears most of the way, and switch down to the granny gears when we get to the steep stuff. We'll leave the bikes at the base of the mountain and walk the rest of the way. Whatever you do, don't ride over any cactus. You do, you might get a whole mess of punctures in your tire all at once."

"You mean Jerry's tire," he replied.

Laura grinned. "Yeah, and I'd never hear the end of it. Let's go."

She lifted her bike over the barbed wire fence adjoining the road, dropped it on the other side and slipped through, carefully avoiding the sharp barbs. Brian followed suit. Laura climbed aboard her bike and began pedaling slowly along a barely perceptible pathway through the jumbled maze. She downshifted and pedaled steadily while skillfully negotiating the faint track meandering toward the butte.

Brian did his best to emulate her. It was a strange feeling, riding a bicycle in such harsh terrain. His most recent cycling experience had been a few weeks back with Michelle, the two of them riding lightweight road cycles on the bike path along Lake Michigan. There, the hazards had been different— a kaleidoscope of pedestrians, bicycles, inline skaters, walkers, joggers, baby buggies and Frisbee throwers. Here, it seemed, the trick was to be loose, look ahead for tire-destroying obstacles and be ready to slow down or swerve abruptly, all while staying in the proper gear and keeping from scraping your legs on the rocks constantly lurching at you. And yet, as they pedaled on, he began to enjoy the ride. Once, he was admiring the taut flexing motion of Laura's tight butt up ahead, and nearly ran into a boulder.

Laura stopped and waited for Brian to catch up several times until they reached the bottom of the steep hillside. She turned and said. "This rock is pretty loose. Set your bike down and put your walking shoes on."

"Wait a second. What's this?" Brian said. The sun glinted off a coppery object partially obscured beneath a gnarled sagebrush plant a few feet to his right. He stooped to retrieve a small twig and inserted it into the open end of the rifle shell lying on the ground at his feet. He held the shell aloft at eye level, supported on the tip of the twig so Laura could examine it as well.

"Interesting. That's pretty recent, and the big game seasons don't open for a while," she said. Hold on. I'll get an evidence bag."

Laura unzipped her fanny pack and pulled out a zip-closure plastic bag. She motioned for Brian to drop the shell in, sealed it, and affixed a label, which she completed in ball-point—date, description and location where found. She stowed the bag in her pack. She marked the spot on the ground with a small cairn-like pile of rocks.

"Let's see what else we can find," she said.

They paced around the area, then slowly picked their way up the steep talus slope on foot, occasionally slipping backward on the easily dislodged stones. A couple of times, Brian began to fall and shot out a hand to steady himself against a rock. They gained perhaps 300 feet of elevation before reaching the spot Brian had been with Scott Noble Stevens the day before. Coming at it from below lent an entirely different perspective. No sign of the dinosaur dig site from here—it would be on the other side of the ridge. He imagined a man coming up this hill as they'd just done, intent on grabbing Darcy. It was a steep, slow climb. Why hadn't she run away? Could she? Or had a rifle bullet crippled her, or even worse? And why hadn't the sheriff or the deputies found the shell casing at the foot of the hill?

Laura said, "Let's work our way out from that rock."

"Okay."

They began to examine the ground in small circles around the large boulder where blood had been found the evening before last. Brian got the compact binoculars from his backpack and glassed the area top to bottom. He concentrated on the base of the hill, where the sun glinted off the shiny handlebars of the two mountain bikes lying on the ground. If a man had parked a truck on the road and walked in on the route they'd bicycled, could he hide down there? Possibly. He could sit under one of those old cottonwoods and be at least partly invisible to someone up here intent on digging. Hell, knowing Darcy, he guessed she'd have been so into her fossil work, she wouldn't have noticed Santa Claus and his reindeer down there, at least not right away. At any rate, such a man would have a good line of sight to this point from down by the bikes. Say someone fired on Darcy. What would she do? Brian looked at his immediate surroundings. Hell, if someone shot at *him* right now, he'd dive behind the nearest cover, which would be the huge boulder a few feet to his right. If the shooter came up the hill, how long would it take? Probably a little longer than it had taken Laura and himself just now. The sheriff had found tracks of a person in western boots, about size twelve. Although he didn't wear such boots himself, Brian guessed they'd be damned awkward for climbing up as they'd just done. It had taken them about ten minutes, not hurrying, but not dragging either. The sheriff had said the boot tracks went both directions—up, then down on top of the upward tracks. The wind had erased them all.

Laura broke into his reverie. "Hey Brian, did your niece carry a notebook?"

"I don't know. Maybe," he said.

"Check this," she said, holding up a wrinkled piece of white paper. "This was wedged under a rock. Damned near missed it."

Laura smoothed out the paper on a flat rock. It was about three by five inches, white with pale blue lines, obviously torn from a spiral notebook. Dirt smeared the surface. Someone had printed in block letters: "BIG COW." The last stroke of the W was not complete.

"Might be Darcy's scrawl," Brian said. "Big cow. Hmmm. Maybe she didn't like her tent-mate so much, after all."

"Yeah, or possibly the person who shot her got here as she was writing the note. She can't keep writing, so she balls this up and tosses it. She hopes someone finds it," Laura said.

"I like it. And, I'm guessing 'big cowboy.' What do you think?"

"Okay, not bad. Now, all we've got to do is narrow it

down to one of the hundreds of big guys who wear cowboy boots from time to time around here." She sighed. "But, it's something." She tucked the paper into an evidence bag.

Brian spotted the pile of rusted metal he'd seen with Stevens. It was slightly above them and about twenty yards away.

"That stuff is from mining, right?" He pointed toward the rusty heap.

"Oh yeah. That's some of the junk from when they closed up the mine I mentioned before. They just walked away when the ore ran out. Left the equipment behind because it wasn't worth moving. People have been prospecting around here over the years, but I don't believe it's ever amounted to anything."

"Think I'll take a look inside that mineshaft," Brian said.

Laura followed his gaze to the crumbling excavation in the hillside, a square-cornered opening about four feet high and three feet wide, supported on the top and sides by weathered timbers, and partially concealed behind the scrap pile. " Be my guest."

Brian carefully sidestepped across loose rock to the metal junk pile. He kicked at a rust-pocked steel rail with a boot toe. The stuff looked like what you'd see at a metal recycling yard on the west side of Chicago. Just beyond, a huge web covered the shaft opening. A spider with a body the size of an eyeball lay in wait near the center of the gossamer trap. Brian peered through the web into the darkness beyond. Once his eyes adjusted, he could make out a rock-walled tunnel disappearing into the gloom. He guessed nobody had been in there in ages. As he turned to retrace his steps to the boulder where Laura waited, he noticed a filtered cigarette butt on the ground. He snapped a few photos of the area.

"Anything?" Laura said.

"Only a deserted tunnel guarded by the mother of all spiders."

"Yeah, not much of a mine, is it? When I was little, we played hide-and-seek up here. I was the only one brave enough to hide in the tunnel—it goes in a few feet and dead-ends where it's boarded up."

"Do you know where Old Horn's cabin is?" Brian said.

"A few miles from here. Want to check it out?"

"Yeah."

They hiked down, mounted the bikes and rolled toward the road, Laura in the lead. Brian grasped the brake levers all the way down, swerving around obstacles and fishtailing on the loose surface. Several times he felt like he was about to wipe out, and gripped the brakes harder. Miraculously, he made it to the bottom intact, though his fingers felt limp from squeezing the brakes. He realized he wore a smile and decided the descent must have been fun.

"Awesome riding, dude," Laura said with a grin.

In the truck, she drove back the direction they'd come, then turned onto a rutted two-track disappearing into woods. A short distance later, she stopped outside a small log building with a peaked roof. The front door was open a crack. It had been padlocked, but somebody had smashed the lock off. It lay twisted on the ground. They entered the gloom of a one-room interior lit only by fading sunlight through the one window.

Brian switched on his penlight. The place had been

thoroughly tossed. A wooden table lay on its side, one leg broken off. The stained mattress had been slit open and its stuffing shaken out. The simple wooden cabinet in one corner had been opened, and the contents strewn on the floor. There were a few canned goods, traces of flour and some metal dishes in the mess.

"I wonder if they found what they were looking for," Laura said.

"I'd guess not."

"What do you mean?"

"Just that they trashed the whole place. Chances are, if they'd found what they wanted, at least some of the stuff in here would still be intact."

Laura nodded.

In the truck on the way back to Clarkville, Brian said, "I'm surprised we found the shell and the note. Didn't you guys go over the area?"

Laura glanced at him. "Yeah. The three of us did. The note was pretty well hid, so I don't feel so bad. As for the shell, I wonder. By the way, Jim told me Sam looked around at the bottom of the hill, but he didn't bother with a detector."

17

Early Saturday, Brian gunned the Grand Cherokee along the highway on his way to Arthur Sands's ranch in the Crazy Mountains. The previous evening, he'd joined Laura and her son for a delivered pizza at her house. He and Laura seemed to be developing some kind of relationship. He wouldn't mind seeing her again. That reminded him, he needed to call Michelle soon. Laura's son had thawed a little during dinner as they discussed mountain biking—the boy had showed off, giving Brian some tips on hill-climbing technique. A bright spot in a sea of worries. He sure hadn't gotten very far, and the sheriff's office hadn't either.

What was going on with the sheriff? He'd apparently tossed the slug in his desk drawer and failed to get a ballistics test done. Why? An oversight? Plus, he'd overlooked the shell Brian had found at the base of the hill yesterday. Maybe the best thing would be for the FBI to come in. Bureaucracy or not, the FBI was still the best police force in the world. Give them a spent bullet and they could search thousands of records of guns used in crimes for a possible match. Maybe James could come out. Nah, they'd send agents from SLC, maybe somebody local as well. Somebody competent, he hoped.

Darcy had been gone for three and a half days now. He tried to convince himself she was still alive. Otherwise, he'd feel guilty the rest of his life. He should never have let her go on the expedition. But then, it really wasn't his decision. How could he have stopped her? He had to stay focused, take this thing one step at a time. He'd find her. She'd be okay. Maybe.

Brian had been lucky this morning—Arthur Sands answered the phone at his ranch and agreed to see him if he'd like to drive over then. The vast Sands ranch began across the road from Bone Mountain and extended eastward for miles. Sands said he'd do anything he could to help, and so on—the graciousness of a rich man with sensitive antennae.

As Brian negotiated the seventeen miles from Clarkville, he found himself enjoying the scenery. A whitetail doe and two fawns, skittish but curious, posed like lawn ornaments, training their big brown eyes on the vehicle as it rolled past. An occasional ranch house with barn and outbuildings punctuated the dry hills and grasslands. Barbed wire fences bordered all the land, separating it from the highway. Large herds of Black Angus and Hereford cattle grazed within their confines. In other places, wheel-lines and pivots sprayed mists of water pumped from streams and the aquifer, allowing thousands of acres of deep green hay and alfalfa to grow in the naturally arid climate.

Topping a rise, Brian looked down on a moving scene: three adult horses and a colt chased after a pickup truck rolling across a fenced pasture with a load of loose hay in the bed. The truck slowed down and a horse caught up, stretching its long neck to attack the hay. The animal struck like a snake and snared a mouthful of lush green fodder. Its peers quickly did the same as the truck coasted to a halt. Brian smiled.

He had seen only a handful of vehicles on the road all the way from town. A vast blue sky overhung the countryside, marked sporadically by feathery white tangles of cloud. The Sands ranch property came into view, bounded by a perimeter fence: seven strands of tight wire linked heavy steel posts painted olive green. A white sign hung from the fence with a message in red block letters: DANGER! ELECTRIC FENCE. Brian was reminded of the *Jurassic Park* movies.

The main entrance of the Sands ranch appeared a few minutes later, a wide opening in the fence blocked by a mammoth steel bar gate on wheels. Varnished pine logs with the girth of 55-gallon drums framed the top and sides of the entrance. Hanging from the massive top beam was a brand symbol: a large plastic hourglass with sand apparently flowing through, locked in time and space.

Brian stopped the Grand Cherokee a few feet short of the gate and waited. In a moment, a metallic voice rasped from an unseen speaker, "Hello. State your business, please."

"Brian McKay. I have an appointment to see Mr. Sands."

"Okay. You're gonna punch a code into the keypad on the left side of the gate. The code is SR15566." The voice sounded Midwestern and hard as a shovel blade.

Brian complied. A moment later, the formidable gate began to rumble sideways on its track, deliberate as a locomotive. In a moment, it stopped, allowing ingress through a space barely wider than the vehicle. As Brian moved through the opening, he noticed a video camera mounted on a log post. Once his rear bumper cleared the gate, it closed behind him, locking home with a solid thunk.

The freshly paved entry road climbed through cottonwoods, pines, aspen and willows for about a mile and culminated at a billiard-table-green lawn surrounding the largest log building Brian had ever seen. The central part of the house was three stories high and contained huge arched windows coated with a coppery reflective substance. You'd be able to see out of the building, but not in. Lacquered pine logs overlapped at the corners. Several one-story wings branched off from the main building. Enormous windows faced the lofty mountains. A vastness of dark green metal roof topped the structure. A separate ten-door garage adjoined the complex, with a dozen outbuildings in view on the surrounding acreage. Brian noticed an airplane hangar next to a long blacktop runway behind the compound. There was also a huge painted white letter H on a round asphalt area beyond the garages, a helicopter landing pad. Gravel roads branched off to the interior of the property. A pair of large red barns with cupolas on the roofs and white trim were visible on the horizon.

Brian pulled the Grand Cherokee into a parking area off the drive a few yards from the main entrance, went to the door and knocked with his key ring. Almost immediately, the door swung inward. A stocky man with a light brown crew cut and flat eyes stepped aside, allowing Brian to enter. He looked like a pile of rocks in a gray sweat suit. For a split second, Brian flashed to the nightmare with the grizzly bear he'd had while trying to sleep in the motel after his flight from Chicago.

"Have a seat. He'll be with you in a few minutes." Without waiting for a response, the man pivoted on a heel and left the room. His was the voice Brian had heard at the gate.

"Nice meeting you, too," Brian muttered to the empty doorway. He had a choice of more than a dozen brown leather chairs in a room about twice the size of his apartment. A fire-place capable of roasting oxen anchored one wall. The stone chimney rose to a peaked cathedral ceiling. Wagon wheel chandeliers dangled from chains fifteen feet above his head. On a wall near the fireplace, a framed plaque proclaimed, "When you come to my lodge, the robe will be spread and the pipe lit for you." The quote was familiar—Brian thought it might have come from Charlie Russell, the Montana cowboy artist of the late nineteenth and early twentieth centuries.

He wandered to a window across from the entrance. A log-framed bench with brown cushions sat in front of the window. Outside, the lawn sloped down to a diaphanous blue lake. A covey of mallards paddled along the near shore, dipping their heads in the water to feed, with the unintended comical effect of pointing their feathered bottoms at the sky.

Tables and lamps were scattered throughout the immense interior space. Paintings of western landscapes and bronze sculptures of cowboys, mountain men, horses and Indians graced the walls and tables—a collection of western art that would have made many a museum director envious. A colorful picture, about 20 by 30 inches, hung on the chimney above the fireplace. Brian walked over to take a closer look. The image was of a cowboy on a bucking horse. The rider's hat had gone flying, and the horse was creating havoc as it pranced through a campfire, scattering men, cooking utensils and food in its wake. An artist's signature appeared in the lower left-hand corner: CM Russell. Beneath it appeared a sketched buffalo skull and the date, 1908. Charles M. Russell, the famous cowboy artist. Brian had seen a piece in the Trib recently about a Russell oil painting that had changed hands for over five million dollars. He was studying the fine details of camp objects in the foreground of the picture when a baritone boomed behind him, "It's one of Russell's better efforts, don't you think?"

The voice belonged to a man just under medium height, deeply tanned, with a wide-shouldered, narrow-waisted build, receding black hair, shrewd dark eyes behind tinted squarish eyeglasses, a prominent straight nose and a brilliant smile dominated by capped teeth. He'd been put together with care; his large head and athlete's physique had the perfection of a Frank Lloyd Wright prairie-style house. "Call me Art," the man said, as he proffered a small hand with manicured nails. He wore a sky blue cotton shirt, black moleskin trousers and soft black leather boots with rounded toes. The entire getup fit flawlessly—it had to be custom.

They chatted for a few minutes. Sands mentioned that the Russell was a reproduction of the famous oil painting, "Bronc to Breakfast." The original hung in the Montana Historical Society Museum in Helena. He let on that he had several smaller Russell originals elsewhere.

Sands led Brian down a long hallway to a library/office room exuding masculinity. An enormous teak desk was flanked by a wall of bookshelves and groupings of framed photographs. Brian noticed a tight arrangement of pictures showing Arthur Sands with the rich and famous: Sands and Peter Fonda straddling Harleys, Sands wielding a silver shovel alongside Chicago's Mayor Richard M. Daley at a ground-breaking, Sands shaking hands with Presidents George H. W. Bush, Bill Clinton and Barack Obama. A bottle of twenty-year-old single malt Scotch whisky and a set of small crystal sipping glasses occupied a corner of the desk.

Sands led Brian to some leather chairs and a couch forming a conversation nook near the fireplace. He took a chair and motioned Brian to the couch, which, Brian noticed, placed him a couple inches lower than his host.

"Cup of coffee or tea? Something stronger?" Sands asked.

"I'm fine. I wanted to speak with you about my niece."

"Anything we can do to help, just ask."

"Well, since this place is right across from Bone Mountain, where she was last seen, I figured it wouldn't hurt to let you know what she looked like and ask you to keep your eyes and ears open. Here's a picture of Darcy—high school graduation, taken a couple years ago." Brian got a print of the photograph he'd given the sheriff from his shirt pocket and handed it to Sands.

The older man regarded the photo and set it on a table next to him. "Nice looking girl. Hang on a minute."

Sands picked up a phone and tapped in three digits. "Will you please stop by my office? Thanks." He hung up and turned his attention back to Brian.

"I'll speak to my security honcho, tell him to keep on the lookout. No doubt, you've already spoken with the sheriff."

"That's right. But Darcy's been gone over three days and they don't have any leads. Anything you can do to help me find her—I'd be very appreciative."

"Certainly. As I say, I'll instruct my staff to be alert."

A knock sounded and a young woman entered the room.

"Here, Gwen. Would you run off a dozen color copies of this?"

The woman disappeared with the photo.

"What staff do you have here?" Brian asked.

"Besides security, there's a ranch manager, some hands, veterinarian, weed-control guy, housekeeper, chef, personal trainer, mechanic and a couple office people."

"What's security do on a ranch?" Brian asked.

Sands sighed. "Unfortunately, a man in my position's got to protect himself from thieves, kidnappers. Even, believe it or not, rustlers." He smiled. "Tom Norton, the gentleman who let you in, takes care of security for me. He's got a couple of men here at the ranch and others in Chicago. Tom's with me wherever I go. Don't be fooled by his gruff exterior—he's invaluable to the smooth running of things. By the way, do you suppose the FBI will come in on this thing with your niece?"

"If they decide it's a kidnapping, there'd be no keeping them out."

"I understand you just left the FBI. What are your plans, if I might ask?"

So Sands had done some checking on him. "Haven't decided. Darcy's my main priority for now."

"Of course. You know, I can always use a man with an impressive background such as yours in my organization. Perhaps, when this is all over—successfully, no doubt—we should sit down, here or in Chicago."

"I'll keep that in mind."

"What else can I help you with?"

"Any chance I could look around your place here?" Brian asked.

"I was about to take a ride-around anyway. Why don't I give you the fifty-cent tour? I'll get Ray Chafee, my ranch manager, to join us. He knows a lot more about the details of the operation than I do. Plus, I'll have Tom join us."

Sands phoned and asked Chafee and Norton to meet them in his office. Gwen returned with the photo of Darcy and some copies, which she handed to Sands wordlessly. Just then, Tom Norton appeared. Sands introduced them, and Norton grasped Brian's hand in a grip like a trash compactor. Brian responded in kind. Their hands were locked for an extra beat. Norton made a point of staring into Brian's eyes, as if taking his measure. "Pleased to meetcha," Norton said.

A moment later, Chafee, a tall, thin man in faded work shirt, jeans and boots came in. A chaw of tobacco bulged in a cheek. He smiled shyly as he shook hands with Brian. "Howdy," was all he said.

The four men climbed into a metallic gray Suburban, Sands behind the wheel. Brian rode shotgun in a front bucket seat finished in dark leather, while Norton and Chafee took the bench behind them. Brian breathed in the new-car smell pervading the cabin—it had been a while since he'd experienced it.

"Is there a map of this place I could look at?" Brian asked.

"In the glove compartment," Sands said.

Brian extracted a folded document on heavy stock. The map showed the headquarters complex in the south central part of a 125-square mile, roughly rectangular piece of land bordered on the west by the gravel county road and Bone Mountain. A mix of private and Geyser National Forest land made up the other three sides. Tiny black squares represented scattered buildings in the interior. There were two squares off by themselves near the northeast corner of the property, a large one and a smaller one.

BONE MOUNTAIN

Sands drove slowly on a gravel road flanked by undulating green and khaki colored fields. Along the way, he proudly pointed out buildings, pastures, fences, equipment, irrigation ditches and pivot lines. Brian followed along on the map.

From creek drainages shot with yellow, red and purple wild flowers, the land swept upward to ridges covered with pines and firs. From there, the eye was drawn further up to the shoulders of the Crazies, still laced with streaks of snow in mid-summer. Icy rivulets of snowmelt cascaded down the mountainsides and sluiced into small streams, lakes and ponds—perpetual water sources in an arid climate. The sharp summits and green valleys reminded Brian of a trip he'd taken to Switzerland shortly after graduating from college. If Darcy's life weren't at stake, the surrounding beauty would have knocked him out.

Sands' voice jogged him out of his reverie. "Actually, we're only the second largest bison operation in the state—Ted Turner's Flying D over by Gallatin Gateway is a little larger. By the way, technically, they're bison, but most people call them buffalo. Either one's fine," Sands said.

The billionaire stopped the vehicle on a wide spot in the road overlooking verdant fields stretching to the base of the mountains. They watched as a dark shape in the far distance slowly edged toward them. In a few moments, Brian could identify the moving mass as a herd of about a hundred grazing bison. They drifted closer, massive heads down, hoovering the lush grass with unflagging industry. If they noticed the truck full of men above them, they gave no sign. Brian felt privileged to observe such a primitive scene.

"What was this land like before you got it?" he asked.

Chafee spoke for the first time. "I worked for the previous owner. Ran a few hundred head of cattle, had a hard time making ends meet. The cows wrecked the pastures. May not look like it now, but some of this ground down below us wasn't much more than bare dirt with weeds when we took over ten years ago. Bison are easier on the land than cattle. They keep moving, never stay put for long. They grow fast, produce nice lean meat, better for you than beef. Thing is though, you can't herd them the way you would cows. You can get a bison to go anywhere he wants to go. The trick is to get him to want to go where you want him to go."

"Kind of like people, in a way," Sands said.

"Do you make a profit on the bison?" Brian asked.

Sands glanced sideways at Brian as if he suspected him of farting. He said, "Wouldn't do it if we didn't."

Chafee said, "We sell some of the older adults for meat. We raise some fairly exotic bulls and sell them at auction for up to ten thousand dollars each. A bull's job is to eat grass and have sex with the cows. They stay around as long as they perform. If you get reincarnated as a bison, you'll want to be a bull." It sounded to Brian like a line repeated many times.

"How big does a bull get?" Brian asked.

"They can be six foot high at the shoulder and weigh a ton," Chaffee said.

"Are they dangerous?"

"Generally not," Chafee said. "But, I wouldn't advise getting between a momma and her calf."

Norton snorted. "They've never given me any shit."

"Over in Yellowstone Park, a bison killed a tourist this summer," Chafee said. "This German guy got too close, trying to take a picture, and the bull caught him on his horns, flipped him in the air, stomped him."

"Are they fast?" Brian asked.

"They can run thirty miles an hour for a short burst," Chafee said. "And they can jump a fence just like a deer. We keep them well fed and watered, so they've got incentive to stick around."

"Art, you mentioned rustling. Seems like it'd be damn near impossible to steal bison," Brian said.

"Not what a couple of local clowns thought, though," Sands said. "Tom, why don't you tell him what happened."

"About a year ago, two assholes knocked out the power on a fence, cut the wires, drove a semi in and tried to get a bull up a ramp and into the trailer. Of course, the security system let us know there'd been a breach, and I ran over with a couple guys." Norton laughed mirthlessly. "Long story short, the assholes tried to take off, got their rig stuck in some mud, and gave it up pretty quick. One of the idiots ended up getting himself busted up pretty bad. And, naturally, we prosecuted. You've got to set an example. Haven't had any problems since." Norton's voice dripped with self-satisfaction.

Mountains lined the horizon in all directions. Brian was amazed at the size and beauty of this magnificent piece of land. He'd seen advertisements in the local newspaper for much smaller ranches in the area with asking prices in the millions. Sands's spread would cost as much as the gross national product of any number of countries, he thought. As they proceeded to the western property boundary, Brian identified reference points on the map. He had a hunch the knowledge might come in handy. Sands stopped along a stretch of fence facing Bone Mountain. Brian noticed a padlocked gate a few yards down the line. The road he and Laura had come in on the day before ran parallel to the barrier.

"This is probably the closest my place comes to the dinosaur dig, Brian," Sands said. "We're about two miles from the base of Bone Mountain here and about ten miles from the main house."

"What are those tracks from?" Brian asked, pointing toward a set of parallel tire indentations through the tall grass on both sides of the gate. They looked to have come from a vehicle about four feet wide.

"Looks like somebody's been driving four-wheelers between here and the butte. Don't know who or why. Any idea, Tom?

"No, but I'll sure as hell check it out," Norton replied.

A little further on, they came to a huge new-looking tan metal warehouse. It reminded Brian of a United Airlines hangar at O'Hare.

"What's that building used for?" Brian asked.

"Equipment storage," Chafee said. "Tractors, dozers, fencing supplies, sprayers, tools, you name it."

Sands drove past the structure and stopped next to a smaller building, a galvanized Quonset-style shed. "C'mon, I'll show you a hobby of mine." The men got out, Sands with a device like a TV remote in his right hand. He pushed a button and an overhead garage door rolled upward on tracks. They walked inside. Sands flipped a switch and the arched interior was bathed in fluorescent light from hanging fixtures.

The building was filled with a collection of rusty picks, shovels, ore cars, metal awls and assorted other tools.

"This is some old mining equipment we either inherited or bought," Sands said. "I store it inside to protect it from the elements, in case it's got any value—I'm thinking it might be good for a museum or restaurant decor. You know, antique ranch and mining stuff is real popular with restaurant designers. You've probably noticed a little of that in Chicago. Which reminds me, I've got to get back. Flying there in a little while. Meetings."

As the Suburban rolled away, a flash of color near the larger building caught Brian's eye. A blue baseball cap with a red letter C on the front lay on the ground near the entry door of the warehouse. Looked like a Chicago Cubs cap. Seemed like there were Cubs fans everywhere.

At ranch headquarters, Sands pulled the Suburban in near Brian's Grand Cherokee. Brian folded the ranch map and tucked it in a hip pocket. Outside, Sands stuck out a hand and said, "Good luck, Brian. Call if you need anything."

Brian backed out and drove slowly down the driveway. In the rearview, he observed Sands trotting to the front door and into the house, Chafee getting into a green pickup, and Norton climbing aboard another large dark SUV.

18

As soon as Brian's vehicle was out of sight, Norton drove to his office in a nearby building and made two phone calls. A few minutes later, after a brief report from Gilstrap and the Gruels about the girl, her escape from the cabin and their trip back to the ranch, he addressed the three men sitting in chairs across the desk.

"Okay, here's the deal. Cody, you fucked up royally. This girl's out there somewhere. If and when she gets to a phone, you've had it. Her uncle, this Brian McKay bozo, is looking for her, and he's a fucking FBI agent. You've gotta disappear for a while, maybe go back to California."

"Man, I need the job. What am I supposed to live on?" Gilstrap said.

"Here's some expense money." Norton pulled an envelope out of a desk drawer and tossed it across to Gilstrap. "You'll need to change your name and appearance."

"My appearance? Ya mean like plastic surgery?"

"Nah. Just shave off your mustache, cut your hair, lose the western duds. Follow me?"

"I guess," Gilstrap said. He opened the envelope. When he saw the wad of bills inside, his expression brightened. He tucked the envelope into a back pocket of his jeans—quickly, as if he were afraid Norton might change his mind.

"I've got a bunch of stuff at my cabin. Can I go back and get it?"

Norton's face flushed red like a raw steak. "Hell no! There's no time for that crap. We'll send it to you later. If anyone connects you to the girl, all of us are up shit creek without a paddle. You can't be seen around here. You've gotta be out of the picture ASAP. Anyone asks, I'll tell 'em you quit, took off." He gave a curt nod, as if confirming a decision.

"What about us?" Shane asked.

"You guys are to report to Crawford at eight tonight. You're gonna be helping him and me wind up the operation. I want the damned thing done like yesterday. Crawford says it's only gonna take two-three nights with four guys. You follow?"

Donny sat fidgeting, head down, kneading the front of his hat brim into a funnel on his lap. He gulped, glanced up at Norton and said, "Uh, what about the girl?"

"Leave her to me. You guys have got plenty to do. In fact, why don't you two go get some rest? You'll need it. Get going."

The Gruels left the office. Norton scowled as he heard the racket they made outside. Donny Gruel's surprisingly tuneful tenor was raised in song: "Ah don't care if it rains or freezes, long's ah got mah plastic Jesus, settin' on the dashboard of mah truck—"

"Shut the fuck up," Shane yelled.

Norton waited until their vehicle was out of sight and he could no longer hear the coughing engine. He stared at Cody Gilstrap. The man had created a hell of a mess. Even if he left town, there was a good chance the feds would eventually track him down. And Cody couldn't be counted on to keep his big mouth shut. The stupid son of a bitch was nothing more than a loose cannon. Norton reached into the desk again. When his hand came out, it was holding a Colt Woodsman .22 Target pistol with a silencer attached to the barrel. Gilstrap's eyes widened. He began to rise from his chair. Norton watched him impassively. He pointed the gun at Gilstrap's face. "Sit down, Cody," he said quietly.

"Hey, Tom, take it easy," Gilstrap said, as he dropped into the chair. "I'll do like you said. Nobody'll be the wiser. Hey, I'm already gone."

"Yeah, you are," Norton said. He squeezed the trigger. There came a sound like a kernel of popcorn popping. A small red hole suddenly appeared in the center of Gilstrap's forehead. His head jerked back, but he remained sitting upright on the chair, his eyes wide open, a look of utter surprise on his face. He tried to say something, but the words came out as a groan. Norton got up, stepped around the desk, placed the barrel against Gilstrap's temple and pulled the trigger twice. Two more muted pops, and Gilstrap's head lolled to the side. His torso jerked, then he went utterly still.

At first glance, he looked like a man who'd dropped off to sleep watching TV after dinner. But now, there were three small entry wounds in his head, oozing blood. All three bullets had lodged in the brain. Tumbled around in there, did a lot of damage and stayed inside—the advantage of small-caliber ammo. Norton imagined he heard a small gasp, but it was probably just a kinetic reflex from the corpse. He pocketed the pistol. It felt warm against his thigh.

He rolled Gilstrap sideways in the chair, dug the envelope of cash out of the man's hip pocket, and returned it to the desk drawer. He retrieved the three ejected shell casings from the floor and pocketed them. No brass, no ammo, drill sergeant.

Norton went outside and backed his Suburban close to the doorway. He went to the rear of the vehicle, opened the lift gate and tailgate and removed an eight-by-twelve-foot brown vinyl tarp. He returned to the office, spread the tarp on the floor, and dragged Gilstrap's body out of the chair and onto the plastic surface. He noted with satisfaction there was no blood visible on the chair, the wall behind it or the floor. Just the same, when he got back, he'd go over the area with soap and water.

He emerged into the cooling late afternoon air and looked around. The coast was clear. He dragged the tarp-shrouded body to the vehicle, lifted it to the tailgate and slid it in. He locked up the office and drove away on a little-used dirt road leading to the northeast corner of the ranch. One good thing about working out here in the middle of goddamned nowhere—there were an unlimited number of places to get rid of pains in the ass.

19

Brian's curiosity had been piqued by his tour with Sands, Norton and Chaffee. Initially, he'd been skeptical. The born-again rancher persona seemed odd for a Chicago businessman. But the guy hadn't given off any of the nonverbal cues of deception. As a veteran interrogator, Brian was alert for the telltale shifting of position, crossing of arms, covering of mouth that liars find hard to avoid. Maybe the guy was just slick. To his credit, Sands had said all the right things about helping find Darcy. What was the deal with the old mining equipment in the Quonset shed? Could such hardware possibly be used in the restaurant décor industry? He knew that half the restaurants in Chicago had some kind of theme and the trappings to go with it. Then there was the Cubs cap on the ground. Reminded him of Darcy—a big fan. And Norton troubled him. The man had looked familiar from the outset and just now, Brian remembered why.

Norton had been known as "Tough Tommy" Norton in his younger days. He'd been on the Chicago police force from the early nineties until sometime in the mid-aughts, a patrol cop out of the Town Hall station near the Cubs' ivied baseball shrine, Wrigley Field. Maybe the cap on the ground was Norton's.

There had been a series of incidents in which seeming-

ly law-abiding citizens complained Norton had screamed ob-
scenities at them, had roughed them up, even in one case, broken a man's neck. That was the incident Brian remembered
most clearly. The story had come out in bits and pieces over
months, culminating in a trial heavily covered by the Chicago
media. A newly married couple, an assistant professor of English at DePaul University, and his young bride, a social worker, were sitting in their car in Lincoln Park, in a legal parking
space, but with an expired parking meter. Norton had pulled up
behind the vehicle in his squad and blocked them in. He'd gotten out and immediately began to write a ticket for illegal
parking. The man in the parked car asked the cop if he could
either feed the meter a quarter to avoid the ticket or just leave
the lot. Tough Tommy had exploded. He'd hit the man on the
head with his ticket book, opening a bloody gash. Words had
been exchanged, and Tough Tommy'd put the professor in a
headlock and rammed his head (witnesses' counts varied from
five rammings to more than a dozen) into the side of the man's
car. With the professor lying in a bloody heap, Tommy'd
kicked him in the legs, face and ribs.

When the wife had protested, the enraged cop grabbed
her and body-slammed her onto the trunk of the couple's vehicle. In court, Norton testified the man and woman had resisted
arrest, and he'd only been using "reasonable and necessary
force" to subdue them. The professor had mostly recovered
after six months in a neck brace, but would limp the rest of his
life, while the woman had needed cosmetic surgery to repair
substantial disfigurement of her face. The lawsuit that followed against the City of Chicago and Norton had resulted in a
5.8 million dollar out-of-court settlement paid by the city and
Norton's being cut loose from the police force after a fifteen-

year career. Brian wondered how Norton and Sands had hooked up.

Brian couldn't get the Cubs cap out of his mind. He exited the Sands ranch the way he'd come in, made a right on the gravel road and drove in the direction of the warehouse and Quonset shed he'd seen during the tour. He wasn't sure what he'd do, maybe just take a look from outside the fence. Now that he knew of the "security monitor" system that had enabled Norton to nab the would-be buffalo rustlers, he decided to be extra careful. If someone came along, he'd tell the truth—he just wanted to take a look around where he'd spotted the cap, and he didn't want to bother the ranch staff. He braked outside the high fence alongside the equipment warehouse. He scanned the area, trying to locate the baseball cap. No sign of it. Either the unceasing wind had taken it away, or someone had picked it up.

20

Darcy hadn't slept much during the night. Now, at mid-morning, she paced around the warehouse, glancing at her watch. Her stomach actually hurt with hunger. She knew how the lions felt in the Lincoln Park Zoo when feeding time was overdue. And she hadn't had any water since her pack bottle ran out the night before. Her mouth felt sandpaper-dry.

It was quiet as dust in the metal building. She kept listening for the sound of a vehicle. Maybe the man with the hammer would be back to work today. It was Saturday, though, and perhaps he had the weekend off. She guessed he must be a geologist or fossil bone preparator, judging from the sounds coming from the little room in the corner. The dental drill noise might have been an air scribe, a miniature jackhammer which preparators used to remove rock from bones.

She'd investigated the exterior doors and walls and found them impregnable. She'd tried to pry open the steel door to the room where the man had been working yesterday, as well as the door leading to the farm equipment room, and had only succeeded in breaking the blade off a screwdriver and scratching up the locksets. Until a few days ago, she'd never been locked in anywhere, never been deprived of her freedom. Between the cabin with barred windows and this place, she'd had more than enough incarceration for a lifetime.

Darcy pricked up her ears. She heard a motor approaching slowly on the side of the building opposite the doors used by the men she'd seen yesterday. She decided to take a chance, to try once and for all to get the hell out of this place. She picked up a hammer she'd spotted in a corner and carried it over to the wall nearest the motor noise. She lifted the hammer, felt a searing pain in her injured shoulder and dropped the tool to the floor.

Outside, a vehicle pulled up, the motor idling. Darcy heard footfalls approaching the building. A man cleared his throat. Darcy picked up the hammer and, ignoring the flash of pain in her injured shoulder, pounded the metal head against the wall with all her might.

Now, it was dead quiet outside. Was someone standing there, listening? She had nothing to lose. She shouted, "Hello!"

"Jesus H. Christ," a man said on the other side of the wall.

Darcy recognized the voice immediately. She shouted, "Brian, it's me! I'm in here."

"Darcy? Are you all right?"

"I'd be a lot better if I could get out of here," she said.

"How the hell did you get in?"

"Long story."

"Well, hang on. I'll open this door. Just a minute."

"Okay," she said. She sighed deeply and paced around the room, wondering how in the world her uncle had found her and where she was, anyway.

Brian ran around to the entry door on the other side of the building and tried the knob. It was locked at the handset, and he could see a thick deadbolt anchored in the jamb above it. He wished he had his lock picks with him. No use kicking it—he'd only end up with a sore foot. He returned to the spot where he'd spoken through the wall with Darcy and yelled, "I can't open it. You've got to wait a few more minutes. Hey, are you hurt?"

"Got a sore shoulder. Worst thing is, I'm starving. Can you *please* get me out of here?" she said.

"Look, I'll get help. Hang on. I'll be right back."

Brian hopped into the Grand Cherokee and peeled away toward the Sands ranch headquarters, his heart racing. If he were religious, he'd be thanking God. Hell, he'd thank Him anyway. How had Darcy gotten into that warehouse? Was Sands behind her disappearance?

21

Brian skidded the Grand Cherokee to a stop near the main entrance to Sands's log castle. He wrenched the front door open and stormed in. Tom Norton sat at a table near the door with his thick arms folded across his chest. A one-liter bottle of carbonated soda water and an open newspaper were on the table. He scowled at Brian.

"There a problem?"

"My niece is locked up in that big warehouse. Help me get her out."

Norton held up a meaty paw. "Hold on, man. You're losing me here."

"Listen, Norton," Brian said through clenched teeth. "I need someone to open the door of that fucking warehouse we drove by a while ago. Are you going to help me or sit there playing with yourself?"

"Hey, wait just a goddamn minute, now," Norton said, as he got to his feet. "Maybe you don't know who you're talking to."

"Actually, I do," Brian said.

Norton looked startled for an instant and then recovered. "Hey, smart guy—"

Brian was in no mood to argue with this thug. He rushed Norton and straight-armed both hands against the ex-cop's chest, knocking him back, and nearly down. Norton straightened and raised his fists in a boxing stance. Brian stepped forward and popped him in the nose with a quick left jab. Norton swung wildly, but didn't connect. Brian jabbed him again, this time in the jaw. Some of the fight seemed to ebb from the big man, but he still held up his fists, ready to swing.

Keeping an eye on Norton, Brian reached over and grabbed the bottle of soda water from the tabletop. He shook it briskly. Norton tried to swat it away, but missed. Brian put a thumb over the top of the bottle, shook it and quickly squirted a jet of soda up the struggling ex-cop's nose. Norton bellowed and brought both hands to his face. Tears streamed down his cheeks and mucous ran from his florid nose.

"Want another blast, Tommy?" Brian said.

"You cocksucker, I'll kill your ass," Norton said. But he kept his hands to his face as tears streamed from his eyes.

"What's the problem here?" Arthur Sands had entered the room.

"This guy—" Norton began.

"My niece is locked up in that big warehouse by the Quonset shed. I want her out of there *now!*" Brian yelled.

"I don't understand. How could your niece possibly be here?" Sands looked puzzled. "And why are you guys fighting?"

"Maybe your 'security honcho' here can answer that. But later. I heard Darcy's voice coming from that warehouse, and I want her out of there now, damn it!"

"Tom, you go unlock the warehouse," Sands said. "I've got to finish packing." Sands checked his watch. "We have to leave in less than an hour." He strode from the room.

Brian regarded Norton with a contemptuous smile. The security man's face was red, especially his nose, which continued to drip soda and snot. He wiped his streaming nostrils on a sleeve, shot a venomous glance at Brian, and stood pouting like a kid unwilling to go to school. Brian had heard about the soda-in-the-nose trick from another agent, who'd said it was a practice commonly used to interrogate suspects in Mexico. Whatever the origin, it worked.

"You heard the man. Let's go." Brian said.

He pointed at the door. Norton slowly walked to the exit and Brian fell in step behind him. Brian got behind the wheel of his Grand Cherokee and Norton took the shotgun seat. In the enclosed space, Brian nearly gagged on the smell of the ex-cop's pungent after-shave. He cracked the driver's side window. Norton blew his nose noisily into a handkerchief. Neither man spoke until they'd almost reached the warehouse.

"Look, don't get me wrong. I've got nothing against your niece," Norton said. "If she's in there, we'll get her out. And I'll look into who's responsible for it."

"Swell."

At the warehouse, Norton selected a key from a ring and unlocked the door. Brian shouldered him aside and burst in. Darcy's voice came faintly from behind a partition wall about halfway down the length of the building. "Hey, I'm over here."

"Come on, man. Open that other door," Brian shouted.

Norton plodded to the door centered in the dividing wall, chose another key and unlocked it.

As soon as the door was open, Brian and Darcy rushed together and bear-hugged. Neither spoke. They just held on tight for a moment. Darcy trembled in Brian's grasp. He thought she might break out crying, but she didn't. There wasn't much to be said. Relief was its own language.

Norton retreated to the warehouse entry door and stood there, awkwardly shifting his weight from one foot to the other.

Brian held Darcy at arm's length and looked her over. Blood stained most of the left shoulder of her filthy tee shirt.

"You were shot?" he asked.

"Some big jerk did it. Just a flesh wound," she added in a flippant movie hero voice. "More like a deep cut on the outside bicep. Anyway, it doesn't hurt as bad as it did. Other than that, and being god-awful thirsty, starved and sleepless and sunburned to a crisp and covered with mosquito bites, I'm fine," she said.

Brian reached a hand to touch her forehead, the sides of her face. "You feel warm, like you've got a fever."

"Well, actually, I don't feel so good." It was true. Her shoulder throbbed. She had a headache. Her stomach felt cardboard-lined. "It's been a bad week," she said.

"I'll take you to a hospital. We've got to get you checked out."

As they neared the door, Norton cleared his throat. "I'm Tom Norton."

Darcy said, "Hello," flatly. She'd sensed the tension between Brian and the other man immediately.

They got into the Grand Cherokee, with Darcy in the back seat and started the drive to the ranch compound.

"What is this place, anyway?" Darcy said.

"A ranch owned by a guy from Chicago," Brian said. Actually, you came full-circle, almost made it back to where

161

you started at the dinosaur dig. Why did you go into that building, anyway?"

"They took my phone. I was looking for one so I could call for help."

"Who locked you in?"

"Some guy in a red vest. He didn't see me. It was an accident, I think."

"Huh. You know, we should call the sheriff, let him know where you are."

"Yeah, and Doctor Stevens," Darcy said.

Brian didn't want to discuss the situation further in front of Norton. He noticed that Darcy seemed to pick up on his reticence, since she remained uncharacteristically silent for the rest of the ride. He glanced over at Norton, who seemed lost in thought.

When they got to the house, Brian said to Norton, "Get her a bottle of water."

Norton mumbled, "Okay. There's a phone there in the corner you can make your calls from." He went outside.

As they moved toward the corner of the massive living room, Darcy spotted a mirror on the wall and stopped to examine her reflection. She let out a wail. "My God, what a mess. My hair looks like a dirty mop. My nose is a mass of peeling skin. And my teeth feel like they're wearing mohair sweaters."

Brian didn't respond. They took chairs at an oak card table containing a cordless phone and several directories. As Brian found the listing for the sheriff's office, Norton returned and wordlessly handed a bottle of water to Darcy. She twisted the cap off and drank half of it at once. Norton disappeared.

Brian got Sheriff Harrison on the phone. "Sheriff, my

niece is back, safe and nearly sound," Brian said.

"Well, that's the best news I've heard all day," Harrison drawled. "Where in the blazes was she?"

"In a warehouse at the Sands ranch."

"What? How'd she get in there?"

"After being shot in the shoulder, she wandered around in the wilderness and somehow walked out onto the ranch. I haven't heard the whole story myself yet. Tell you what, I'm going to take Darcy to the hospital, get her examined. How'll it be if we stop by your office in the morning?"

"Fine. I'm looking forward to hearing about this one. Not too early, though, seeing as how it'll be Sunday, and I've gotta go to church. Say eleven?"

"See you then." Brian broke the connection.

"Let's go," he said. "The sooner we get you treated at the hospital, the sooner we can get you some eats—if you're up for it, that is."

Darcy just gave him a look.

As they were leaving, Sands and Norton appeared, each pulling a black overnight rolling suitcase. Norton carried a larger suitcase as well.

"Brian, sorry I'm not being more hospitable, but we've got to get to Chicago ASAP," Sands said. He walked over to them, bowed to Darcy. "You must be Darcy. Arthur Sands."

"Thanks for putting me up last night," Darcy said. She raised her water bottle in a mock toast, then finished off the contents.

Sands blinked. "Oh, yes. Uh, your uncle said you somehow got into one of my storage buildings. I'm looking forward to hearing all the details. But now, I've got to go. Tom, where's Scott?"

"He's already aboard, Mr. S," Norton said. He seemed to have recovered most of his composure, but still wouldn't make eye contact with Brian.

"Talk to you both soon." Sands smiled. "All's well that ends well," he added over his shoulder, as he and Norton headed toward the door.

Brian followed them. "Darcy seems to be all right, Art, in case you're interested," he called.

"Good, I'm glad to hear that. I really am. Bye now," Sands said, waving a hand as he left.

The billionaire's sleek Hawker 4000 waited on the airstrip, dual jet engines revving smoothly in preparation for takeoff. As Sands and Norton boarded, Brian glanced up at the round passenger windows. A third passenger looked down at him blankly. Brian managed a grin and waved at Scott Noble Stevens. The paleontologist waved back, then turned his head away, possibly to greet Sands.

A moment later, the jet's potent engines powered up with a deafening roar. The graceful craft edged forward, turned slowly to point up the runway and blasted away like some NASA rocket. Brian watched as the plane rose steeply, banked and then headed east.

22

The nurse who checked Darcy into the emergency room at Beacon Hospital was unabashedly curious. She told Darcy her disappearance had been the top story in the Clarkville Times for days. Darcy wouldn't have been surprised if the woman had asked for her autograph.

As the doctor on duty cleaned and re-bandaged the gunshot wound, he told Darcy it had become slightly infected. He gave her a prescription for an antibiotic and pain pills and recommended she go easy on the booze and get plenty of rest. When she passed this intelligence on to her uncle, he recommended a light supper at the town's best restaurant, the Clarkville Grille.

"Light?" Darcy looked incredulous. "What's this 'light'? Are you kidding? How about a huge steak? As an appetizer, I mean."

"Okay, but let's get you a room first."

They rode to the Masters, where Darcy booked a room down the hall from Brian's. They separated, with a plan to meet downstairs in a little while. In his room, Brian grabbed his camera and examined each picture from the previous day. He'd only taken seven shots, but they'd all come out clear and sharp. He studied each print carefully, zooming the images in the LCD screen. Nothing jumped out at him, but he had the feeling there was something of interest. He just couldn't focus on it at the moment. He'd try again, later. Time to meet Darcy for dinner—he'd better hurry, or she might start gnawing on the furniture.

Darcy filled Brian in on the events of the last few days, between bites of Caesar salad, a huge New York strip steak encrusted in black pepper, julienne vegetables and a dark chocolate torte with raspberry sauce. She ate like a famished wolf.

"Not bad for a small town," she said as she wiped her mouth with a starched cloth napkin.

"Hell, it's respectable for any town."

Over coffee, he advised her on the discussion they'd have the next day with Sheriff Harrison. "Answer all his questions truthfully, but don't volunteer anything extra and don't ramble."

"Sort of like an expert witness, huh?"

"Yup. Keeps you from getting in trouble."

"But I haven't done anything wrong."

"I know, but the sheriff's kinda hinky."

"What do you mean?"

"I can't put my finger on it, except he seems kinda negligent in keeping track of slugs and shells."

"What slugs and shells?"

"One of each was found near where you were shot. The slug may actually be the one that went through your shoulder."

"Cool. I'd like to get it as a souvenir."

"I'd rather see it as an exhibit in court...evidence against the shooter."

"That reminds me. I may have a picture of the damned shooter." Darcy pulled Cody Gilstrap's driver's license from her backpack and handed it to Brian.

"Crude-looking monkey. You know, this guy probably killed Old Horn, too.

"Who?"

"Old Horn. An Indian got whacked there last year."

"Wow. What's the deal, anyway?"

"I think it's got something to do with digging on Bone Mountain. Your *T. rex* dig seems legit, and nobody's bothered the people working on it, except you of course. So, I don't think the dinosaur is the issue. I'm thinking there's something else up there, maybe something you got too close to for comfort."

"Well, I did uncover a neat duckbill bone."

"Yeah, there's that. You didn't see any gold nuggets, diamonds, stuff like that up there, did you?"

"Nothing that exciting. Here, try this: what if there's a Mafia graveyard up there? You know, say the Nevada mob's been sinking corpses in Bone Mountain, and I was about to dig up Joey the Clown Lombardo's earthly remains."

"Actually, he's in the Metropolitan Correctional Center in Chicago."

She grimaced. "What's our next move?"

"*Our*? I think *I'll* find an expert, check some stuff out."

"How about me? I'm an expert."

"You're going to Chicago with me. You go back to that dig and this Gilstrap guy might try something again. Anyway, it's almost time for school to start.

"No way. I'm back at the dig tomorrow. There're not

that much left to do. We've gotta get the rest of the bones out."

"Bullshit. You're going back to Chicago, if I have to drag you there myself."

"Look, I'm not some kid you can order around. Besides, "I'll stay with the group. Don't worry about me, I'll be fine," Darcy said.

"Plus, I'm worried about Gilstrap," Brian said. "You see him, you'll probably kill him with your bare hands. I want him alive to stand trial."

"Anyway, I've already decided. I'm staying here."

They finished dinner in silence. Brian knew Darcy could be as headstrong as a child queen. At the Masters, he called the Sheriff's cell and got voicemail. He left a brief message about the identity of the shooter. Next, he clicked through all his Bone Mountain photos on the LCD screen of his camera, with no additional insights. He undressed, got under the covers and lay awake for a while. Thoughts came and went— how to find Cody Gilstrap? He had some ideas. Maybe he should call James. And he'd damn well better call Michelle tomorrow—he hadn't spoken with her in days. He felt good, though. Didn't miss the FBI a bit. And with Darcy back and reasonably healthy, catching the kidnapper would be gravy. He wondered whether he'd have to kidnap her again to get her to go back with him to the city.

23

Brian and Darcy arrived at the County Courthouse in downtown Clarkville shortly before eleven Sunday morning. Once again, the building was nearly deserted. They entered the Geyser County sheriff's office and found the reception desk deserted, the inner door unlocked. Brian led the way back to Sheriff Harrison's office. Halfway there, a young crew cut deputy sat at a desk with a landline phone wedged between his chin and shoulder. He looked up as they walked by. The smell of scorched coffee still dominated the air.

Two men, white shirt collars visible above their jackets, occupied chairs facing the sheriff with their backs to the door. Harrison looked past them and broke off in mid-sentence. Both seated visitors turned quickly to see what was behind them.

Harrison said, "Got the prodigal niece with you?"

"Yep. Sheriff, this is Darcy," Brian said.

"Pleased to meet ya," Harrison said. He remained seated and eyed the young woman impassively. "These two fellas here," he said, gesturing toward the seated visitors, "are with the FBI. Mr. Morgan's up from Salt Lake. Mr. Thorsten's from Bozeman. They'll want to talk with you folks."

The two agents stood. Brian and Darcy shook hands with them. Albert Morgan, a blocky, balding man in his late forties, with gold-framed glasses shielding watchful eyes, looked bored. Bill Thorsten, muscular, about thirty, with short sandy hair, looked like a television casting director's idea of an FBI agent. Morgan's suit, radiant white dress shirt and red silk tie seemed out of place in this small western town where, Brian had ascertained, dress-up meant a shirt with a collar and clean blue jeans. With the addition of a cheap-looking navy sport coat, that's how Thorsten was attired.

Morgan took charge. "Ms. McKay, we came here to investigate a kidnapping. We'll still do that, of course, even though, thankfully, you've returned." His eyes stayed on Darcy. He'd all but ignored Brian. "We're going to ask you some questions. It could take a while."

"That's okay. I'm not due back at work until tomorrow," she said, glancing at Brian, who raised his eyebrows. They hadn't discussed the matter since the night before.

After the men had poured themselves mugs of muddy-looking coffee and Darcy had gotten a Diet Coke from a machine, the group moved to the department's conference/interrogation room. A long rectangular table with a fake wood-grain top and chromed metal legs took up half the room. Six worn vinyl-covered chairs surrounded the table. Morgan claimed one at the end. The sheriff took the other end and commandeered the ashtray. The McKays sat side by side across from Thorsten, who placed a Dell laptop on the table and booted it up.

As Brian had anticipated, Morgan assumed control of the meeting. Addressing the McKays, the agent said, "We're going to interview both of you in-depth now. Is it okay if we record this discussion?"

"All right by me," Darcy said.

"Yes," Brian said.

Brian knew that FBI policy now required agents to electronically record interviews of people in custody, but the procedure was optional for non-arrested individuals, for whom old-fashioned pen and paper notes were still allowed. He figured an electronic record would protect Darcy and him from later misinterpretation. It looked like Thorsten was doing the recording on his laptop.

Morgan asked Darcy and Brian if they were there of their own free will. He leaned forward so his elbows rested on the table. He asked each of them to identify themselves for the record.

Then, Morgan said, "Darcy, please tell us in your own words what happened from the time you began digging on the east side of Bone Mountain last Tuesday afternoon, until the time you arrived here this morning. Don't leave anything out. Mr. Thorsten or I may ask questions from time to time. Please." He nodded at the young woman.

Darcy launched into an abbreviated account of the events of the last five days, excluding what she considered un-important details. Morgan interrupted occasionally with ques-tions. The agents seemed particularly interested in her de-scription of the man who'd abducted her.

Darcy retrieved Gilstrap's driver's license from her backpack and handed it to Morgan. "Here he is in living col-or."

Morgan took the Montana license, holding it by the edges. He examined it, grunted and carefully set it down on the table next to Thorsten. "Log in and see what's in the sys-tem on this guy."

Thorsten tapped a few keys and clicked his mouse several times. He pressed more keys, clicked the mouse and waited. Finally, he said quietly, "All right," and turned the computer slightly so Morgan could look directly at the screen.

Morgan nodded, then addressed his colleague, "Show it to Darcy here."

"Why don't you come around and take a peek at the screen. The display doesn't work very well if you look at it from an angle," Thorsten explained.

Darcy walked around so she could look over Thorsten's shoulder. Displayed on the monitor was a crisp full-color head-and-shoulders shot of the man who'd wounded and imprisoned her—an unsmiling, shaved-headed man with a thick neck and a two-day-old beard. He looked different without the cowboy hat. She shuddered. Seeing that man again, even in a picture, creeped her out.

"That's him," she said

Thorsten moved the cursor on the computer screen, scrolling down to a paragraph of text. He read aloud from the display: "Travis Bright, a.k.a. T. C. Bright, a.k.a. C. Travis, a.k.a. T. C. Gilstrap, a.k.a. Cody Gilstrap. A man with a lot of names."

"Question is, where's the guy now?" Morgan said, as if talking to himself.

"Is this character known at all in Geyser County?" Brian asked the sheriff.

"Well, a Cody Gilstrap works at the Sands place," Harrison said. "Let me take a look at the picture you've got on that computer. He got up and peered at the image. "Yep. He's the guy."

172

"What's his job?" Brian asked.

"Security, odd jobs, whatever Tom Norton asks him to do."

"Interesting. We'll need to see Mr. Sands," Morgan murmured. "And Mr. Norton."

A discussion of Cody Gilstrap followed, Morgan asking Darcy and the sheriff a series of detailed questions about the man. The sheriff indicated Gilstrap had joined the Sands operation about two years before. Darcy gave them directions to the cabin as best she could. The sheriff said he knew the place and could guide the agents to it later, if needed.

Morgan said the FBI was still interested in the Old Horn case. Brian knew FBI policy required follow-up on major cases at least annually. Each summer, Detroit agents interviewed everyone still alive who'd been at the Machus Red Fox restaurant in Bloomfield Township, Michigan the evening of July 30, 1975, when Jimmy Hoffa had showed up in the parking lot and then dropped off the face of the earth.

Morgan went over with Darcy the details of her escape from Gilstrap's cabin, her actions at the outfitter's tent, how she got to the Sands ranch and into the warehouse. Darcy mentioned the plaster-covered object and the man working in the closed off room. She didn't volunteer her suspicion that fossil bones might have been contained in the plaster, and no one asked her—she'd gone over these matters with Brian the previous evening.

The conversation ebbed. Brian glanced at his watch. Almost noon. "Al, have you got any more questions for us?" he asked.

"Yeah. What have *you* got?" Morgan said. "Walk us through your activities here."

"I've spent a little time with Sands and Mr. Tommy Norton at the Sands ranch. I know of Norton from a previous life." He proceeded to outline his contacts with the two men for the agents. As he did, Thorsten began working keys on his laptop again. He nodded at the screen and Morgan studied it carefully.

"I'm reading about some of Mr. Tough Tommy Norton's exploits as a Chicago police officer." He peered at the screen for a moment. "Interesting."

As if he'd been waiting for his turn, Thorsten finally spoke up. "Brian, what else have you done besides visiting the Sands place since you got the news Darcy was missing?"

Brian told of his initial visit to the dig site, his meeting with Russell Eagle Feather, his visit to Bone Mountain with Deputy Laura Jensen, his conversations with Professors Holt and Bakeno, his tour of the Sands ranch, and his second visit to that property, culminating in finding Darcy in the warehouse. Thorsten asked good follow-up questions. Brian held nothing back except his conversations with James St. Claire.

"Are Sands and Norton still at the Sands place?" Thorsten asked.

"They left for Chicago yesterday," Brian said. "They took Stevens with them. Told us they'd be back in a few days." Turning to Harrison, he said, "You'll be getting the results of the ballistics test on the slug recovered by Deputy Jensen any day now, I suppose."

Harrison said, "We haven't heard back from Missoula yet."

Morgan raised an eyebrow. "I know you folks are kind of casual here, but what the hell's taking so long?"

Harrison scowled. "Damn lab's backed up. If you guys read the newspaper, you'd a seen an article the other day about how they're crying to the legislature to give 'em money to get up to speed."

"Let us have the results ASAP when you get them," Morgan said. "Any other comments, Brian?"

"A request for Sheriff Harrison: could you have a deputy keep an eye on Bone Mountain for a while?"

Harrison flushed. "This is isn't Chicago here. We've got nine sworn officers in the department, including me. We patrol a county that's 2,900 square miles. Between the domestic incidents, property disputes, shots reported, accidents, goddamn cows on the road and general hell-raising, we manage to keep pretty damned busy. There's more crystal meth around here than you could imagine. We've got our share of felony drug cases and bad check investigations, too. There's just not enough of us. Our response time has been going to hell in a hand basket. Then there's the goddamned paperwork, which we never get caught up with." He sighed. "But I'll ask whoever goes up the Castle Mountain road to peek in on the dinosaur place."

"Thanks. I appreciate it." A ghost of a smile passed across Brian's face.

Morgan stretched and yawned. "Well, that's a wrap for the time being." He nodded at Thorsten, who clicked the mouse, presumably ending the recording of the conversation.

"We'll be in touch," Morgan said. "Where can we reach you folks?"

"We're checking out of the Masters Hotel tomorrow morning," Brian said. "Darcy and I have some things to do during the day, then I guess we're off to Chicago." He wrote his home address and his phone numbers on a piece of paper and gave it to Morgan.

Brian and Darcy rose simultaneously. "We're outta here," she said.

24

They decided to spend the rest of the day exploring. Brian piloted the Grand Cherokee through rugged foothill country along the Boulder River, where they took pictures of each other standing in front of a 100-foot waterfall gushing beneath a partially collapsed natural bridge spanning the water. Large rainbow trout finned in the current below. Lunch was at a rustic bar called the Roadkill—slogan: FROM YOUR GRILL TO OURS. That afternoon, they hiked five miles along the river and up into the wilderness, where they spotted a cow moose nursing a calf. The pair of animals posed like a tableau near a pond covered with lily pads. Uncle and niece joked and roughhoused, got caught up and smiled more than either had in a long time. But they avoided the topic of Darcy's next destination.

Brian and Darcy returned to the Masters after dark. They agreed to meet in the coffee shop at 7:00 a.m. for breakfast and retired to their rooms.

Brian was relieved his cell had no messages. He'd wanted to phone Michelle before she had a chance to call and leave a message for him. They'd never been into texting. Feeling a twinge of guilt, he dialed her number.

She picked up after one ring. "Hello?"

"In case you wondered, I'm still alive."

"That's good."

"Yeah, well, I found Darcy."

"Is she all right?"

"She's been shot in the shoulder and she's tired and malnourished, but we're working on all that. She'll survive."

"What do you mean shot?"

"Slight wound—what they call a graze. Well, that's easy for me to say, but she's healing up, and she'll be okay."

"So, when will you two be home?"

"Tomorrow. Well, at least one of us. I told Darcy she's coming with me, but she wants to stay on the dinosaur dig till it shuts down."

"You know, I think you're right. It seems idiotic to take another chance. And yet—

"I know. She's an independent young woman capable of making her own choices."

"Yes."

"Hell, you two're ganging up on me."

"Only when you deserve it. So when's your flight?"

"Tomorrow, Delta, supposed to get in at eight."

"Good. I'll meet you at the gate. Watch for me."

"All right."

"I've missed you."

"Yes, well, you can show me how much."

"I like the way you think."

"Don't take chances. Stay with the group. Under no circumstances should you go onto the other side of the hill," Brian said. They were in the Grand Cherokee, heading to

Bone Mountain on a beautiful morning. Fluffy clouds scudded over the mountains. The air was clear and deliciously clean.

"Yes, Mom," Darcy replied.

Brian realized he must sound like a tremulous old fart. "You know I'm right," he said, a little defensively. "And you might even be okay if you listen to me. If anything goes wrong, give me a call ASAP."

"What are you going to be doing in Chicago, I mean, now that you've blown off your job?"

"Tell you the truth, I'm not sure. One thing is, I'm going to find the bozo who snatched you."

"How are you going to do that back there?"

"This Sands guy's in the city, and he took his charming and lovely assistant Norton with him. I plan to find out more about what those guys are up to. They've got to be mixed up with this Gilstrap psychopath."

"Don't detectives usually have employers or clients or something, somebody who pays them?"

"So I hear, but this one's *pro bono*."

"Meanwhile, the FBI and sheriff are doing the same thing, out here. Right?"

"Yeah, and somehow, I'm not brimming with confidence, although, one of the sheriff's deputies is pretty sharp, and Thorsten might have a few operative brain cells."

"Yeah, and he's kind of a hunk. But what are you going to do? Look for another job?"

"Nah. Something on my own. I've got some ideas along the lines of contract work for businesses—security systems, industrial espionage, that kind of thing. I haven't sorted it out yet."

They pulled into the dig site camp around ten and went

to the large central teepee. This time, the oversized guard shambled out of the shelter unbidden.

"Can I help you?" he asked, blinking into the sun behind them.

"Hey, Colten," Darcy called.

"Oh, I didn't recognize you guys at first?" Colten said, continuing his irritating habit of posing statements as questions.

"Darcy needs to drop a few things off at her tent," Brian said. "I'll wait here."

Colten shrugged. "Hey, no problem?"

"What's new? Any more excitement the last couple days?" Brian asked.

"Nah, it's been quiet, man. Uh, I'm like, glad to see your niece came back? Where'd she go, anyway?"

"Actually, she was kidnapped. Does the name Cody Gilstrap ring a bell?"

"Wow. Jeez, I hope she's okay?"

"She'll be all right. What about Gilstrap?"

"Don't know him, but I've heard the name? I'm thinking he like, works over at that big ranch?" Colten pointed his chin in the general direction of the Sands place.

"What do you know about him?"

"I wouldn't know him if he hit me on the head? He's not from here, I guess?"

"No. I understand you work nights, guarding the dig."

"Yup."

"Run into any problems?"

"No, man. Hardest part's like, stayin' awake? I mean, who's gonna try to steal dinosaur bones at night? I can't even find them in the daytime?"

Brian was tired of listening to the burly guard. Plus, the man wasn't much of a source. He was glad to see Darcy returning, wearing her small backpack and looking pleased.

"Onward and upward, then," she said.

Brian frowned. "You're beginning to sound like that Stevens schmuck."

They went up to the dig site, where Stevens's second-in-command, Bill French, was busy supervising the other workers. He seemed to have readily adopted Stevens's role, down to the laconic stance and crossed arms. When the crew members spotted the McKays, the work stopped. Several of them hurried over to greet Darcy. She and Becky Stanton hugged and fell into conversation. While Darcy and her friends got caught up, Brian pulled French aside.

"You're getting your best worker back, but a little worse for wear," Brian said. "Take good care of her this time, will you?"

The younger man reddened. "Absolutely. I've been given strict orders that like, nobody goes away from the site. It's non-negotiable. Everybody stays together. And I've got this." He patted the pistol holstered at his side.

Brian regarded the new-looking firearm. Young Indiana Jones.

"And, besides, we can't afford to lose any more help. We're under a lot of pressure to stay on schedule," French said.

Brian noticed the young woman who'd given him directions on his first visit, looking his way. She caught his eye and waved. He waved back.

"Well, I'll let you all get back to work," Brian said.

181

"Darcy knows where to reach me if there's any problem."

Brian pointed the Grand Cherokee toward Clarkville. Several times, he began to slow down as if to turn around. He could still get back there, grab Darcy and they could make the flight together. By the time he reached the town limits, the idea had vaporized. But he'd still fret like a nudist at a porcupine convention until she was safely back in Chicago. He decided to grab a quick bite at a burger joint before the run to the airport. He was polishing off the last of a delicious greasy double cheeseburger when a familiar voice came from behind him.

"You keep eating like that, you'll lose your girlish figure."

He turned to find Laura Jensen, in uniform and wearing a gray ball cap with the white letters GCSD on the front.

He stood up. "Hey, I like the hat," he said.

"Know why we locals wear baseball caps instead of cowboy hats?"

"I'll bite."

"So people don't mistake us for tourists."

Brian grinned. "All right. Any progress on the slug or the shell?

"Missoula says the slug's a .30-06, and they've got ballistics records, in case we find a weapon. No matches with known weapons in the system. The local ET says no prints on the .30-06 shell. And no sign of Mr. Gilstrap. We've put out a BOLO on him nationwide, and I imagine your federal friends have done the same. What's next for you?"

"Got a flight home in a couple hours. Going to see if I can stir up some excitement there."

"Well, I guess this little town must be kind of slow for a guy like you. I can't picture you living here."

"That reminds me, I've got some pictures I'd like to show you, if you've got a minute. These're from Thursday at Bone Mountain." He retrieved his SLR from the pack sitting on the floor next to his chair.

They took seats at the table. Brian brought up on the LCD display screen the images he'd taken on the hillside where Darcy'd been taken. He handed the camera to Laura. She examined each photo without comment, until she reached the last, an image of the entrance to the old mine tunnel in the hillside.

"You know, this one looks a little funny," she said.

"Funny how?"

"I don't know. It's been a few years." After peering at the print a bit longer, she said, "The opening looks bigger than I remember it."

"That's odd. You'd think that over the years something like that would get smaller if it changed. Wouldn't weather cause rocks to fall into it? Hell, it could even cave in after what—ninety years?"

"That's what I was thinking." She shrugged. Could just be the angle of the picture, though." She handed the camera back. "So, when are you coming back out?"

"I might when Darcy's finished up at the dig, depending on what's going down in Chicago."

"Look, keep me in mind for a biking buddy. And stay in touch," she said.

"You can count on it."

"Well..." Laura stuck out her right hand, and they shook.

Was it Brian's imagination, or did she hold on for an extra beat? The image of James's mischievous face formed in his mind. James was speaking: "Hey, this is a sheriff's deputy, big guy. Is this what you call cooperating with local law enforcement?" Finally, Brian pulled away. On the way to the Bozeman airport, he couldn't get Laura out of his mind.

25

The Delta Airlines 757 made a wide turn over Lake Michigan and cruised down the shoreline north of the city. Brian peered out the window as familiar landmarks flowed by below. Bright lights framed the emerald green playing surface of Wrigley Field, where a night game was in progress. He remembered the days long before August, 1988, when lights had been installed at the old baseball shrine. He'd grown up in a five-room apartment in a two-flat a couple blocks south of the park. As a boy, he'd sit on the front steps watching fans stream by to the game. Occasionally, he and a friend would score a few tickets to the game in advance and hawk them to passersby at a tidy profit. Then, scalping became a blip on the CPD radar screen, and they'd had to cool it.

After the games, especially the drawn-out extra-inning ones, drunken fans would wobble down the street, some unable to locate their cars. Brian recalled his dad going bananas one time, when a drunk had lurched between their two-flat and the adjacent building and taken a leak on the old man's prize tulips. It was the only time Brian had seen his father strike another man. He'd decked the interloper and dragged him into the street. Brian knew he had inherited some of the senior McKay's self-righteousness—he hated to see anyone get away with destructive nastiness. This had been a helpful attitude in his chosen profession, but it spilled over into his personal life as well, making him seem a little priggish to some. He used this perception to advantage whenever possible.

The jet skimmed over downtown Chicago, then made a wide circle to the west before descending toward O'Hare. Brian gazed down at the tall buildings illuminated by the last slanting rays of light. He admired the incredible view of the metropolitan area by night as the aircraft drifted ever lower. Mercury vapor streetlights glowed orange in a series of interlocked grids, defining the street pattern. Unbroken processions of traffic pumped along the main arteries. Dozens of arriving and departing flights streaked by, their outboard lights like the bellies of fireflies. The complex network of O'Hare runways came into view below. The ponderous plane seemed to home in on one as the whump of the deploying landing gear sounded below Brian's feet.

The plane touched down on schedule, just after eight P.M. The final streaks of sunlight faded away as the plane rolled to a stop.

As Brian retrieved his carryon from the overhead compartment, he wondered if Michelle would be waiting for him at the arrivals area, sitting in her Lexus outside or still be tied up in traffic. She was notoriously late for appointments. A night person, Michelle loved to stay up into the wee hours of the morning, reading, working at her laptop or just watching old movies on TV. This seemed to influence her entire schedule—late to rise, skipped breakfast, late lunch, typically still in the office when the Polish cleaning lady arrived, late dinner, and on to repeat the cycle. They'd sparred good-naturedly about her owlish proclivities and procrastinating disposition. Brian had once predicted her tardiness at her own funeral, to which she'd quoted Thomas Jefferson: "Delay is preferable to error."

Brian emerged from the passenger tunnel and walked through the terminal to the arrivals area. He spotted Michelle on the edge of the crowd, easily the most attractive woman in the gathering. She stood apart, dressed in dark suit and heels, talking on her phone. She hung up as he rushed to her and wrapped her in his arms. They locked mouths in a lingering kiss.

"Been here long?" he asked.

"I got here five minutes early," she said, ruefully. "I've been working."

"Got to keep those billable hours up."

"Speaking of hours, when did you eat last?"

"They served a half-ounce bag of pretzels on the plane, but the flight attendant was nice—she gave me two bags."

"Probably noticed the hungry look in your eyes."

He did an eye-roll. "Anyway, I'm starved."

"In that case, let's go to the Frontera Grill, my treat."

The restaurant was crowded as usual, but they managed to snare a table after a one-margarita wait in the bar. In the dining room, they ordered a second round of margaritas and chose appetizers from the lengthy menu—a miniature enchilada stuffed with fresh crab and scallions for Michelle and mussels steamed in a saffron-chile sauce for Brian.

"Tell me what happened to Darcy, and what you're

planning to do," Michelle said.

"Okay, but It'll be between bites. This stuff is delicious. They should open a branch in Montana."

"But then wouldn't Montana be too much like Chicago?"

"Well, the scenery would still be better there. Although, I have it on good authority that you can't eat it. The scenery, I mean."

"Stop stalling. Is Darcy all right? And how could you leave her there?"

"The doc said it was about as slight a wound as you can have with a gunshot, and it's healing up fine. She's taking an antibiotic for infection, but she says the pain's gone."

"But still, why didn't you make her come with you? What if that creep comes back?"

"Not my choice, really. She can take care of herself. Gotta give her credit. The kid's got better judgment than a lot of agents I've worked with."

"That's a compliment?"

Brian ignored the barb. "You know, I think maybe this could be her career. This dinosaur field, I mean."

"Have they at least tightened security where she's working?"

"The guy in charge is keeping the staff all together— no more solo excursions. For what it's worth, he's packing, and they've got an armed guard on nights, though I'll admit he's not the sharpest knife in the drawer."

The handsome young waiter returned and took their plates. Brian wasn't sure if the guy had winked at Michelle, but he let it go.

Brian sipped his margarita. "How have you been doing? Are you being appreciated at the firm?"

Michelle shrugged. "Yeah, I'm okay. Generating my ten billable hours a day, sometimes more. I'm heading up the team handling the Chicago Board of Trade suit against some New York exchanges."

"What's the suit about?"

"Several of the smaller exchanges are trading derivatives based on CBOT contracts without the proper permission. We're going to make the cheeky easterners desist."

"Nice. And I thought the bureau got into hardboiled stuff."

"Well, actually, it's a lot of paper pushing. But some of the questions of commodities law are interesting. And I've got the cutest intern from Harvard Law helping me."

"Huh. You should see the sheriff's deputy I worked with in Montana. Makes Scarlet Johansson look like a bag lady."

Their entrees arrived. Brian had roasted pork loin with red chili lentils and grilled pineapple. Michelle's main course was marinated striped sea bass with roasted tomatoes, green chilies and a sauce of chipotle peppers and dried cherries. The conversation ebbed as they tucked into the delicious food. The restaurant was known for some of the most sophisticated south-of-the border cuisine available in the United States. The chef-owner had recently won an annual nationwide competition as "most innovative chef of the year." They passed on dessert, and finished up with cups of strong coffee with a hint of cinnamon.

"Are you up for a nightcap at my place?" Michelle asked.

"Well...I suppose."

They sat on the couch in Michelle's town house, nursing small glasses of coffee-flavored liqueur. His carryon case was on the floor just inside the front door.

Brian did a stage yawn. "Must be time for bed," he said.

Without speaking, Michelle set down her drink, stood, took him by the hand and led him to the master bedroom. He was always taken aback by the undiluted femininity of the room—white gingerbread-carved headboard and flowery bedspread, fuzzy brown teddy bear sitting propped against a pillow, a paperback romance novel on the nightstand.

They were out of their clothes in seconds. Brian loved the look of her full, high breasts. A small blue capillary passed near one of the stiff red nipples. They locked into a clinch next to the bed, their bodies drawn together like magnets. As they kissed, Michelle opened her mouth, and their tongues met. They edged to the bed in a slow dance, never releasing the hold they had on each other.

In bed, they let go fully, holding nothing back. Brian got on top and guided himself into her. They remained motionless for a moment, then he began to thrust, slowly at first, then building speed gradually. Michelle encouraged him with whispers, her head back and eyes closed. Brian willed himself to hold out as she grasped his hips and pulled him further down into her. Soon they were in perfect sync. Michelle rocked upward, yelled out, raked fingernails along Brian's back, worked him deeper into her. They sped up, breath coming in short gasps now. Finally, they climaxed together, a sweet bliss of intertwined limbs and mingled breath.

After resting in comfortable silence for a few minutes, they started all over again. The second time was slower, more tender.

Michelle fell asleep, but Brian lay on his back, his hip touching hers, his eyes slits. He wondered if it were time to settle down. Neither he nor Michelle had ever mentioned the M-word. It would be a huge step to even consider such a drastic move. He knew several guys who'd let marriage wreck wonderful relationships. Maybe he'd think more about it when this case was over. But, what case? He didn't have an employer or a client. And Darcy was okay. He tried to tell himself the Old Horn shooting was none of his affair. He realized he'd like to see Laura again and felt a flash of guilt for thinking it, especially then. About an hour later, he quietly sat up and placed his feet on the floor. He glanced over at the motionless form of Michelle beneath the sheets. He wondered if he should stick around for a while. As he began to rise, she trailed a finger along the taut muscles of his back.

As if reading his mind, she said, "Why don't you stay?"

"Sorry, I've got to get home, take care of some stuff before I meet with James. It's been heaven being with you again. We'll spend more time together, now that I'm back."

"Uh-huh."

"No, I mean it."

"It's just that it would be nice if, once in a while, we could spend an entire night together."

"I've got to go, really."

She decided to not press him further. Besides, she had

to be at a meeting at the ungodly hour of eight-thirty. She sighed. "Okay, but I expect you to pop for the next dinner."

He turned and gave her his most boyish smile, then he leaned over and kissed her, a long, lingering kiss. At that point, he almost changed his mind about leaving. She returned his kiss with urgency and ran her fingertips along the base of his neck.

"You're the very best," he said.

"Did you say best or beast? Don't answer. Anyway, you're not bad yourself."

Brian extricated himself and got dressed. Not wanting to be left alone, Michelle got out of bed and put on her robe. Brian pulled on his shoes and they headed out of the bedroom holding hands. They kissed again at the front door, and then he clopped down the front stairs and into the street to hail a cab.

26

Brian entered the Nook Café, took a booth near a big window facing North Halsted and turned a heavy white china mug upright on the table. Harold, a waiter who'd worked at the place for as far back as Brian could remember, sauntered over with a full pot of coffee.

"You awake yet, Brian?"

"Just barely, but that'll help," he said, as Harold filled his cup.

"So where's the beautiful girlfriend?"

"Which one?"

Harold gently bopped him on the head with a menu, then handed it to him.

He gave it back. "I already know what I want."

"I'm spoken for," the waiter said with a grin.

It was a ritual they'd played out at least weekly for years. Harold had served many breakfasts to Brian, alone and with Michelle. He'd met Harold's boyfriend, Larry Bambenek, a skinhead biker, on several occasions at the Nook. Brian ordered a Greek omelet with hash browns and a large glass of grapefruit juice. Harold retreated to the kitchen.

Brian folded open the Sun-Times and scanned through it. On page six, there was a short article on the Chicago Museum of Natural History's quarterly board meeting, to be held that day at noon at the museum. Doctor Scott Noble Stevens would be giving a lecture at the CMNH at three o'clock and would report on progress at the *T. rex* excavation underway in Montana. The rest of the news was unsurprising—the weather would be sticky with a chance of rain; a study showed Chicago had three of the nation's ten most congested limited-access highways and the Cubs had broken even on the last road trip. When Harold returned with his steaming breakfast, Brian abandoned the paper. It was a luxury to have two consecutive good meals served at table, no less.

Out on the street, Brian was accosted by a familiar-looking panhandler, a stocky black guy of indeterminate age known to one and all as "the Burlap Man." The beggar wore a suit of rough brown burlap bags he'd salvaged from behind a nearby coffee shop that roasted its own beans. He carried a huge boom box tuned to a rap station, with the volume cranked to ear-splitting level. Sometimes the Burlap Man smiled cordially; other times he'd shout racial epithets at the top of his lungs, so as to be heard above the din of his music. Today was a cordial day. He approached Brian, bowed, tipped an imaginary hat and held out a hand. Brian pressed a crumpled five-dollar bill into the outstretched hand and continued on his way. When he'd gone about fifty feet or so, the music behind him suddenly stopped, and a cultivated English-accented voice called out with bell-like clarity, "Much obliged, my good man." Brian smiled and continued on to a corner drugstore where he bought a Tribune. Outside, he got out his phone and dialed James St. Claire's number at the FBI Chicago field office.

James picked up after two rings. "Hello?"

"What kind of a greeting is that, Special Agent St. Claire?" Brian demanded in a mock-stern voice.

"Hey, Brian. Let me buzz you back," James said.

Five minutes later, his phone rang. Recognizing James' cell number, he picked up and said, "McKay's Mortuary. You kill 'em, we chill 'em. You drain 'em, we displayin' em."

"Hey, brother," James said. "I'm outside. Never know who's listenin' in the office."

"Can you meet for lunch today?" Brian said.

"You buyin'?"

"You're the employed one, the one with the lavish expense account."

"True, but that's available only for official bureau business."

"This is official all right. How about Grant Park?"

"Okay, good idea to get away from this place, so we aren't anywhere near J. Edgar. I'll cab it over there. Meet at the fountain?"

"Sounds good. Bring some dogs."

"You got it."

They rang off, and Brian went to get a long-overdue haircut. Mid-morning, he returned to his apartment and fired up his laptop. There was an e-mail, sent the previous night, from Darcy. The expedition must have a satellite uplink, like the Himalayan mountain-climbing expeditions.

Darcy reported she'd been working on the *T. rex*'s caudal bones, which were a hundred percent intact. She'd also found a stray tooth the size of a dagger. This was really a big moment, because it was the one of the last teeth needed to make a complete set. She looked forward to seeing Brian, but he shouldn't worry about her. No mention of danger, nothing negative at all. It struck him that Darcy seemed happy but, reading between the lines, maybe a little bored, now that things were going so well.

Brian sent a responding e-mail, warning her to be careful, and asking what she planned to do when the dig was over. She'd have a little time before returning to classes at the university. Perhaps she'd like to join him and Michelle for an RD before the semester started up (RD was Darcy's term for "real dinner," a relatively rare event for her).

Next, he Googled the name Arthur Sands. The screen displayed the first ten of more than 810,000 hits. He began to browse through them, learning that Sands and his first wife, Barbara, had had a son named Scott, who'd be about forty now. Popular name, that Scott. Seemed like half the guys he bumped into these days were Scotts. There was a lot of information about Sands's business interests, not that much about the man's personal life, and only a few references to criminal connections. After reviewing the first few hits, his eyes began to glaze over, so he logged off. James should have gotten more concise information on Sands, anyway.

Around eleven o'clock, he shouldered his backpack, went down to the street, walked the two blocks to the Brown Line elevated train station and waited on the raised platform for the next train bound for the Loop.

In a hard plastic seat aboard a gently rocking el car, Brian examined the urban scene through a dirty window. The train tracks were elevated twenty feet above the ground, affording a bird's-eye view. The route wound through residential neighborhoods dominated by two and three story buildings and small retail businesses. Signs of affluence abounded on the rapidly gentrifying North Side. Starbucks shops and other havens for upwardly mobile young professionals appeared in every block along the primary arteries.

As the train drew closer to downtown, the buildings got taller. Two-flats, town homes and four-unit luxury condominiums gave way to residential high-rises as tall as sixty stories. A cluster of glass-sheathed skyscrapers framed the eastern horizon along Lake Shore Drive. Brian noticed some of his favorites among the architectural behemoths—the black, tapered John Hancock, the nearby One Magnificent Mile, the 108-story Willis Tower and the white granite-clad bulk of the huge Aon Center. These gigantic structures, along with dozens of others, formed precipitous canyons that saw sunlight only briefly each day. Brian compared the sheer cliffs of concrete and glass with the mountains he'd been in the day before. It seemed a bit presumptuous of man to construct these artificial peaks.

The train stopped at the massive Merchandise Mart, then crossed the Chicago River and made its way into the northern Loop. The tracks looked down on busy streets lined with unbroken rows of lofty edifices. Pedestrians scurried about below, hustling between dashing taxis like adrenaline junkies running with the bulls in Pamplona. The train proceeded south down Wells, then into a square pattern along the Loop perimeter, east on Van Buren, then north up Wabash. Brian got off at the Wabash/Adams stop, descended the stairs to the street and headed east a block on Adams toward Michigan Avenue and the Art Institute of Chicago. A large banner over the Art Institute entrance advertised an exhibit of Cail-lebotte paintings. Brian mused that the museum's permanent collection included Caillebotte's "Paris Street, Rainy Day," one of the world's great oil paintings. Maybe he should see the exhibit with Michelle.

He shouldered his backpack containing the dinosaur bone he'd received from Russell Eagle Feather and crossed Michigan, walked around the Art Institute and entered Grant Park, the green front yard of Chicago stretching for more than a mile along Lake Michigan. Tourists and locals frequented Grant nearly around the clock. The park, in turn, home to Millennium Park, was filled with trees, lawns, a music pavilion, tennis courts and Buckingham Fountain, the world's largest. Thousands of gallons of water gushed from pale green bronze seahorses set in the bottom of three circular levels within the fountain. A southerly breeze fanned a misting spray into the air, where it watered the grass nearby. Brian angled southeast past tennis courts, toward a grouping of white stone tables just west of the fountain. James St. Claire, clad in a charcoal Armani suit, sat at one of the furthest tables, leaning back and surveying the scene through a pair of dark Ray-Bans. He spotted Brian and smiled.

As Brian approached, James lifted a grease-stained white paper bag off the table and said, "Good thing I tapped the lavish expense account." He set the bag down on the tabletop and got to his feet.

"I knew I could count on you," Brian said.

They executed a homie handshake and sat in the stone chairs. James opened the bag and extracted two cans of Coke and several packages wrapped in greasy white paper—a pair of hot dogs and a couple of overflowing bags of rough-cut French fries. He shook the bag, and a pile of ketchup packets and napkins poured onto the table.

"I assume these dogs are properly garnished," Brian said.

"Hell, yes. What do you think I am, uncouth?"

"No, you're couth enough, but I'm always a little nervous when I see ketchup in the general vicinity of hot dogs."

James frowned, pulled off his shades and squinted until his eyes were narrow slits. "Nobody, I mean absolutely nobody, puts ketchup on a hot dog," he said through gritted teeth. "Okay, what movie?"

"'Sudden Impact.' And he didn't say 'absolutely.'"

James grinned, put his glasses back on. "Let's eat."

They devoured lunch quickly. Brian always appreciated that unique delicacy, the Chicago-style hot dog. A poppy seed bun cradling a red Vienna Beef link adorned with mustard, relish, onions, tomato wedges, a pickle spear, hot peppers and a dash of celery salt. Every sandwich shop in town served them; none applied ketchup to the dish unless it was demanded by some wayward tourist, and then, only grudgingly. Ketchup was reserved only for the fries, and not even then, for a purist. The dogs were delicious, but Brian was reminded he hadn't worked out for a long time. He vowed to himself he'd visit the health club the next morning. He took a swig of Coke, wiped his mouth and fingers on a napkin and said, "Find anything interesting?"

"Yeah. J. Edgar's an even bigger asshole than we thought. He was all jazzed that one day about where you were, what I thought you were doing, that kinda shit. I'm assuming my office phone's tapped. Same for e-mail."

"But that's normal—for him, I mean. He's always assumed agents'll leave him in the dark. Which they do, of course. Ah, fuck him, anyway. My life's none of his damned business." Brian waved a dismissive hand. "What about Sands?"

"Ran him through NCIC and UCR. Dude's got his fingers in all kinds of shit. In there like swimwear. No sheet, though. Closest was that deal in '02, when the U. S. Attorney indicted him for bribing public officials to help keep a union out of one of his manufacturing plants. Later dropped due to lack of evidence. He's done business with some mobbed-up materials suppliers, though not lately, far as we can tell. Early aughts, he was seen a few times with Rocco DiPonio."

"DiPonio? They say he ordered hits like he'd order spaghetti and meatballs," Brian said. He wasn't surprised at the lack of anything on Sands in the National Crime Information Center or Uniform Crime Reporting databases—the man would be too slick to get caught up in the low-rent crime normally captured there.

James went on to outline a series of Sands's business interests, contacts, possible links to organized crime figures, ex-wives, relatives and biographical information. "Oh, and here's some news. Sands is a graduate of Northwestern University, class of '84."

"So?"

"I ran J. Edgar, too. Guess what. He was in the same class."

"There were probably a few thousand other people in that class."

"Yeah, but not in the same fraternity, and not room-mates for two years."

"No shit?"

James smiled. "Had to dig a little to get the roommates part. Ginny—J. Edgar's assistant—sweet lady, knows lots of interesting stuff. And she admires my smooth style."

"You did good. Any idea how this translates into Edgar's interest in me and Darcy?"

"Ginny tells me the J-man and Sands talk on the phone every now and then. Says they're tight. Doesn't know, or won't say, what they talk about. Can't blame her, she doesn't want to get canned."

"So, Sands might be telling Edgar to watch me so he can cover his ass accordingly."

"Could be. You know about Norton, of course. Sees himself as a hard-ass, but really fucked himself, career-wise. Makes me think less of Sands, he relies on the guy."

"I wouldn't underestimate Norton. He's come a long way from his cop days," Brian said. "And even then, he had his strong points. Guy worked with him once told me Norton didn't give up easy—something about him being persistent as a pit bull with two dicks."

"Yeah? Anyway, my contact in Salt Lake gave me the skinny on the two agents on the case—same guys who were there for the Old Horn thing. Morgan's smart but iffy. Man's livin' large—drives a Jag on the job instead of a bucar. Cuts corners. You know, he started out in the Chicago office, 'bout same time as J. Edgar. And he's a KMA. Only got a year to go."

Brian knew this meant, "Kiss my ass." "Interesting. I wonder if Morgan and J. Edgar keep in touch, too."

"I was getting to that. This gal in Salt Lake says they've been calling back and forth lately—she doesn't know what about."

"How about the other guy?"

"Thorsten grew up in Montana, got sent to Salt Lake straight out of the Academy, part of the RAT program."

"Wait a minute. What in hell is RAT?"

"Rural American Training. Supposed to provide opportunities for hicks."

"Fucking FBI acronyms. You know, I'm a member of CRAP, myself."

"That right?"

"Yeah, Council for Resisting Acronym Proliferation."

James grimaced. "Well, anyway, four years later, they put this Thorsten dude in Bozeman all by himself—a one-man resident agency. Man's got a reputation for some smarts. Clean. Plays by the book and all that shit. Him and Morgan were on the Old Horn investigation together. Didn't find dick."

"What about Sands's ranch?"

"Dude paid seventy-five mill cash 'bout four years back. Parties with business pals there. Hizzoner da mare showed up last fall for fly-fishing, along with Max McGinty, head honcho of McGinty Construction. I'd guess our man owns a piece of both of 'em."

"That McGinty outfit does a lot of city work, don't they?"

"Everything from resurfacing Lakeshore Drive to the new runways at O'Hare."

"What else you got?"

"Woman shows up at his Montana place from time to

time is, weird enough, one of his exes, lady uses her maiden name, Barbara Hardy. And he's part sponsor of your dinosaur dig, being a huge contributor to the Museum of Natural History."

"How huge?"

"Over three mill last year. I figure him for trying to score points with the old-money crowd."

"That kind of dough might do the trick."

"Impresses the ladies, too. Guy's got a little condo on the Gold Coast, nothing fancy, maybe ran him a couple mill. Live-in's that anchor woman on Channel 6, what's her name, the brunette with the bodacious bod."

"Gina Stablow?"

"Yep."

"Huh. Can't fault the man's taste. Anything about Old Horn, other than the bureau came up empty?"

"No, 'cept his only family's a nephew, dude name of Russell Eagle Feather. Colorful name, huh?"

"I met him. He got a sheet?"

"Nah."

"Well, let me know if J. Edgar asks anything more about me."

James looked offended. "Man, that goes without sayin'." He ate his last French fry. "That's about it, big guy. I'll keep you posted. I'd best get back. Give Michelle my love."

"Okay. Let's grab a drink one night soon."

"Cool. Later."

Brian headed out of Grant Park and flagged down a taxi.

27

L ew Milton, Chairman of the Board of Directors of the Chicago Museum of Natural History, sat at the head of a long mahogany table in the center of the museum's posh new boardroom. Ten white men, a black man and a white woman sat in high-backed maroon leather chairs lining both sides of the table. Most of them had angled themselves to face the chairman, attired in the power uniform of dark suit, white shirt and deep red silk tie.

Not a particularly striking man, Milton still had one of those faces that seem to belong at the head of the table when power brokers convene. He had a prominent jaw with a hint of jowls, a wide joke-telling mouth, thin nose and lips and small ears ringed by a fringe of white hair. His belly sagged over his belt as if trying to find a place to rest.

The skin around his pale gray eyes crinkled as he emitted a small chuckle and said, "All right, I've bored you enough with financial matters. Suffice it to say, the fundraising effort is on track, but we can't let up if we're to make this institution world-class. And now for the interesting part of the program. Doctor Scott Stevens here is going to give us a progress report on his efforts to glean an exhibit for the museum that will make history. I'm sure you'll all agree, this building's not worth a hoot in a hot place unless we've got a best-in-show dinosaur to show off. Without further ado, I'll turn it over to Scott."

Stevens got behind a podium in a corner of the room and turned on the microphone clipped to his shirtfront. "Thank you for giving me this opportunity to update you on how the museum's valuable resources are being deployed. You'll be happy to know we're on schedule and below budget." He paused to acknowledge a smattering of polite applause. "We've got a wonderful crew of volunteers with an impressive amount of field experience. The weather's cooperated, the skeleton's confined to a relatively compact area, and, despite the extreme density of the surrounding matrix, we've done fantastically well in extricating bones without any major mishaps, knock on wood. I've got some shots of our dig activities that I think you'll find compelling. If I could have the lights dimmed, please."

A museum employee turned the recessed ceiling lights down to a pale glow while Stevens brought up the first image in a PowerPoint presentation. A picture of the striated bulk of Bone Mountain filled the screen next to Stevens.

"This is Park Butte, Montana, but everyone calls it Bone Mountain. It's located just west of the Crazy Mountains, a few miles from the town of Clarkville. For years, locals have found fossils here, mainly Cenozoic fish and turtles. Those fossils are much more recent than the Cretaceous period, the final time of the dinosaurs, which ended around 70 million years ago. Our *T. rex* represents the first Cretaceous dinosaur bones found in close proximity to the Crazies."

Stevens clicked a button and the scene changed to a tight shot of the *T. rex* skeleton protruding from rock. A half dozen workers crouched, sat or stood around the osseous framework like vultures picking a carcass clean.

"This picture was taken a few days ago," he said. "The animal ended up more or less upright, with its skull and tail separated from the torso. We've exposed most of the major bone groupings of the top three quarters of the animal, and we're nearly done with freeing the rest. When the upper part of each set of bones is exposed, we tunnel down along the sides to the bottom and then underneath to create, in effect, a mushroom-shaped pedestal."

The next shot showed two young women forming a protective plaster shell around some bones. "We'll end up with quite a few of these plaster casts," Stevens continued. "It's more efficient to bring out large groupings of cast bones and separate them back in the lab. As you can imagine, this is a tedious task, but, for our crew, it's a labor of love. And they work cheap." There were appreciative chuckles from the board members.

Next came a picture of Stevens standing by a pair of young men working on the nearly six-foot-long skull of the *T. rex*. "I was worried at first the skull might have been lost, but I found it one morning, near the rear-end of the animal. It apparently became detached and washed away from the neck, but, thankfully, not far. It's in great condition and will make a super exhibit in the museum. Our *rex* will outshine all others in the world, no question."

Stevens was interrupted by enthusiastic applause. Someone called out, "Hear, hear." A man at the far end of the table murmured to the guy next to him, "Sounds like the dinosaur had its head up its ass. I hope this guy isn't the same."

Stevens guided the Board through another dozen images—shots of the skull, the ribcage, the other bones, workers using all sorts of tools to separate bone from rock, everything from paint brushes to jackhammers. Stevens commented briskly on each image. He stressed the efficiency of the operation and assured his audience the dig team would be loading the bones onto trucks for delivery to Chicago within a couple of weeks. "And now, if we could have the lights again, I would be happy to entertain any questions you may have," Stevens said.

A silver-haired man in a blue suit near the far end of the table spoke up. "Thank you, Doctor Stevens, for a most enlightening presentation. I'm curious, though, will our *T. rex* be larger than the Field Museum's?"

"Yes, ours is definitely bigger than theirs." More polite laughter.

The sole woman at the gathering cleared her throat and caught Stevens' eye. She was about fifty, lean, with a permanently tanned face from long exposure to sunshine. She wore a bright red jacket in vivid contrast to the dull plumage of her male counterparts. "Could you please give us an update on the young woman who disappeared from the dig last week? I understand she's turned up but she was hurt. Is this something we should be concerned about, exposure-wise?"

Stevens gave her an earnest smile. "Yes, Ms. Sommers, Darcy McKay was injured very slightly, but she's fine now, and the injury was incurred away from the dig. Mr. Sands and I saw her just Saturday." Arthur Sands, sitting midway along the table, nodded in agreement.

"As a matter of fact," Stevens continued, "she's back at work on those bones, even as we speak. I've talked at length with her uncle, her only living relative, and I'd say we're in very good shape on this."

The woman persisted. "But wasn't she shot? What was that all about? And is there danger of such incidents disrupting things further, or, God forbid, resulting in additional injuries to staff?" She regarded Stevens expectantly.

"From what we understand, Ms. McKay wandered off from the dig proper and encountered a stranger. She left with him, and only recently returned. I understand she suffered a minor gunshot wound, but she's fine now. We don't know the man's whereabouts, but the FBI and local authorities are investigating. We've taken appropriate precautions, and have an armed guard on duty."

Sommers was not easily mollified. "Why on earth should such a thing happen?"

Stevens rubbed his jaw, thoughtfully. "Well, with the recent highly-publicized run-up in value of *T. rex* skeletons, I can only hypothesize someone might have wanted to steal bones. Perhaps he thought Ms. McKay was working on some bones independently, and saw it as an opportunity for a quick theft." He shrugged. "In any case, we don't foresee any additional problems along those lines. Are there any other questions?"

The woman looked as if she might venture another question. Before she had a chance, Arthur Sands leaned forward, resting his steepled hands on the table, and spoke quietly. People at the ends of the table had to strain to hear him. "I can assure you the dig site is in a safe neighborhood. I've got a place nearby and have never experienced any such problems, and I'm not aware of them occurring anywhere else in the vicinity." He raised his voice a little. "More important, I believe we all owe a debt of gratitude to Doctor Stevens here for proceeding with such professionalism and dispatch in guiding our expedition toward a successful end." He clapped his hands, and the others joined in.

Milton stood, thanked everyone present and adjourned the meeting. The board members exchanged small talk as they retrieved their electronic devices and briefcases. The group gradually dispersed. In the hallway, Stevens, Sands and Milton huddled.

Milton said, "Scott, are we okay PR-wise on this thing? Is the girl's uncle satisfied, or is there anything out there that could bite us?"

"I'm not a lawyer, but the girl's back at work, without any complaints. Like I said earlier, the uncle used to be an FBI agent here. I understand he dropped the girl off at the dig while I was en route to Chicago, and no one's heard boo from him since," Stevens said.

"Scott's right. We're in the clear. By the way, our friend Elgar says the uncle left the bureau just last week," Sands said.

"What's this about the girl turning up at your ranch?" Milton said.

"We were literally on our way out the door, leaving for Chicago Saturday afternoon, when the uncle, this Brian McKay, showed up all hot and bothered, claiming his niece was in one of our ranch's storage buildings. I sent my security man to go with him and check it out. The girl was there, all right. She told us, including the local sheriff, she'd been kidnapped by a character named Gilstrap, who'd been working at the ranch. He's disappeared. The sheriff's looking for him, and the FBI sent a couple of agents, including a guy I know, from Salt Lake City," Sands replied.

"FBI? Jesus, let's just hope they don't pull a 'Sue' on us," Milton said, referring to the FBI's seizing of *T. rex* bones a few years earlier, when two competing institutions disputed ownership of the valuable bones.

"Don't worry about that. I'll be in touch with Elgar. There shouldn't be any problems with the bureau," Sands said.

"Good, good," Milton said. "By the way, Scott, do you think you should beef up security for the duration of the expedition? I'm sure we could free up the funds from the budget."

"We already have. We've got an armed guard onsite and we've tightened up procedures for the staff. They're being supervised closely—no more freelance stuff. I'd say we're covered pretty well."

Milton smiled, grasped Stevens's hand in a firm handshake, and put his left hand on the younger man's shoulder. "We've got every confidence in you," he said. But his eyes remained questioning.

Stevens raised a wrist, glanced at the gold Rolex. "I've got to take care of some business before the lecture. You gentlemen are welcome to join us in the auditorium."

28

Brian walked along the Lake Michigan shoreline en route to the Chicago Museum of Natural History's recently christened building. The lake shimmered under a sapphire blue sky. Little white sails studded the azure water to the horizon and tacked slowly across the water in the offshore wind. Brian wondered, not for the first time, who were these guys who had the time and money to go sailing on a weekday afternoon? Not unemployed ex-FBI agents, for damned sure. He strolled along the harborside walkway, admiring sailboats anchored at star-shaped metal docks. A forest of aluminum masts swayed in the slight breeze, halyard fittings jingling against metal. Maybe someday he'd take sailing lessons. But then what? He remembered the old saw, "A boat is a hole in the water you pour money into."

Summer-warmed water lapped the vertical concrete seawall bordering the pedestrian path. A few yards inland, joggers, bicyclists and inline roller skaters bustled along paved pathways curving through Lincoln Park. Tourists sat on the grass, talking, examining maps, plotting their next moves. Ahead, on a small beach, lifeguards preened in their watchtowers. Children played, ran, hollered, floated in inner tubes. Teenagers lolled on towels, languorously soaking up the cloud-filtered rays of sunlight. The smell of suntan lotion wafted through the air. The museum lay just beyond, anchoring an expanse of emerald lawn and set back from the water about a hundred yards.

Brian climbed smooth granite steps to the main entrance, went in and paid the thirty dollar admission fee, which included a ticket to the lecture, DINOSAUR ADVENTURES: THE RESURRECTION OF *T. REX*, FEATURING RENOWNED PALEONTOLOGIST, DR. SCOTT NOBLE STEVENS. He had to check his backpack in a locker at the entrance. He pocketed the key and wandered among the exhibits of life-size dinosaur models and fossil bones and played a couple of interactive computerized games, "Can you read the rock clocks?" and "What's your Mesozoic IQ?" A large open space near the center of the exhibit area contained a sign perched atop a giant faux dinosaur bone standing on end: FUTURE SITE OF SCOTT, WORLD'S LARGEST *T. REX*. Scott? Brian made his way down a side hall to check out an exhibit called the "Hands-on Preparation Lab."

A large room with a window cut into the wall facing the hallway, the prep lab appeared to be empty at first. Brian found a side door and entered. Two men sat hunched forward on folding chairs in a corner playing chess. They looked up when Brian came in. The older of the two, perhaps thirty, slim and goateed, said, "Sorry, we're on our break."

As Brian approached them, he noticed that the chess pieces were miniature carved dinosaurs. The kings were, naturally, *T. rex*es.

"That's all right," he said. "I'm just diddling around, waiting for Dr. Stevens's lecture to start."

The younger man spoke up, "Cool. You play chess?"

"No, I never learned. Mind if I sit in, maybe pick up a little about how it's played?"

"Hey, no problem."

Several minutes elapsed in silence as the players each made a move.

"Are you the guys who'll prepare the *T. rex* bones?" Brian asked.

"If they ever get them in here," Goatee said out of the corner of his mouth. "Meanwhile, we play chess and, when a tour group comes through, we work on those Diplodocus bones on the bench there, answer questions, let the tourists touch our bones, whatever turns 'em on." He smirked. He pointed with his chin toward the workbench under the window. A few bones reposed under bright light from a long-armed architect's lamp. A circular magnifying glass on a gooseneck arm was centered over the work area. Metal probes and other tools lay on the work surface near the bones.

"You ever heard Stevens speak?" Goatee asked.

"Well, only in conversation. Matter of fact, I met him recently out in Montana," Brian said.

"Oh, then you know," Goatee said.

"Know what?"

"Well...you've probably noticed he's a little—how can I put this? Self-important."

"Hey, the guy thinks he's hot shit," the younger man said. "To him, the rest of us are a bunch of stooges."

"Is he good?" Brian asked.

"Yeah. He's smart and stuff. It's just that he like, could care less about the people that do the work. I mean, he'd rather be on the Channel 2 News than actually get into the nitty-gritty."

213

"Maybe you fellas can help me," Brian said. He pulled his phone out of his pocket and brought up a photo of the dinosaur bone Russell Eagle Feather had given him. The image included a metal ruler next to the bone to indicate size, about ten inches long and six inches across at the wide end. "What do you suppose this is?"

Goatee studied the picture carefully. "If it's real, it could be the first installment of our *rex*," he said. "Looks like a humerus. And I don't say that just to be humorous." He waggled his eyebrows.

The other man said, "Hey let me see that thing." Brian handed the phone to him. "Something weird about this bone, man. It doesn't look like any *rex* bone I've ever seen. This sucker's almost a foot long, and it's only about half of the bone. That's way longer and fatter than the other humeri. I'd guess it's like, a third again bigger than Sue's."

"But it is from a *T. rex*, right?" Brian said.

"Sure looks like it, except for the size," the younger man said. "But what else could it be?"

"Where'd you get this bone, man?" Goatee asked.

"A friend found it in Montana."

"Well, if he found the rest of it, could be he's got us beat."

Brian checked his watch, noticed it was about time for the lecture to start. He got his phone back, thanked the two prep lab employees and headed for the lecture hall.

Brian scanned the large bowl-shaped auditorium, looking for a seat near the front. Rows of terraced spectator seats arched in a semicircle facing a stage. The room was already nearly full. He claimed a front-row seat a few feet below the speaker's podium. He settled in to wait as the room filled to capacity, and dozens of people unable to find seats stood along the rear and side walls.

A few minutes later, Lew Milton took the stage, strode confidently to the podium, smiled at the full house like a kindly teacher sizing up his class on the first day of school.

"Thank you very much for joining us today, ladies and gentlemen. We're about to hear from one of the most prominent figures in international paleontology today, Chicago's own Doctor Scott Noble Stevens. Doctor Stevens is an esteemed professor of Paleontology at the University of Illinois. He'll be discussing his exciting discoveries on the life and times of that fearsome tyrant lizard, *Tyrannosaurus rex*. As you may know, Doctor Stevens is heading up the expedition in Montana for what is, by all accounts, the most complete *T. rex* skeleton ever discovered. We look forward to displaying that magnificent dinosaur right here in the CMNH come next spring. Following his formal remarks, Doctor Stevens will field questions from the audience. And now, I am honored to present Dr. Stevens." He turned sideways and led the applause as Stevens approached the podium.

Stevens smiled disarmingly as he took the measure of the eager audience. A natural speaker, he modulated his voice to easily reach the last row. A trace of British accent seeped into his words, occasionally. "My thanks to all of you for attending today. We're proud of the *T. rex* we're taking out of the ground in Montana. It's shaping up as the world's first 100% complete *T. rex*. And frankly, it's a monster. I feel privileged to have discovered such an impressive animal, especially in an area where not one significant large dinosaur skeleton had ever been found before."

He put his hands in his pockets and shrugged modestly. "But then, one of the neat things about paleontology is, if you know the geologic history of a particular area, you can find previously undiscovered fossils." He rocked back on his heels, grinning, pleased with himself, as the audience applauded.

Stevens then launched into his slideshow, well-honed from his earlier session with the Board. When the lights came up, he spoke for another few minutes, emphasizing the "incredible importance" of the expedition and the "virtually perfect" *T. rex* skeleton that would follow.

"Ladies and gentlemen, we'll deliver the bones to this museum next week. Then, the painstaking task of preparation begins. Skilled professionals will work on each bone until it is ready for inclusion in the mounted skeleton. It takes several hours of preparation work for every hour we spend digging up the bones in the field. I will supervise assembly of our giant tinker-toy. I think you'll find the pose of our *rex* will be as unique as its size. I know the Chicago Museum of Natural History will be proud of this display for decades to come. And now, if there are any questions..."

Stevens took queries for another fifteen minutes. Brian admired the guy's ability to make each person feel as if his question were important. Stevens exuded sincerity. He never lapsed into jargon, nor did he talk down to the audience. Must give one hell of an undergrad paleontology seminar, Brian thought.

Stevens finished up, thanked the audience and graciously acknowledged enthusiastic applause. He was unclipping his lapel mike, when Brian said, "Hey, Doctor Stevens."

Stevens looked startled for a moment while he searched for the source of the greeting. When he recognized Brian, he recovered quickly. "Ah, good to see you again, Brian. What's new?"

"Wondered if you wouldn't mind taking a look at this." Without waiting for an answer, Brian held out his phone with the photo of the bone to Stevens. The paleontologist took the phone and studied the image intently for a moment.

"Is this real? A replica?"

"It's real. I've got the bone."

"Hey, where'd you get this?"

"Bone Mountain."

"Huh? What the hell?" He hesitated. "Well then, you'll need to turn that bone over to me. Might as well keep all of our animal together."

"Hang on. Do you notice anything odd about it?"

Stevens peered at the picture again. "Well, for one thing, it's awfully large." He hesitated. "Actually, it seems a bit uh, oversized."

"Might be from an oversized animal, huh?"

Stevens looked perplexed. "Well, it could be. I'll have to compare it to the skeleton we're currently excavating."

"I'm no dinosaur expert, but, the way I understand it, there are two of these humerus bones on each dinosaur. Haven't you folks already got your two?"

"Well...yes, I believe we have. That means—"

"Yep, it does." Brian leaned on the edge of the stage, reached a hand up toward Stevens. "If you don't mind, Doctor, I'll take my phone back, now."

Stevens rallied. "It's kind of big for a *T. rex*, but there isn't any larger known tyrannosaurid in the U.S. I mean, Gi-

217

ganotosaurus is in Patagonia, and *Carcharodontosaurus* and *Spinosaurus* are both in Africa."

"That's nice," Brian said.

As if in a trance, Stevens bent and handed the phone back to Brian. As he took it, Brian said, "If you've got a minute, I'd like to buy you a cup of coffee. I've got something else to show you."

"Okay, sure."

After Brian reclaimed his backpack from the locker, they walked a block to a Starbucks and got French Roasts in large paper cups. Once they were situated in plush living room-style chairs, Brian reached into his pack and retrieved the dinosaur bone.

Stevens gasped. "Brian, you're shocking the shit out of me. Can I see it?" He held out a hand, and Brian gave it to him.

After rotating the bone and running his hands over the striations and protrusions, Stevens spoke. "Where exactly did it come from?"

"From the nephew of the man who was killed on Bone Mountain last year. I'm guessing the guy found it there, but over on the east side of the hill, where they found his body."

"Jesus."

"Has anyone else from your group been digging on the east slope, I mean, other than Darcy?"

"No, I don't think so."

Brian drained his cup. "Doc, wouldn't you or Sands, or anyone, for that matter, have to file for a permit with the

218

feds, to be able to dig up bones?"

"If you're on Federally-owned property. Not if you're on private, and the landowner gives you the okay. But you don't need a permit to prospect."

"What if there are more bones on the east side?"

"I'd think the museum would want us to return next year for another dig. In fact, I'd be willing to bet a lot on it."

"Darcy'll be happy to hear that."

"Have you heard from her? How's she doing?"

"She's okay. We've been in touch. You know, she says she's thinking of getting an advanced degree in paleontology."

"That's great. I'll have a chat with her. I can help her with information on programs, contacts and so on." Suddenly, Stevens seemed ingratiating.

"So, you guys are close to winding up the dig?"

"Have to. We lose most of our workers when the fall semester starts. Plus, the weather can get funky real quick out there. We got into a blizzard last September."

"When do you head back out?" Brian said.

"Tomorrow afternoon. I've got to take care of some business here in town first. Hey, what are you going to do with that bone?"

"Hang onto it for now." He held out a hand and the paleontologist reluctantly placed the bone in it.

"Gotta run," Brian said, as he stood.

Stevens slumped back in his chair.

29

John Elgar picked up the phone. "Special Agent in Charge Elgar speaking."

"Art Sands. We've got a problem in Montana."

"I beg your pardon. I thought everything had settled down. After all, the girl's returned unharmed, and—"

"Listen, John. That part's okay, but it's a little more complicated. It seems your boy McKay got hold of a dinosaur bone from the nephew of the old Indian that got killed on Bone Mountain last year."

"He's not my boy. Matter of fact, he's not my anything. You know I no longer have any control over McKay."

"Obviously."

"Hey, wait a second. That's not fair."

"Listen to me," Sands said. "Scott thinks the Indian found the bone someplace near his dig, probably on public land, but he's not sure."

"Can't McKay be compelled to turn it over to him?"

"Nah. Scott says it's not part of his dinosaur. McKay showed it to him a little while ago, but wouldn't let him keep it," Sands said.

"Is this a problem?"

"I knew you'd catch on. I see it as unhealthy competition."

"What do you mean?"

"We've worked too goddamned hard to get this trophy exhibit." Sands's voice gained volume. "What if there's another one just like it—or even better—and somebody else gets it out? All of a sudden, we, I mean the CMNH, look like bush leaguers. We can't let that happen."

"I see. Well, you'll be happy to know I've had a couple of agents surveilling Mr. McKay since he came back to town," Elgar said. "They're keeping me informed."

"What's he been up to?"

"He and one of our agents, a minority fellow, have been in contact. They had a sort of lunch meeting today. I don't know what it was about yet."

"Listen to me. Find out what McKay and your guy were talking about and let me know. See what McKay told him about the bone. Where did it come from and where is it now? What's he going to do with it? Does he know where the rest of them are? Speaking of agents, what's Morgan doing?"

"He's trying to find *your* boy, Mr. Gilstrap," Elgar said.

"Good. That's appropriate. What's he got so far?"

"Not much. He and Thorsten—he's the resident in Bozeman—interviewed McKay and his niece. They looked around at the alleged kidnap scene. They've been to Gilstrap's cabin. They've interviewed Tom Norton and, of course, yourself and your staff. I understand they plan to see the Indian's nephew again—can't remember his name."

"Okay. What's all this add up to?"

"Essentially nothing," Elgar said. "I'd think the most they'll do is apprehend Gilstrap, and even that's problematic."

"Don't bullshit me, John. We go too far back. Do

these guys think he's still around?"

"Probably not, according to Morgan. He hypothesizes Gilstrap may have returned to his home state, California. The feeling is the man would have surfaced by now, otherwise."

"Wouldn't bother me if he weren't found."

"I understand."

"On the other hand, he kidnapped the McKay girl, so he deserves what he gets. What is it with these guys? Something in the water?"

"A background check would have revealed that Gilstrap had a criminal record."

"Gotta admit you're right on that one. I'll ask Tom how the hell he let the bozo slip through. Meanwhile, keep me posted, John. You know I hate surprises."

"All right, but sometimes the best course of action is to wait and see what develops."

"I'd rather do the developing," Sands said. He hung up.

Elgar rang James St. Claire and asked him to come in. James replaced the receiver and glanced at his watch. Nearly five o'clock. Elgar was known to leave the office promptly at five most days, so he could catch his commuter train to Lake Forest. Chances were this would be a short meeting. James had spoken personally with the SAC only two times—the day he started work with the bureau and last Friday, when Elgar grilled him about Brian.

James entered the SAC's outer office, where Ginny Clements tapped at a computer keyboard. Without looking up, she said, "Hi, James."

"How do you do that?"

"Do what?"

"Know who's coming in without looking at 'em."

She eyed him with the hint of a smile. "With our friend around"—she nodded over her shoulder at Elgar's closed office door—"you develop *very* good peripheral vision. Besides, there aren't that many of you guys around here."

"You guys?" James put on a hurt look.

"Minorities."

"You got that right."

"It was up to me, I'd hire more of you."

"Why?"

"Better dressers. Hell, you're the best-dressed agent in this place, no contest."

"Well, anyway, I'm proud to be a BMW."

"BMW?

"Yeah. Black man working."

The secretary's phone buzzed. She picked up, listened and said, "He's just arrived. I'll send him in." She hung up and said, "He seems a little edgy today. Don't jerk his chain too much."

"I'd rather be the jerker than the jerkee," James said. He smiled at her and walked to the closed inner office door. He knocked and entered.

"Have a seat, St. Claire," Elgar said.

St. Claire? Not Special Agent St. Claire. What—had he been demoted? James pasted on a smile and took a seat across from the older man.

Elgar's own smile reminded James of a corpse in the hands of an adroit mortician. As before, he focused on a spot a few feet past James' left shoulder. Elgar settled himself in his high-back leather chair, got a paper clip from a desk drawer and waited with crossed arms, as if either trying to decide how to begin or expecting James to initiate the conversation. Then he examined the paper clip and began to bend it open. He seemed intent on making it into a completely straight piece of wire.

James marked time, calmly at first, then with increasing nervousness. He'd been vaguely uncomfortable since his last conversation with Elgar and the subsequent visit from the HR guy, Blevins. Was he about to be pressured to rat on Brian? What did he know to rat about, anyway? He *had* given Brian some information on Arthur Sands from bureau files; passing on confidential information to non-bureau employees was an offense punishable by disciplinary action, possibly suspension. James wondered if his conversations with Brian had been the subject of surveillance. Well, at least his two-year probationary period was over with.

Finally, Elgar broke the silence. "I'll cut to the chase. Have you had any discussions with Mr. McKay since he returned to Chicago last night?"

James considered the question. It occurred to him that either he or Brian might have been tailed to Grant Park that afternoon. In fact, he should probably assume that was the case.

"Yes. We had lunch today."

"Ah, then you're up to date on his doings, I suppose."

"He hasn't been doing much, now that his niece has been found and all. I think he plans to take it easy before going on to the next thing."

"What is 'the next thing?'"

"He didn't say. Actually, sir, with all respect, isn't what Mr. McKay does with his personal life none of the bureau's worry?" He smiled to soften the force of his words.

Elgar frowned. He seemed satisfied with the linearity of the first paper clip, and began working on another. "Normally, that would be true. However, when ex-agents of this office breach federal laws, I am concerned because I am sworn to uphold the law, and I am also concerned for the sake of the bureau's good name, of course. Has Mr. McKay indicated to you his intentions regarding the dinosaur bone he's brought back from Montana?"

James was puzzled. "Actually, sir, I'm not aware of any dinosaur bone. Brian didn't mention one to me." It was a relief to be frank—although James wondered why Brian hadn't confided in him about the bone. Could Elgar be mistaken?

Elgar digested this, then nodded. "Very well, but let me know if you find out anything further about this matter."

Elgar asked a few more questions about Brian—what had the ex-agent said about Darcy, about the dinosaur dig, etc. James kept his answers as short and uninformative as possible, while trying to appear earnest and helpful. He'd learned this technique early on, as he'd questioned white-collar crime suspects. Whatever you say can and will be used against you. He didn't mention Arthur Sands or the information he'd given Brian about the man or about the Old Horn murder.

"If Mr. McKay contacts you in the future, I'll expect you to inform me immediately," Elgar said.

"I'll keep that in mind, sir. Is there anything else?"

"Not at the moment. Oh, one thing. About your personnel evaluation. I understand your friend McKay forgot to prepare one for you before he left. Would you be so kind as to complete a self-evaluation? I'm sure Del Blevins can provide the blank form to you."

"I'll do that. Thank you, sir."

The SAC stood, signaling the end of the conversation. He had nearly completed straightening the second paper clip—only one curved portion remained. Maybe I should bring him a new box of clips, give him something to do for a while, James thought. James reached his right hand across the desk and the men shook. He'd heard Elgar was averse to physical contact. The younger agent offered an insincere smile, turned and left for Blevins' office.

30

When Brian got back to his apartment, he put on Tom Petty and the Heartbreakers, the *Hypnotic Eye* album, slumped to the couch and listened for a while. The hard-driving tunes and sardonic lyrics always made him feel good. By the time the second track, "Fault Lines," had ended, he remembered he hadn't checked his phone messages recently. There were two—Michelle reminding him it was his turn to buy dinner, and James demanding to know what was this bullshit about a dinosaur bone. He punched in Michelle's number, and was happy to hear her voice on the second ring.

"What is this? You're tapping me for dinner already? I'm the one with no means of support," he said.

"Except a kind-hearted girlfriend you mooch meals from."

"Isn't it wrong to end a sentence with a preposition?"

"Maybe, but, as Sir Winston Churchill said, "The rule which forbids ending a sentence with a preposition is the kind of nonsense up with which I will not put."

"Since when is put a preposition?"

"You're changing the subject."

"The subject being?"

"Dinner."

"And?

"And you're buying."

"How about Chinese carryout?"

"Depends."

"On what?"

"Whether it's good, who's buying and who's doing the carrying."

"It'll be good, and I'll buy and carry."

"Well...okay, but you've got to come up with a really nice white wine, too."

"All right. Where?"

"Rooftop deck. Seven. Okay?"

"Perfect."

Brian tried James, got his recording and left a message. As he boarded the cab for a top-notch Chinese joint near Michelle's Lincoln Park townhouse, he took note of the cabby's appearance. The fiftyish man had a silver slicked-back haircut, an undershirt with a pack of smokes tucked into the rolled right arm over a tattoo of an eagle clutching a lightning bolt in one claw. He turned out to be one of those native Chicago characters with an opinion on everything from the Federal Reserve chairman's latest pronouncement on the economy (dumb—they should break up the Wall Street banks) to the best way to fight terrorism (nuke the entire Middle East). Brian jousted good-naturedly with him and, before he knew it, they'd arrived at the House of Hunan.

The sun was setting as Brian and Michelle carried the wine and a tray of steaming food out her second floor master bedroom patio door to a small wooden deck. From there, they climbed wrought iron fire escape stairs up another level to a wooden platform covering half the roof of her narrow building. A circular table sported a Corona Beer umbrella and four cedar chairs. Brian placed the ice bucket cradling a bottle of Sauvignon Blanc on the table, along with a pair of wine glasses. Michelle set down a tray containing white cardboard containers of pot stickers, hot and sour soup, shrimp lo mein and mushroom egg foo young. She assembled place settings—straw place mats, napkins and lacquered chopsticks. When everything was arranged, Brian poured wine.

"You know, it doesn't get any better than this," he said, raising his glass.

"Or cheaper," Michelle added, as she clinked her glass against Brian's.

"I've been looking forward to this kind of food."

"Why? You didn't have any Chinese out west?"

"I'll put it this way: the local Chinese joint in Clarkville provides packets of ketchup with your order instead of soy sauce."

She laughed. "Serves you right for abandoning me."

They ate in silence. The food was delicious. When Michelle had finished the modest portions on her plate, she set her chopsticks down, patted her mouth with a napkin and reclined in her chair, her wine glass cradled in the fingertips of both hands. Brian followed her gaze over the rooftop to the spectacular cityscape. Lights came on gradually in the surrounding buildings, forming urban constellations. The sun faded in orange mist, the hazy air forming a thin layer of gauze on the horizon. The concrete and glass towers of the North Side and Loop were lit up like cruise ships in an island port. A half moon glimmered over Lake Michigan. Stars studded the purpling sky. The wind carried faint traffic noise up to them—honking horns and pedestrians' voices punctuated the stillness below.

Brian helped himself to seconds and replenished their wine glasses.

"Are you going to make me eat alone? he said.

"I've had enough."

Brian knew something was troubling her. Normally, she'd be right with him, helping finish up the food.

"How're things in the office?"

Michelle sighed, shook her head. "I'm thinking it's time I explored other options, as they say."

"That bad, huh?"

"The work's okay, still interesting, challenging. It's that goddamned Abernathy. I've about had it with the guy."

She'd mentioned Ted Abernathy on other occasions. The ambitious partner in charge of the firm's litigation department and she were like oil and water. His antipathy had stymied her career.

"He's done something lately?"

"I've got the highest billable hours in my class. I get assigned to the toughest clients. My evaluations are outstanding. And yet, word is, I'm to be passed over for partner."

"How do you know? I mean, isn't that stuff top secret until they announce it?"

Michelle gave him a look. "Lawyers are the biggest gossips on the planet. If you want free publicity, tell it to a lawyer, and make sure he knows it's hush-hush."

"Why in hell would this bozo treat you like that?"

"I'm a woman."

"I've noticed. But, that's all the more reason they'd want to showcase you."

"Abernathy's got a wild hair."

"Why?"

"He damn-near ignores me in the office. But, a week ago, I went to a party given by one of the partners. He was there, too. Keep in mind, the guy's married, has four kids. Anyway, he corners me in the kitchen, gives me a big grin, says he'd like to get to know me better, puts his grimy hands on me."

"Is he still alive?"

"Unfortunately."

"So, you kicked his ass and now, he's out to roadblock your career."

"Probably not that drastic. But there's more."

Brian waited.

"One of Ted's young geniuses, kid graduated near the top of his law school class at Harvard last year, was helping me on a case recently. Turns out the budding genius is a lazy little shit and a slimeball. I ended up re-doing everything I delegated to him. Then he gives me his expense report to approve, and I see he's made up expenses—things like a trip to Florida for case research, commuting mileage, dinners that had nothing to do with the work. Naturally, I bounce the report back to him. A few days later, I hear he's taken it to Ted, complained about me and had Ted approve the expenses. Ted calls me, tells me I need to improve my supervisory skills. I bring up the genius' bogus expenses. He reminds me the kid is brilliant, his family has tons of connections, and what are a few insignificant charges the client will never even notice? The conversation deteriorated rapidly at that point."

"I can imagine," Brian said. "So, what are you going to do?"

"See what happens. Abernathy's no dummy. I'm getting outstanding job evaluations from other partners and I don't think he wants a nasty discrimination suit or a harassment suit, for that matter."

"You'll be okay. In fact, I almost feel sorry for Ted."

She gave him a look. "Your empathy is overwhelming."

"Not to change the subject, but, do you know anything about the law related to federal land rights?"

"Let me guess. This is something to do with the dinosaur business."

"Yeah. See, I have a dinosaur bone, exact source unknown. It could be controversial."

"Great. People eat that stuff up. Write a book about it, and make millions."

"Not so fast. I said I found one bone—not the whole skeleton. My guess is, it's related to the deal with Darcy. Land ownership's kinda complicated. I've got to find out who has the rights to what—I already know some of it—and the legal implications."

"Well...I've got a friend who might be able to help you. She's a lawyer, does some real estate work." She paused, as if in thought. "You know, she also has a problem you might be able to help her with."

Michelle gave him the phone number of her friend, Christine Pellas. They stayed on the rooftop talking for another hour or so. While Michelle went inside to brew a pot of coffee, Brian called Christine Pellas and made an appointment at her office for nine the next morning. After dinner, they ended up in Michelle's bedroom.

BONE MOUNTAIN

31

Brian took the stairs to his second-floor apartment, was reaching into a pocket to retrieve his keys when he noticed the door was open a crack. His handgun was in a box in the bedroom closet—a lot of good it would do him. He started to push the door open but it wouldn't give. Angry, he put a shoulder to the door and slammed into it, crashing inward. He stepped in, ready for action. The remains of a small straight-back wooden chair from the kitchen lay on the floor just inside the entrance. Someone had propped the chair under the inside doorknob, probably as an early warning system.

He stopped to look and listen. And sniff. He noticed a faint perfumy odor, something like the Old Spice aftershave his father used to wear. Funny how you'd notice smells when you entered your home after being out for a while. But neither he nor Michelle used a scent like that, and he hadn't had any other visitors lately. Maybe the neighbor upstairs was using air freshener to get rid of the stench from her cigarettes, but he doubted it. Then he recalled catching a whiff of a similar smell in a vehicle in Montana. The odor had come from Tom Norton as Brian drove him to the warehouse to release Darcy. Could Norton have done this? Lots of guys used Old Spice aftershave. Brian listened intently before moving further into the apartment. The only sounds were his own breathing and the quickening thud of his heart.

Brian surveyed the mess that had once been his home. The intruder had trashed the place, knocked every picture off the walls, turned the furniture upside down and slashed it open, tossed books on the floor. Brian walked cautiously through every room, opening closet doors, looking under the bed. He even ripped the shower curtain aside. The back door remained closed and locked from the inside. He stood in the kitchen, amazed at the quantity of destruction. Everything in the refrigerator had been thrown on the floor—eggs, butter, cheese, milk, juice and jelly had mixed together, forming an intricate omelet at his feet.

In the bedroom, the mattress had been pulled off the bed and slashed open. The nightstand was upended. The dresser drawers lay on the floor, the contents strewn randomly. He went to the closet and tossed aside the clothes on the floor to get to the boxes where he kept valuable things out of sight—things like his gun and the dinosaur bone and pottery shards he'd gotten from Russell Eagle Feather. The fireproof box that had held both of these items was empty.

The bathroom was almost as bad as the kitchen. The contents of the medicine cabinet had been tossed in the tub. The magazines and books that he kept piled on the hamper now shared the toilet bowl with dirty clothes. Nothing was missing except the box containing his gun and the dinosaur bone.

He went into the tiny guest room that served as his home office. There too, a hurricane had hit. The bottom half of the double-hung window was missing and shards of glass littered the sill. He looked out and saw the indentations of large, plain footprints in the ground below, surrounded by ragged bits of glass. The burglar had left that way, probably to cut down on the risk of bumping into Brian coming in.

Fortunately, the computer remained in place. Brian checked his e-mail. A message from Darcy said the *T. rex* dig would be finished in a matter of days now. Stevens was due back Thursday morning. They'd actually gotten more work done with him away. She was looking forward to going home. She missed deep-dish Chicago-style pizza and Italian beef sandwiches with hot peppers. Oh, and her uncle, too. The cute female sheriff deputy, Laura something, had visited the site that morning, and asked her a few questions about Gilstrap. Laura had also asked about Brian. Kind of sexy-looking for a cop, Darcy observed. Darcy said she hadn't mentioned that Brian had a girlfriend in Chicago—didn't want to disappoint the deputy. Brian smiled, tapped out a brief reply indicating his undecided travel plans, and logged off.

As he was about to shut down the computer, Brian glanced at the floor where the desk contents now resided. He didn't see the dozen or so flash drives he'd used for file back-up over the past couple years. After pawing through the mess, he concluded they'd been taken by the burglar. He clicked open the security program which showed the most recent usage of computer programs and data files. According to the information displayed on the screen, the computer had been turned on and the intruder had attempted to log on, but had been thwarted by not knowing Brian's password.

Brian sniffed. Was it his imagination, or was the aftershave smell stronger in this room? He called the landlord, an older man named Plotnik, who occupied the apartment next door. Plotnik said he hadn't seen or heard anything unusual.

He suggested Brian call the police now and the insurance company in the morning. Good advice, but he didn't plan on following it.

How would Norton know he had the dinosaur bone? He'd told Russell Eagle Feather, of course. And the two professors at Montana State, the lab workers at the CMNH and Scott Stevens. His theory had been that it would be good to get the word out he had the thing, maybe spark a reaction. Well, it had worked...too well. Now what? Why would Norton—if it was Norton—go through his computer files? Having his handgun in the intruder's possession was another worry.

Brian checked the phone in the kitchen for transmitting devices, found none. Then he did a cursory search of the apartment for bugs in the light fixtures, sound system, electrical outlets, behind pictures, on the bottoms of lamps, tables and chairs. Nothing.

Before going to bed, Brian examined the front door. The prowler had picked the locks, done a good job—the deadbolt was a decent one. Was the goddamned dinosaur bone really worth that much? Didn't the experts make fakes for the missing bones? And where was the rest of the dinosaur? Why would Norton want his computer files? No classified information in them—unless it was something in a bureau file that might implicate somebody. Sands, maybe? There wouldn't be much of interest to an outsider in the e-mails with Darcy and James and others. After locking the front door and wedging a doorstop under it, he gave it up and went to bed.

Sleep was elusive. He dreamed of burglars picking locks, rifling desk drawers, stealing fossil bones and computer files and using them, along with his gun, as evidence to convict him of a murder he didn't commit. The murder victim was female, someone familiar. He was in a jail cell, by himself, pondering an impossible question: why would he kill anyone? He hadn't killed anyone. It was a frame-up. He needed a lawyer. He was taken to a room with a phone on a table. He called Michelle's office, but she didn't answer. Ted Abernathy came on the line and said Michelle had decided to move into his house with him, his wife and children. It didn't make sense. He had to get her out of there. But first, he had to get himself out of jail. He began to look for another lawyer in the yellow pages. He found a defense lawyer listed, a man by the name of Nathan Plotnik. He punched in the number, but the call wouldn't go through. A gruff male voice told him all circuits were busy, to hang up and try his call later, perhaps in a year or so. He began to argue that he'd be in prison at least that long, unless a lawyer could find a way to get him out. The voice advised him to engage in an impossible sexual act. Then came a click, and the line went dead.

Brian awoke suddenly and looked at the bedside clock. 8:05 a.m. He rubbed sleep from his eyes, wished he could doze for a while. After a few minutes, he got out of bed and staggered to the bathroom. He was due at Christine Pellas' office in less than an hour.

32

Brian found the address Christine Pellas had given him on the phone the night before. The building was a small Near North redbrick loft in an industrial neighborhood undergoing rapid gentrification. Restaurants with affected names and stores catering to those with money to burn were displacing machine shops, shoe repairs, greasy spoons and seedy residential hotels. The three-story building had been recently sandblasted and tuck-pointed.

A new-looking framed directory in the small lobby informed Brian "The Pellas Law Firm" was on the second floor. He took the elevator up. The smell of fresh paint made him want to sneeze. The narrow hallway was punctuated by dark wooden doors with film noire-style frosted glass panels bearing the names of lawyers, accountants and interior design consultants. The rehab job had been done recently, and not on the cheap. The lawyer's offices occupied a small suite at the far end of the hall. Brian entered and found himself in an anteroom containing two modest chairs and a chrome and glass table bearing that day's edition of the New York Times and a few magazines. The door to the inner office was open, and he could hear someone handling paper. In a moment, a dark-haired young woman appeared in the doorway.

She smiled a welcome. "Hi, Chris Pellas."

"Brian McKay. Good to meet you."

"Come in. Coffee?"

"I'd love some. Black, please."

In her office, she set down a couple of cups of strong-looking coffee, went to her desk and motioned him to sit. "Michelle tells me you're interested in some issues of federal land law," she said.

"That's right. I need to know the ins and outs of digging up dinosaur bones on Montana land owned by an Indian."

"I can tell you that, as a white guy from Chicago, you rank low on the totem pole, pun intended."

"That's what I thought."

"Give me some facts."

"A Crow Indian named William Old Horn, now deceased, lived in a cabin on a piece of private land in south central Montana bordered by a privately-owned ranch and public land. This is according to the county sheriff and the Indian's nephew. I haven't looked at any records. I've got reason to believe there are fossilized dinosaur bones on the land. I'm wondering if the nephew has the right to dig up the bones.

"Did he inherit?"

"Claims he did, says he's the only living relative."

"Do you know whether there was a will?"

"The nephew says no."

"If the uncle died intestate, Montana law would prevail as to disposition of the assets of the estate, including real estate, of course. The nephew would probably inherit, if he is, in fact, the only living relative. It would be interesting to know whether the uncle actually had full title to the land. Sometimes, the government holds land in trust for Indians. If that's the case, they might control any digging of fossil bones."

"I don't know if it's in trust."

"You might want to ask the nephew."

"What are the general rules about digging up dinosaur bones, like permits, and so on?"

"You've got to have a permit to dig on federal land, but not on private. If it's owned privately, you just need permission of the owner. I remember that, after Sue got so much publicity, some landowners began asking for thousands of dollars just to do prospecting, let alone actual removal of bones. That's died down a bit since then."

"So I need to find out about the land title and whether there's a trust agreement?"

"Yes. The easiest way would be to get that from the nephew. Alternatively, you could check with the local county clerk's office."

"Any idea of what your fees will run?"

Chris waved a hand as if shooing a fly. "I'm afraid I haven't been able to provide much assistance."

"No, you've been quite helpful."

"Listen, Michelle tells me you're an ex-FBI agent. Maybe you can advise me on a...problem."

"What kind of problem?"

"I'm a little embarrassed to say, actually." She sighed. "But here's the situation. I used to date a guy named Ted Abernathy. He's the partner in charge—"

"Of litigation at Briggs, Coleman and Davenport."

"So, Michelle's told you about him."

"Just her own dealings with the guy. Nothing about you," Brian said.

"Well, I had a relationship with Ted for a while. I

241

stopped seeing him about two weeks ago. I realized neither of us was in it for the long run, and I decided it was time to move on." She sighed. "So I broke it off and he didn't handle it very well."

"How so?"

"He's called me here and at home several times a day. He's been abusive. I've made it clear I won't see him, but he's kept calling. Two nights ago, he was waiting outside the door downstairs when I left. He took hold of my arm, and actually tried to steer me to his car. He said we'd have a nice quiet drink and discuss our relationship. I told him there was no relationship and nothing to discuss, hailed a cab and left him standing on the sidewalk."

"Heard from him since?"

"I think so."

"You're not sure?"

"I got an envelope, anonymously. It probably came from Ted."

"What sort of envelope?"

"Well, yesterday, when I got back from lunch, this had been delivered to the outer office." She opened a desk drawer and extracted a nine by twelve-inch brown envelope. Her face colored as she opened the flap and took out a photograph. She held it by a corner, between thumb and forefinger, as if grasping a dead rat by the tip of its tail, and set it down on the desktop in front of Brian.

An eight by ten color photo depicted a couple on a large bed. The woman had her head between the man's legs, and her lips encircled his stiff penis. He was on his back, propped up on his elbows, watching the woman intently, a strange light in his eyes. The woman's cheeks were pulled in, as if she were providing suction on the man's engorged member. The man in the picture was slender, fortyish, with dark hair and an eagle beak. The woman in the picture was Christine Pellas. There was something about the picture that made it seem especially pornographic. Maybe it was the weird expression on the man's face.

"This is the man we were discussing just now?"

"Yes."

"Ah, hell. What could he hope to gain with this stuff? I mean, it's obviously not going to win any points with you. And you're in a better position than he, I'd think, in terms of caring about keeping this quiet."

"Well, it's embarrassing—not what we're doing in the picture, so much. It's the fact that I was ever with such a loser. What if it ended up on the Internet?"

"You think that's what this is about? He wants to embarrass you?"

"I don't know. I could send this to his wife. Wouldn't you think he'd be worried I could use this picture against him?"

"Maybe the picture came from someone else. Where did this, uh, incident take place?"

Christine reddened. "A hotel room near here."

"Who chose the room?"

"He did."

"Chances are, either Abernathy sent this, or there's a blackmailer at the hotel."

"What should I do?"

"Let me know if you get a follow-up note or email or phone call. And call me when it comes. I'll respond on your

behalf. Let me borrow this. I might need to use it as a lever."
He rolled the picture up loosely and tucked it in an inside jacket pocket.

"I hope you don't think I—"

"I don't think anything, except maybe I can give you some help on this."

"What will you do?"

"I'm going to have a little chat with your uh, ex-friend."

33

Brian got home around noon. While he was trying gamely to restore order to his train wreck of an apartment, James called.

"Hey big guy, you gonna clue me in on your dinosaur bone?"

"You out of the office?"

"Yeah."

"Okay. The bone's gone," Brian said.

"What? You donated it to a museum?"

"I don't know who I donated it to. Somebody tossed my place while I was at Michelle's last night. Took some computer files, my gun and the bone. How'd you hear about it, anyway?"

"You failed to share news of the uh, dingus with me on Friday. I got the word from our buddy, the J-man."

"How would he know about it? I mean, I only told some guys in the bone business, including Stevens. Did J. Edgar pump you about me again?"

"Well, yeah, as a matter of fact, he hauled my ass into his office and threw salt in my game. Asked me what you were doing with the dinosaur bone you brought back. For once, I didn't have to play it cool. I told the dude the truth: I didn't know dick about any dinosaur bone."

"Shit. What else?"

"Asked what did we talk about at lunch yesterday."

"How'd he know about that?"

"I'm guessing one of us was tailed to Grant Park. Couple of slick muthas we are, not noticing."

"I'll say. What did you tell him?"

"Damn little as I could. But what's the four-one-one on this dinosaur bone?"

"It's part of some kind of *T. rex* arm bone I got from the nephew of the Indian was killed last year."

"Man, is this thing part of Stevens's dinosaur?"

"I don't think so."

"Maybe it's got something to do with the problem with your niece."

"What I was thinking, too."

"Could be J. Edgar is still a close bud of Stevens," James said. "Or maybe he's just bein' a mullethead. By the way, he said something about federal laws being broken by ex-agents of this office. Meaning you, sure as shit. Probably expected I'd pass it on, maybe get you thinking."

"Christ," Brian said. "What else?"

"He asked for a rundown of our conversations since you got back. Naturally, I kept it short, mostly the truth and never mentioned Sands."

"Good. Based on the bullshit J. Edgar's been slinging your way, looks like he's real interested in the bone. Do you suppose they'd do a B and E to get it?"

"You told me about a case a few years back, called 'Kinky Cashbox.' Remember? Some agents B and E'd an after-hours betting club on the West Side during the day, when no one was around. Couldn't use what they found in court, but it gave 'em a lever to crack the case open like a fucking walnut."

"That's right. I was one of the agents manning the lock picks."

"No shit? Man, the legend grows."

"But now, I'm not part of any case, least as far as I know."

"But somebody wanted that bone awful damn bad. You think Gilstrap's in Chicago?"

"I've got a theory on this thing. Let me run it by you."

"Go for it."

"Okay. Let's go back a little over a year ago. William Old Horn lives in a cabin near this Bone Mountain. Call the spot BME, for Bone Mountain East. Anyway, he explores, diddles around, looks for pottery scraps, arrowheads, whatever. One day, he digs up a dinosaur bone—the one I had until last night. He suspects this could be important, so he stashes the bone someplace, maybe buries it on his property. Then he hits town and, after a few pops, lets it drop he's found something sweet—part of a *T. rex*, he thinks. Word gets to Sands or one of his gofers. Gilstrap's assigned to watch the old guy like a fish hawk, see if he digs up any more bones, and where. Sands figures a big-time dinosaur skeleton might be worth *maximo dinero*—especially after Sue brings in the eight million in Chicago. Old Horn goes back to the spot where he found the bone, starts digging, maybe finds another one. Gilstrap moves in, whacks him, takes whatever he can find on him, which isn't much. He drags the body to the brush at the bottom of the hill, tosses the guy's cabin, but still doesn't find diddlysquat. Old Horn's nephew gets the first bone later, from the hidey-hole his uncle's told him about. Sands waits for Old Horn's death to blow over. He figures the overworked, semi-competent sheriff's not gonna bust his balls on it. The FBI comes and goes. Sands figures he can buy BME from Eagle Feather if he inherits it. Or better yet, maybe he can pick it up for back taxes. Meanwhile, Gilstrap's still keeping an eye on BME. His marching orders are to report if Eagle Feather or anyone else shows up and starts digging. Or maybe he's supposed to stop them."

"Sounds okay, so far," James said. "This where Darcy comes in?"

"Yeah. She's looking for fossils on BME, probably not that far from the bones. Gilstrap gets excited, shoots her, barely dings her shoulder. He gets creative, decides to take her alive, use her, then get rid of her. He's not going to mention any of this to his bosses. But Darcy's more than he's bargained for—you know that story. When she gets away, he tries to find her, and can't. He knows she's got his driver's license, so his ass is in a sling. He panics and splits."

"So, then you get the bone from Eagle Feather, start showing it around, Sands finds out, and now, you're the loose cannon."

"Right, they don't want to kill me—the FBI's already been called in twice—but they steal the bone because they think it might implicate them in the two shootings. Hard to get fingerprints off a dry bone, though. Of course, I've told Stevens about the bone and where it came from."

"You think Stevens told Sands?"

"Makes sense. They flew to Chicago together, went to the museum board meeting together. And Sands is bankrolling

Stevens's operation. One of those two tells J. Edgar, probably Sands."

"Where's this going next?"

"Sands nails down a permit to dig, soon as he can. Stevens heads up an expedition next year, and the CMNH gets another world-class bag of bones that, combined with the first one, makes Sue look like a wannabe. Five'll get you ten the bone I had miraculously shows up when they put together the second skeleton."

"I like it, except, why wouldn't they take the bone away from Eagle Feather way back when?" James said.

"They didn't know he had it."

"Sands's got more dough than most third-world countries. Why's he want to get in the middle of this dinosaur shit?"

"Guys like him can never have too much, but that's not what he's after here. See, he gets a tax write-off and tons of good press if he donates the dinosaur to the museum. Plus, he's a booster of the museum, anyway."

"Okay. So what's *our* next move?"

"I'm looking into the legal points on this," Brian said. "Could be Sands doesn't get the dinosaur after all."

"That'd be cool. You gonna finger Sands for having Gilstrap shoot Darcy?"

"I'm thinking along those lines, but he's probably too smart to leave tracks. And Norton's in the middle. Plus, I'd like to see the dinosaur end up with the right owner, which might not be Sands or his pet museum."

"Hey, you're on a roll, big guy. What else you got?"

"I'm wondering about J. Edgar's part in this. He seemed to be interested in me and what I was doing about

Darcy from the get-go. Why would he care? And he knew about the bone right after I told Stevens about it. I keep coming back to: what's the relationship between Stevens and these guys? Maybe you could dig into that."

"I'll check with my usual sources."

"Be careful. J. Edgar's a snake and he's not your biggest fan."

"I can handle him. What's your plan, man?"

"I'm gonna get on the paper trail—see who owns what as to the land the bone came out of."

"You got anything else going?"

"I've got sort of a client, lady needs my help."

"Uh oh. What kind of help?"

"She's being harassed by some jerk she used to date. It's escalating, and she needs him out of her life."

"You a bodyguard now?"

"Something like that. But you know me. I'll try to finesse the dude first."

"And, if that doesn't work you'll kick his ass."

"Exactly."

"How far we gonna take this dinosaur thing?"

"To the end of the line. I'm going to punch Gilstrap's ticket for what he did to Darcy, and I'll get whoever else was in on it. And now I owe Eagle Feather for losing his uncle's stuff. Bottom line is, I hate to see these assholes get away with it."

34

A few minutes later, Laura Jensen called.

"Brian, thank God I caught you." She sounded keyed up.

"How are you doing?"

"I guess I'm OK."

"Something wrong?"

"We still haven't gotten a report on the bullet I sent to Missoula a week ago."

"Ah, it probably wouldn't do much good, anyway. I have a feeling we'll never see the rifle Cody Gilstrap fired at Darcy."

"I'm beginning to think we'll never see Cody Gilstrap either."

"Oh?"

"Sam told us to not waste any more time looking for him. Says we've got ten million other things to do and, besides, the feebles are looking for him."

"Feebles?"

She laughed. "You know, FBI."

"Uh huh. What else?"

"Weird thing happened last Thursday. I didn't think to mention it to you before. Tom Norton came here and met with the sheriff for about an hour. They holed up in Sam's office with the door closed. I don't know what it was about, but Norton was grim-looking when he got here, and even grimmer when he left."

"Have you ever seen them together before?"

"Not in the office, but I saw them drinking together once."

"When was this?

"About three weeks ago, in a local hangout called the Redtail. They were in a booth in the corner, which seemed a little odd."

"Any idea what they'd have to talk about?"

"The first occasion, no. Thursday, it could have been Sam questioning Norton about the shootings at Bone Mountain. After all, it's across the road from the Sands place and Norton's the security guy."

"Who all's the sheriff interviewed, so far?"

"He talked to a bunch of folks from the Sands place. There was Mr. Sands, himself, and Ray Chafee, the ranch manager. Also, Hank Crawford. He's some kind of geology expert, bunks at the ranch, but I don't know if he's on the payroll."

Brian wondered why Art Sands hadn't mentioned Crawford. "Any idea what he's doing there?"

"From what I hear, he looks for remains of early human cultures—prehistoric people and the like. Supposedly, he used to work for the Museum of the Rockies, but they pink-slipped him."

"Anyone else?"

"There's a couple of brothers work for Norton, used to pal around with Gilstrap. Talking with them's like supervising a special ed class."

"What? They slow or something?"

"These guys—Shane and Donny Gruel—are what I call mouth-breathers, guys with the manners of pond slime. I'd have to say they weren't involved. Not that they're harmless—they're both plenty capable of raising hell, but not something like that."

"Did you ever find out whether Gilstrap's got a white pickup?"

"You bet—a 2007 Dodge crew cab dually. We found it at the Sands place. His four-wheeler was in a storage shed at the bottom of the road to his cabin."

"And the cabin?"

"Sam and Jim went up there with Bill Thorsten from the FBI. From what I heard, everything Darcy told us jibed. They checked out Cody's little jail room. Man, he must be one sick puppy."

"Sounds like the sheriff's at least gone through the motions. It's possible he interrogated Norton that day, but you don't think so."

"Well...no, I don't.

"Why not"

"Sam and he seem to be...what's the word? They're not opponents, and they're sure not friends. They're more like—"

"Co-conspirators?"

"Something like that. Like they have something to hide. Maybe Sam doesn't want to be seen talking with Tom, like he knows he shouldn't be associating with him."

"Could be something dirty?"

"I don't know. Norton's not someone I'd want to be

alone with, though." There was a shudder in her voice.

"Why?"

"I'll put it this way: he's a nasty guy and none too well-liked around here."

"What's the buzz on him? Does he pal around with anybody? Have a girlfriend? Tear the wings off flies?"

"He mostly keeps to himself. I don't know of any friends he might have, male or female. And he's a mean drunk. Beat the hell out of a couple of guys."

"Was he charged with anything?"

"Nah, but that's not unusual."

"So, you think the sheriff's not a hundred percent behind solving the Bone Mountain case?"

"Right. And it's not like him. When it comes to department business, he's usually a straight shooter, conscientious, follows up on details."

"And now, he seems to have a different agenda."

"In a way. For example, his handling of that slug seemed a little careless. He just hasn't been busting his butt on the Darcy case. Come to think of it, he was kind of lax about the Old Horn shooting, too."

"And you wonder why."

"I've got a bad feeling. Look, I'm talking out of school here, but it's almost like he's making Bone Mountain a low priority, regardless of the two major crimes we've had there. Far as I know, you and I are the only ones still give a damn about it. And the FBI, I guess."

"Did the FBI agents search the area where Darcy was shot?"

"Yeah, on Sunday. Those two agents went out with

Sam. I got this from Dave, one of our deputies."

"Did Dave go with them?"

"No. He just happened to be in the office Sunday, catching up on paperwork when you and Darcy came in for your session. He says Sam took the two agents out to Bone Mountain right after you left."

"Any word on how it went?"

"Nope."

"Anything else of interest?"

"I've been thinking about the old mineshaft opening up on Bone Mountain."

"And?"

"And after we were up there and you'd left my place, I was thinking it looked different than I remembered it from way back when. Anyway, it may be far-fetched, but I think I'll go back up there and take a look."

"Good. Let me know right away if there's anything."

"Okay."

"And, could you do me a favor, check something out at the county clerk's office there?"

"Sure. I've got a girlfriend in the clerk's office."

"Could you see if title to Old Horn's property was transferred to his nephew, Russell Eagle Feather? Also, whether there's any kind of trust agreement on the property—something between the government and Old Horn? I understand the feds hold land in trust for Indians, sometimes."

"I'll see what I can do."

"I'd be infernally grateful."

"Where are you going with this, Brian?"

"Okay, no secrets. Eagle Feather gave me a dinosaur bone his uncle found near where Darcy was digging. Looks like part of a *T. rex*. Ownership of that land and any trust deal would probably determine who's got the right to take out the bones, if there are more. There might be the proverbial shitload of money at stake. Incidentally, I'd keep this to myself. There's no reason for the sheriff to get involved at this point."

"As far as I'm concerned, this whole conversation is confidential to the hubcaps."

"What conversation?"

"Okay. I'll call you back in a little while. By the way, when are you coming out to visit us?"

"I'm not sure. It may depend on what you tell me later."

35

Brian called Briggs, Coleman & Davenport and asked to speak with Ted Abernathy.

A secretary came on the line. "Mr. Abernathy's office."

"Brian McKay here. I need to speak with him right away."

"He's in a meeting."

"Tell him it's extremely urgent."

"May I take a message?"

"How about taking a message to him in his meeting. Tell him I need to talk with him right now about his involvement in distribution of pornography."

"What?"

"You heard me."

"Uh, just a minute."

A few seconds later, the lawyer was on the line. "Abernathy speaking. What is this all about?" The voice was one of those smooth, deep-timbered ones designed to instill confidence in jurors.

"You know damned well what it's about, Abernathy. I'm representing Christine Pellas."

"Who?"

"Don't be a dumbass. I haven't got the patience. Chris

showed me the picture you sent her."

"Forgive me, but, frankly, I don't know who you are or what you're talking about."

"My name's McKay. Maybe I should just show the picture to your wife."

"Now just a goddamned minute. Are you threatening me?"

"Yes. And I'll back it up if you don't start talking sense. What'll it be?"

There was silence on the other end for a few seconds. Then Abernathy spoke quietly, "What do you want from me?"

"That's better. I want you to meet me at five p.m. in Washington Square Park. It's a couple of blocks from your office, just west of—"

"I know where it is."

The lawyer broke the connection. Brian smiled. He'd stirred up the scum-sucking lowlife. Interesting that he hadn't asked more about Brian's identity or how they'd recognize each other in the park. He glanced at his watch. After three. He grabbed a quick bite from the meager stores in the refrigerator. As he was finishing, his phone rang again.

"I got a copy of the title on that land," Laura said.

"What's the scoop?"

"Russell Eagle Feather has title. I asked about a trust agreement, and they told me there wasn't any."

"Good. I owe you one."

"You got that right. You'd better get out here and pay up."

"I'll let you know. Be careful, Laura. You're my favorite Montana sheriff's deputy."

"Thanks, I think."

36

Brian arrived at the skyscraper housing the 175-lawyer firm of Briggs, Coleman and Davenport at 4:40 p.m. The 60-story office tower jutted skyward on Delaware, west of the world-class shopping strip along North Michigan Avenue known as the Magnificent Mile. He waited outside the north entrance, where he had an unobstructed view of the glass-walled lobby. Business people hurried by. Shoppers with bags from the exclusive shops sauntered along, laughing and talking. Every other person on the street clutched a phone and was using it. He kept an eye on the elevator bank serving the top ten floors.

Security was tight, with armed guards shepherding everyone through metal detectors before gaining access to the elevators. Brian knew that Briggs, Coleman inhabited floors 57 through 60, with a pretentious cathedral-ceilinged library and conference room at the peaked summit of the office tower. Michelle had given him the grand tour a few months back. He'd seen the plush digs as a sign of excessive hourly billing rates, but figured most clients would be impressed that their lawyers displayed the trappings of success.

At 4:55, the lobby elevator doors opened and a tall, lean man wearing glasses and a dark suit stepped out. Brian recognized the hawkish face of the man in the picture with

Christine Pellas. As the guy came through the revolving doors, Brian studied him further. Looking straight ahead, Ted Abernathy marched west toward Washington Square Park. He purposefully threaded his way through the sidewalk crowds. Brian followed a few yards behind, not bothering to be discreet. Abernathy reached the city block-square park, known informally as "Bughouse Square" because of the crazy soapbox orators who'd held forth there decades earlier.

The lawyer stood on the periphery of the green oasis of parkland, swiveling his head about like an owl. A few people occupied iron park benches, enjoying the mild afternoon. Abernathy moved a few steps into the park and stopped in the middle of the sidewalk. A young black woman pushed a wheelchair toward him. Her passenger, a pale older matron, sat swaddled in a gray blanket. As they approached, the lawyer seemed to register their presence, but he didn't move aside. The nurse was forced to detour around him, so that the wheels on one side of the wheelchair went off the edge of the sidewalk. The nurse struggled to keep momentum, but the wheelchair slowed nearly to a stop in the thick grass. She finally made it around the man, glaring at him as she passed.

"Nice guy," Brian muttered, as he closed on his quarry.

Startled at the sound of footsteps behind him, Abernathy spun around. His dark eyes were cold, challenging.

"You're Abernathy," Brian said. It wasn't a question.

"I'm kind of busy. Let's get this over with."

"Follow me," Brian said. Turning his back on Abernathy, he strode into the park and found a vacant bench largely shielded from the surrounding streets and other benches by trees. Abernathy came up behind him. Brian turned, gestured at the bench. As if addressing a dog, he said, "Sit."

Abernathy obeyed and Brian took a seat beside the lawyer, a little too close, invading his space.

"Ted, Christine Pellas says you've been harassing her. She wants it stopped. So you're going to stop. You will keep your sorry ass away from her. Follow me?" Brian's face was as close to Abernathy's as a baseball manager's arguing a bad call with an umpire.

Abernathy stuck out his chin in a defiant pose. "I haven't the foggiest idea what you're talking about."

Brian kept his voice level, businesslike. "Don't play dumb, Ted. I asked you a simple fucking question and I want an answer right now. Do you follow me?"

Abernathy started to say something, checked himself and looked at the ground between his feet. "I admit she and I had a completely consensual relationship, but it's over. I'm the one who broke it off. Why would I want to harass her?"

"Because you're an insecure, egocentric asshole. She was happy to be rid of you, and you didn't like it. You wanted to get back together with her, and she told you to fuck off."

"I don't have to sit here and take this." Abernathy began to stand, but Brian grabbed a handful of the fine cloth on his shoulder and hauled him back down to the bench.

"So why the harassment, Ted?"

"That's not true. That bitch—"

Brian brought a hand up deliberately and slapped Abernathy's face, knocking his glasses off. The lawyer's eyes watered and his chin quivered. Once again, he started to speak and then clamped his thin-lipped mouth closed. There was a bright red spot on his left cheek where he'd been struck. He reached to the ground to retrieve his glasses with a trembling hand.

Brian knew that bullies caved real fast when you threw their own tactics back at them. When he was about seven, a bigger kid in the neighborhood buried his fist in little Brian's stomach. Brian had cried and felt bad. Word got to Brian's dad, who advised the youngster to hit back next time, harder. Next day, the bully approached Brian with clenched fists. When he was within reach, Brian decked him with a blow to the nose. Bloodied and tearful, the bully retreated home. That was the last of that problem. Brian didn't feel the least bit guilty giving Ted Abernathy a dose of his own medicine.

"Ted, you've got a problem with women. I think you're afraid of them. You're threatened by a strong woman like Christine."

"She's just trying to stir up trouble for me because I dumped her. She—"

Brian raised a hand. Abernathy shrunk into the collar of his suit coat like a turtle withdrawing into its shell. Brian withdrew the hand. "Did you take the picture to her office yourself?"

"What picture?"

Brian cuffed the lawyer on the back of his head. As he did so, the Three Stooges came to mind and he smiled inwardly. He extracted the photo of Abernathy and Christine Pellas in bed from a pocket and smoothed it out. This one. Recognize it?"

"Someone must have...I mean, I don't—"

"Can the theatrics. How do you suppose the members of your firm's management committee would react to getting copies of this, Ted? Better yet, what if it went to your wife?

Or maybe Facebook? Think it would hurt your chances of making managing partner some day?"

Abernathy's tongue darted out, licked his lips. "I, uh, well..."

"Why'd you take this to Chris's office?"

Abernathy shrugged. "I don't know. I guess I wanted to give her a memento of our relationship."

"Memento, my ass."

Abernathy put his glasses on and rubbed his temples with slender fingers. "Well, I knew she'd be embarrassed."

"She was, but not for the reason you think. She was embarrassed because there was documentation she'd ever been with a piece of shit like you, Ted. She'd rather forget you ever existed. You stay the hell away from her. Understand?"

Abernathy muttered something and began to stand up again. Brian grabbed the collar of his custom-made suit, and jerked him back down. "He put his face inches from the lawyer's and said, "I didn't hear you, Ted."

"Okay, okay. Yeah, I understand. Are you satisfied?"

"I'll be watching, Ted. You send anything to her, call her, text her, email her, come anywhere near her, I'm going to be all over you like flies on shit. Got it?"

Hesitation. Sulk. Then, almost inaudibly: "Yeah, I've got it."

Brian suddenly rose and walked away. He tossed over his shoulder, "Have a nice evening."

As he exited the park, Brian drew his cell phone and punched in Chris Pellas' office number.

She answered right away. "Pellas Law Firm."

"Chris, I talked with Mr. Snapshot. He agreed to stay away from you."

"What did you say to him?"

"I accused him of harassing you. At first, he denied it, but then he had a change of heart."

"You didn't use violence, did you?"

"Not so much. I may have suggested violence would be forthcoming if he didn't behave, though."

"Hmmm. Well, thanks. I really appreciate this." She paused. But I'd still trust him about as far as I can throw him."

"Sounds like a good policy. Let me know if you hear from the jerk. By the way, I used the photo to refresh his memory that he'd taken it. Want it back?"

"You can burn it."

Brian hailed a cab and got home a few minutes later. He did, in fact, burn the photo. Then, after a quick shower, he dressed in a dark blue short-sleeved shirt, jeans and black New Balance leather walking shoes. He was brushing his hair when his phone rang. James, ready to leave work. They agreed to meet at a bar called The Duke of Earl, near Brian's apartment.

Brian and James sat on stools at the bar, a dark, carved monstrosity from the 1890s. The crowd was light—it was still early. They drank mugs of pleasantly bitter Bass Ale. The jukebox in the corner played the Rolling Stones song, "Miss You," at low volume. The bartender busied himself taking glasses from a dishwasher and wiping them with a towel before setting them on a rack under the counter. The bottles on the back bar were neatly aligned, the bar top clean. The promise of the evening had yet to be corrupted by the crush of drinkers and drunks that would inevitably follow. Brian mused that later the perfect anticipatory glow would be obliterated; it would be just another North Side bar.

James tapped a foot to the beat coming from the jukebox. "Okay, what happened with this pervert lawyer? Or is that redundant." He began to drum four fingers on the bar top, in time to the music.

"I 'fronted the dude in Washington Park. First, he played dumb, so I slapped his glasses off his face."

"That make him any smarter?" James laughed and started tapping both hands on the bar like a bongos-player.

"Faster than a building inspector pockets his grease money."

"What happened to finesse?"

"I decided to go with ass-kicking."

"Man, the wild west must've gotten into your blood," James said. Now, his torso was twitching rhythmically in time to the music, while he continued drumming both hands on the bar. He eyed Brian, deadpan.

Brian took the bait. "All right. If you want to dance with me, why don't you just fucking say so?"

James gave him a gotcha smile. "You know, that tune's not bad. For old white guys, I mean."

They'd debated the relative merits or lack thereof of each other's music many times—Brian defending classic rock and James hip-hop. Brian couldn't imagine what James saw in Jay-Z. James failed to dig what was so great about the Stones.

Brian nodded. "Damn fine tune. Glad you appreciate it."

"Anyway, sounds like you ruined the perv's day. Way to go, big guy."

"Hell, that was just my feeble training in action."

"Feeble? Don't sound feeble to me."

"That's a word the wild westerners use meaning you FBI agents."

"Huh. So what's your plan?"

"I might fly back to Montana—there're too many loose ends, and now I've got some ideas on how to pull 'em together."

They ordered burgers at the bar, had some more beer, got caught up on bureau gossip. Brian ran the idea of a private detective practice by James, who offered samples from his repertoire of private eye jokes, and then admitted Brian was qualified, although there couldn't be much money in it, and most of those guys were, in James's opinion, bottom-feeders. Brian got home late, thought of calling Michelle, decided to wait until morning.

37

Arthur Sands's Hawker 4000 knifed through the atmosphere west of the Chicago metropolitan area, cruising at 30,000 feet en route to Montana. A pilot and copilot/mechanic manned the controls. Two passengers sat in leather-bound luxury in the aft cabin designed to carry as many as ten. Tom Norton reclined his considerable bulk on a couch along the starboard wall of the fuselage. He cradled a can of Bud in a meaty fist, sipping from it as he peered out the window. Scott Noble Stevens lounged in a large padded seat across the aisle, his crossed ankles propped on a square tabletop. Norton frowned as Stevens pulled the latest iPhone from his brown calfskin briefcase and began to poke at the screen.

"Hey, won't that thing fuck up the plane's navigation system?" Norton bellowed.

Stevens paused in his keying. "No. They tell you that on commercial planes to scare you. It's perfectly safe." He completed placing his call, and made himself comfortable. "Hey, Bill. Yeah, it's me. How are you guys doing? You are? Awesome. What's left? Yeah? Cool. How's Darcy McKay doing? She is? That's good. Yeah. Tomorrow. I'm in the air right now. At the Sands place tonight. Yep, bright and early. See you then." He smiled as he clicked off the phone.

"What, don't tell me your kids are on schedule," Norton said.

"Tom, you're such an optimist. Actually, they're ahead of schedule. Don't see how they managed with me away."

Norton laughed. "Prob'ly the only way they fuckin' got anything done."

Stevens was about to fire back a barb about Norton's own less-than-stellar staff, but checked himself. Tom Norton wasn't a man to piss off, and he seemed to have the confidence of Art Sands, God knew why. The paleontologist consulted his Rolex, sighed and removed a laptop computer from a padded nylon case on the seat next to him. He booted up and retrieved a Word document he'd been working on for quite some time, an article for *Scientific American, Tyrant King in the Rockies—T. rex Redux*. It was Stevens's contention that *T. rex* migrated many miles away from the ancient seas of the Cretaceous and into the surrounding upland forests some 67 million years ago. He was quite proud of his discovery of a magnificent *rex* in a place where colleagues had long ago concluded none would be found. Horner, Rigby and others had concentrated their efforts in the eastern half of Montana, where, in the Cretaceous period, fearsome *tyrannosauridae* had indeed thrived.

Stevens saw himself as a brash young paleontological pioneer, sort of a modern-day Edwin Drinker Cope. In the late nineteenth century, Cope had launched a series of independent fossil-seeking expeditions, with amazing results. He'd named dozens of dinosaur species and battled mightily with his older, more established rival, Othniel C. Marsh of Yale. Stevens had another trait in common with Cope: he paid local landowners and amateur bone hunters for tips on where to find fossils in the ground. That's how he'd come upon the *T. rex* bones currently being excavated—he'd paid a local elk horn hunter who also dabbled in the occasional dinosaur fossil for information. This fact would not be mentioned in the magazine article.

The journey was much quicker than a commercial flight. The Hawker touched down on the ranch's blacktop runway a scant two and a half hours after departure from O'Hare. As the sleek craft taxied toward the main house, a slender figure observed its progress from a window. Barbara Hardy was looking forward to seeing one of the plane's occupants. As the passengers stepped off the boarding stairs and came toward the house, she walked swiftly toward them.

Scott Noble Stevens quickened his pace when he spotted Barbara. Norton detoured around them on the way to his Suburban. Stevens and the woman hugged each other tightly just outside the door.

"I've missed you so much," she said. "How was Chicago?"

"Fine. I did my PR bit and they ate it up. I'm back to work on the bones tomorrow. Gotta get an early start. All the PR in the world's not worth much if I don't deliver the goods."

"Come in and have something to eat," she said. "Here, let me help you with your bags. You'll stay here with me tonight, won't you?"

"Sure."

The attractive middle-aged woman preceded him inside. Suitcase in hand, Stevens followed her to the bedroom he customarily used. A small framed picture of Stevens sat on the dresser top. She placed his computer case on the bed, kissed him on the cheek and went to the kitchen to dish up the food she'd prepared. Norton had driven off, probably to his own cabin. Stevens was glad to be rid of him for the evening.

Barbara Hardy flitted around Stevens as he ate a bowl of homemade soup and bread. She refilled his wine glass, asked one question after another. How had the board meeting gone? What about the presentation at the museum? Had he been eating well? Sleeping? Was his dig on schedule? Had things been going smoothly with the crew? Was Darcy McKay all right? She showed all the concern a mother normally feels toward a favored son she seldom sees.

They'd always been close. She'd doted on Scott throughout his childhood—he'd been the sole offspring from her brief marriage to a geologist named Mark Stevens. She'd fallen in love with Arthur Sands and married him shortly after the divorce from Stevens. That second marriage had lasted four years and fallen apart a decade ago, due mainly to Sands's inability to be monogamous. Most people wouldn't understand, but she and Art had remained more than good friends in the years since they'd divorced. Barbara had remained single after they'd split. She and Art had lived together off and on in the ensuing years, brought together by friendship and their common interest in doing everything possible for Scott. When she'd learned of Scott's heading up the *T. rex* dig near Art's Montana place, she'd called her ex-husband and he'd welcomed her to the ranch. She'd moved there the day their son's work had begun. Sands visited sporadically, never for more than a few days. The unspoken understanding was that Barbara would be going back to her Chicago condominium when the dig ended.

Barbara poured herself a cup of coffee and sat at the

table across from Stevens. "You be careful up there," she said.

Stevens grinned impishly. "Always. I've worked in lots more extreme sites. Where we're digging's relatively solid and flat. We've got it made in the shade."

"That's not what I mean." She looked into her cup of coffee thoughtfully. "I'm worried more about...violence." She met her son's eyes. "Someone else is after something up on that hill." She lowered her voice, as if afraid of being overheard. "I'd be damned careful around Tom. He's—"

She broke off suddenly. Her face whitened.

"What?" Stevens said.

He read the fear in his mother's face, and turned to look behind him. Nobody there.

She shook her head. "Thought I heard something. Probably just the wind." The only other person around was Tom Norton. He'd made crude passes at her twice, and she'd rebuffed him without a second thought. She didn't relish the idea of being alone in this house, especially with Art away and Tom coming and going unannounced.

Stevens wiped his mouth, rose and put a hand on her shoulder. "Hey, would you like to come with me and see what we're up to? There's going to be a crew from the Discovery Channel shooting today. I'll make you a star, sweetheart. With your looks and my brains, we could go places." He leered mock-suggestively.

She managed a smile. "Thanks, but no. I wouldn't want to be underfoot. You'll have enough to do without keeping track of an old lady. I'll be fine."

As she spoke, they heard an engine nearby. A moment later, Tom Norton's Suburban rolled past the kitchen window, headed toward the ranch entrance. Barbara thought the occupant had been looking toward them when he drove past, but she couldn't be sure.

38

After Laura Jensen had gotten Jerry onto the school bus she had a second cup of coffee at the kitchen table. Her shift would start in an hour at eight. Jerry, a smart but trouble-prone boy, took after his Dad. Her parents were going to pick Jerry up at school and take him to their place for a rare over-night visit. The divorce had been messy. She seldom thought of her ex—had it really been two years? Jesus.

She was glad she'd talked with Brian McKay on the phone the previous day. She'd been worried and upset when she'd called but his calm professionalism gave her confidence. He didn't have blinders on. It wasn't him just trying to catch his niece's kidnapper—he obviously felt obligated to find William Old Horn's murderer as well. And he seemed to care about her. Brian was single and not that much older than herself. He'd be back, if only because of this damned case. Maybe they could go out somewhere. Maybe she could get her parents to let Jerry stay over again, and then Brian could come by and…she shook her head. Had to concentrate, decide what to do.

She'd been the only deputy in the bullpen when she'd called Brian yesterday. Later, with both the sheriff and Kelly out on another long lunch break, she'd sneaked into the sher-iff's office and gone through his papers. Strangely enough, there didn't seem to be a file on the Darcy McKay kidnapping case. Maybe Sam hadn't had time to set one up, but still…

And Kelly was a blabbermouth to the point of being a department liability. Laura used to wonder why Sam kept her on. There was an all-but-confirmed rumor the two of them were sleeping together, which Laura had suspected for some time. Had Kelly listened in on her conversation with Brian? God—all she needed was for Sam to get a replay. That would give him cause for firing her. Laura knew he wouldn't hesitate to do so. Where would she find another job in law enforcement? She'd have to move somewhere else, away from her aging parents, which she didn't want to do.

What would draw Sam and Tom Norton together? Norton had been a cop, but so what? As Sands's ramrod, he'd been Cody Gilstrap's supervisor. She'd have been willing to bet Gilstrap killed William Old Horn. He attacked Darcy at the same location. The FBI had searched the area, and so had she and Brian. What was there worth killing for? Laura played hide-and-seek on that parched hill as a girl. The old mineshaft kept coming to mind. Why? It dead-ended a few feet in. As she'd mentioned to Brian, she'd get back up there, see if there might be something going on there.

The front doorbell interrupted her reverie. Funny, most people around here knock, they don't ring the bell. Probably a salesman or a Jehovah's Witness, she thought.

Laura knotted her bathrobe belt before going to the door. A person she'd been thinking about stood on the threshold, expressionless. Without speaking, he pushed his way in.

"Hey, what do you think you're doing?" Laura yelled.

The man said, "Are you alone?"

She flushed with anger. "No. Johnny Depp's in the

275

kitchen. We were just having tea and cookies."

The intruder smiled mirthlessly. "You've got a mouth on you, I'll say that." He looked toward the hallway, listening. "I need to use the john," he said. Without waiting for her assent, he went to the hall and back toward the bathroom. He stuck his head in each room on the way to the bathroom in back. Laura followed him until he went into the bathroom and closed the door.

A few minutes later, he returned to the living room, where Laura stood by the still-open front door.

"Thanks for stopping by," she said. She held the door open and gestured the way out, like an usher in a theater.

The man walked deliberately to her, and slammed the door closed with her hand still on the knob. Without warning, he locked rough hands around her neck and threw her to the floor. He straddled her as she lay on her back and hit her in the mouth with a hard fist. Blood gushed from her lower lip. She struggled like a fish in a net, but the deadweight of her attacker pinned her to the carpet. When she tried to raise her arms, he batted them aside like a man opening a pathway through saplings. He hit her in the nose with a short punch, and more blood streamed out. He hauled back and, grunting with effort, struck her a third time, this one in the upper face. More blood, warm and insistent, ran into Laura's eyes, blinding her. She was on the verge of blacking out. She remembered her gun in the kitchen. Why hadn't she gotten it when he barged in? Now, it was too late.

Pain became a dull bludgeon, overwhelming, without the mercy of putting her under. For a split-second, her vision went black, then the man's bulky shape loomed again. She felt as helpless as a bug impaled on a pin. And yet she had to somehow get free, had to marshal her fading strength for a last struggle. She knew that she wouldn't live to see her son again, not unless she could fight off this animal. She forced herself to go limp, pantomimed exhaustion, surrender. The man picked her up and carried her into her bedroom.

For Brian, the puzzle pieces were starting to sort themselves by color and shape, although they weren't falling into place, not just yet. But he had some ammunition now. He picked up his phone and punched in Laura Jensen's cell number. No answer. He checked his e-mail. There was a message from Darcy.

"Last night after dinner, everybody hit the tents early," she wrote. "We've been working long hours the last few days, and even the nightly campfire get-together has turned into a pain. I couldn't sleep. The moon was full and it was like a floodlight was on outside the tent. Becky was snoring and I tossed and turned 'til after midnight. I got up and walked around outside for a while. Thought I heard voices off in the distance, but then I guessed it must have been coyotes. (There are tons of them around here. Some of them hang around so much, we've given them names.) Anyway, just as I was finally falling asleep, I heard a motor, like a bulldozer or tractor or something. It wasn't anything from the dig site, I know that. It was just for an instant, and then it was gone. Maybe I'm just hearing things. It's so quiet here, I'm looking forward to getting back to the city. I think it'll be easier to sleep in my apartment. And maybe my favorite uncle will treat me to an RD!"

Brian texted a quick reply to Darcy. He asked about her shoulder. He promised to spring for an RD if she'd follow his advice to stay with the group and keep healthy.

He tried Laura's phone again. No answer. He called her home number and got her recording. Then he tried the sheriff's office. The receptionist said that Laura wasn't in.

"Do you expect her today?"

"Well, I don't know what to tell you. I mean, she was supposed to be here at eight, but we haven't heard from her. Maybe she's taking a sick day."

"Huh. Well, please ask her to call me." Brian gave the receptionist his cell number.

What the hell was going on? Laura had sounded scared yesterday. In a rural county sheriff's office, it would no doubt be hard to keep secrets. Hell, it was damn near impossible to keep a secret in the Chicago FBI office. Maybe she'd stuck her neck out too far. How private had their phone conversation been yesterday? That receptionist didn't seem to have a whole lot of work to do. Would she listen in on the deputies' phone calls? Suddenly, he felt nervous, ready to get moving, anxious to start prying up rocks to see what was underneath. He logged onto Delta Airlines and booked a coach seat on the next flight to Bozeman, leaving in a couple of hours.

39

The flight was on time. Brian called Laura's cell phone again from the Bozeman airport with the same result—no answer. He rented a Ford Escape at the airport and made it to Laura's little house in Clarkville in record time. It was nearly dark, and the temperature had dropped into the fifties. He parked out front and made his way to the door.

He noticed Laura's pickup wasn't in the driveway. He rang the doorbell and waited. No response. He rang again, then rapped his knuckles sharply on the door. After a moment, he stepped off the porch and went around to the side of the house, stopping at the first window. He peered in at an old oak dining table and chairs. No sign of activity inside. He continued to the garage in back. Brian cupped his hands against the small window next to the door and looked into the gloom at Laura's pickup. He returned to the front of the house and tried the doorknob. It was unlocked, probably not unusual in a quiet small town neighborhood like this where, Laura had told him, everyone knew everyone else, and serious crime was generally something you watched on the evening news. He turned the knob and went in.

"Hello. Anybody home?" he shouted.

Dark red stains flecked the living room floor just inside the door. Brian's heart sank. He moved into the dining room, following a trail of smaller red splotches on the carpet. Continuing into the hallway, he could see lights in the kitchen. There were breakfast dishes on the kitchen table. Laura and Jerry had had cold cereal, and there was an opened loaf of cinnamon-raisin bread on the countertop next to a toaster. A mountain biking magazine had been left open by one of the place settings and a half-full mug of coffee was at the other.

Brian left the kitchen and made his way to the first room off the hallway. An unmade bed with rumpled covers occupied the room along with discarded clothes and a desk containing a computer and stacks of magazines and books. A *Hunger Games* poster dominated the wall adjacent to the bed. This was obviously Jerry's lair. Brian continued to the next room.

A fat black housefly drifted lazily from the master bedroom as he entered. He could hear birds singing through the screen in the south-facing window. An inexpensive land-scape print hung on the wall over the queen bed.

The body of Laura Jensen lay supine on the bed, clad only in a terrycloth bathrobe, open to her waist. He hardly recognized the battered red pulp that had once been her face. Her head lolled at an unnatural angle. The eyes were wide open and looked a darker blue than he'd remembered them. The mouth gaped. Blood drenched the pillow beneath her head. A long, thin horizontal slit extended from just beneath one ear and across the jugular area nearly to the other ear. Her throat had been slit. The flow of arterial blood had stanched some time ago. Her face had been battered and bruised with something blunt. There were livid bruises on her arms and chest. Her heels and the backs of her legs were a deep purplish-red, the result of pooling of blood in the lowermost parts.

The uniquely horrible smell of death—stale raw meat, metallic liquid and combined feces and urine—assaulted Brian's nose. He fought back a wave of nausea as he stepped away from the bed. He realized he'd been hyperventilating. Bent at the waist with his head between his legs, he took several deep breaths, until the urge to puke his guts out subsided.

After the initial shock, Brian stood alert for a moment, listening. Was he really alone in this house? No sounds but his own rasping breath. He scanned the room quickly, avoiding Laura's staring eyes. The eyes seemed to be imploring him: why hadn't he gotten there sooner? Why had he egged her on, pushing her until she'd become the target of a murderer?

Calling the law could wait. He needed some time to look around. He couldn't tell whether Laura had been sexually assaulted. He decided he didn't really want to know and gave it up. Gingerly, he grasped her nearest wrist and lifted it. The skin was cool to the touch and dry as bread crust. The arm was stiff and hard to move, indicating *rigor mortis* had been progressing for a while. He knew that rigor normally peaks within four to twelve hours. He quickly examined her fingernails. No sign of skin, cloth or anything else connected to fighting off the killer. He glanced at his watch. A little after five. Where was Jerry? School must have gotten out a couple of hours ago. Maybe the kid was riding his bike or over at a friend's house. If he'd come home and found his mom like this, what would he have done? Would he have called someone?

No clues sprang up and slapped him in the face. He'd seen victims of lethal violence before, but never anyone he knew or cared about. He discovered he cared more than a little for Laura Jensen.

Brian wondered where Jerry was. In a little while, the boy's world would be shattered, if it hadn't been, already. Good people would cry, wonder why. How could this happen here? To such a nice person? Anger began to build jet-like. People had a habit of getting hurt and killed around him. Why did he have to be the one to find her? He felt the leaden weight of guilt. Why hadn't they come after him instead?

Enough self-pity. Time to act like a professional, to get to work. Spots of ferrous blood, nearly dry now, dappled the bedroom floor. The spatters made an irregular line nearly all the way to the front door. He tried to reconstruct how it went down. She'd answered the door, been struck in the head just inside, struggled, been beaten to the floor, probably pounded some more as she struggled to survive. Then the attacker had carried her into the bedroom, dumped her on the bed and—this was getting him nowhere. He got down on hands and knees and examined the pooled blood more closely. The sharp outline of a partial shoe print was just barely visible on the edge of the largest bloodstain. Since Laura was barefoot, the murderer must have stepped in her blood. It looked like the impression of a wide, smooth sole, possibly from a man's causal shoe. Jesus Christ—had he made the rookie mistake of stepping in the blood in his rush to see if there were signs of life? He examined the soles of both shoes—clean, thank God.

He prowled around for a few more minutes, found nothing more. He sighed, got his phone and dialed the Clarkville police department. He then went out the front door and took a seat on the steps leading up to the porch.

Brian knew well that people who find corpses are in for, at a minimum, a severe bout of questioning from the local authorities. And he'd been, technically at least, trespassing in another's home. He could even expect to be charged with murder. He had no qualms. Sticking around and doing his duty wasn't too much to ask. He knew deep in his gut that Laura Jensen had put her safety on the line, at least in part, at his direction. And he'd failed her. He balled his fists in frustration.

Five minutes later, a white Clarkville police car with flashing blue lights pulled into the driveway. Brian rose from his perch on the front steps as a pair of young uniforms got out and started toward him. The one in front rested a meaty hand on the butt of his holstered revolver.

Brian kept his hands in view and stood slowly as the policemen approached.

"I'm the one called it in," he said. "I'm going to get my wallet out to show you ID."

"Okay," the first policeman said. They waited nervously while Brian extracted his wallet. He handed the license to the cop who'd spoken, while noting the name on his badge, Oates. The other cop's badge displayed the name Johnson.

"Chicago, eh? You're a long way from home, aren't you, Mr. McKay?" Oates said. He tucked the license into a breast pocket. "Let's all go inside."

Oates led the way into the house, with Brian in the middle and Johnson bringing up the rear. Oates hesitated when he caught sight of the blood spots on the carpet in the living room. Brian was encouraged by the fact that the officers seemed to avoid stepping in the blood. He waited outside the bedroom door while the two cops peered in.

"Holy shit," Johnson said, his face pale as bleached cotton. Brian guessed the young cop had never seen a murder victim before. It was a scene he'd remember the rest of his life. Hell, all three of them would.

Oates, affecting world-weariness, approached the corpse, checked for a pulse and grunted affirmation when he found none. He turned to his colleague and said, "Go ahead and call Newhouse. Tell him we got a white female, about thirty, victim of a knife wound. Give him the address and tell him we're here with Mr. uh, McKay. Oh, and take this and check it out." He handed Brian's license to Johnson, who left to carry out his orders.

"Mr. McKay, while we're waiting, how about running this down for me, starting with how you happened to be here," Oates said. He stepped out of the bedroom and stood next to Brian in the hall. His right hand never strayed more than an inch from the butt of his Smith & Wesson, and he kept his bulk between Brian and the front entrance.

"Okay. The deceased is Laura Jensen, a deputy with the Geyser County Sheriff's Department. I'm ex-FBI, Chicago. Ms. Jensen was working on the investigation of the kidnapping of my niece from the Bone Mountain dinosaur dig."

"Oh yeah. I heard about that. Your niece came back, right?"

"Yes."

"So what are you doing here?"

"I've been discussing the case with Laura—Ms. Jensen—who's been trying to track down the kidnapper. I believe the abduction is related to the homicide of William Old Horn over a year ago at the same site."

"Okay, but what are you doing in her house?"

"I talked with her on the phone yesterday about the investigation. I was in Chicago at the time. We traded information. This morning, I tried calling her at the office, and they said she hadn't shown up or called in. I called her home phone and cell, too. Nothing. I was kind of worried about her, and was planning on coming to Clarkville anyway, so I got on a plane to Bozeman. I arrived here about thirty minutes ago."

"You just hopped on a plane and flew all the way to Montana? Just like that?" He snapped his fingers. "And you say you entered the premises half an hour ago?"

"Well, actually a few minutes more than that. First, I rang the bell a couple of times and then I knocked. Nothing. So I checked the garage, saw her truck inside. Then I tried the front door knob and found it unlocked. I thought maybe she was ill or something. I pushed the door open and called out. When there was no answer, I went in. I found her just as you see her."

There was sudden commotion in the front room. A few seconds later, a big red-faced man of about fifty joined them.

Oates turned to the new arrival and said, "Sir, Mr. McKay here found the body. He was just explaining how he happened on the scene."

"That's nice. Have you frisked him?"

"Well, no, I—"

"Do it. Now." Detective Newhouse's tone was matter-of-fact, like a man requesting a tablemate to pass him the salt.

Oates beckoned Brian into the dining room. Johnson joined them and Oates patted Brian down.

Newhouse's voice came from the bedroom: "Mirandize him."

285

Oates drew a three by five card from his wallet and began to read, "You have the right to remain silent. Anything you say can and will be used against you..." He labored through the reading of rights as if reciting from a textbook.

"You guys going to interrogate me?" Brian asked.

"Not us. Him. Oates nodded toward the bedroom, where they could hear Newhouse moving around.

"McKay, come in here, please," Newhouse called. "And watch where you step."

Brian joined the detective, who stood next to the bed, carefully avoiding the copious bloodstains on the floor.

"Turn around and lift your feet one at a time, so I can see the soles."

Brian complied.

"Okay. You know what I think? I think you need to make a statement."

"I'll be happy to. I'm on your side." Brian considered clamming up and getting a lawyer, but that would waste valuable time. He wanted the son of a bitch who'd killed Laura, and he was willing to help the police any way he could. What could he possibly fear from an investigation, anyway? He gave Newhouse the short version of how he happened to be there, his finding the blood, which led him to the body and calling the Clarkville police department.

"Did you touch anything?"

"I checked for a pulse—neck and wrist. That's it."

"That's how you got the blood on your fingertips?"

Involuntarily, Brian looked down at his right hand. There was a dried red substance the color of spilled wine on the pads of his right forefinger and thumb.

"Yes, it must be."

"Any idea who did this?"

Brian summarized his two conversations with Laura the previous day. "I think she believed her working on these cases—the murder of Old Horn and the kidnapping of my niece—somehow put her in danger. My impression was she didn't trust the sheriff to investigate the cases. She said he told the deputies to stop working on them."

"You're accusing Sam Harrison of this?" Newhouse cut his eyes toward the corpse.

"No, I'm not. There's another guy I like for it." Brian explained Cody Gilstrap's abduction of Darcy and the likelihood he'd killed William Old Horn.

"You're saying you think Gilstrap did her, then." Newhouse said.

"I don't know. Are you going to gather evidence here?"

"You don't need to worry about us. We're hicks, of course, but we do have a competent ET. He's on the way."

"Am I going to be booked?"

"We'll see. You're gonna come to the station and we'll talk some more, and I'll get your statement on record. Understand?"

"Fine by me."

The evidence technician, a tall guy with a permanent expression of amusement, arrived and conferred with Newhouse, while Brian waited silently in the dining room with the two uniforms. A few minutes later, Newhouse reappeared. He shepherded Brian out the door and into the back seat of a well-used black Chevy Impala sedan, which he drove to the Clarkville police station. During the short ride, Brian mentioned Jerry and expressed concern as to his whereabouts. Newhouse just grunted.

40

When Brian woke up the next morning, his brain felt too big for his head. He looked at his watch on the nightstand. Seven a.m. They'd cut him loose around midnight. He'd picked up his rental car at Laura's and made it to the hotel around one. The air was warm and stale in the room. He got up, went into the bathroom, emptied his bladder and downed a couple of aspirin. In a few minutes he began to feel a little better.

In the shower, he ruminated about the night before. After a while, Newhouse had seemed to believe him. Like all good cops, he'd been skeptical at first. He called John Elgar at home to check out Brian's FBI background. This had brought a grim smile to Brian's face—he could imagine Elgar's irritation at being disturbed at his residence in the middle of the night for law enforcement business. On the other hand, the SAC would have finally gotten his long sought-after first-hand report on Brian's activities in Montana.

Newhouse dragged Brian through the sequence of events at Laura's house over and over, seemingly ready to pounce on any inconsistency. The detective was especially interested in Brian's last phone conversation with Laura. After several hours, Newhouse became almost human. He pumped Brian for information related to the Darcy kidnapping, apparently believing, as did Brian, the murder of Laura Jensen was somehow related. The evidence technician, who, it turned out, worked for both the town police and the county sheriff's department, returned from Laura's house and sat in on the interrogation for a while.

Brian asked if they'd found the murder weapon, but they wouldn't tell him, which he took to mean they hadn't. After Brian had asked about Jerry Jensen several times, Newhouse let him know they'd tracked down Laura's son at her parents' house, where he'd gone after school. The boy went to his grandparents' place occasionally after classes. The older couple would keep the boy there indefinitely. A county social worker had been dispatched to provide counseling.

Brian felt dejected. Even if the police were to look into Laura's suspicions about the sheriff dragging his heels, it probably wouldn't go anywhere. Harrison was smart enough to deflect them. He wondered why Harrison had apparently not checked on Laura when she didn't show up for work the day before. And Brian's dislike of Tom Norton wasn't a reason to arrest him. Maybe Gilstrap had switched from gun to knife.

Brian got dressed and went down to the hotel lobby, where he picked up the slim local newspaper. A front-page story from the day before caught his eye: "Local Men Leave Twelve Deer to Rot on Road." An account followed about the court trial the day before of a pair of brothers named Shane and Donny Gruel. Brian recognized the names—Laura Jensen had mentioned they were employees at the Sands ranch. They'd been fined $2,400 for illegally shooting twelve deer and leaving the carcasses to rot along a rural road north of

Clarkville. The two were described as 25 and 22, respectively. They'd been cited the previous fall for hunting without permission on private land. This time, they were guilty of hunting during a closed season and abandoning game animals in the field.

Game warden Monte Redding said the Gruels shot the deer at night from a pickup truck with .30-06 rifles after shining them with a hand-held spotlight. Redding said he'd driven toward the sound of shots and then followed a trail of beer cans to the brothers. He remarked, "This is one of the biggest wastes of wildlife I've seen in my eighteen years on the job." Donny Gruel's explanation: "We just started out shooting a few rabbits, but we must've got carried away, 'cause it escalated to deer."

41

Tom Norton parked next to a new log building with a green metal roof and an oversized rock chimney. He rapped his knuckles on the door while trying the knob. Inside, Hank Crawford staggered across the floor naked, wiping sleep from his eyes. The intrusion frosted his ass—a man works nights should be able to catch a few zees during the god-damned day. He noticed the doorknob turning slightly, and was damn glad he'd locked it.

"C'mon, c'mon, let's go," Norton yelled.

"Hold your horses," Crawford mumbled, as he pulled on a pair of purple warm-up pants with white stripes on the outside seams. He scratched the hairless crown of his head, reached a callused hand back to make sure his gray ponytail had been banded together.

As soon as the door was open, Norton pushed his way in, almost knocking Crawford off his feet. "When are you guys gonna be done?"

"Don't waste time on small talk, do you?" Crawford said.

"Fuck that." A flush crept up Norton's face. He poked a stiff finger into Crawford's chest. "The shit's about to hit the fan, unless we get those bones the fuck out of there. Now, what's your ETA?"

Crawford's eyes flitted to the door, back to Norton's iron gaze. His thin mustache twitched nervously like a worm suddenly exposed by a gardener's shovel. He tried for a placating tone. "Hey chill, man. We're doing good. We have a productive time tonight, it's a wrap tomorrow night."

"Good. Where do we stand on plastering?"

"Got everything done that's come out. Plus, we've got some loose bones we're just gonna wrap in newspaper and transport in boxes."

"I thought you said we had to do 'em all, even though they're not going that far."

"Yeah, the vibrations from the chopper and moving them around could turn the punky bones to dust, we're not careful. But I sorted through—a lot of them are protected enough to move wrapped in paper. Don't worry, I know my job."

"You damn well better."

"Speaking of the chopper, is it all set up?" Crawford asked.

"Yep, paid my guy today. He'll have the bird gassed, signed out and ready to go. You'll pick it up at hangar ten, just like we saw when we were up there the other day. You're sure you can fly the thing?"

Crawford looked offended. "No problem. I flew one a lot like it in Iraq with ragheads firing AK-47s at me. This'll be cake compared to that."

"Okay. What's left in the ground?"

"Just part of the neck. We're having a hell of a time getting it out without pulverizing it. There's bone hash all over the place, and I don't want to make more of it."

"Don't waste a lot of time on it. Whatever's missing,

293

you can make up out of sawdust and glue—that's what you guys do half the time anyway, isn't it?"

"Well, sometimes you have to use fillers," Crawford admitted.

"People are starting to talk, saying they hear noises up there at night," Norton said.

"Where'd you get that?"

"Harrison says a local yokel driving by mentioned it to a deputy. You know how nosy they are around here. Some explorer-type is gonna start lookin' around, sure as shit."

"After that girl got shot? You think so?"

A muscle twitched in Norton's out-thrust jaw. "Yeah, I do. The girl prob'ly saw the shit you worked on in the equipment warehouse—she was in there all last Friday night. Plus her uncle, that ex-FBI asshole, is still dicking around, trying to find out what's happening. We don't get the bones out soon, we're gonna get taken out our fucking selves. You follow?"

"Yeah, sure, Tom, if you say so."

"You guys start earlier tonight. Get going while it's still light, and plan on keeping at it hot and heavy till dawn."

"Christ, my ass is already dragging."

"Work those two douche bag brothers harder, then."

Crawford rolled his eyes. "I'll try. Man, those guys'd fuck up a wet dream. I paid their goddamned poaching fine out of my own money, you know. They'll never pay it back."

"I'll add it to your share."

"You realize, of course, those jerks are gonna talk when this is over. If not before."

"Don't worry. I'll take care of that. You don't have to

tell me *my* goddamn business, either. Hey, the old Indian didn't talk, did he?"

Crawford looked into those flat eyes and shuddered inwardly. He scratched the stubble on his chin. "Well, that's your department. I'm just a bone doctor here."

"Fine. Get this operation done and everything will be copacetic. We understand each other?"

Crawford nodded. "Yeah, sure, Tom."

Norton formed a pistol with a thumb and index finger, pointed it at the smaller man and made an explosion noise with his mouth. "Catch you later."

42

Brian stood across from Sam Harrison, the sheriff sitting at his desk with his arms crossed—a classic defensive posture.

"Have you guys got anything on Laura's murder?" Brian asked. "Any little thing at all?"

"The Clarkville police are in charge," Harrison said. "That happens to be in their jurisdiction. Newhouse knows what he's doing. Tell you the truth, we're doing what we can to cooperate, but—"

"What—you can't squeeze it into your overworked, understaffed schedule?" Brian had run out of patience.

"They'll collar the son of a bitch who killed her, you can rest assured," Harrison said.

"Are you serious? Someone guts one of your deputies in her house, and you say the police will take care of it? What kind of a law enforcement officer are you? Or do you just not give a damn about Laura?"

Harrison reddened. "What's that supposed to mean?"

"I don't have a lot of confidence in you, Sheriff."

"Look, winning your confidence ain't exactly at the top of my list. The voters elected me to do a job. In fact, maybe I could get it done a little better if you'd stay the hell out of my hair."

"What kind of job have you done on Darcy's abduction? The Old Horn killing? A big pile of nothing. That's county jurisdiction, meaning you guys, not the Clarkville police. Looks to me like you're oh for two and about ready to strike out."

Harrison's face bunched like a fist. "That's enough out of you." He stood and jabbed a forefinger at Brian. "We did a proper investigation of that problem with your niece. Gilstrap's disappeared into thin air. We did all we could with Old Horn at the time. And we're not giving up on Laura, though, like I said, our buddies down the hall are riding point on that one. Maybe you should go bother them. Unless you got something we can use, I don't have time to jaw with you."

"Laura told me you were lax on the Old Horn case. With Darcy, you said the slug was banged up, but turned out it was in good shape. And you didn't even send it in for testing—Laura had to get the damned thing out of your desk drawer and send it. Plus, you didn't find the damned shell lying on the ground—I had to do *that* for you. You say you've got no idea what the motive would be for somebody shooting two different people at the same damned location on Bone Mountain. You call this law enforcement? Bullshit."

A muscle throbbed in Harrison's neck. "Hey, McKay, the almighty FBI hasn't found anything, either. Are they deadbeats, too?"

Brian shook his head in disgust. "Okay, Sheriff. I'll get out of your hair. Have a good life."

As Brian stalked out of the office, Harrison tossed at him, "Let us know us when you get it all figured out, hotshot."

297

Brian called Bill Thorsten in Bozeman. After a moment, the agent picked up.

Brian got to the point quickly. "Bill, are you still working my niece's abduction?"

"Uh, well I'm the case agent, but I'm on some other things at the moment."

"What about Old Horn?"

"That one's still open, naturally, but there's nothing active."

"A sheriff's deputy was killed here yesterday—Laura Jensen. She's the one who—"

"Yes, I know, Clarkville PD has promised to keep me informed. What's your involvement?"

Brian gave him a recap of his conversations with Laura the day before she was killed, his finding the body the previous night and his experience with the Clarkville police as well as Harrison.

"Seems like it's got to be connected to the other two incidents," Thorsten said.

"The way I read it, too. Aren't you going to investigate? Supplement what the locals are doing?"

"May be difficult. Morgan doesn't see any of this stuff as *numero uno* for me."

"Why's that, you suppose?"

"Just between us girls, he says Chicago gave him the word to back off. Plus, he's got me doing an admin project related to case load stats in the SLC region. Far be it from me to understand the ways of the muck-a-mucks. You know how it is, Brian."

"Yeah, but since when does Chicago give orders to

Salt Lake? Must have been one hell of a reorganization in the few days since I left the bureau."

"Hey, I sympathize," Thorsten said. "Gilstrap's the obvious suspect for all three, but there's more to it, the way I see it. Someone was pulling his strings, maybe still is."

"Right. Who's his boss? Norton. And Sands."

"True. The police talked to them. But those boys aren't dumb enough to implicate themselves, and there's no evidence linking them."

"What did you guys find on Bone Mountain?" Brian said.

"Same as you, I guess. Not much."

"What about the mineshaft?"

"Nothing but a little half-assed tunnel, dead-ending after a few yards. Morgan made me crawl in with a flashlight. Only thing in there besides monster spiders was mouse turds and a couplea empty Richard's Wild Irish Rose bottles."

"You think there could possibly be gold left to be mined? Is that maybe what this is about?"

"I looked into that. The mine closed ninety years ago, a small operation that didn't yield a whole lot. Nobody's filed a claim anywhere around there since. Of course, that doesn't mean people haven't looked. The sheriff volunteered this stuff, and the records backed it up."

"When I talked with Laura that last time, she said she thought the entrance to the mine tunnel might have been somehow changed."

"But she didn't bring it up when you two went up there together?"

"No. Anyway, I'm going to take another look."

"How about letting me know how it comes out?"

ROBERT D. HUGHES

"Okay. You know, my impression is Laura Jensen knew something, or at least, someone thought she did. She sounded scared in that last phone conversation. Said the sheriff and Tom Norton were hanging together. Since Norton was Gilstrap's boss, and he's an all-around asshole, I'm taking another shot at him."

"For what it's worth, my take on the sheriff is he's an okay guy but he's lazy. He'd just as soon let us clean this mess up and let him take credit in the eyes of the voters. Norton, I don't know. But, he's a hard-ass, for sure."

"Hey, would you like to join me on my little expedition?"

"Nah, just let me know if you come up with anything I can use. I could get involved pronto, you gave me an excuse."

Brian decided to cruise out to the Sands ranch to rattle Norton's cage, maybe meet Crawford, the geologist, see what he was working on. As he cleared the town limits and headed north, rain began to come down. The Crazy Mountains, shrouded in mist, looked like rotund, pointy-headed monks in gray robes. Bright yellow slashes of lightning streaked the darkening sky. The wind picked up and rain pelted down so fast, the windshield wipers could barely keep up. Brian suspected Darcy and her cohorts were racing for cover at the dig site. The Doors were on the radio, doing "Riders on the Storm," which seemed appropriate.

He parked near the main house, ran to the shelter of the roof over the main entryway. In response to his knock, an attractive blonde woman of about fifty pulled the door open. She looked familiar, but he couldn't place her.

The woman smiled uncertainly. "Hi. Help you?"

Brian identified himself and asked to speak with Arthur Sands. Might as well start at the top.

"He's still in Chicago, but I'm expecting him to call. Would you like to leave a message?"

Suddenly he knew why the woman looked familiar. James had mentioned that Scott Stevens' mother was Sands's ex and that she lived on his ranch. "Are you related to Scott Stevens, by any chance? Sister, maybe?"

The woman smiled. "Aren't you kind. Actually, I'm his mother. Barbara Hardy."

"I'm the uncle of the young woman who was kidnapped on Bone Mountain—Darcy McKay."

"Oh, yeah. Art mentioned he gave you a tour. You're from Chicago, right?"

"Right."

"I heard the girl—your niece—was found. I sure hope she's doing okay."

"Yeah, she's back working for your son up there." He nodded in the direction of Bone Mountain. "But I'd still like to track down the character who abducted her, guy name of Cody Gilstrap."

A trace of wariness clouded her frank eyes. "I never met the man, but well, good luck to you."

"Is Tom Norton around?"

She averted her eyes, took a deep breath. "I think he went to his cabin."

"Could you tell me how to find it?"

"Sure. Take this road to the first junction, and make a right. Go about another three-quarters of a mile. It's a log building, kind of new-looking."

"Thanks a lot, then."

Barbara flashed a smile. "Why don't you stop by and have something cool to drink on your way out. I'm almost done with my bookkeeping work, and I always enjoy chatting with a fellow Chicagoan. I mean, if you've got the time."

"Sounds good. See you in a while."

Brian followed Barbara's directions to the cabin in the trees. Dark gray clouds blocked out the sun. The tall aspens and pines lining the road swayed in the quickening wind. As he reached the log building, raindrops the size of ripe grapes began to spatter the windshield. Brian grabbed the Montana road map on the car seat and used it as an umbrella as he dashed to the building.

There was no response to his repeated knocking, so he tried the door handle. Locked. Holding the map over his head, he went around to the side. By staying under the overhanging eave, he was able to keep mostly dry. Thunder cracked, and he looked toward the mountains in time to see a jagged lightning streak knife through the sky behind the high peaks.

He turned his attention to the first window he came to and peered inside. A ceiling fixture illuminated a masculine office with an L-shaped desk, a computer and a wall of shelves containing a few books, stacks of magazines and papers and an ancient-looking red clay pot.

Brian's heartbeat quickened. The bulbous pot was slightly larger than a two-liter pop bottle, but with a wide top opening. The exterior was a faded orange and deeply cracked. Apparently, someone had found the thing in fragments and glued them together. It reminded Brian of the pottery scraps Russell Eagle Feather had given him, but this pot was unlike any he'd ever seen. It had a skull carved into the side, the skull of a monster. He thought of Godzilla terrorizing Tokyo. Why would someone mess up an old pot by tacking on a monster face? Maybe it was a gag gift from a souvenir shop. But then, Godzilla was based on *T. rex*. The face could be a crude depiction of a *T. rex* skull. Could the pot be old? Could the dinosaur face be original equipment?

He returned to the Escape, got his camera and retraced his steps to the window, ignoring the rain. He screwed a polarizing filter to the end of the 80-200 millimeter telephoto zoom lens to cut through the reflection from the windowpane. He zoomed in and focused on the pot and took a couple of frame-filling shots. As he was about to turn away, he noticed a series of lines carved into the lower part of the clay vessel. He stretched his neck to get a better view. The lines could be a crude map, like one drawn in mud with a stick. He took another tight shot, focusing on the lines.

Brian returned to the ranch house, where Barbara Hardy greeted him with a fleeting smile. She had be lonely, spending time by herself in this big place. He accepted a beer. She fixed herself a vodka tonic, mostly vodka, in a tall glass. They sat in the front room overlooking the small man-made lake out front. Ducks and geese paddled about in the water, feeding and engaging in noisy territorial disputes accompanied by energetic wing flapping.

"Any idea where Hank Crawford is?" Brian asked.

"Sorry, no."

"What about those other guys, the Gruel brothers?"

"I haven't the foggiest. The staff all stay in their own cabins and I don't have much to do with them."

"What do Norton and his guys spend their time on these days?"

"Well, I only hear bits and pieces, but I think he's supervising them on some night project, God knows what. I wouldn't feel...comfortable asking Tom about it. He's very private. I did ask Art the other day, and he said there's nothing special going on that he's aware of. I think he keeps out of Tom's way, lets him run his own show."

"Look, sorry to be such an inquisitor, but have you seen or heard any activity on Bone Mountain at night?"

"Activity? No. Why?" She looked puzzled.

"Just trying to be thorough. I'm still on the trail of that bastard who shot my niece, and it happened up there."

Barbara took a healthy swig from her glass. Brian noticed her face had become slightly flushed and a thin mist of perspiration had formed above her upper lip. He guessed this was not her first drink of the afternoon.

"You know I'd like to help," she said, carefully. She appeared to be having trouble making the consonants come out right. "I read about that sheriff's deputy, that Laura Jensen being killed. This place is beginning to remind me of Chicago—kidnappings, shootings, murders. What's next?" She shuddered.

"A little smaller scale here, but yeah, I know what you mean," Brian said.

"I worry about Scott and his workers. I'll be glad when the dig is over."

"We've got something in common. I'll feel a whole lot better when Darcy's out of there, too."

"She's pretty brave to stick around after what happened."

"Tell me about it."

304

"Scott says there may be more dinosaur bones up there." She looked out the window in the general direction of Bone Mountain.

"I wouldn't be surprised," Brian said. "From the little I know about that stuff, they tend to find clusters of bones all in one place."

"Are you staying around for a while, then?

"Until I get some results. What about you? Will you go back to Chicago with Scott?"

"Yes, I live there, actually."

"I'm a little puzzled about one thing. How come Scott's last name is Stevens?"

"That was my first husband's name."

"Oh. So Art's his step-father."

"Yes."

"By the way, do you know what Cody Gilstrap's job was here?"

"Not really. Art or Tom could tell you more."

"Have you met an FBI agent named John Elgar, by any chance?"

"Sure. He and Art go way back. Why?"

"Elgar used to be my boss. I'd heard he knew your ex."

Barbara drained the last of her drink. "How about another?" She reached for Brian's empty bottle, her fingers grazing his on the glass surface. She smiled at him, a little brightly.

"Hey, I'd like to, but I've got to take care of some business."

Brian got up and Barbara walked him to the door.

"Drop in again," she said.

"I will. Thanks."

As Brian started the Escape, he glanced back at the log home. Barbara Hardy, framed in the doorway, lifted a hand in a languid wave as he backed out.

43

Brian took the Interstate past Clarkville and continued west another ten miles. As he drove, he mused about the Sands-Elgar relationship. Elgar might be a pompous suit, but dirty? Not likely—it just didn't fit. So...if he were helping Sands somehow, perhaps Elgar thought it was all legit. What if Sands had something on Elgar, a lever of some kind? He'd have to find out.

The rain had let up and the sun was breaking through the late afternoon clouds. He kept the side window cracked as he drove, allowing the sweet, rain-washed mountain air in. He took an exit with a sign reading, WEST END NO SERVICES. The only buildings in view were a green doublewide and a large one-story galvanized steel building. GUNS GALORE had been painted on all sides of the structure in huge black letters clearly visible from the highway. A white ambulance with orange lettering was just leaving the parking lot as Brian pulled in. He left the Escape near the building's door and entered.

A burly, bearded man in a swivel chair behind a counter looked up from his magazine when Brian came in. He sported a dirty white ball cap with the inscription "Old Town Tavern" and a picture of a mule on the front. The breast pocket of his shirt bore the name, "Dale."

"Help you?" he said.

"I noticed an ambulance leaving as I came in. Trouble?

"Nah, just a customer, paramedic out of Bozeman."

"Well anyway, I need a handgun," Brian said.

"You've came to the right place. I've got a good selection and the best prices in town."

Town? What town? "Good. I'm thinking in terms of a semi-auto, possibly a Sig Sauer."

"I've got a nice P226. That work for ya?"

"Let me take a look."

Dale unlocked a case behind him and extracted an angular black pistol with checkered grips. He set it on the counter in front of Brian. "This baby was owned by a guy in law enforcement. You can see it's in great shape, hardly ever used. Fires standard nines."

Brian picked up the weapon, worked the slide, clicked out the ten-shot magazine and replaced it. He aimed the gun toward the doorway, homing in on the door handle with the little front blade atop the barrel lined up in the rear notch site. The gun felt right in his hand, a lot like his personal P228 stolen from his apartment in Chicago, the one he'd had during his entire FBI career. This one had a slightly longer barrel and weighed just a touch more. Carrying a handgun is a very personal thing. To some, it makes a statement: don't mess with me; to others it's a security blanket. To Brian, it was simply a tool, like a carpenter's level—nothing more, nothing less. "Mind if I fire a few rounds?" he asked.

"Hell, any guy didn't would be damn careless. C'mon." Dale led Brian out a door in back.

A firing range had been set up outside the gun shop, facing away from the highway. Dale hung two dark man-shaped silhouette targets about fifty feet from the firing station. Each target was divided into sections with white lines. The sections were numbered one through ten. The head and central trunk were tens, and the numbers dropped down for the less vital areas of the body. The outside edges of the shoulders and the hips came in at two.

Dale handed Brian a pair of sound-dampening ear-muffs and a package of ammunition, then stepped back and donned muffs himself. Brian loaded the magazine, locked it home and went into a two-handed stance facing the target on the left. He slowly squeezed off five shots, lowered the pistol and moved to his right a few feet. He fired the second set more quickly at the next target. With the last few shots, a bit of the old feeling came back, the sense of the gun as extension of hand.

The proprietor removed his earmuffs and went out to fetch the targets. He plucked them from their hangers easily, like a man who'd done it thousands of times. He lined the targets up on the shooting counter in front of Brian. "Looks like you were a little rusty on the first batch. Nice tight grouping on the second. What are you planning to shoot?"

"I don't know...yet."

Brian purchased the gun for $500 cash after filling out the required paperwork. Easier than buying a car, he mused. But then, a car in the hands of the wrong person was just as deadly a weapon. Hell, even more so. He wasn't impressed with the driving skills of the locals here, but their errors tended to be of a sloppy or careless nature, rather than the rabid aggressiveness all too common on Chicago streets. He appreciated Montana's lack of a sales tax, too—in Chicago, tax would have added another fifty bucks or so. Dale threw in a small leather belt slide for carrying and a fresh box of nine-millimeter ammo.

Back in Clarkville, Brian ate a candy bar, picked up a few supplies and returned to the Masters for a nap. He wanted to be well-rested for the evening's activities.

44

Brian was up by six p.m., took a quick shower and got dressed. He couldn't stop thinking about the dubious characters working for Art Sands. The names and faces kept playing in his mind like an old hit song you'd rather forget, but can't—like that one about piña coladas and being caught in the rain. Gilstrap certainly hadn't been acting on his own when he kidnapped Darcy—or could he? Norton had been a bad cop, and he'd probably tossed Brian's apartment. He'd been reluctant to go to the warehouse to unlock it and let Darcy out—why? The Gruels might be lowlifes, but there were no laws against it. He needed to invade their territory, shake something loose. He'd been tense, worried, looking for a phantom kidnapper, a ghostly killer. But something would pop soon, he somehow knew. Suddenly, he needed to feel the burn of whiskey in his throat.

He took the stairs down to the popular Murray's Hideout just off the hotel lobby. A sign on the swinging doors advertised live entertainment starting at nine—a rock n' roll band called Juno and the Paycocks. Happy hour was in full swing. After-work singles ranging in age from early twenties on up occupied barstools. Most drank draft beer; a few worked on hard drinks. A noisy pool game involving two men and two women as well as kibitzers of both sexes was in process. When somebody made a shot, cheers erupted. Raspberries and boos greeted misses. Brian flagged down the bartender and ordered a bourbon rocks.

He sipped from his glass standing with his back to the bar, watching the pool match idly. He scanned the place, half-hoping to spot somebody from Sands's empire. No familiar faces. He ambled out to the lobby and carried the drink upstairs to his room. He sat in the only chair, facing out the window toward Main Street, and slowly sipped. The alcohol melted into his veins like mountain snow in the hot sun. He'd only have the one. Had to stay sharp.

Traffic was light in the street below. Most of the vehicles passing by were four-wheel-drive pickups, SUVs or crossover wagons. Brian felt a pang of loneliness. He wondered what it would be like to live in a town like Clarkville. He decided it would make a good base camp for playing in the mountains, but it would be tough to earn a living and difficult for an urban guy like himself to adjust. The people were friendly enough, but he knew he'd miss the amenities of Chicago—the restaurants, the blues bars, world-class architecture, pro sports teams, Lake Michigan. Plus, this country, though beautiful, was dry as a bone. The trees and flowers one took for granted in the Midwest couldn't make it here. Sagebrush, junipers and grasses ruled the countryside. Hardwood trees seemed to be about as common as chicken lips.

Though he'd managed to save a few bucks, he'd need some source of regular income, and soon. One possibility to cut his living expenses would be to move in with Michelle. She'd probably go along with it, and his love life would improve. Nah—they'd drive each other nuts before long. He was beginning to get comfortable with the idea of setting up a private investigation practice in the city. Most places, starting a PI business would be iffy. In Chicago, with its steady economy and unlimited supply of criminals large and small-time, the business could be profitable, especially for an experienced ex-FBI agent. There'd be a few former colleagues who'd refer business his way. James could tap into FBI information for him, but not too often—he didn't want to derail the young agent's career. Brian's dorm roommate from his freshman year at Michigan was now an area commander in the Bureau of Detectives in the Chicago Police Department. He'd have an inside track with local law enforcement.

Brian opened the map he'd gotten during the ranch tour the previous Saturday. He studied it carefully, noting the location of the various features in relation to the headquarters complex. With a ballpoint, he marked the building where he'd found Darcy and the nearby gate in the electric fence along the western border. He felt a pang of guilt at the thought of Darcy—he needed to enlist her help tonight. He tried to memorize as much of the map as possible, especially the location of gates in the perimeter fence and the few scattered buildings.

The sun would be down in less than an hour. Darcy and the group had probably knocked off for the day at Bone Mountain. Brian folded the map and called her cell.

"Hey, Babe, are you up for an excursion?" he asked.

"Sure. Where we going?"

"One of your favorite places, the Sands ranch."

"What's happening there?"

"That's what I'd like to find out. By the way, this is an unannounced visit."

"Cool. When?"

"How's an hour from now?"

"Awesome. I'll grab a bite and be waiting for you near the HQ tent."

Brian ate a bag of potato chips and a candy bar, watching TV. A well-coifed anchor was reading copy about the drought in the western states, particularly Montana. Local farmers and ranchers were concerned they'd lose a big chunk of their crops—hay, winter wheat and barley—unless the rain began to catch up soon.

Brian loaded the magazine of the Sig Sauer, made sure the safety was on. He cinched a black leather belt around his waist and worked the slide carrier onto it within easy reach on his right hip. He slipped the gun into the slide and practiced drawing a few times. He wore his shirt with the tail out—it was just long enough to hide the gun. He stuffed the Sands ranch map, a small flashlight and a nylon pouch containing slender steel lock pick tools in a pocket. He went to the hotel garage, got the rental and eased onto the street.

Darcy was waiting for him at the parking area near the large administrative teepee. Flames leapt from a campfire out front. Dig workers ringed it, sipping beer from cans. Through the open driver's side window, Brian could hear somebody strumming a guitar and singing the Beatles' "Across the Universe." Darcy got into the Escape, leaned across and pecked Brian on the cheek. She wore a black short-sleeved tee shirt, blue jeans and hiking boots.

"We look like twins," she said.

"Great minds, and all that. We'd best try for inconspicuous. There could be watchers. They've got sensors out there but I've got a pretty good idea of where they are and how they work."

Brian levered the car into drive and they rolled slowly down the bumpy dirt road.

"What are we looking for?"

"I'd like to check out that plastered bundle you saw in the warehouse. Also, maybe take a look at the room where you heard the dentist drill noise."

"You mean my second prison?" Darcy asked.

"Yeah. I've got a hunch there's more than one dig going on."

Darcy nodded. "What I was thinking, too. Where's the other one? On the Sands place?"

"Maybe. Or nearby."

"Like I said in my e-mail, I keep hearing noises like construction machinery at night. It happened again last night," Darcy said.

"Yeah? What time was this?"

"Around three in the morning. I couldn't sleep, so I went for a little walk out of the camp and up the trail to the dig. I'm standing there listening to the coyotes yelp. There's no wind. Then, I can just faintly hear an engine—maybe more than one—and a clunking noise like a road grader makes."

"What direction?"

"The other side of the hill."

"On the hill, or farther away?"

"A little farther, I think."

"That could mean the county road, or the Sands property on the other side," Brian said. "Speaking of which..."

He pulled the Escape off on the right and braked to a stop in a wide flat spot near a clump of cottonwoods. When they opened the rental car doors, the dome light remained dark—Brian had switched it off earlier. Outside, they eyed their surroundings. Barely visible in the deep indigo sky, Bone Mountain rose up several hundred feet above the plains in the west. Brian switched on his flashlight and stepped forward. A sturdy fence with high-tensile wire suspended from stout wooden posts paralleled their side of the gravel road. They were outside the western border of the Sands property. The gate and warehouse would be nearby. Brian patted his pockets to make sure he had the map and tool pouch.

Darcy noticed the pistol and said, "I'm armed, too."

"Yeah? Whatcha got?"

She took her Swiss Army knife from a pocket and held it up. "This little sucker saved my life, you know."

"Makes me feel better, you've got it with you," Brian said. "Let's go."

They moved to the fence.

"Don't touch that thing unless you want curly hair," Darcy said. "The gate should be just a little ways from here."

They walked quietly along the fence to the south. A few minutes later, they came to the gate, the same one Brian had noticed during his tour. A heavy steel chain and chromed padlock secured the gate to a heavy post.

"This is where I came in last Friday," Darcy said. "But it looks different at night. I had no idea I was so close to the dig site. And another thing, the gate's locked this time."

Brian studied the gate mechanism carefully. No sensor wires visible. Opening the gate wouldn't set off an alarm, but cutting the fence wires might. He removed the nylon case of thin stainless steel picks from his pocket and went to work on the padlock, with Darcy training the flashlight on it. A few minutes later, the shackle popped out of the lock body. In the distance, coyotes howled mournfully. The only other sound was the wind sighing through the treetops.

Brian grabbed the insulated handles, pushed the gate in and listened. He went in and Darcy followed. He closed the gate behind them and replaced the chain. He hung the lock carefully in place, its shackle around a link of the chain, but he didn't click it closed. From a distance, it would appear to be secured but if they had to leave in a hurry, they could barge through without stopping to fiddle with the lock.

They walked along the fence in dim light, the moon a metallic yellow crescent to the east. Soon, they came to the large warehouse and went to the entry door, which was also locked. Brian got out his picks again and began manipulating them in the keyhole. Several times he thought he had it, only to have a pick slip at the last second. This was a competent, expensive lock set. Finally, after nearly ten minutes of coaxing, the mechanism gave and he was able to swing the door open.

Brian kept his flashlight focused on the warehouse floor. They proceeded to the partition wall and found the next door unlocked. Anxious to show Brian where she'd been trapped and the plaster-wrapped package she'd seen, Darcy led the way. Brian shined the flashlight around the floor and walls. The room was completely empty.

"Somebody cleared this place out," Darcy said. That door over there is the room where that man was working when I first came in."

That door was unlocked as well. They went in and found another completely empty space. A barren wood workbench and shelves lined the wall opposite the door, abandoned as old newspapers. The floor was spotless.

"What was going on in here last week, do you suppose?" Brian said.

"The dentist drill noise reminded me of an air scribe. That's a tool used by bone prep people in the bone lab, sort of a miniature sand blaster. And the man in here was hammering, sounded like chipping at rock with a point of some kind. The plaster deal sure looked like a bone cast. I thought maybe Doctor Stevens had rented space in here, trying to get a head start on the prep work."

"I suppose it's possible. By the way, I found out your Doctor Stevens is Arthur Sands's stepson."

"He does seem like the kind of guy who grew up with plenty of money around. Hey, do you think I should ask him whether he's stored anything offsite?"

"Yeah, let me know what he says."

They retraced their steps, closing doors, leaving all as they'd found it. Brian locked the entry door.

"What's that?" Darcy said in a quiet voice.

"What?"

"Listen. That noise again. Hear it? Like road construction."

Brian listened intently but couldn't hear anything. "Your ears must be better than mine."

They hiked along the fence line, stopping frequently to listen. They boarded the car and moved a short distance along the road. They were now across from the base of the eastern slope of Bone Mountain. The Stevens dinosaur dig would be directly opposite their position, on the other side of the hill.

Brian shut off the engine, eased his door open and listened. Now, he could hear very faintly the sound of a diesel engine tractor or dozer coming from the hill above. Plus, a steadily throbbing motor, like a generator. But there were no lights, no movement. All looked serene.

"This is where that son of a bitch must have parked his truck," Darcy said.

"Gilstrap? Yeah, must be. Okay, Babe, we got what we came for. Time to take you home." Brian said.

"What are you gonna do?"

"Get some rest. You need to do the same. When's the dig supposed to wind up?"

"Couple of days is what I heard. We're down to the last bones now, but there's a lot of housekeeping—bagging up some of the surrounding rocks, documentation. I don't mind. All of it's new to me, and I'm learning tons of cool stuff."

"You want to join me for Bull-a-rama tomorrow evening?"

"Bull-a what?"

"Bull-a-rama. Annual event at the Geyser County fairgrounds. Big-time bull-riding competition. You'll probably like it. They tell me it's one of the most dangerous sports on earth."

"Works for me. What time?"

"Starts at seven. Can you get away around six?"

"Sure. See you then."

45

Tom Norton lowered the night vision binoculars and let them hang from the strap around his neck. The car receded from view on the gravel road below, headed in the direction of town. Although he couldn't see any facial detail, he knew the two snooping along the western perimeter fence were that motherfuckin' pest Brian McKay and his niece. By the time he'd spotted them they were almost to their car. They left a few minutes later. He wondered if they'd breached the fence. He took his cell phone from a pocket, hit the speed-dial for Sam Harrison.

"Yeah?" Harrison sounded sleep-fogged. Or drunk.

"FYI, McKay and his niece just left for town. I saw them dicking around near the warehouse."

"Huh? Which warehouse do you—"

"The one Crawford was working in until I had him move the hell out."

"Oh. It's a good thing you—"

"Yeah, it is. Keep an eye on McKay. See if you can pick him up at the hotel. We're too close to the end to let some ex-law fuck us up."

"I hear you. Look, I can't tail him away from town. There's no traffic around here. He'd pick me up in a heartbeat."

"The other side of the coin's everybody watches everything around here. You'll figure out a way to keep tabs on him. He comes out this way again, you let me know pronto. I might need to get in touch with you real quick. Carry the goddamned burner phone I gave you, and leave it on. You got me?"

"Okay, okay. Are we on for the wrap tomorrow night?"

"Hell, yes. Just make sure *you're* ready. No fuckups allowed from here on out."

"Speaking of fuckups, any word on Gilstrap?"

"Forget him. He's history."

Norton hung up and turned back to the rocky hillside. He walked a few yards and disappeared, like a man stepping into an elevator.

46

E arly Saturday morning Brian called Michelle, who related that Ted Abernathy had become a virtual recluse since his run-in with Brian. She asked him when he would be coming home, and he told her he planned to return with Darcy in a few days.

He called Doctor Anton Holt next and gave him a report on the pot with the *T. rex* image on the side. Holt got excited and wanted to see it. He'd heard of pots with images carved on the outside, but never a dinosaur skull. He hypothesized the skull and apparent map carvings might be related. Brian told him the pot was inaccessible, but that he had taken photos and would e-mail them to Holt. He sent the email after he got off the phone.

That afternoon, Brian drove into the countryside south of town and took a washboard gravel road into the Geyser National Forest. The route climbed into the foothills of the Absarokas. He'd read that the word "Absaroka" meant Crow, as in the Crow Indians. As he gained elevation, the temperature dropped, and small patches of snow appeared along the road. The day they'd met, Sam Harrison told him that winter came "early and often" to the high country. He was inclined to believe the sheriff on that one.

The road dead-ended at a place called Otter Creek

Campground, where Brian got out. There were no other vehicles in sight. A mule deer doe and two fawns bolted away when they caught his scent. Their pale rumps rose and fell like waves as they melted into the trees.

At the edge of the campground a steep cliff overlooked the valley floor a thousand feet below. Brian trained his binoculars in the direction of the Crazies and picked out Bone Mountain, some thirty miles away. From this vantage point, the hill jutted up in triangular profile, like the blunted tip of an arrowhead. The dig site wasn't visible on the gradual west slope. He surveyed the steeper eastern side from top to bottom. The sun glinted off a shiny object half way down, possibly the abandoned mining equipment. But that stuff had been rusty as hell. Brian focused more precisely, but couldn't locate the shiny spot. He estimated the mountain to be perhaps two hundred feet thick at that level. There were several higher peaks adjacent to Bone Mountain. The landscape appeared lumpy, wrinkled like an unmade bed from this angle. There would be lots of little hidden spots up there. He lowered the glasses.

Brian mused about the challenge to come. He felt ready for Norton, Gilstrap, Sands, whoever the hell came at him. It would happen soon; he could feel it—the thrill of anticipation that always descended on him before a battle. Like any law enforcement job, FBI work meant day after day of tedious routine broken unpredictably by sudden flashes of excitement. He felt like he was back on the job. He'd stirred up enough hornets—one should try to sting him soon.

At the Masters, Brian stowed several items in his small daypack, so he'd be ready to act when the time came: binoculars, energy bars, cell phone, flashlight, lock picks, the map of the Sands ranch and the Sig with extra ammo.

At the Stevens *T. rex* dig, the crew members were subdued. Tired and fed up with the micromanagement of Scott Noble Stevens, their mood was snappish. A couple of shirtless young men had nearly come to blows that morning in an argument over how to operate a portable winch. Several of the crew looked to be on the verge of desertion. Stevens, seemingly oblivious, prowled the site, urging the workers to be careful but to keep up the pace. He smelled completion of fieldwork.

Darcy and Becky Stanton worked quietly together, forming plaster casts around the last clusters of tailbones. Darcy soaked burlap strips in water and patted them around a bone bundle, mummy-style, while Becky mixed plaster of Paris with water in a five-gallon white plastic bucket. They both applied the white outer coat with their hands. When the surface was nearly dry, they carved documentation in the surface with an ice pick: location, date, bone numbers and their own initials. While they were thus engaged, Stevens came over and watched from a few feet behind them.

"Did you girls measure the angle to the datum stakes from both ends?" Stevens asked.

Darcy continued working, head down.

Becky spoke up. "Yassuh, boss. We done measured our little hearts out."

Stevens grunted and moved on.

"That guy creeps me out big-time," Becky muttered.

"Well, he can be a pain in the ass, but he's under a lotta pressure. And he's a major force. Hey, did you hear anything weird last night?"

"Actually, yeah, I thought I heard like a truck, but then I thought I might have been dreaming."

"Same here."

"What's going on? What did you guys find out, anyway?"

"We went back to that big warehouse. Everything was gone—the plaster thing, everything. I mean the place was like, totally empty."

"What do you think they're doing?"

"Well, either someone else has got a dig going around here, or Doctor Stevens sent some of our bones to outside storage, I guess. Reminds me, I'm supposed to ask him about that."

"Could be. See anybody over there?"

"No, but my uncle's on it, for sure."

"He's a cool guy."

"Yeah, but a little old for you. Hey, he's taking me to this bull-riding thing, Bull-a-rama, tonight. Want to go?"

"Thanks, but I'm gonna crash after dinner. I'm like too wiped out for nightlife. When I get home, I'm making up for lost time."

"What—sleep or nightlife?"

"Both."

Tom Norton looked across his desk at Hank Crawford and the Gruel brothers, all three in folding chairs. "Okay, tonight's the wrap," he said. "We start at 8:30, and keep going 'til it's done. All four of us are gonna bust our butts. I'm on the loader. Hank, you're going to go get the chopper soon as we're finished here. When you get back, you'll supervise loading.

You two guys are feeding the loader, plus you're gonna help clean up and load the cargo into the bird. Understand?" He looked a challenge at the Gruels.

"Uh, Tom, why do we need to clean up? I mean, there was everything from bat shit to boulder piles up there when we started."

"Don't fucking worry about the old stuff that's been there forever. What I'm talking about's the shit we brought in. I want that place to look like we never been there. All the McDonald's boxes, the beer cans and anything else you bozos've dropped on the ground's gotta be picked up. Even though I don't expect it, somebody could get in there some day. The less there is to connect it to us, the better off we are. Got it?"

"Everything goes to Building D tonight—right?" Crawford said.

"Yep," Norton said.

Shane raised a hand like a schoolboy. "Uh, When do we get paid?"

"Don't worry about that. After he returns the bird, Hank's going to get going on the prep work in D, which'll take a while. Then the bones take a long boat ride across the ocean. The buyer's gonna wire funds to me as soon as he gets the shipment. I'll dole out your shares the same day."

"Ah shit," Donny said. "You mean we gotta wait to get our goddamned rightful due?"

"I'll see if I can make it quicker," Norton said. He gave Crawford a look.

After dismissing them, Norton called Sam Harrison. "Come on by tonight. You can help us mop up."

"I'll be there, loaded for bear," Harrison said.

In their slovenly truck, the Gruels lit cigarettes. The cab was littered with beer cans, cigarette ashes, fast food wrappers and shotgun shells. An unopened package of condoms topped the dashboard.

"Yahoo! It's Bull-a-rama for this cowboy!" Donny cried.

At the wheel, Shane looked over with baleful eyes. "Yeah, but we only got—" he looked at his Timex—"about two and a half hours. Shit, we'll only have time for a few beers before we gotta be back here."

"Then, get your ass in gear, bro."

47

A little after six, Brian swung by the dig site and collected Darcy. They'd dressed in long-sleeved shirts, jeans and hiking boots. After driving to the county fairgrounds, he eased the car into a parking space along a chain-link fence. They located a refreshment stand, where Brian bought them hot dogs and cans of beer. They found seats near the top of the metal bleachers arced around the circular dirt arena.

The P. A. system emitted a loud crackle. A cowboy-hatted announcer leaned out of the mini-press box and informed the crowd in a made-for-radio baritone, "You folks are in for a real treat—the 18th annual Bull-a-rama extravaganza! Some of the best bull riders in the west will compete for prizes ranging from fancy belt buckles to plenty of cash money to a brand new GMC three-quarter-ton pickup."

Families, couples and singles had nearly filled the stands. The atmosphere grew festive as beers were downed and the sun dropped lower toward the western horizon behind the McKays. Brian noticed a message on the back of a young man's white tee shirt a few rows below: FORGET THE BULLS, RIDE A COWGIRL.

Finally, after pretty teenage girls on horses had galloped around the dirt arena carrying U.S. and Montana flags on poles held high, the bull-riding competition got underway. One after another, 2,000-pound bulls with ornery attitudes thundered into the arena carrying 150-pound cowboys clutching braided bull ropes for dear life. The object was for the rider to stay on the animal until the eight-second whistle sounded. Once past that goal, points were awarded based on style, both for the bull and the rider. Cowboys came and went; only a few managed to remain planted for the required time. Bulls with names like Cap'n Crunch, Burger Time and Hannibull Lecter tossed off would-be prizewinners like yesterday's underwear.

After a particularly pugnacious white-horned black bull had hurled a slender rider over the fence, the announcer commented, "That young man nearly got himself an ivory enema."

Another bull performed an intricate dance involving swift changes in direction and a straight-up jump resulting in an ashen-faced cowboy in a fetal tuck beneath the animal's substantial gut. As the agitated bovine whipped his massive head to and fro, looking for his tormentor, two brave and highly skilled "bullfighters," formerly called rodeo clowns, distracted the bull by swatting him on the snout and prancing in multicolored baggy pantaloons. The contestant managed to squirm between restless taurine legs to safety. The announcer chimed in with, "That bull had more moves than a chicken on Ex-Lax."

After weeks of working with fossil bones in near-monastic circumstances, Darcy welcomed the boisterous atmosphere of the bull riding. She gawked around like a schoolgirl on vacation. The sights, sounds and smells were all new. She happened to be looking toward the refreshment stand below and to the right of the bleachers when a familiar-looking man in a stained straw hat passed by with a beer can tilted against his mouth. Was he someone she knew? Something about the way he carried himself. She returned her attention to the current bull ride, which ended almost before it began. A moment later, it came to her—the beer-drinker was one of the men on ATVs who'd raced up the trail to the cabin in the woods while she hid, fearing for her life.

"Ready for another?" Brian raised his empty can.

"If you're buying."

Brian threaded his way through the crowded bleachers and got in line at the refreshment stand. While he waited, two men in front of him discussed the intricacies of bull riding. One observed that there wasn't a hell of a lot of money to be made by the young bull riders.

"Why in God's name do they do it?" he asked his companion.

The other man, affecting superior knowledge, explained, "Well, it's sort of like having fun, only different."

Brian purchased a couple of beers and started back to the stands. Someone bumped his right arm hard, knocking one of the cans from his hand. He looked into the pinched red face of a skinny man decked out in western duds.

"Hey, whyncha watch where yer goin'," the man said.

"I will, if you will," Brian said. He bent to retrieve the can on the ground.

"Fucking asshole," the man said, as he wiped at a liquid stain on the elbow of his pearl-button plaid shirt with a grimy bandana.

"Watch your mouth," Brian said.

"Yeah? Hey, what's yer fuckin' problem?"

Brian had seen plenty of guys like this in Chicago—

long on in-your-face attitude, short on staying power. He grabbed the man's shirt under his chin and twisted hard. "How'd you like me to kick your ass from here to town?" Brian said.

The bellicosity drained from the guy like water through a sieve. Without another word, he wrenched free from Brian's grip, spun on a high boot heel and stalked off. Brian shrugged and made his way back to his seat.

"Here you are, kiddo. Be careful, they got shaken up on the way back." Brian handed a can to Darcy and kept one for himself.

"What do you mean? What was all that yelling down there with that cowboy?" Darcy said.

"No big deal. Some idiot who'd had too much to drink, I guess."

"That was one of the guys riding up the trail near that cabin," Darcy said.

"Really?" Brian looked around beneath the stands.

"There he is, over there," Darcy said. "With the other one. The two that kind of look like twins."

Brian followed her gaze. The guy he'd had the altercation with and a near double were ambling away from the arena toward the parking area.

Brian turned to the man next to him, a weathered fellow in work clothes. "Do you happen to know who those guys are?" he asked, pointing toward the receding duo.

"Them? Oh, they're brothers. Name's Gruel. Shane and Donny, I believe." He turned his attention back to the arena, where a young, Kevlar-vested cowboy ran for the fence and climbed it hastily, narrowly avoiding the horns of an angry bull. Brian remembered Laura Jensen's comments on the Gruels—something about them working for Sands. And they were familiar for another reason—they were the guys he'd read about in the local newspaper, the ones who'd shot a bunch of deer and left the carcasses to waste. Shane would be the elder, Donny the younger, the belligerent guy in the straw hat.

The announcer bellowed, "Anybody heard about the fella was milking a cow over east of town the other day? A fly flew in the cow's ear and came out into the milk bucket. In one ear and out the udder." The crowd groaned.

"On that note, what say we make a move," Brian said. "Let's go see what our buddies are up to." He nodded toward the parking lot, where the last rays of sunlight were nearly gone and night was coming on fast.

48

They boarded the Escape. Brian could just make out the taillights of the Gruel brothers' old truck exiting the parking lot. He waited until they'd rounded a bend, then followed. The truck headed west, then north in the direction of the Sands place. There was no other traffic, so Brian stayed as far back as he could while keeping them in sight. The pickup passed the ranch's main entrance and continued on the dirt road along the property line. A few minutes later, it pulled off near the place where Brian and Darcy had been the night before. Brian shut off his lights, killed the engine and rolled to a stop in the grass next to the road. They were still about a quarter mile from the other vehicle. If anyone came along, they'd wonder where the occupants were, but that couldn't be helped.

Through his binoculars, Brian could see the glow of two cigarettes near the parked truck. Raucous voices carried clearly through the night air. One of the men screamed at the other in falsetto, calling him a sick fuck. A flashlight beam appeared. Brian lowered the glasses and watched as the light bobbed across the road and slowly up Bone Mountain. When it was well over half way to the top, the light disappeared. Brian reckoned the spot to be near the place where Darcy had been abducted, not far from the entrance to the abandoned mine the FBI had checked out and found to dead-end after a few feet.

Brian's instincts told him he should follow the men up the mountain, find out what they were up to. By now, he had a pretty good idea, but he needed first-hand proof. He wanted to take Darcy back to the Stevens camp and return by himself, or call for help. But who? Not the sheriff. And he'd need something solid to get Thorsten involved. He hesitated to put Darcy at risk again—hadn't she been through enough already? But what if these guys were pulling out tonight? Time might be getting short. Chances were, if he went up now, he could get a look at the action, get enough hard evidence to convince Thorsten to bring in the FBI. The backpack with his gun was in the trunk. He made a decision, hoping he wouldn't live to regret it.

"Want to join me for a short hike?" he said.

"Well, you need backup."

He convinced himself she was right. "Okay, let's go."

Brian strapped on the Sig Sauer and slung the small pack over his shoulders. They left the car and began making their way on foot to the Gruels' truck. They came upon the old pickup, where Brian paused and scanned the slope above through the binoculars. No lights or movement. No sounds except the night creatures—crickets chirped, an owl said who and a small object whipped by Darcy's head, lifting her hair.

"What the hell was that?" she said in a stage whisper.

Brian looked around. Diminutive objects careened in the air above them with jerky, awkward movements. One came within a couple feet of Brian's head and veered away.

"Bats," he said. "I recognize 'em from my days in Ann Arbor. The little buggers used to get into the house where I lived with some guys. We'd swat 'em with tennis rackets."

"Yuck."

"Don't worry about them. Let's go up. This is a fact-finding mission. Our object is to see and not be seen. No lights, no talking unless it's absolutely necessary. Okay?

"Okay."

Brian led the way from the road, through the rough terrain choked with rocks and brush to the bottom of the east flank of Bone Mountain. The moon provided enough light that they were able to follow the faint path winding steeply upward without a flashlight. They stopped to watch and listen after gaining about a hundred feet of elevation.

Brian put his mouth near Darcy's left ear and said quietly, "Hear anything?"

She listened for a moment, then shook her head.

Brian continued upward, moving carefully in the moonlight. Another hundred feet of elevation gain, another stop.

"You hear that? Darcy said quietly.

Brian listened for a moment. Yes, there were sounds coming from above, possibly from inside the hill. Inside? Sounded like an engine and the rasping of a front-end loader bucket on rock. The engine sound died down, then stopped. A second, lower-pitched motor continued to chug away.

"Let's take it real slow and easy from here on," Brian said. C'mon."

They continued climbing up to the huge boulder marking the spot where Darcy had been abducted almost two weeks ago. It seemed to Brian like years had passed since then.

They went single-file along a flat traverse to their right, angling slightly upward to the rusty mining gear and the deserted tunnel. In the luminous rays of the moon, they could see the rotted wood framing the mineshaft opening. One of the splintered vertical supports leaned so the top timber canted down at one end. It looked as if a solid blow could collapse the supports, sealing off the entrance forever. The cobweb with the cookie-sized spider was gone. Squatting on his haunches, Brian aimed the flashlight into the hole.

"Let's go in. Stay in the middle and keep away from the support timbers," Brian whispered.

He crawled in with Darcy on his heels. The passageway was about four feet high. They stood, heads bowed, and shuffled further into the shaft. Brian played the light beam ahead. Nothing but rocks, dust, animal droppings and the occasional old bottle or can. In the dustier parts, there were scuff marks that might have come from shoes. Shortly, they reached a solid-looking rock wall. Brian moved the light over the surface.

"That one rock looks like it's rigged up," Brian whispered.

"Where?"

He reached a hand to a rectangular dark gray rock about the size of a brick. As his palm closed over the rock, it gave a little. "This thing turns," he murmured.

The rock rotated about ninety degrees clockwise and suddenly, a door-sized section of the wall began to open toward them on recessed hinges. Brian stopped the door from moving more than a couple of inches. Light edged the rectangular barrier. On the other side, voices echoed as if bouncing off the walls of a large room. A diesel engine revved and backed down. Men yelled. They could make out phrases: "Over here. No, to your right a little." It sounded like a construction crew, with men on the ground guiding an equipment operator.

"Hey, why'm I the one's gotta bust his balls liftin' this shit every time? Whyn't you do it for a fuckin' change." Brian recognized the voice of the man who'd bumped him and knocked his beer loose at the bull-riding competition, Donny Gruel.

"Hey, eat me, shit-for-brains." A similar voice—probably the older brother, Shane Gruel.

"Would you assholes knock it off. The both of you, get that thing up there so I can load it." Definitely Tom Norton.

Brian cautiously pulled the door open a few more inches. A larger, more recently crafted tunnel went straight ahead a few yards, then veered to the left. He motioned for Darcy to wait outside the door. "I'm going to see what's at the end of this tunnel," he whispered in her ear. "Go down and wait for me at the car. If I'm not back in an hour, call Bill Thorsten. Here, take this." He handed Darcy his phone, with Thorsten's phone number in the directory.

"No way. I'm stoked. Gotta stay with it."

"Look, I'll be out in a. little while. If we both go in, there's no backup, and this thing could end up in the loss column. Go on."

"Crap," Darcy muttered. She knew Brian was right, but she hated to miss out. She took Brian's phone, found Thorsten's number, and entered it into her own phone. She handed Brian's phone back. Reluctantly, she turned and began retracing her steps out of the tunnel.

Brian crept through the doorway and moved silently into the newer tunnel. In another few yards, the passageway turned left. Twelve feet later, it gave onto a larger arched portal. Brian inched forward, careful to not dislodge loose rock or soil. Keeping his body obscured in shadow, he extended his head forward just enough to view beyond the arch with one eye. He was now looking into a huge cavern lit with portable floodlights on metal stands. A commercial Honda generator throbbed steadily, loud in the enclosed space. Across the room, perhaps a hundred feet from the door, a towering rock wall appeared. Shadows of three men danced on the wall.

Cautiously, Brian poked his head into the room for a better look. Now, he could see the entire space, a large chamber with a rough domed ceiling perhaps twenty feet high at its rounded apex. Along the wall to the right, Donny Gruel wielded an over-sized pry bar wedged under an irregularly shaped white object about the size of a corpse. He pushed the bar down onto a rock fulcrum in an effort to lift an edge of the white thing off the rock floor. A lookalike man—had to be the other Gruel—pulled the top of the bundle toward himself with gloved hands. It gave a few inches. They rocked their burden back and forth, until finally it rolled partway into the toothed bucket of a large yellow front-end loader displaying a brand name in black letters: TEREX. Brian found the name ironic— or actually, appropriate. Tom Norton occupied the operator's seat, scowling.

"Well, it's about fucking time," Norton bellowed. He revved the loader's engine. It stumbled, then caught and roared thunderously loud in the enclosed space. Norton worked levers to extend the twin hydraulic arms which moved the bucket forward a foot then raised it off the stone floor, cradling the white object. He turned the big machine in a tight circle and lumbered it to the other end of the room, disappearing through an opening the size of a garage door in the far wall.

Brian noticed a pair of industrial fans facing away from his spot, one on each side of the huge cavern. As gray smoke belched from the loader and the generator powering the lights, the fans pushed most of it in the direction Norton had driven the loader. Piles of rubble, as if taken from a hole, were concentrated against the pitted rock wall to the right. There were signs of recent digging all along the wall. It reminded Brian of the parts of the Stevens dinosaur dig where the bones had been removed. Was this the source of Eagle Feather's dinosaur bone? Maybe. And, if there'd been a dinosaur skeleton there, it must have been huge. The excavation was much larger than the one at the Stevens *T. rex* site.

In any case, he'd seen enough, had something solid to give Thorsten and the FBI.

Brian was just about to turn to go back, when the generator motor began to sputter and the lights in the cavern flickered. An unfamiliar voice came from just inside the cavern entrance. "Hey, the generator's dying. Where's the gas?"

"Oh shit. I left it outside in the tunnel." Donny Gruel.

"You better hump it in here quick. Tom's gonna be pissed."

As if on cue, Norton's angry voice came from farther away. "Somebody better gas up that goddamn generator right fucking now."

"Okay, okay. I'm gettin' the gas." Donny Gruel again.

Brian retreated a few feet backwards toward the entry door. He stopped, motionless in the dark. He eased the Sig Sauer from the belt slide and held it in front of himself, pointed toward the arched entryway to the cavern. The generator continued to run raggedly, the lights in the cavern wavering unevenly like a guttering candle in a stiff breeze. Seconds later, a slender man appeared in the entryway, backlit by the flickering work lights. Brian recognized the outline of the character he'd had the altercation with earlier, Donny Gruel. He began to move in Brian's direction, on a collision course in the dark. He scuttled forward, bumped his head on the low ceiling and cursed. When he'd come within arm's length, Brian gripped the Sig by the barrel and struck Donny on his head, as if hammering in a nail. Donny sunk to his knees, then keeled over onto his side, motionless.

The cavern lights dimmed, nearly went out. Someone inside yelled, "Hey, where's the fuckin' gas?"

Brian turned and began making his way in the gloom toward the spot where he'd left Darcy. Just after he'd made the right turn, but before reaching the hidden door, he heard noises behind himself as if someone else had entered the tunnel. A flashlight beam played on the walls. There were noises of men scrambling around in the cramped corridor.

Tom Norton's voice came from behind Brian and around the bend. "Get out of the way. Lemme see. The dumb shit must've bumped his head on the beam, knocked himself out."

Then Donny Gruels' whiny voice: "Some guy slugged me."

Brian hustled forward as fast as the claustrophobic passageway permitted. He bumped a shoulder on a rotting vertical wall beam, setting loose a cascade of rock and dust. He didn't pause for an instant, just kept going. In a moment, he glimpsed a hint of faint light ahead. He knew he must be almost to the door. Suddenly, the crack of a gunshot came from behind, ear-splitting in the tunnel. A bullet sang past Brian's head and ricocheted of the wall. He was still short of the camouflaged door.

Brian made his way out of the mineshaft and burst into the cool night air a few seconds later. Staring down the mountain, he tried to catch a glimpse of Darcy. He could barely make out her form in the gauzy moonlight far below as she worked her way down to the car.

As Brian began to descend, he heard a sudden noise behind him—someone outside the tunnel moving over the rocks on foot. Backlit by the moon was the figure of a bulky man just outside the tunnel entrance. From the way he carried himself, Brian knew it was Tom Norton. He appeared to be holding a handgun. Brian ducked behind a large boulder and waited in silence for a few seconds. It occurred to him that this was probably the same boulder Darcy had shielded herself behind after she'd been shot.

Cautiously, Brian peaked around the boulder. Norton had stopped, was now looking intently in Brian's direction. He seemed to be listening, trying to detect movement, like a nocturnal owl homing in on prey. Brian propped the Sig on a level rock and took careful aim, just as he'd done at the firing range at GUNS GALORE. His forefinger tightened on the trigger as he held his breath to ensure steadiness. Just a split second before he would have squeezed off the shot, the man above did an about-face and walked back into the tunnel. Brian let out his breath slowly as he removed his finger from the trigger.

As Brian straightened a moment later, a muffled explosion came from the tunnel entrance. A large cloud rose slowly in the moonlight, as an avalanche of rocks and stones cascaded down the hill below the mineshaft. For a moment, he was concerned about being swept up in an avalanche, but only small pebbles reached him, rolling over his shoe tops. He watched as the dust cloud gradually dissipated and silence returned to the hillside.

With the flashlight in one hand and the Sig in the other, Brian retraced his steps to the tunnel. The shaft opening no longer existed. Someone had set off an explosion from inside—probably dynamite—closing off access to the cavern. That meant there had to be another entrance—but where? He tried to locate Darcy in the darkness below but could neither hear nor see her. He had to find the other entrance. According to the luminous hands of his watch, he and Darcy had split up a little over a half hour ago—she'd call for help in thirty minutes. If these guys were shutting down entrances, they probably planned to be out of there tonight. There was no way he'd let them get away with the goods.

49

When Darcy heard the explosion above, sounding like a bomb blast, she stopped moving. She wasn't sure if the earlier cracking noise had been a gunshot. Should she keep going or turn back to rejoin Brian? She checked her watch. A Thirty minutes until she was supposed to call Bill Thorsten. What could she do against explosives and guns anyhow? She continued downslope.

Just as Darcy reached the bottom, the sound of an approaching vehicle drifted up from the road. As she watched, a patrol car with a rooftop light bar eased to a stop behind the Gruels' truck. A heavyset man wearing a Stetson emerged, slammed the car door and made his way in her direction. Brian had bad-mouthed the sheriff, said he wasn't worth a damn. Could this be him? Suddenly, the man switched on a handheld searchlight, which bathed the area in front of him like the midday sun. Darcy went prone on the rocky ground. A large sagebrush provided some cover.

She recognized Sheriff Harrison trudging along, now pointing the brilliant light at the ground in front of him as he lumbered uphill in her direction. Darcy didn't trust Harrison, especially after what Brian said. And she'd found the sheriff's manner kind of gross. She'd play it cool, see what happened. Pungent sage leaves tickled her nose as the wind picked up.

Soon, her eyes began to water and she felt the first inkling of a nascent sneeze. Her nose wrinkled and she had the uncontrollable urge to let loose with a full-fledged spasmodic honk. She covered her nose and mouth with a hand and muffled most of the involuntary expiration, which escaped as an affricative whoosh.

At the sound, Harrison stopped and swiveled with the searchlight. The beam just missed Darcy and kept going in a ragged arc. Harrison stood still for a moment, apparently listening. Then he pivoted and continued up the slope.

Darcy waited until the sheriff was at the level of the tunnel entrance, then resumed her journey to the deserted Escape. She got her phone and called Bill Thorsten. No answer. Should have been a voicemail message. She had cell coverage, but it was weak. Was there a technical glitch?

Darcy sat down in a grassy patch off the side of the road near the car. She'd wait a few minutes and try the number again. Every few seconds, she looked up toward the place she and Brian had gone inside the mountain. Harrison's light was moving along to the right now. Why hadn't he entered the tunnel? *Was* it still there, after the explosion? Where would he be going? What had happened to Brian? She hit redial. Still no answer. According to her watch, an hour and twenty-five minutes had gone by since she'd left Brian. She settled down to wait, trying redial every minute or so. She could hear nothing except the moaning wind rocking the vehicle next to her gently on its springs.

50

Brian wondered if Darcy was worried. Was she waiting for him at the car? She should have called Thorsten by now. He'd climbed about fifty feet above the former tunnel opening and was working his way to the north, angling around the roundish hump of mountaintop. There was a sketchy route along the hillside, probably a game path made by bighorn sheep. Brian kept the flashlight clenched in his teeth and pointed down at his feet. He needed both hands to grasp the random protrusions and crevices that served as handholds along the craggy rock wall. He stopped every few minutes and listened with his ear to the steep wall next to him. The third time he did so, he heard the distinctive clatter of the diesel engine revving inside. Then, very faintly, voices became audible. He estimated he must be outside the spot along the wall of the cavern where the dug-up rubble had been. He worked his way further along the curving contour of the mountainside.

A short time later, the noises emitting from inside the earth became louder. An engine throbbed steadily—the generator. Another revved—the loader. Then light became visible a few yards ahead and slightly below his position. Brian crept forward, clinging to the precarious slope with feet and fingertips. He could make out a brightly lit square opening in the slope below. He pocketed his flashlight. As he began to descend toward the opening, a moving light came into view. Brian caught a glimpse of a bulky man carefully stepping to the lighted opening and disappearing inside. Sam Harrison? Was he linked up with Norton? Brian stayed put, watching what was apparently the second cavern entrance.

Harrison had been surprised to see the old mineshaft opening gone. That had been the entrance to the subterranean dig he'd always used, it being the shortest approach on foot. Norton had warned him they'd have to blow it if someone wised up. Maybe that fucking troublemaker McKay had wandered in and lucked onto it. That would account for the empty rental car below. If so, he hoped Norton had taken care of him. It hadn't been fun getting to the so-called shipping dock at night, even with his department-issue heavy duty flashlight, and even having checked out the alternate foot route during the daytime. Harrison entered the huge rock-walled room to find Norton at the controls of the massive diesel loader, piloting the machine back for another load.

When he spotted Harrison, Norton parked near a plastered bundle and stepped down. Diesel smoke sputtered out of the machine's smokestack and eddied toward the large exit, pushed by the humming fans. The two men put their heads together and conversed in low tones as the Gruels horsed a bulky plaster bundle onto the toothed edge of the loader bucket. Donny Gruel's forehead was stained red from the wound inflicted by the butt of Brian's handgun.

"What happened to the shaft?" Harrison asked.

"Somebody came in and slugged Donny. I took a shot

at the fucker, but he got away. You see anyone out there?"

"Nope, just a Ford Escape parked a ways back from the geniuses' rig. Rental, I'd guess."

"Gotta be McKay," Norton said. "Hope he got scragged when I blew the entrance. If not, he's out there. Ah, fuck him. Anyway, we're using Plan B. Got to move our asses before this whole thing goes kablooey all over our face."

Norton nodded toward the opening in the cavern wall. "Hank went to get the chopper. We should be about ready to load 'er up by the time he gets back. Your people in line?"

"I let 'em know I'm handling things up the Shields tonight. All this way from town, ain't none of 'em's gonna come by. There won't be any problems," Harrison said.

"I hope to Christ you're right. All we need's another nosy deputy like that Jensen broad."

Harrison flushed. "Don't worry. Everything's under control."

"It better be." Norton rubbed his chin with a blocky fist.

Someone screamed like a pig being disemboweled. It came from the other side of the cavern, where the Gruels were wrestling with a bone bundle.

"You stupid fuck! You smashed my goddamned foot."

Donny Gruel hopped in a small circle next to the loader bucket, massaging his left foot with both hands. Inevitably, he lost his balance, and sat down with a thud. His brother doubled over and howled with laughter.

Norton and Harrison regarded them silently for a moment. Norton yelled, "You two assholes better get back to work. I want those bones on pallets in the loading area fucking ASAP. Get to it."

"Fuckups," Harrison said.

Norton nodded grimly. "C'mon, help get this done."

Harrison pitched in with the work, spelling the injured Donny Gruel. Out of shape, he wheezed and grunted with effort as he helped wrestle the bone parcels into the loader bucket. They'd gotten most of them onto pallets in the loading area when the distant thwack-thwack of helicopter blades beating thin air came through the stone walls. The sound built to a crescendo. Bits of stone fell to the cave floor as thunderous vibrations rocked the walls. Gradually, the sound dissipated as the powerful motors powered down.

51

Brian watched as a huge twin-rotor helicopter with a single red running light thundered into view and hovered for a moment like a prodigious beast of prey. Pale patches of luminescence that looked like solar-powered patio lights one might buy at Costco formed a rough circle on the ground outside the cavern doorway. Suddenly, a powerful white light beam projected from the belly of the machine, revealing a flat surface below. The chopper dropped slowly like a spider hanging from a thread and landed on the makeshift landing pad.

The prop wash sent stones down on Brian's head, and he covered his face with both hands to protect his eyes. When the rotors had nearly stopped spinning, he looked between fingers. Light from the opening in the rock wall spilled out onto the landing area. Brian noticed the inscription *U.S. Army* on the bulging flank of the machine. The twin-rotor behemoth had to be a hundred feet long. It had four sets of landing wheels. The rotors were mounted on stubby towers, the one on the back higher and shaped like a whale's tail. The machine looked like the ones he'd seen on TV, the craft used to transport U. S. troops leaving the Middle East. How the hell had these guys managed to get ahold of it? And how were they able to construct a landing pad up here among the peaks?

A man Brian hadn't seen previously emerged from the

helicopter. He was short and pudgy with a gray ponytail and an Adidas warm-up suit. Must be the pilot. Tom Norton and Sam Harrison came out to meet him. The rotors wheezed to a stop. Brian could hear Norton's voice clearly as he said, "Hank, go inside and see how those two are doing. Should be about done."

When Brian heard the name "Hank," he remembered Laura Jensen telling him about the geologist named Hank Crawford. Must be the pilot as well—a real versatile guy. As Brian watched from his precarious perch about fifty feet from the cavern entrance, the chopper pilot went inside. Without warning, Norton drew a long-barreled pistol from his shoulder holster and shot Harrison in the side of the head. The crack from the small-caliber gun sounded like a dry twig snapping in the night air. Harrison sagged to the ground, facedown. Norton bent over the sheriff and fired two more shots into the base of his skull, squeezing them off, taking his time. Harrison twitched, then lay still. Norton removed Harrison's keys from his belt clip and his wallet from his trousers. After stowing these items in his own pants pockets, Norton dragged the body to the right side of the helicopter. He opened the passenger door and then, grunting with effort, he lifted the corpse, and pushed it into the cabin behind the cockpit seats. He rummaged around for a minute, then backed out and slammed the door. He reentered the cavern.

For Brian, the scene he'd just witnessed was an eye-opener. Harrison had been in on the scheme, whatever it was, and Norton appeared to be the ringleader and executioner—the most stone-cold killer Brian had ever encountered. He'd shot Harrison with as much emotion as a normal man would swat a fly.

Brian worked his way to the landing pad and approached the immense craft on the side furthest from the cave entrance. He located a metal handle on the pilot's door, carefully worked it open and climbed in. He felt the rough canvas cover of the pilot's seat and made his way behind it. He stumbled on something soft but unyielding and realized it was the corpse of Sam Harrison, covered with a tarp. He skirted the body and wended his way back into the massive cargo area. Light from the cavern opening came through the chopper's porthole-style side windows, revealing sets of three-wide olive drab seats piled on the floor, along with stacks of first aid kits, gas masks, ammo boxes and other military gear. The stuff took up about ten feet of space just behind the cockpit area. From there to the end of the cargo hold was all vacant metal floor.

Suddenly, voices came from outside. Brian crunched down behind the army gear as Hank Crawford opened a door up front and climbed into the pilot's seat. He operated some controls, causing an opening to appear in the tail. There was the whoosh of hydraulics as a stout metal loading ramp slid out the rear end of the craft's massive cargo hold and scraped onto the rocks beneath it. Overhead lights flashed on, illuminating an interior space about seven feet high, just as wide and thirty feet long.

Shane Gruel drove the front-end loader up the ramp with a palletized plaster-coated man-sized bundle dangling from thick nylon straps mounted on the loader bucket. Brian stayed hidden in his cocoon of canvas-clad equipment as Shane drove load after load into the long cargo hold within the rear quarters of the chopper. There were a dozen pallets of large bundles and six pallets with several smaller bundles on each. Crawford stood at the rear opening yelling instructions as to where each load should be placed. The Gruels and Crawford then toted in several cardboard boxes containing small items wrapped in newspaper. These were stashed in among the palletized plastered objects.

"Must be twenty thousand pounds of cargo," Norton said. "Can this thing handle it?"

"Piece a cake," Crawford said. He looked around. "Hey, where's Harrison?"

"He had to go back to town. C'mon, let's close this place down and haul ass."

52

Brian remained out of sight sandwiched between the piles of materiel and the cockpit, in the forward portion of the cargo hold. Norton supervised the Gruels and Crawford in the final stages of loading. They wheeled in the generator, the industrial fans, the work lights and stands, heavy electrical cords, tools and plastic bags of trash. Norton took over the loader and drove it back into the cavern for what he called a "final inspection." He returned a few minutes later and drove the machine up the ramp into the chopper. Even with the bone bundles, equipment and the loader, there was room to spare inside the immense space. After the four men had left the craft, Brian raised his head just enough to see what was happening outside. All four were standing near the entry to the cavern, a few yards from the chopper.

As Brian watched through a circular window, Norton went to the opening in the rock wall and pulled the big steel overhead door closed. The door was camouflaged to look like gray rock. He reached into the rocks to the right of the door and tugged out the end of a slender white plastic pipe. It looked like the PVC piping used by plumbers. The pipe came from a point in the rocks a foot from the log support beam on the right side of the doorway.

Norton drew his pistol and said, "You two, get over

there." Brian could hear the voice clearly—They'd left the cargo ramp and passenger side door in the cockpit open.

"Who—us?" Donny Gruel said.

"Get your asses over by that door, right now."

Donny and Shane Gruel shuffled to the cavern doorway, cutting nervous glances over their shoulders at Norton.

"Okay, turn and press your ugly faces against the door. Come on, hurry up."

"But Tom, this ain't fair. We worked our asses off on this thing. You can't just—"

Norton strode forward and raked the gun barrel across Donny Gruel's scalp. The wound began bleeding. "Shut up and turn toward the door, jagoff," Norton said.

Norton stepped to the plastic pipe, pulled off the end cap and extracted a length of white cord, all the while keeping an eye on the Gruels, who stood fidgeting with their chins pressed against the steel door.

Shane turned to look at the cord and said, "Jesus, Tom, what's that?"

"Oh, just something you guys'll get a charge out of." He barked a sound that might have been a laugh.

Norton unpocketed a disposable lighter and thumbed the spark wheel until an orange flame shot from the top. He bent and carefully touched the flame to the white cord, dropped it to the ground and quickly stepped away.

"You guys move an inch and I'll put .22 longs up your asses," Norton said. Then, in an undertone, he addressed Crawford. "Get on the other side of the chopper. Hurry up."

While Crawford hustled to the far side of the helicopter, Norton backed away, keeping the Woodsman trained on the Gruels. The light from the rear of the chopper's cargo hold lit a macabre scene—the brothers shaking in fear, their faces tight to the cavern door, while the fuse near their feet burned steadily up the white cord like a Fourth of July sparkler.

Shane Gruel glanced over at his younger brother, standing there shaking like an aspen leaf in the breeze. He'd never seen Donny so scared. Dumb as Donny was, he'd figured out the boss man was gonna kill the both of them even before he'd lit the fuse. Shit, this was just not fuckin' right. Shane had never claimed to be any kind of hero, but hell, he had to do something. Maybe if he was to make a cool move, at least one of them could get away in the dark. What's that they say—no pain, no gain? Well, here she goes...

Suddenly, Shane Gruel screamed, "Run!" He bolted to his right and began to scramble away among the scattered rocks. He disappeared in the gloom beyond the illumination from the chopper. Norton fired a shot at him and quickly backed around the rear of the machine as a muffled explosion came from the chamber inside the cave exit. The portal collapsed and disappeared in a chalky dust cloud. Rocks slid down from above, completely engulfing Donny Gruel, who hadn't moved.

Debris streamed down like a waterfall for a moment. When it finally stopped, a cloud of dust hung in the air like the aftermath of an avalanche. The dust gradually disappeared as the breeze carried it off. An eerie silence descended. The entrance to the cavern had been completely obliterated.

Norton came around the chopper, quickly noted the devastation with satisfaction, then clicked on his flashlight and moved into the scree to hunt down Shane Gruel. He couldn't hear footsteps—the jagoff must have holed up somewhere. As

Norton passed a boulder the size of a pickup truck, a pair of wiry arms shot out and wrapped around his left leg. Norton's momentum tumbled him to the ground, where he cracked a knee on the sharp edge of a rock. He screamed in pain and rage, as he struggled to his feet.

Shane Gruel was a man possessed, his arms like steel bands around Norton's leg. "You killed Donny, you cocksucker," he yelled.

Shane suddenly sank his head into Norton's captive leg like a striking rattlesnake. He pressed his teeth deep into the flesh of the meaty thigh.

Norton grabbed a handful of Shane's long, stringy hair and jerked it back with all his strength, but the smaller man's teeth held, and his grip would not be dislodged. Norton reached to the ground and picked up a melon-sized rock, raised it high and crashed it down on the back of Shane's skull. He grunted with effort as he methodically smashed the rock down over and over, until the head was a pulpy mess barely recognizable as human. Shane went slack, but his incisors retained their vise-like grip on Norton's leg. Norton bent down, grabbed the upper and lower rows of yellow teeth in thick fingers and tried to wrench the mouth open enough to extricate his thigh. The clenched jaws continued to hold.

"Jesus Christ," Norton yelled. He labored back toward the chopper, dragging Shane Gruel with him, like a whale carrying a parasitic remora.

As Norton came into the light, Crawford blinked, unsure of how to react to the apparition before him. "Uh Tom, what's going on?"

"Help me get this worthless piece of shit offa me,"

Norton said.

With the aid of a pair of pliers and a screw driver from the helicopter's tool kit, Crawford and Norton managed to work Shane Gruel's clamped jaws open a fraction of an inch, enough to free the larger man's thigh. The battered body slumped to the ground.

In the flashlight beam, Norton appraised the damage to his leg. There were punctures where the teeth had bitten in, and a small amount of blood had soaked through the pant leg. He'd live. His mind flashed on the specter of AIDS, but he shrugged it off. Oughta get a rabies shot, though, just to be safe.

He looked at Crawford with a mean smile. "Well, it's me and you, now."

Crawford tried to grin, but he came off more like a man who'd swallowed a fish bone.

"Help me load this—thing—into the chopper," Norton said.

At this utterance, Brian sank further into his lair of seats and gas masks.

A few minutes later, Norton and Crawford had stowed Shane's body in the rear of the cargo hold next to the TEREX loader. The cargo ramp was retracted and all doors closed.

"Oaky, let's blast off," Norton said.

"What about that rental car Sam mentioned? Should we just leave it sitting on the road?" Crawford said.

"I'll get it after we take this stuff over, if it's still there. First priority's to get to D, unload this shit and get the machine back."

53

Bill Thorsten had been troubled since his phone conversation with Brian McKay the day before. He leaned back in his easy chair and aimed his eyes at the ceiling overhead. The TV's volume played low from across the small living room. The more he thought about it, the more he knew he hadn't heard the last of Bone Mountain. There'd been too much shooting and killing up there to just walk away and pretend everything was fine. And the killing of the sheriff's deputy, Laura Jensen, seemed likely to be related to the previous murders. At least, Detective Newhouse of the Clarkville PD seemed competent. Why was Morgan so negative? It wasn't as if Thorsten had much else on his plate. He wondered if Brian was next on the hit list. *You keep sticking your head into business like that, at some point you get it chopped off.* He'd tried to call the ex-agent again, but there'd been no answer.

Suddenly, his phone rang, an unknown number. "Bill Thorsten."

"This is Darcy McKay." She sounded upset. "Brian said to call you if he didn't get out."

"Huh? Out of where?"

Five minutes later, Darcy had given Thorsten the short version. He told her to wait near the rental car, but out of sight. He rushed out of the house and got behind the wheel of his bureau Chevy.

On the highway, Thorsten held to a steady ninety. As he drove, he considered his own role in this troubling case. The one-man Resident Agency in Bozeman, he enjoyed a higher degree of autonomy than agents in larger cities. He seldom saw his nominal boss, Morgan, for which he was thankful. On the other hand, as the sole FBI agent in four counties, an area of thousands of square miles, he had certain community obligations for which training at the Academy hadn't prepared him. He sat on the dais with mayors and various county commissioners at community events. When locals had questions on federal government issues—anything from Social Security to the President's email address—they didn't hesitate to call or stop by to get the straight dope from Thorsten. Sometimes, he thought how nice it would be to have a partner, maybe a seasoned guy like Brian McKay. He knew that, a few years back, there had been two agents stationed in Bozeman. But, with federal funds drying up, he figured he'd be on his own for a while.

This Old Horn-McKay case, as he thought of it, had the potential for major personal recognition if he could bring it to resolution. But if he took the lead and the thing dribbled into oblivion, it would do nothing to advance his career beyond Bozeman. Still, it could be worse; they could assign him to some big city like New York or L. A. He'd grown up in a Montana town so small, Bozeman seemed like the big city. His two years in service there had brought him a handful of fraud cases, a few bank robberies and one case that got national attention, the kidnapping and murder of a waitress at a local restaurant. Thorsten had solved it quickly, apprehending a police officer who'd been making salacious phone calls to a series of waitresses before working up the nerve to take one. The guy had confessed after Thorsten got a warrant, searched his trailer and found the victim's panties. Amazing how these creatures liked their souvenirs.

That last conversation with Brian had gotten him thinking about Sam Harrison. Not the most gung-ho law officer Thorsten had ever seen, but the man didn't strike him as a kidnapper or a killer. And yet he seemed to have some kind of conflict of interest. What?

The taillight reflectors of a new-looking Ford Escape appeared ahead. Thorsten coasted to a stop behind the vehicle. Montana plate on the rear. He turned off the engine and got out. A quick perusal with a flashlight showed him the Escape was empty. As his eyes adjusted to the dark, he scanned the area between the vehicle and Bone Mountain, looking for Darcy McKay. A familiar voice in the brush off the road said, "Hi" and Darcy materialized out of the darkness. He spun around to face her.

"Darcy. Anything from Brian?"

She shook her head. "He's up there somewhere." She pointed at the dark hillside above.

"How long since you heard the first explosion?" Thorsten asked.

"About two hours ago, maybe a little more."

"And the chopper?"

"It landed a little after the first explosion."

They looked up the dark hill across the road. No sounds or movement. Thorsten checked the safety on his holstered Smith & Wesson .45.

"Show me where you guys were and where that explosion came from," he said.

They began to make their way up to the old mine entrance. Before they'd gone more than a few yards, the sound of jet engines starting up, accelerating and running smoothly came from above. They stopped and peered upward, trying to locate the source. Then came the staccato racketing of helicopter blades, slowly at first, then building to a steady thrum. A moment later, an immense tandem-rotor helicopter rose from between a pair of rounded peaks to the right and hovered above them in the moonlight. Outlined atop the craggy skyline, it held motionless, with a bright spotlight shining from beneath the cockpit. The chopper circumscribed a lazy circle around the top of Bone Mountain.

The agent and young woman were in the open, with no cover nearby. Intense light raked the ground as the chopper labored by overhead. They stayed motionless, heads down, as it passed over. The machine completed the circle then accelerated abruptly and flew off in an east by northeast direction over the Arthur Sands ranch.

Thorsten and Darcy hurried down to the bureau car and took off for the main entrance of the ranch. By the time Thorsten had punched in the security code he'd been given on his first visit and entered the property, the helicopter had thundered out of view. He raced past the main compound and kept going into the ranch interior. He'd always had a keen sense of direction and he had a pretty good idea of the machine's flight path. If it were bound for a destination on the ranch, he'd be on it in a little while. But, for all he knew, it could be on its way to Canada.

Thorsten drove with only his parking lights—headlight beams could be easily seen by whoever was in the helicopter.

The lack of illumination made him limit his speed to thirty on the winding dirt road. After a few miles, they came to a cross-fence spanning the roadway. Thorsten braked to a stop and Darcy got out to open the gate, a tubular metal barrier built into the fence. She swung it open and Thorsten drove through. Now, with their side windows open, they could just barely hear the helicopter motor several miles away and dwindling. As they progressed through the open country along a small creek, the night sky was visible intermittently; other times it was blotted out by cottonwood branches overhead.

54

In the helicopter, Norton said, "I thought I saw something down there near the tunnel just before we picked up speed."

"Probably deer," Crawford said. "That hillside's rotten with mulies. Reminds me, I should get back up there and bag some meat."

The men in the cockpit were silent as the big craft approached the high peaks of the Crazy Mountains. Below, permanent snowfields glowed white in the moonlight. For the city-bred Norton, it was difficult to imagine a man voluntarily climbing from road level to the summits of mountains such as these—what could possibly be the point? They veered away from the mountains, and all appeared flat and dark below. The powerful twin-turbine engines throbbed steadily.

Behind them on the floor, Brian clung to a circular cargo tie-down ring to keep from sliding around. The faint glow of the cockpit instruments provided a modicum of light to the cabin. The engine roar made it impossible to hear the occasional words exchanged by Norton and the pilot. Brian decided to lie low until the chopper landed, wherever that might be. Then, when the opportunity arose, he'd take the two assholes up front, one at a time. No sense in making a move while they were airborne—he had no desire to crash and burn in the Rocky Mountains, or anywhere else, for that matter.

Norton abruptly swung around in the co-pilot's seat and shined a flashlight into the cargo hold. Still facing the rear of the craft, he shouted, "I'm gonna see if the bones are staying put back there, see if you know what the hell you're doing."

Crawford said nothing.

As Norton got up, the chopper suddenly lurched sideways as if swatted by a giant's hand. Brian held onto the tie-down ring like a rush-hour commuter on a bus. He could hear the wind raging outside now.

"Hey, take it easy," Norton screamed at Crawford. "What are you tryin' to do—kill me?"

"Sorry, couldn't help it," Crawford yelled.

Norton worked his way around the seat, staggered and nearly lost his footing as the craft rocked in choppy air. As Norton drew even with the pile of seats and gas masks, the flashlight beam flickered, dimmed and went out.

"Jesus Christ on a pogo stick," he said.

Norton smacked the flashlight against the ceiling and the light came back on. He continued into the cargo hold with the flash shining at the floor, just missing Brian's nest. The big man carefully picked his way among bone bundles, the flashlight beam moving back and forth over the plaster packages. After a few moments, he retraced his steps toward the front. The ex-cop stopped within an arm's length of Brian. The light played about in the piles of military gear for a moment, then froze.

In the murky glow, Brian could barely make out Norton's feet and lower legs, about a yard from his right elbow. He held his breath, hoping to hell he hadn't been spotted. Suddenly, with a grunt of exertion, Norton knocked over a stack of canvas gas mask cases, scattering them about the floor. As Brian peered up, the flashlight beam hit him full in the face.

Brian reached for the handgun at his back. The flashlight fell away as Norton went for his weapon. Brian's night-vision remained impaired by the light. He sensed as much as he saw Norton pulling a long-barreled handgun from his belt and aiming it at him. He rolled to the rear as Norton fired the Woodsman. The bullet whizzed by Brian and drilled into the left-side fuselage wall. The chopper suddenly rocked in an updraft. Norton teetered and fell, landing on his back atop a plaster-cast bone bundle. His pistol and flashlight clattered away among the encased bones. The cast the ex-cop landed upon fractured open with a loud cracking sound like a frozen river breaking up in spring. As Norton attempted to regain his feet, Brian went to a knee, pointed the Sig in the general direction of the noise and snapped off a shot.

The bullet narrowly missed Norton's head and obliterated a side window. Suddenly, wind was alive and howling through the cargo hold. Pieces of newspaper used to protect loose bones were lifted from cardboard boxes and swirled about the interior like gigantic snowflakes in a blizzard.

Hank Crawford called from the front, his voice unnaturally high with stress. "Tom, what're you shooting at?" Then, "Hey, you better sit down. We're landing."

Brian got to his feet and trained the automatic where he guessed Norton to be in the gloom. At that moment, the chopper dropped abruptly, causing Brian to lose his footing. This time, he went down on his side, still clutching the pistol.

The helicopter's descent accelerated until it felt almost like free fall to Brian. What—was there a mechanical problem? But the engine note remained steady. *Was* Crawford trying to kill them? The craft pivoted and then dropped straight down like an elevator car whose cables had snapped en route to the ground floor. He wondered if he'd feel anything upon impact. Nah, it would be over quickly. At least Norton and his buddy up there would go with him.

A strange orange light washed in through the windows. Suddenly, the engines revved louder and the chopper's descent slowed. A few seconds later, the craft struck the ground lightly and bounced once. Brian was tossed about like a rag doll. His head thudded against the metal floor and he nearly blacked out. But he retained his vise-like hold on the Sig's checkered grips. The chopper teetered on the ground, wobbling back and forth like a bowling pin about to topple. It finally came to rest on all tires with the engines throbbing and the whirling rotors threatening to launch it skyward again.

As the engines throttled back and the rotors slowed, the ponderous craft settled down firmly on the ground. A blocky figure was visible in the orange glow, staggering to the front.

Brian heard Norton scream, "C'mon, Crawford, get the fuck outa this thing!"

In a semiconscious fog, Brian struggled to stand. He heard metal doors squeak open on hinges, then the sound of scrambling feet as the two up front exited.

Brian crawled forward until he bumped into the pilot's seatback, found his way around it to the open door and looked out.

The Chevy rounded a bend and rolled into a clearing.

Thorsten and Darcy hadn't spoken since they'd passed through the gate. Ahead, they heard the racket of helicopter blades slapping air. Faint engine noise—it must be on the ground and shutting down. Then the blade noise stopped. The agent crested a rise, doused the parking lights and stopped the car. He and Darcy listened. A dim light glowed through the trees straight ahead.

"Voices. Hear them?" Darcy said.

"Yup."

They got out of the car and continued on foot.

55

The orange glow came from a mercury-vapor yard light illuminating a flat clearing flanked by a two-story wooden barn. Neither Norton nor Crawford was in sight. Suddenly, Brian heard a shout.

"Go get your rifle outa the cabin."

Brian saw Norton slide open a door and enter the barn as Crawford sprinted toward a smaller building in the trees a few yards away. He guessed Norton was after a weapon as well, having lost his pistol in the chopper.

He swung his legs out of the cockpit and dropped to the ground with the Sig in his fist. The barn entrance was about fifty feet away. A large block letter D had been painted in white over the doorway. He moved forward silently, the gun held out in front of him in the classic two-handed Weaver stance.

Just before Brian made it to the barn, Norton stuck his head out. His eyes got big when he saw Brian coming. "Hank, get out here!" he called toward the small building to his left.

Brian smiled. "What's the matter, Tommy? You look like you've seen a ghost."

"*You're* gonna be a fuckin' ghost," Norton said through gritted teeth. But doubt clouded his eyes. The glow of the yard light above him formed an improbable halo around his crew cut head. Norton backed off, glanced over his shoulder at the cabin. "Get out here and waste the motherfucker!" he yelled.

As Brian trained the pistol on Norton, he noticed movement at the front of the other building. He quickly cut his eyes that way. In the moonlight, Hank Crawford was barely visible, standing on a low deck with a rifle raised uncertainly in his hands. Brian aimed at the pilot and squeezed a shot off. He was gratified to see the rifle slip from Crawford's hands and clatter on the boards at his feet. The ponytailed man clutched an elbow and screamed in pain.

In the instant when Brian's attention was diverted to Crawford, Norton rushed forward with a long knife held low in a fist. Brian turned back to him, too late. The razor-sharp serrated blade ripped through his shirtfront and cut into the flesh just above the navel. Norton jerked the knife upward, but Brian had already stepped back, and the blade whistled straight up into the chilled night air. Blood seeped through the front of Brian's shirt, and soon it was soaked. He could barely feel the pain but, when he put a hand to his belly, it came away covered with blood. He wiped it on the side of his trousers. It flashed in his mind that he'd likely been stabbed with the knife used to murder Laura Jensen.

Brian kept his eyes on Norton and the knife. The gut wound had started to hurt, and the bleeding had not slowed. But nothing felt loose inside down there. He felt unnaturally hot. Sweat rolled down his forehead and into his eyes. Norton was only a blur in front of him. The Sig felt like a lead weight at the end of his right arm.

Brian willed his arm and wrist and fingers to keep the gun pointed toward Norton's torso. The blur that was the ex-cop began to back away.

"Stop right there," Brian said. He blinked sweat from his eyes and tightened his finger on the trigger, preparing to fire.

Norton abruptly pivoted and began to run toward the barn. Brian quickly put the front site, as well as he could, on the receding figure. As he pulled the trigger, Norton's feet got tangled up with a rock on the ground and he sprawled on all fours. Brian couldn't tell if the shot had struck home. The report echoed in the distance for a moment. Norton began to drag himself to his feet.

Brian heard footfalls approaching from the opposite direction. He whirled to face the two dark figures now moving quickly into the yard. One was big, the other shorter and slightly built. They reached the area lit up by the yard light and Brian could see that Bill Thorsten had an automatic in his right hand. Darcy, empty-handed, looked tense as a plucked violin string.

Thorsten stared at something past Brian's shoulder. He raised the automatic and yelled, "Freeze! FBI."

Brian about-faced in time to see Norton disappearing around the corner of the cabin in the trees, to be swallowed up in darkness. He did not appear to be wounded. They could hear him crashing through dry brush as he fled.

Brian spied movement in the periphery to his left. Hank Crawford was staggering away from the cabin, holding onto his damaged elbow.

Knowing he had plenty of time as well as backup, Brian carefully turned toward Crawford.

"You, pilot-man, get your ass over here right now," he

yelled.

Crawford looked his way and swore softly. He turned and stumbled into the lighted area near the barn, still cupping his bloody elbow in a hand.

"Assume the position against that wall," Thorsten said.

Crawford leaned forward against the rough planks, awkwardly braced with his good arm, his wounded one dangling, legs spread slightly. Thorsten came over and kicked the legs farther apart, then frisked him thoroughly with a rough hand. Satisfied, he cuffed the wrist of the pilot's good arm to the door handle.

In a pleading tone, Crawford said, "Hey, I'm bleeding to death over here."

They ignored him.

"Brian—*you're* bleeding," Darcy said. "I'll see if there're some first aid supplies around." She hurried to the cabin.

"Jesus, looks like the Army got here first," Thorsten said.

Brian turned to check out the colossal helicopter. The Army insignia was partially visible in the pool of light from the bulb over the barn door, and the paint job was the unmistakable olive drab *de rigueur* for stateside Army equipment. "Our buddies must be well-connected," he said.

56

Tom Norton ran until each breath burned his lungs. Sitting on his ass at a desk sure wasted him for this aerobic shit. He had to slow down and walk. Good thing he knew his way around this godforsaken place in the dark. He'd be okay. Had to get to his cabin, grab some dough, a gun and ammo. How'd that song go, lawyers, guns and money? Well, he'd get by without the lawyers—wouldn't do him a hell of a lot of good at this point.

Obviously, the show here was over. The deal with the dinosaur bones had turned to shit, and what a goddamned shame. This had been the big one, the once-in-a-lifetime chance to grab the fuckin' brass ring, to not be anyone's gopher anymore, forever. But he hadn't counted on that lucky prick McKay. The guy'd damn near shot him. He'd had one good piece of dumb luck himself, though: tripping and falling had probably saved his ass. But McKay'd nailed Crawford in the arm. Too bad he hadn't killed him—the weak son of a bitch would probably spill his guts to the feds, might've started already.

Anyway, there'd be other games to play and win. He had to grab the Suburban and hit the highway. He could change vehicles in town and head south. He'd have to alter his appearance and glom onto some high-quality fake ID—he knew where to get it in Denver. Then down to Mexico, and the feebs would be suckin' wind. Let's see, the shortest way would be through the east pasture, then to the gravel road leading to the compound. He'd have to haul ass, get there before the fuckwads at D figured out where he'd gone.

A few minutes later, Norton charged through a gate into the largest of the grassy fenced-in pastures used by the Sands ranch bison. The moonlight seemed bright, now that his eyes had fully adjusted. A mass of bison was visible now, perhaps a quarter mile ahead. The shaggy beasts were working their way in his direction, dumbly cropping grass, seemingly oblivious to his presence. No time to detour around them; every moment counted. He kept going in a straight line toward the herd. When he'd closed to about two hundred feet, Norton noticed the animals had stopped and were looking at him. They stood motionless as he approached—a hundred feet out, now fifty. Some of the animals began to snort, emitting clouds of vaporous breath. One or two pawed at the earth.

Norton hollered, "Get out of my way, you mangy shit machines."

Still, the herd stood its ground. Almost on them, now—damned if he'd go around. The ammonia stench of freshly deposited urine and feces filled the air and steam rose from pie-sized brown piles. As Norton approached a huge bull, he made eye contact. The animal's large brown eyes showed no fear, maybe a little curiosity. What was the expression on that massive face? Norton recalled the recent news story about a German tourist who'd tried to sit on a bison's back in nearby Yellowstone National Park. The enraged bull had chased the hapless idiot, swiftly overtook him and gored him in the back, flipping him in the air. The tourist had lived, but the incident had gotten a lot of press. Some had called for killing the bison in question—others applauded its actions.

Norton eased to the right a little, intending to pass closely on the herd's left. He figured he'd be okay if he minded his own business. As he came even with the leading animal, it suddenly bellowed, charged and whipped its massive head toward him. The forward-pointing left horn ripped into his side, piercing the flesh to a depth of about three inches. He stumbled, fell, got back up, clutching the ragged wound. Blood oozed between his fingers. It felt as though his guts were leaking out.

"Get away from me, you stupid fucks!" Panicking, Norton scrambled away to his right. The nearest fence was more than seventy-five feet distant. By reflex, he reached down for the handgun he'd earlier jammed into his waistband, but, of course, it was long gone. Probably wouldn't be much better'n a peashooter against these monsters, anyway. No sense in trying the knife in the belt sheath, either. The fence seemed to be a mile away now. He felt weaker as the blood flowed steadily from the gaping wound in his side. As he staggered away from the nearest animals, the bison froze for a moment. Then all hell broke loose. The herd thundered forward en masse. He tripped on a rock, lost his balance and went down hard on his belly.

Norton cut a look over his shoulder as he struggled to his feet. A few yards behind him, massive brown shapes surged forward, sending up swirling dust clouds. Confused and panicking, the herd surged forward at full speed. Ironically, they seemed to want to get away from this human-caused commotion. Hooves pounded the dry grass, rolling thunderclaps breaking the stillness. A few seconds later, the first animals got to Norton. Without breaking stride, they ran over him like a steamroller on fresh blacktop. Dozens of sharp-hoofed legs carrying tons of solid flesh and bone overwhelmed him. Hooves landed on his head, his back, his flailing arms and legs. His full-throated scream of horror and pain was cut short. The limbs stopped flailing, went limp before a dozen animals had passed. By the time the entire herd had trampled by, he might have been a discarded scarecrow of cloth and sticks, its red stuffing eviscerated by a flock of crazed ravens.

In the still air, they heard a distant rumble.

"Thunder, sounds like. Though the sky's clear," Thorsten said.

"Was that a scream? " Darcy said.

"Let's go check it out," Brian said.

"Wait a sec. How's the gut?" Darcy asked.

"A little sore, but, thanks to your bandage job, I'll survive."

"I've had some practice," she replied.

Thorsten herded Crawford into the back seat. With his cuffed hands and wounded right elbow, the pilot sat leaning forward awkwardly, gritting his teeth in a pained grimace. They'd tied a towel around the wounded elbow, but plenty of blood had leaked through.

Brian sat opposite Crawford in back. He kept an eye on the prisoner, ready to react if he man tried to make a move. But Crawford looked as deflated as a popped balloon.

Thorsten took the wheel and Darcy piled in at shotgun. Halfway to the main house, they came upon an eddying herd of bison, some inside the fence, others outside it, blocking the roadway. The animals' eyes glowed large and brown in the headlights. There was a gaping hole in the fence where the bison had crashed through. Thorsten jerked the car to a stop, causing Crawford to pitch forward and crack his forehead against Darcy's headrest. He swore softly.

Something beyond the fence line caught Brian's eye. "What's that in the field?"

Visible in the moonlight, a ragged lump lay on the ground not far from the road. Thorsten and Brian got out, keeping their open doors between themselves and the milling bison. Thorsten trained his field glasses on the tattered form. He gave a low whistle. "That's your pal Norton. Looks like he got caught in rush hour traffic."

"Poetic justice," Brian said. "He told me the bison had never given him any trouble, said he was too tough for them."

57

Later Sunday morning, Brian's knife wound was treated at Beacon Hospital. The young surgeon told him the stitches would come out in a week. He'd given Brian some hydrocodone to combat the pain but he hadn't used it.

That afternoon, Brian, Darcy and Bill Thorsten gave statements to Jim Reid, the second-in-command and new acting sheriff of the Geyser County Sheriff's Department. The fresh-faced young lawman was harried, trying to step into his new role while covering the huge expanse of Geyser County with the much smaller sheriff's department in the wake of the deaths of the sheriff and Laura Jensen.

Thorsten had checked in with Al Morgan at the Salt Lake City FBI office, and the senior agent had flown up on a bureau plane with an FBI agent named Risley. The three agents were staying at the new Comfort Inn on the edge of Clarkville.

Thorsten contacted the Malmstrom Air Force Base in Great Falls, Montana, some 170 miles to the north. Yes, as a matter of fact, they were missing a CH-47D cargo helicopter on loan to them from the Army, and were quite anxious to get it back. He told them that would have to wait until the bureau was finished with it.

Morgan ordered the helicopter cargo seized as part of

the FBI investigation. Agent Risley was to watch over the chopper near the D barn on the Sands ranch until given the order to release it to Malmstrom. The agents recovered the bodies of Sheriff Sam Harrison and Shane Gruel from the chopper. Based on Brian's eyewitness account, they chalked up both Harrison's and Shane Gruel's murders to Norton. But Shane's brother Donny remained missing under the rubble of the second blown entrance to the secret dinosaur dig cavern. Morgan indicated the FBI would be re-opening that dig site to recover any bodies and to further investigate the entire crime scene. Hank Crawford was charged with accessory to murder and jailed in Clarkville. When Morgan, Thorsten and Risley examined the cracked-open plaster package in the helicopter, they determined the contents to be "rocks and fossils." Thorsten commented wryly that digging for fossils on public land without a permit was another of the many crimes carried out by Norton and company.

After giving his statement, Brian had called Doctor Dave Bakeno, who came over to the Sands place and preliminarily identified the bones in the opened plaster as belonging to a previously-unknown tyrannosaurid of the Cretaceous era, an animal substantially larger than the largest known *T. rex* found to date. The find represented a most spectacular holotype, the first bones of a new species, in recent memory. With Arthur Sands's consent obtained over the phone, the bones were to be unloaded the next day and stored in the barn near the helicopter until legal ownership could be determined. The FBI would provide secure locks and an armed guard. Brian also called Doctor Holt at MSU, and the professor said the pictures of the face pot showed a map related to a *T. rex* image.

Monday morning, Brian, Darcy, Thorsten, Morgan and Risley sipped coffee at a circular table in the back room of the Crazy Café in Clarkville. They'd finished brunch, Morgan's treat.

Morgan addressed Brian, "How'd you know about Norton's dinosaur dig? And how the hell did you find it?"

"Actually, Darcy smoked it out two weeks ago when she got shot. When I obtained that fossil bone from Russell Eagle Feather, I guessed his uncle'd found it nearby. But where? We may never know for sure, but it had to be close to the mineshaft. Then Darcy mentioned hearing machines at night on Bone Mountain, and I knew that shaft must lead to something other than a dead-end. We owe Mr. Old Horn thanks for finding the first bone."

"What's the deal on the old pottery thing from Norton's cabin?" Darcy asked.

"He must have stolen it from William Old Horn's place around the time he iced him," Brian said. "Old Horn's journal says he found a 'face pot' May 10th of last year, which was just before he died. Anyway, as you guys noticed, this pot had a dinosaur skull carved on it. The markings on the bottom will probably tell you where the cavern with the dinosaur's located, as long as you have a reference point to work from. The Indians who lived around here hundreds of years back found the dinosaur skeleton in a cave and recorded the location, but they sealed it up. The gold miners stopped short of punching through to it."

"So those markings in the surface of the pot are some kind of map," Thorsten said.

"Must be. I spoke with an expert on that kind of stuff over at Montana State, professor name of Holt, after I e-mailed him photos of the pot," Brian said. "Maybe you can let him look at the real thing."

"Norton found out where the bones were and extended that old mineshaft right into the cavern," Brian continued. "Those guys must have spent some time punching through on the far side and then leveling off a helipad. Cargo helicopter was the only way to get the bones out all at once. Hank Crawford can no doubt tell us how they got that loader up there— maybe another chopper loan. That, along with dynamite's what they used to break through to the cavern on the other side to create the second entrance. With the jumble of hills up there, you can't see anything from the road."

"Cody Gilstrap's still unaccounted for," Thorsten noted.

"I'm willing to bet Gilstrap's body's somewhere the Sands place, wherever was convenient for Norton," Brian said. "I wonder where an ex-Chicago cop like Norton got the know-how to pull this off."

"He managed to hook up with Crawford. I checked him out—the guy's a bone expert of sorts," Thorsten said. "No degrees, but plenty of experience. He's done some geologic work and freelance bone prospecting around Montana the last couple years, found some stuff and sold it to collectors. He admitted Norton hired him to dig out the bones and do a rough prep job before shipment to the customer. Claims he didn't have anything to do with Old Horn or Darcy. I'm inclined to believe him."

"But he's the one that recognized the meaning of the

pot they took from Old Horn—right?" Brian said.

"He says Norton showed it to him and asked what it meant. He seems proud of the fact he used it to find the bones," Thorsten said.

"Who gets the bones, then?" Darcy asked.

"Ah, there's the real question," Brian said. "I called Eagle Feather this morning, to fill him in. He thinks they might be his."

"That reminds me," Morgan said. "We found this inside that pot." He pulled a cylindrical dark object with a protuberance on one end from his briefcase and set it on the table in front of Brian.

"Well, I'll be damned. That looks like the bone I got from Eagle Feather. Proves Norton tossed my apartment. You might as well lock it up with the rest of them," Brian said.

"Appears Norton put the sheriff on the payroll, too. Nice little moonlighting job," Morgan said.

"He and Norton were in cahoots, according to Laura Jensen," Brian said. "Seems Harrison's role was to deflect attention away from Bone Mountain, to keep a lid on everything, and help with the final wrap-up in exchange for a cut of the proceeds from the bones. But he wasn't needed toward the end, and Norton blew him away Saturday night. In fact, he only needed Crawford until the bones were ready to ship. His days were probably numbered, too."

"I wonder who their customer was," Darcy said.

"We found some records in Norton's cabin, showed a possible buyer," Thorsten said. "He'd been in touch with an Irish guy, a movie actor name of Richard O'Carran."

"Wow. He starred in "The Legend of Shakespeare" last year," Darcy said. "He's got like an awesome castle in Ireland."

"Probably where the dinosaur was going," Thorsten said. "There were documents indicating planned shipment of cargo, New York-Dublin, in a Liberian-registered vessel. Probably planned on using a few trucks to get the bones to the Big Apple. Norton thought the thing through, I'll say that for him."

"Something bothers me about the FBI's involvement in this case," Brian said to Morgan. "Why was John Elgar interested? Only thing I can think of is his connection with Sands and his pet Chicago Museum of Natural History."

Morgan looked into his nearly empty coffee cup as if he might find the appropriate words there. "This doesn't go beyond this room. Sands and Elgar are old pals. Sands has got so much dough, he couldn't spend it all if he lived to a hundred. But Elgar's from old money; Sands isn't. He's after respectability for himself and, more important, for Stevens and the museum. He's clean now, has been for years. Told me once he made his fortune by having more information than anyone else. Knowledge is power, and all that stuff. He always wants to know what's going on that might affect him. So, when Darcy was kidnapped, and Stevens and the museum were likely to be caught up in the bad publicity, and it happened right across the road from his ranch, he wanted to be kept posted. Guys like him manage the news, minimize the damage. He asked Elgar to help—that's all it was. But he damn near got up to his ass in alligators, anyway. He trusted Norton—way too much, as it turned out."

"You all realize Stevens is Sands's stepson?" Brian said.

"Yup. And the museum in Chicago is like another son," Morgan added. "So, when you started stirring the pot out here, Sands got hyper. I was just trying to keep the lid on and reassure Sands through Elgar. Both of 'em worked me over, in their own ways, you know." Morgan looked a little embarrassed.

"I still don't see how Sands could be so clueless about what Norton and those guys were up to." Darcy said.

"He didn't spend much time around here," Brian said. "Plus, it's funny how a man can turn a blind side to anything that might be trouble."

"I'd say this hasn't been the bureau's finest hour," Thorsten put in.

"Could have been worse, though my buddy James St. Claire's gonna be really disappointed," Brian said. "I think he was hoping I'd find out Elgar'd conspired to steal a dinosaur."

Morgan offered a bit of a smile and said, "He wouldn't do a thing like that."

"Only because he couldn't find his ass with both hands," Brian said.

Nobody disagreed. Thorsten covered his mouth with a hand. His eyes were smiling.

58

Three weeks later, Brian was happily settling into a new routine in Chicago. He and Michelle had made love twice the first night. She'd been gentle, reserved, almost too much so, in recognition of Brian's gradually healing stomach wound. In any case, he'd been so occupied with pleasure he hadn't noticed the pain.

The second night back, Brian, Michelle, James and Darcy had a stupendous Real Dinner at a restaurant on the Gold Coast called "Gold Mine." The décor reminded Brian of Arthur Sands's collection of old mining equipment, and of the pile of rusted stuff near the former tunnel into Bone Mountain. He didn't mention his observation. Darcy had been working out in anticipation of the fall UIC softball training, which would be starting soon.

The network TV affiliates and national cable had gone bananas over the story—what they called the "Dino-Murders." A carnival atmosphere surrounded the coverage. It came as no surprise to Brian and Darcy that the center of media attention had been Scott Noble Stevens, who enthusiastically jumped into the spotlight, ready to explain to anyone with a microphone and camera crew the paleontological importance of the holotype dinosaur behind all the violence. A casual viewer might think he'd discovered it himself.

BONE MOUNTAIN

Brian had checked in with Chris Pellas, who seemed relieved she hadn't heard from Ted Abernathy. She'd sent Brian a check for $2,000. She asked if he would be interested in helping a friend of hers, a trial lawyer who needed an investigator on a murder case. Brian had followed up, and now had his second client, this time with the welcome prospect of a good payday.

Darcy had returned to classes at the University of Illinois Chicago campus. She had decided to, after her undergraduate degree in biology, go on to graduate studies in vertebrate paleontology. Stevens showed keen interest in mentoring her. Brian had to admit to being a little jealous—Darcy seemed to take Stevens's words as gospel, now that they were back in civilization. James had been quite amused by Brian's explanation of Elgar's strange interest in the Montana goings-on. Good news, though—he'd gotten a respectable raise and assignment to a high-profile new case involving investment fraud, called "Operation Made Off."

Brian kept in touch with Bill Thorsten. The day before, Thorsten told him the FBI had engaged a forensic investigation outfit called NecroSearch, which used ground-penetrating radar to analyze underground anomalies such as buried bodies on the Sands ranch. They went to work, radiating out from the barn labeled D in the northeast corner of the ranch. Bingo—they found Cody Gilstrap's body in a camouflaged grave, accompanied by a .30-06 rifle. Gilstrap had been buried forty yards from the barn. The crime lab in Missoula finally came through with the ballistics test requested by Laura Jensen more than a month earlier—the slug she'd found near the place of Darcy's abduction did, in fact, come from the weapon fired at Darcy and also used to kill Old Horn. The bullets in Gilstrap's head matched up with Norton's target pistol, as did the ones taken from Harrison. The wicked knife recovered from Norton's body had been examined in the lab. No doubt, it had been used in the killing of Laura Jensen, but her family wouldn't give permission to exhume her body for testing, and the FBI wasn't pushing. Thorsten had filled in Detective Newhouse of the Clarkville Police Department, at the request of Brian. "And that knife was probably the one that perforated my tender hide," Brian told Thorsten.

On a lazy October Saturday morning, Brian was about to go out to run errands, when his phone rang.

"Hello. This is Russell Eagle Feather." The voice had a different quality, a confidence Brian had not noticed when he'd met the young man in his campus apartment.

"Good to hear from you. Y'know, I've been kind of wondering how you were doing and whether you got some dinosaur bones."

"Hey, I'm calling to give you an invitation," Eagle Feather said.

"What—you're having a graduation party?"

"Even better. There's going to be a dedication ceremony a month from now for the "William Old Horn Dinosaur Museum.""

"Got a nice ring to it. Where's it going to be?"

"The bones aren't traveling very far after all. I inherited the right to them from my uncle. Sands and those guys backed off, and a judge sealed the deal. Turns out, my uncle asked around about whether he needed a dig permit from the feds, after he found the first bone. But he never got the chance to do any digging. Probably wouldn't have had the means to do it anyway. Actually, Norton and those guys did me a favor, digging them up. Mr. Sands donated the land and funding for a museum building on his ranch. And the building's coming along on schedule. Everything's going through our new non-profit organization, the Old Horn Institute."

Brian considered. Why would Sands finance a new museum in remote Montana? Of course, the man would get a hell of an income tax deduction. And the publicity would be better than cash to him—he'd be associated with a great new dinosaur species. "Who's preparing the bones?" Brian asked.

"Professor Bakeno is going to supervise getting the main exhibit ready."

"Oh, yeah?"

"Yep. They're calling it *Hornosaurus Ancienus* in honor of my uncle. This baby makes *T. rex* look like a wea-sel." His voice was tinged with pride. He sounded so happy, so unlike the dour young man Brian had met before.

"Are all the bones there?"

"Well, almost all of 'em, the Professor said. But some of them were damaged when they took them out. He's kind of pissed about it, says it'll be tough to figure out how it died."

"They gonna make any knockoffs for road shows, that kind of thing?"

"Yeah, actually, part of the deal is the Chicago Muse-um of Natural History gets a full-sized replica to exhibit per-manently. No road shows. That's how Mr. Sands wanted it."

"Okay if I bring a guest?

"Sure, you can bring anybody you like. I've invited some faculty members from MSU. And Doctor Stevens will be there, Mr. Sands and a bunch of other people. I'll mail you the invitation, but I just wanted to tell you about it first, and to, uh, say thank you. I hope you can make it."

"Count me in."

59

B rian hardly recognized the setting when he drove in on the new entry road near the northeast corner of the Sands ranch. The D barn was gone, replaced by a substantial new redbrick two-story structure with a bronze metal roof. A rectangular sign out front read, WILLIAM OLD HORN DINOSAUR MUSEUM. The property had been landscaped with freshly planted small evergreens and deciduous trees. The air was chilly, and there were patches of snow on the ground. But the late afternoon sun was bright, and the intense blue dome overhead lived up to the name Big Sky.

Beside him, Michelle said, "It's not like I pictured it. Seems so peaceful here."

"Believe me, it was anything but, last time we were around," Darcy said from the back seat.

"Amen," Brian said. He didn't want to talk about what happened weeks before. Better to enjoy the moment, the birth of a dream, the resurrection of a, to quote a certain old-time movie star, "fascinatin' monster."

Inside, smells of new drywall and freshly-poured concrete mixed with the musty fragrance of very old bones. Display cases had been erected along the walls. A preparation laboratory with plate glass windows occupied a large space on one side of the interior. A stage with a closed curtain dominated another wall. Brian was amazed at the speed with which the place had been transformed. Ah, the power of big bucks well spent.

A crowd of two hundred or so people milled around in the vast space. A bar had been set up in a corner and many of the guests carried drinks and bottles of beer as they mingled. Arthur Sands, with Barbara Hardy in tow, held forth nearby. Brian spotted Scott Noble Stevens, Dave Bakeno and Anton Holt engaged in an animated discussion. The flavor of the crowd was mixed, with a good representation of people who appeared to be Indians scattered about the room in small groups, talking quietly, pride evident in their bearing.

Brian, Darcy, Michelle and Bill Thorsten stood together near the stage, sipping local microbrew beers.

"I see the cargo helicopter went away," Brian remarked to Thorsten.

"Yeah, the Air Force guys were very happy to get it back."

"How'd Norton get his mitts on it?"

"The way you'd expect a bent ex-cop to do it—bribed an officer five thousand bucks to let him borrow it for an evening. The officer copped a plea, but his career's over. Oh, and you were right about the landing pad. They built it with picks and shovels—quite a job, according to Crawford." Thorsten laughed. "Maybe he'll get to use those skills in the pen, though I doubt it. Anyway, that's how they delivered the loader to make the second entrance to the cavern and clear it out—they'd borrowed the chopper once before you showed up.

"Is Crawford cooperating?" Brian asked.

"Yup, speaking of plea-copping. To save his worthless

ass, he's been singing like a contestant on that TV show, *The Voice*." Thorsten shook his head.

Russell Eagle Feather approached them, smiling. "Brian, glad you could make it."

"It's good to be here in happier circumstances," Brian said. He introduced Eagle Feather to the others.

"So, are you going to show us some dinosaur bones?" Darcy asked.

"Some. In fact, I'd better go get ready for the unveiling."

A few minutes later, Eagle Feather got behind a lectern in front of the stage with a cordless microphone in hand, seemingly comfortable as a game show host. He beamed at the crowd.

"I'd like to thank you all for coming here today. This is a happy occasion for me and all the people of the Crow Nation." There was a polite round of applause.

"When the full skeleton has been prepared and the other exhibits completed over the coming months, the museum will officially open to the public. Although the museum is part of a non-profit organization, it will directly benefit the people of the Crow Nation, providing jobs for many tribal members, as well as hopefully funding projects such as a new healthcare clinic for the people." Louder applause.

"I'd like to especially thank Mr. Arthur Sands for donating this beautiful facility for our museum. Also, a heartfelt thank you to Doctor Dave Bakeno and his staff at Montana State for preparing the bones of our world-class dinosaur. And a million thanks to two people without whose help the dinosaur would have been taken away and ended up in the hands of a foreign collector. Please give it up for Mr. Brian McKay and his niece, Ms. Darcy McKay." More applause.

"And now, I'd like to show you something that hasn't seen the light of day for over 65 million years—the magnificently restored skull of the largest known predator to ever roam the earth, *Hornosaurus Ancienus*."

Eagle Feather clicked a button in front of him. The stage curtain rolled open slowly, revealing a dark fossilized skull big enough for a large man to curl up and take a nap in. A deep rusty brown, the skull was mounted on a sturdy wooden platform. The beast's head seemed to grin maliciously as spotlights illuminated open jaws and jagged banana-sized teeth. Brian had recently seen "Sue," the colossal *T. rex* at the Field Museum in Chicago. She seemed like a little sister to this *Gargantua*.

Darcy let out a low whistle. She turned to Brian and said, "Now you see why I'm going into paleontology."

"Yeah, I guess I do. Was this worth us getting shot, knifed and nearly killed over?"

Her eyes danced with mischief. "You tell me, big guy."

Brian and Darcy embraced, grinning like school children. Michelle and Thorsten exchanged a look and smiled. The crowd erupted in applause, first for the dinosaur skull unveiled for their approval, then for the spectacle of the supremely happy man and younger woman who might have been brother and sister, wrapped in an embrace as tears streamed down their laughing faces.

ACKNOWLEDGMENTS

Writing a novel is a daunting experience. You conceive the story in solitude, work on the manuscript in installments over considerable time and re-read, revise and restructure until your fingers are in danger of falling off. Ultimately, you hope to come up with a book that will entertain your readers.

With *Bone Mountain*, none of this could have happened without the support of fellow writers Dave Hayes and Mary Corrigan, who read every word and generously offered comments and ideas that profoundly strengthened the story. A special thanks to Dr. Dave Trexler of the superb Two Medicine Dinosaur Center in Bynum, Montana for his advice and dinosaur lore. Kudos also to the folks at the Wyoming Dinosaur Center in Thermopolis, Wyoming who provided invaluable instruction in the fine art of excavating *Allosaurus* bones within a grid-mapped dig site.

Thanks to loyal friend and distinguished author Arthur Plotnik for sage advice on the writing business. Also, thank you to novelists Elwood Reid and Larry Watson, who offered helpful criticism of the manuscript early on. Mystery short story king Michael Bracken mentored me in the fine art of storytelling.

I owe the highest degree of gratitude to my wife and pal, Sally, who patiently reviewed the pages of the story as they emerged and provided endless help in producing the finished book.

And heartfelt thanks to you for reading my novel—I hope you enjoyed it. There's another one on the way…

To learn more about Bone Mountain and other stories of mine, please stop by my website:
www.robertdhughesauthor.com

ABOUT THE AUTHOR

Robert D. Hughes is the award-winning author of short stories of crime and mystery appearing in numerous anthologies and magazines. He earned an MBA from the University of Michigan. As a financial professional in Chicago, he investigated white-collar crime, bringing several embezzlers to justice. He has a special affinity for the works of Lee Child, James Lee Burke and John Sandford. An Active Member of the Mystery Writers of America, he lives in Livingston, Montana.